MOSCOW RULES

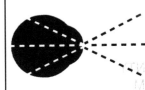

MOSCOW RULES

DANIEL SILVA

LARGE PRINT PRESS
A part of Gale, Cengage Learning

GALE
CENGAGE Learning

Detroit • New York • San Francisco • New Haven, Conn • Waterville, Maine • London

GALE
CENGAGE Learning

LIBRARY OF CONGRESS CATALOGING-IN-PUBLICATION DATA

Silva, Daniel, 1960–
  Moscow rules / by Daniel Silva.
    p. cm.
  ISBN-13: 978-1-59722-703-2 (alk. paper)
  ISBN-10: 1-59722-703-X (alk. paper)
    1. Allon, Gabriel (Fictitious character)—Fiction. 2. Terrorism—Prevention—Fiction. 3. Intelligence officers—Fiction. 4. Moscow (Russia)—Fiction. 5. Military weapons—Fiction. 6. Large type books. I. Title.
  PS3619.I5443M67 2008b
  813'.6—dc22   2008021446

ISBN 13: 978-1-59413-336-7 (pbk. : alk. paper)
ISBN 10: 1-59413-336-0 (pbk. : alk. paper)

Published in 2009 in arrangement with G.P. Putnam's Sons, a member of Penguin Group (USA) Inc.

Printed in the United States of America
2 3 4 5 6   23 22 21 20 19

For Jeff Zucker, Ron Meyer, Linda Rappaport, and Michael Gendler, for their friendship, wisdom, and guidance. And as always, for my wife, Jamie, and my children, Lily and Nicholas.

Don't look back. You are never
completely alone.

THE MOSCOW RULES

■ ■ ■ ■

PART ONE
THE SUMMONS

■ ■ ■ ■

1
COURCHEVEL, FRANCE

The invasion began, as it always did, in the
last days of December. They came by armored caravan up the winding road from
the floor of the Rhône Valley or descended
onto the treacherous mountaintop airstrip
by helicopter and private plane. Billionaires
and bankers, oil tycoons and metal mag-
nates, supermodels and spoiled children:
the moneyed elite of a Russia resurgent.
They streamed into the suites of the Cheval
Blanc and the Byblos and commandeered
the big private chalets along the rue de Bel-
lecôte. They booked Les Caves nightclub
for private all-night parties and looted the
glittering shops of the Croissette. They
snatched up all the best ski instructors and
emptied the wineshops of their best champagne and cognac. By the morning of the
twenty-eighth there was not a hair appointment to be had anywhere in town, and Le
Chalet de Pierres, the famous slope-side

restaurant renowned for its fire-roasted beef, had stopped taking reservations for dinner until mid-January. By New Year's Eve, the conquest was complete. Courchevel, the exclusive ski resort high in the French Alps, was once more a village under Russian occupation.

Only the Hôtel Grand Courchevel managed to survive the onslaught from the East. Hardly surprising, devotees might have said, for, at the Grand, Russians, like those with children, were quietly encouraged to find accommodations elsewhere. Her rooms were thirty in number, modest in size, and discreet in appointment. One did not come to the Grand for gold fixtures and suites the size of football pitches. One came for a taste of Europe as it once was. One came to linger over a Campari in the lounge bar or to dawdle over coffee and *Le Monde* in the breakfast room. Gentlemen wore jackets to dinner and waited until after breakfast before changing into their ski attire. Conversation was conducted in a confessional murmur and with excessive courtesy. The Internet had not yet arrived at the Grand and the phones were moody. Her guests did not seem to mind; they were as genteel as the Grand herself and trended toward late middle age. A wit from one of the flashier hotels in the Jardin Alpin once described the Grand's clientele as "the elderly and their parents."

The lobby was small, tidy, and heated by a well-tended wood fire. To the right, near the entrance of the dining room, was Reception, a cramped alcove with brass hooks for the room keys and pigeonholes for mail and messages. Adjacent to Reception, near the Grand's single wheezing lift, stood the concierge desk. Early in the afternoon of the second of January, it was occupied by Philippe, a neatly built former French paratrooper who wore the crossed golden keys of the International Concierge Institute on his spotless lapel and dreamed of leaving the hotel business behind for good and settling permanently on his family's truffle farm in Périgord. His thoughtful dark gaze was lowered toward a list of pending arrivals and departures. It contained a single entry: *Lubin, Alex. Arriving by car from Geneva. Booked into Room 237. Ski rental required.*

Philippe cast his seasoned concierge's eye over the name. He had a flair for names. One had to in this line of work. *Alex . . . short for Alexander,* he reckoned. *Or was it Aleksandr? Or Aleksei?* He looked up and cleared his throat discreetly. An impeccably groomed head poked from Reception. It belonged to Ricardo, the afternoon manager.

"I think we have a problem," Philippe said calmly.

Ricardo frowned. He was a Spaniard from the Basque region. He didn't like problems.

"What is it?"

Philippe held up the arrivals sheet. "Lubin, Alex."

Ricardo tapped a few keys on his computer with a manicured forefinger.

"Twelve nights? Ski rental required? Who took this reservation?"

"I believe it was Nadine."

Nadine was the new girl. She worked the graveyard shift. And for the crime of granting a room to someone called Alex Lubin without first consulting Ricardo, she would do so for all eternity.

"You think he's Russian?" Ricardo asked.

"Guilty as charged."

Ricardo accepted the verdict without appeal. Though senior in rank, he was twenty years Philippe's junior and had come to rely heavily upon the older man's experience and judgment.

"Perhaps we can dump him on our competitors."

"Not possible. There isn't a room to be

had between here and Albertville."

"Then I suppose we're stuck with him — unless, of course, he can be convinced to leave on his own."

"What are you suggesting?"

"Plan B, of course."

"It's rather extreme, don't you think?"

"Yes, but it's the only way."

The former paratrooper accepted his orders with a crisp nod and began planning the operation. It commenced at 4:12 p.m., when a dark gray Mercedes sedan with Geneva registration pulled up at the front steps and sounded its horn. Philippe remained at his pulpit for a full two minutes before donning his greatcoat at considerable leisure and heading slowly outside. By now the unwanted Monsieur Alex Lubin — twelve nights, ski rental required — had left his car and was standing angrily next to the open trunk. He had a face full of sharp angles and pale blond hair arranged carefully over a broad pate. His narrow eyes were cast downward into the trunk, toward a pair of large nylon suitcases. The concierge frowned at the bags as if he had never seen such objects before, then greeted the guest with a glacial warmth.

"May I help you, Monsieur?"

The question had been posed in English.

The response came in the same language, with a distinct Slavic accent.

"I'm checking into the hotel."

"Really? I wasn't told about any pending arrivals this afternoon. I'm sure it was just a slipup. Why don't you have a word with my colleague at Reception? I'm confident he'll be able to rectify the situation."

Lubin murmured something under his breath and tramped up the steep steps. Philippe took hold of the first bag and nearly ruptured a disk trying to hoist it out. *He's a Russian anvil salesman and he's brought along a case filled with samples.* By the time he had managed to heave the bags into the lobby, Lubin was slowly reciting his confirmation number to a perplexed-looking Ricardo, who, try as he might, had been unable to locate the reservation in question. The problem was finally resolved — *"A small mistake by one of our staff, Monsieur Lubin. I'll be certain to have a word with her"* — only to be followed by another. Due to an oversight by the housekeeping staff, the room was not yet ready. "It will just be a few moments," Ricardo said in his most silken voice. "My colleague will place your bags in the storage room. Allow me to show you to our lounge bar. There will be no charge for your drinks, of course." There would be a charge — a rather bloated one, in fact — but Ricardo planned to spring that little surprise when Monsieur Lubin's defenses were at their weakest.

Sadly, Ricardo's optimism that the delay would be brief turned out to be misplaced. Indeed, ninety additional minutes would elapse before Lubin was shown, sans baggage, to his room. In accordance with Plan B, there was no bathrobe for trips to the wellness center, no vodka in the minibar, and no remote for the television. The bedside alarm clock had been set for 4:15 a.m. The heater was roaring. Philippe covertly removed the last bar of soap from the bathroom, then, after being offered no gratuity, slipped out the door, with a promise that the bags would be delivered in short order. Ricardo was waiting for him as he came off the lift.

"How many vodkas did he drink in the bar?"

"Seven," said Ricardo.

The concierge put his teeth together and hissed contemptuously. Only a Russian could drink seven vodkas in an hour and a half and still remain on his feet.

"What do you think?" asked Ricardo. "Mobster, spy, or hit man?"

It didn't matter, thought Philippe gloomily. The walls of the Grand had been breached by a Russian. *Resistance* was now the order of the day. They retreated to their respective outposts, Ricardo to the grotto of Reception, Philippe to his pulpit near the lift. Ten minutes later came the first call from Room 237. Ricardo endured a Stalinesque tirade before murmuring a few soothing words and hanging up the phone. He looked at Philippe and smiled.

"Monsieur Lubin was wondering when his bags might arrive."

"I'll see to it right away," said Philippe, smothering a yawn.

"He was also wondering whether something could be done about the heat in his room. He says it's too warm, and the thermostat doesn't seem to work."

Philippe picked up his telephone and dialed Maintenance.

"Turn the heat up in Room 237," he said. "Monsieur Lubin is cold."

Had they witnessed the first few moments of Lubin's stay, they would have felt certain in their belief that a miscreant was in their midst. How else to explain that he removed all the drawers from the chest and the bedside tables and unscrewed all the bulbs from the lamps and the light fixtures? Or that he stripped bare the deluxe queen-size bed and pried the lid from the two-line message-center telephone? Or that he poured a complimentary bottle of mineral water into the toilet and hurled a pair of chocolates by Touvier of Geneva into the snow-filled street? Or that, having completed his rampage, he then returned the room to the near-pristine state in which he had found it?

It was because of his profession that he took these rather drastic measures, but his profession was not one of those suggested by Ricardo the receptionist. Aleksandr Viktorovich Lubin was neither a mobster nor a spy, nor a hit man, only a practitioner of the most dangerous trade one could choose in the brave New Russia: the trade of journalism. And not just any type of journalism: *independent* journalism. His magazine, *Moskovsky Gazeta,* was one of the country's last investigative weeklies and had been a persistent stone in the shoe of the Kremlin. Its reporters and photographers were watched and harassed constantly, not only by the secret police but by the private security services of the powerful oligarchs they attempted to cover. Courchevel was now crawling with such men. Men who thought nothing of sprinkling transmitters and poisons around hotel rooms. Men who operated by the creed of Stalin: *Death solves all problems. No man, no problem.*

Confident the room had not been tampered with, Lubin again dialed the concierge to check on his bags and was informed they would arrive "imminently." Then, after throwing open the balcony doors to the cold evening air, he settled himself at the writing desk and removed a file folder from his dog-eared leather briefcase. It had been given to him the previous evening by Boris Ostrovsky, the *Gazeta*'s editor in chief. Their meeting had taken place not in the *Gazeta*'s offices, which were assumed to be thoroughly bugged, but on a bench in the Arbatskaya Metro station.

I'm only going to give you part of the picture, Ostrovsky had said, handing Lubin the documents with practiced indifference. *It's for your own protection. Do you understand, Aleksandr?* Lubin had understood perfectly. Ostrovsky was handing him an assignment that could get him killed.

He opened the file now and examined the photograph that lay atop the dossier. It showed a well-dressed man with cropped dark hair and a prizefighter's rugged face standing at the side of the Russian president at a Kremlin reception. Attached to the photo was a thumbnail biography — wholly unnecessary, because Aleksandr Lubin, like every other journalist in Moscow, could recite the particulars of Ivan Borisovich Kharkov's remarkable career from memory. *Son of a senior KGB officer . . . graduate of the prestigious Moscow State University . . . boy wonder of the KGB's Fifth Main Directorate . . .* As the empire was crumbling, Kharkov had left the KGB and earned a fortune in banking during the anarchic early years of Russian capitalism. He had invested wisely in energy, raw materials, and real estate, and by the dawn of the millennium had joined Moscow's growing cadre of newly minted multimillionaires. Among his many holdings was a shipping and air freight company with tentacles stretching across the Middle East, Africa, and Asia. The true size of his financial empire was impossible for an outsider to estimate. A relative newcomer to capitalism, Ivan Kharkov had mastered the art of the front company and the corporate shell.

Lubin flipped to the next page of the dossier, a glossy magazine-quality photograph of "Château Kharkov," Ivan's winter palace on the rue de Nogentil in Courchevel. *He spends the winter holiday there along with every other rich and famous Russian,* Ostrovsky had said. *Watch your step around the house. Ivan's goons are all former Spetsnaz and OMON. Do you hear what I'm saying to you, Aleksandr? I don't want you to end up like Irina Chernova.*

Irina Chernova was the famous journalist from the *Gazeta*'s main rival who had exposed one of Kharkov's shadier investments. Two nights after the article appeared, she had been shot to death by a pair of hired assassins in the elevator of her Moscow apartment building. Ostrovsky, for reasons known only to him, had included a photograph of her bullet-riddled body in the dossier. Now, as then, Lubin turned it over quickly.

Ivan usually operates behind tightly closed doors. Courchevel is one of the few places where he actually moves around in public. We want you to follow him, Aleksandr. We want to know who he's meeting with. Who he's skiing with. Who he's taking to lunch. Get pictures when you can, but never approach him. And don't tell anyone in town where you work. Ivan's security boys can smell a reporter a mile away.

Ostrovsky had then handed Lubin an envelope containing airline tickets, a rental car reservation, and hotel accommodations. *Check in with the office every couple of days,*

Ostrovsky had said. *And try to have some fun, Aleksandr. Your colleagues are all very jealous. You get to go to Courchevel and party with the rich and famous while we freeze to death in Moscow.*

On that note, Ostrovsky had risen to his feet and walked to the edge of the platform. Lubin had slipped the dossier into his briefcase and immediately broken into a drenching sweat. He was sweating again now. *The damn heat!* The furnace was still blazing away. He was starting to reach for the telephone to lodge another complaint when finally he heard the knock. He covered the length of the short entrance hall in two resentful strides and flung open the door without bothering to ask who was on the other side. *A mistake,* he thought immediately, for standing in the semidarkness of the corridor was a man of medium height, dressed in a dark ski jacket, a woolen cap, and mirrored goggles.

Lubin was wondering why anyone would wear goggles inside a hotel at night when the first blow came, a vicious sideways chop that seemed to crush his windpipe. The second strike, a well-aimed kick to the groin, caused his body to bend in half at the waist. He was able to emit no protest as the man slipped into the room and closed

23

the door soundlessly behind him. Nor was he able to resist when the man forced him onto the bed and sat astride his hips. The knife that emerged from the inside of the ski jacket was the type wielded by elite soldiers. It entered Lubin's abdomen just below the ribs and plunged upward toward his heart. As his chest cavity filled with blood, Lubin was forced to suffer the additional indignity of watching his own death reflected in the mirrored lenses of his killer's goggles. The assassin released his grip on the knife and, with the weapon still lodged in Lubin's chest, rose from the bed and calmly collected the dossier. Aleksandr Lubin felt his heart beat a final time as his killer slipped silently from the room. *The heat,* he was thinking. *The damn heat . . .*

It was shortly after seven when Philippe finally collected Monsieur Lubin's bags from storage and loaded them onto the lift. Arriving at Room 237, he found the DO NOT DISTURB sign hanging from the latch. In accordance with the conventions of Plan B, he gave the door three thunderous knocks. Receiving no reply, he drew his passkey from his pocket and entered, just far enough to see two size-twelve Russian loafers hanging a few inches off the end the bed. He left the bags in the entrance hall and returned to the lobby, where he delivered a report of his findings to Ricardo.

"Passed out drunk."

The Spaniard glanced at his watch. "It's early, even for a Russian. What now?"

"We'll let him sleep it off. In the morning, when he's good and hung-over, we'll initiate Phase Two."

The Spaniard smiled. No guest had ever survived Phase Two. Phase Two was always fatal.

2
UMBRIA, ITALY

The Villa dei Fiori, a thousand-acre estate in the rolling hills between the Tiber and Nera rivers, had been a possession of the Gasparri family since the days when Umbria was still ruled by the popes. There was a large and lucrative cattle operation and an equestrian center that bred some of the finest jumpers in all of Italy. There were pigs no one ate and a flock of goats kept solely for entertainment value. There were khaki-colored fields of hay, hillsides ablaze with sunflowers, olive groves that produced some of Umbria's best oil, and a small vineyard that contributed several hundred pounds of grapes each year to the local cooperative. On the highest part of the land lay a swath of untamed woods where it was not safe to walk because of the wild boar. Scattered round the estate were shrines to the Madonna, and, at an intersection of three dusty gravel roads, stood an imposing wood-carved crucifix. Everywhere, there were dogs: a quartet of hounds that roamed the pastures, devouring fox and rabbit, and a pair of neurotic terriers that patrolled the perimeter of the stables with the fervor of holy warriors.

The villa itself stood at the southern edge of the property and was reached by a long gravel drive lined with towering umbrella pine. In the eleventh century, it had been a monastery. There was still a small chapel, and, in the walled interior courtyard, the remains of an oven where the brothers had baked their daily bread. The doors to the courtyard were fashioned of heavy wood and iron and looked as though they had been built to withstand pagan assault. At the base of the house was a large swimming pool, and adjacent to the pool was a trellised garden where rosemary and lavender grew along walls of Etruscan stone.

Count Gasparri, a faded Italian nobleman with close ties to the Vatican, did not rent the villa; nor did he make a habit of lending it to friends and relatives, which was why the staff were surprised by the news that they would be playing host to a long-term guest. "His name is Alessio Vianelli," the count informed Margherita, the house-keeper, by telephone from his office in

Rome. "He's working on a special project for the Holy Father. You're not to disturb him. You're not to talk to him. But, most important, you are not to tell a soul he's there. As far as you're concerned, this man is a nonperson. He does not exist."

"And where shall I put this nonperson?" asked Margherita.

"In the master suite, overlooking the swimming pool. And remove everything from the drawing room, including the paintings and the tapestries. He plans to use it as his work space."

"Everything?"

"*Every*thing."

"Will Anna be cooking for him?"

"I've offered her services, but, as yet, have received no answer."

"Will he be having any guests?"

"It is not outside the realm of possibility."

"What time should we expect him?"

"He refuses to say. He's rather vague, our Signore Vianelli."

As it turned out, he arrived in the dead of night — sometime after three, according to Margherita, who was in her room above the chapel at the time and woke with the sound of his car. She glimpsed him briefly as he stole across the courtyard in the moonlight, a dark-haired man, thin as a rail, with a duffel bag in one hand and a Maglite torch in the other. He used the torch to read the note she had left at the entrance of the villa, then slipped inside with the air of a thief stealing into his own home. A moment later, a light came on in the master bedroom, and she could see him prowling restlessly about, as though looking for a lost object. He appeared briefly in the window, and, for several tense seconds, they gazed at each other across the courtyard. Then he gave her a single soldierly nod and drew the shutters closed with an emphatic thump.

They greeted each other properly the next morning at breakfast. After an exchange of polite but cool pleasantries, he said he had come to the Villa dei Fiori for the purposes of work. Once that work began, he explained, noise and interruptions were to be kept to a minimum, though he neglected to say precisely what sort of work he would be doing or how they would know whether it had commenced. He then forbade Margherita to enter his rooms under any circumstances and informed a devastated Anna he would be seeing to his own meals. When recounting the details of the meeting for the rest of the staff, Margherita described his demeanor as "standoffish." Anna, who took an instant loathing to him, was far less charitable in her depiction. "Unbearably rude," she said. "The sooner he's gone, the better."

His life quickly acquired a strict routine. After a spartan breakfast of espresso and dry toast, he would set out on a long forced march around the estate. At first, he snapped at the dogs when they followed him, but eventually he seemed resigned to their company. He walked through the olive groves and the sunflowers and even ventured into the woods. When Carlos pleaded with him to carry a shotgun because of the wild boar, he calmly assured Carlos that he could look after himself.

After his walk, he would spend a few moments tending to his quarters and laundry, then prepare a light lunch — usually a bit of bread and local cheese, pasta with canned tomato sauce if he was feeling particularly adventurous. Then, after a vigorous swim in the pool, he would settle in the garden with a bottle of Orvieto and a stack of books about Italian painters. His car, a battered Volkswagen Passat, gathered a thick layer of dust, for not once did he set foot outside the estate. Anna went to market for him, resentfully filling her basket with the air of a virtuoso forced to play a child's simple tune. Once, she tried to slip a few local delights past his defenses, but the next morning, when she arrived for work, the food was waiting for her on the kitchen counter, along with a note explaining that she had left these things in his refrigerator by mistake. The handwriting was exquisite.

As the days ground gloriously past, the nonperson called Alessio Vianelli, and the nature of his mysterious work on behalf of the Holy Father, became something of an obsession for the staff of the Villa dei Fiori. Margherita, a temperamental soul herself, thought him a missionary recently returned from some hostile region of the world. Anna suspected a fallen priest who had been cast into Umbrian exile, but then Anna was inclined to see the worst in him. Isabella, the ethereal half Swede who oversaw the horse operation, believed him to be a recluse theologian at work on an important Church document. Carlos, the Argentine cowboy who tended the cattle, reckoned he was an agent of Vatican intelligence. To support this theory, he cited the nature of Signore Vianelli's Italian, which, while fluent, was tinged with a faint accent that spoke of many years in foreign lands. And then there were the eyes, which were an unnerving shade of emerald green. "Take a look into them, if you dare," Carlos said. "He has the eyes of a man who knows death."

During the second week, there were a series of events that clouded the mystery further. The first was the arrival of a tall young woman with riotous auburn hair and eyes the color of caramel. She called herself Francesca, spoke Italian with a pronounced Venetian accent, and proved to be a much-needed breath of fresh air. She rode the horses — *"Quite well, actually,"* Isabella informed the others — and organized elaborate games involving the goats and the dogs. She secretly permitted Margherita to clean Signore Vianelli's rooms and even encouraged Anna to cook. Whether they were husband and wife was unclear. Margherita, however, was sure of two things: Signore Vianelli and Francesca were sharing the same bed, and his mood had improved dramatically since her arrival.

And then there were the delivery trucks. The first dispensed a white table of the sort found in professional laboratories; the second, a large microscope with a retractable arm. Then came a pair of lamps that, when switched on, made the entire villa glow with an intense white light. Then it was a case of chemicals that, when opened, made Margherita feel faint from the stench. Other parcels arrived in rapid succession:

two large easels of varnished oak from Venice, a strange-looking magnifying visor,
bundles of cotton wool, woodworking tools,
dowels, brushes, professional-grade glue,
and several dozen vessels of pigment.

Finally, three weeks after Signore Vianelli's arrival in Umbria, a dark green panel
van eased its way slowly up the tree-lined
drive, followed by an official-looking Lancia
sedan. The two vehicles had no markings,
but their distinct SCV license plates spoke
of links to the Holy See. From the back of
the van emerged a vast, ghastly painting
depicting a man being disemboweled. It was
soon propped on the two large easels in
Count Gasparri's drawing room.

Isabella, who had studied art history
before devoting her life to horses, recognized
the canvas immediately as *Martyrdom of St.
Erasmus* by the French painter Nicolas
Poussin. Rendered in the style of Caravaggio, it had been commissioned by the
Vatican in 1628 and resided now in the Pi-
nacoteca at the Vatican Museums. That
evening, at the staff dinner, she announced
that the mystery was solved. Signore Alessio
Vianelli was a famous art restorer. And he
had been retained by the Vatican to save a
painting.

■ ■ ■ ■

His days took on a distinctly monastic rhythm. He toiled from dawn till midday, slept through the heat of the afternoon, then worked again from dusk until dinner. For the first week, the painting remained on the worktable, where he examined the surface with the microscope, made a series of detailed photographs, and performed structural reinforcements on the canvas and stretcher. Then he transferred the canvas to the easels and began removing the surface grime and yellowed varnish. It was a markedly tedious task. First he would fashion a swab, using a blob of cotton wool and a wooden dowel; then he would dip the swab in solvent and twirl it over the surface of the painting — *gently,* Isabella explained to the others, so as not to cause any additional flaking of the paint. Each swab could clean about a square inch of the painting. When it became too soiled to use any longer, he would drop it on the floor at his feet and start the process over again. Margherita likened it to cleaning the entire villa with a toothbrush. "No wonder he's so peculiar," she said. "His work drives him mad."

When he finished removing the old varnish, he covered the canvas in a coat of isolating varnish and began the final phase of the restoration, retouching those portions of the painting that had been lost to time and stress. So perfect was his mimicry of Poussin that it was impossible to tell where the painter's work ended and his began. He even added faux craquelure, the fine webbing of surface cracks, so that the new faded flawlessly into the old. Isabella knew enough of the Italian art community to realize Signore Vianelli was no ordinary restorer. He was special, she thought. It was no wonder the men of the Vatican had entrusted him with their masterpiece.

But why was he working here at an isolated farm in the hills of Umbria instead of the state-of-the-art conservation labs at the Vatican? She was pondering this question, on a brilliant afternoon in early June, when she saw the restorer's car speeding down the tree-lined drive. He gave her a curt, soldierly wave as he went hurtling past the stables, then disappeared behind a cloud of pale gray dust. Isabella spent the remainder of the afternoon wrestling with a new question. Why, after remaining a prisoner of the villa for five weeks, was he suddenly leaving for the first time? Though she would never know it, the restorer had been summoned by other masters. As for the Poussin, he would never touch it again.

3
ASSISI, ITALY

Few Italian cities handle the crush of summer tourists more gracefully than Assisi. The packaged pilgrims arrive in midmorning and shuffle politely through the sacred streets until dusk, when they are herded once more onto air-conditioned coaches and whisked back to their discount hotels in Rome. Propped against the western ramparts of the city, the restorer watched a group of overfed German stragglers tramp wearily through the stone archway of the Porto Nuova. Then he walked over to a newspaper kiosk and bought a day-old copy of the *International Herald Tribune.* The purchase, like his visit to Assisi, was professional in nature. The *Herald Tribune* meant his tail was clean. Had he purchased *La Repubblica,* or any other Italian-language paper, it would have signified that he had been followed by agents of the Italian security service, and the meeting would have been called off.

He tucked the newspaper beneath his arm, with the banner facing out, and walked along the Corso Mazzini to the Piazza del Commune. At the edge of a fountain sat a girl in faded blue jeans and a gauzy cotton top. She pushed her sunglasses onto her forehead and peered across the square toward the entrance of the Via Portica. The restorer dropped the paper into a rubbish bin and set off down the narrow street.

The restaurant where he had been instructed to come was about a hundred yards from the Basilica di San Francesco. He told the hostess he was meeting a man called Monsieur Laffont and was immediately shown onto a narrow terrace with sweeping views of the Tiber River valley. At the end of the terrace, reached by a flight of narrow stone steps, was a small patio with a single private table. Potted geraniums stood along the edge of the balustrade and overhead stretched a canopy of flowering vines. Seated before an open bottle of white wine was a man with cropped strawberry blond hair and the heavy shoulders of a wrestler. Laffont was only a work name. His real name was Uzi Navot, and he held a senior post in the secret intelligence service of the State of Israel. He was also one of the few people in the world who knew that the Italian art restorer known as Alessio Vianelli was actually an Israeli from the Valley of Jezreel named Gabriel Allon.

"Nice table," said Gabriel as he took his seat.

"It's one of the fringe benefits of this life. We know all the best tables in all the best restaurants in Europe."

Gabriel poured himself a glass of wine and nodded slowly. They did know all the best restaurants, but they also knew all the dreary airport lounges, all the stinking rail platforms, and all the moth-eaten transit hotels. The supposedly glamorous life of an Israeli intelligence agent was actually one of near-constant travel and mind-numbing boredom broken by brief interludes of sheer terror. Gabriel Allon had endured more such interludes than most agents. By association, so had Uzi Navot.

"I used to bring one of my sources here," Navot said. "A Syrian who worked for the state-run pharmaceutical company. His job was to secure supplies of chemicals and equipment from European manufacturers. That was just a cover, of course. He was really working on behalf of Syria's chemical and biological weapons program. We met here twice. I'd give him a suitcase filled with money and three bottles of this delicious Umbrian sauvignon blanc and he'd tell me the regime's darkest secrets. Headquarters used to complain bitterly about the size of the checks." Navot smiled and shook his head slowly. "Those idiots in the Banking section would hand me a briefcase containing a hundred thousand dollars without a second thought, but if I exceeded my meal allowance by so much as a shekel, the heavens would open up. Such is the life of an accountant at King Saul Boulevard."

King Saul Boulevard was the longtime address of Israel's foreign intelligence service. The service had a long name that had very little to do with the true nature of its work. Men like Gabriel and Uzi Navot referred to it as "the Office" and nothing else.

"Is he still on the payroll?"

"The Syrian?" Navot, playing the role of Monsieur Laffont, pulled his lips into a Parisian frown. "I'm afraid he had something of a mishap a few years back."

"What happened?" Gabriel asked cautiously. He knew that when individuals associated with the Office had mishaps, it was usually fatal.

"A team of Syrian counterintelligence agents photographed him entering a bank in Geneva. He was arrested at the airport in

Damascus the next day and taken to the Palestine Branch." The Palestine Branch was the name of Syria's main interrogation center. "They tortured him viciously for a month. When they'd wrung everything out of him they could, they put a bullet in his head and threw his body in an unmarked grave."

Gabriel looked down toward the other tables. The girl from the piazza was now seated alone near the entrance. Her menu was open but her eyes were slowly scanning the other patrons. An oversize handbag lay at her feet with the zipper open. Inside the bag, Gabriel knew, was a loaded gun.

"Who's the *bat leveyha?*"

"Tamara," said Navot. "She's new."

"She's also very pretty."

"Yes," said Navot, as though he'd never noticed that before.

"You could have selected someone who was over thirty."

"She was the only girl available on short notice."

"Just make sure you behave yourself, Monsieur Laffont."

"The days of torrid affairs with my female escort officers are officially over." Navot removed his spectacles and laid them on the table. They were highly fashionable and

41

far too small for his large face. "Bella has decided it's time we finally get married."

"So that explains the new eyeglasses. You're the chief of Special Ops now, Uzi. You really should be able to choose your own glasses."

Special Ops, in the words of the celebrated Israeli spymaster Ari Shamron, was "the dark side of a dark service." They were the ones who did the jobs no one else wanted, or dared, to do. They were executioners and kidnappers, buggers and blackmailers; men of intellect and ingenuity with a criminal streak wider than the criminals themselves; multilinguists and chameleons who were at home in the finest hotels and salons in Europe or the worst back alleys of Beirut and Baghdad.

"I thought Bella had grown weary of you," Gabriel said. "I thought you two were in the final throes."

"Your wedding to Chiara managed to rekindle her belief in love. At the moment, we are in tense negotiations over the time and place." Navot frowned. "I'm confident it will be easier to reach agreement with the Palestinians over the final status of Jerusalem than it will be for Bella and me to come to terms over wedding plans."

Gabriel raised his wineglass a few inches

from the white tablecloth and murmured, "*Mazel tov,* Uzi."

"That's easy for you to say," Navot said gloomily. "You see, Gabriel, you've set the bar rather high for the rest of us. Imagine, a surprise wedding, perfectly planned and executed — the dress, the food, even the place settings, exactly what Chiara wanted. And now you're spending your honeymoon at an isolated villa in Umbria restoring a painting for the pope. How's a mere mortal like me ever supposed to live up to that?"

"I had help." Gabriel smiled. "Special Ops really *did* do a lovely job with the arrangements, didn't they?"

"If our enemies ever find out Special Ops planned a wedding, our vaunted reputation will be ruined."

A waiter mounted the steps and started up toward the table. Navot stilled him with a small movement of his hand and added wine to Gabriel's glass.

"The Old Man sends his love."

"I'm sure he does," Gabriel said absently. "How is he?"

"He's beginning to grumble."

"What's bothering him now?"

"Your security arrangements at the villa. He thinks they're less than satisfactory."

"Precisely five people know I'm in the

country: the Italian prime minister, the chiefs of his intelligence and security services, the pope, and the pope's private secretary."

"He still thinks the security is inadequate." Navot hesitated. "And I'm afraid that, given recent developments, I must concur."

"What recent developments?"

Navot placed his big arms on the table and leaned forward a few inches. "We're picking up some rumblings from our sources in Egypt. It seems Sheikh Tayyib is rather upset with you for foiling his well-laid plan to bring down the Mubarak government. He's instructed all Sword of Allah operatives in Europe and the Middle East to begin looking for you at once. Last week, a Sword agent crossed into Gaza and asked Hamas to join in the search."

"I take it our friends in Hamas agreed to help."

"Without hesitation." Navot's next words were spoken not in French but in quiet Hebrew. "As you might imagine, the Old Man is hearing these reports about the gathering threats to your life, and he is fixated on one single thought: Why is Gabriel Allon, Israel's avenging angel and most capable secret servant, sitting on a cattle ranch in the hills of Umbria restoring a painting for His Holiness Pope Paul the Seventh?"

Gabriel looked out at the view. The sun was sinking toward the distant hills in the west and the first lights were coming up on the valley floor. An image flashed in his memory: a man with a gun in his outstretched hand, firing bullets into the face of a fallen terrorist, beneath the North Tower of Westminster Abbey. It appeared to him in oil on canvas, as if painted by the hand of Caravaggio.

"The angel is on his honeymoon," he said, his gaze still focused on the valley. "And the angel is in no condition to work again."

"We don't get honeymoons, Gabriel — not proper ones, in any case. As for your physical condition, God knows you went through hell at the hands of the Sword of Allah. No one would blame you if you left the Office for good this time."

"No one but Shamron, of course."

Navot picked at the tablecloth but made no reply. It had been nearly a decade since Ari Shamron had done his last tour as chief, yet he still meddled with the affairs of the Office as though it were his personal fiefdom. For several years, he had done so from Kaplan Street in Jerusalem, where he had served as the prime minister's chief adviser on matters of security and counterterrorism. Now, aged and still recovering from a terrorist attack on his official car, he pulled the levers of influence from his fortresslike villa overlooking the Sea of Galilee.

"Shamron wants me locked in a cage in Jerusalem," Gabriel said. "He thinks that if he can make my life miserable enough, I'll have no other choice but to take over control of the Office."

"There are worse fates in life, Gabriel. A hundred men would give their right arm to be in your position." Navot lapsed into silence, then added, "Including me."

"Play your cards carefully, Uzi, and someday the job will be yours."

"That's the way I got the job as chief of Special Ops — because you refused to take it. I've spent my career living in your shadow, Gabriel. It's not easy. It makes me feel like a consolation prize."

"They don't promote consolation prizes, Uzi. If they didn't think you were worthy of the job, they would have left you in the European post and found someone else."

Navot seemed eager to change the subject. "Let's have something to eat," he suggested. "Otherwise, the waiter might think we're a couple of spies, talking business."

"That's it, Uzi? Surely you didn't come

all the way to Umbria just to tell me that people wanted me dead."

"Actually, we were wondering whether you might be willing to do us a favor."

"What sort of favor?"

Navot opened his menu and frowned. "My God, look at all this pasta."

"You don't like pasta, Uzi?"

"I love pasta, but Bella says it makes me fat."

He massaged the bridge of his nose and put on his new eyeglasses.

"How much weight do you have to lose before the wedding, Uzi?"

"Thirty pounds," Navot said sullenly. "Thirty pounds."

4
ASSISI, ITALY

They left the restaurant in darkness and joined a procession of brown-robed Capuchin friars filing slowly along the narrow street toward the Basilica di San Francesco. A cool wind was chasing about the vast forecourt. Uzi Navot lowered himself onto a stone bench and spoke of death.

"His name was Aleksandr Lubin. He worked for a magazine called *Moskovsky Gazeta*. He was killed in a hotel room in Courchevel a few days after Christmas. At the time, the rest of the world didn't take much notice. As you may recall, its attention was focused on London, where the daughter of the American ambassador had just been rescued from the clutches of the Sword of Allah."

Gabriel sat down next to Navot and watched two boys playing football near the steps of the basilica.

"The *Gazeta* claimed that Lubin went to

Courchevel on holiday, but the French police concluded otherwise. They said he was there on an assignment. Unfortunately, there was nothing in his room to indicate exactly what that assignment might be."

"How did he die?"

"A single stab wound to the chest."

"That's not easily done."

"Better yet, the killer managed to do it in a way that no one heard a thing. It's a small hotel with poor security. No one even remembered seeing him."

"A professional?"

"So it would appear."

"Russian journalists are dropping like flies these days, Uzi. What does this have to do with us?"

"Three days ago, our embassy in Rome received a phone call. It was from a man claiming to be Boris Ostrovsky, the *Gazeta*'s editor in chief. He said he had an important message to pass along regarding a grave threat to the security of the West and to the State of Israel. He said he wanted to meet with someone from Israeli intelligence in order to explain the nature of this threat."

"What is it?"

"We don't know yet. You see, Ostrovsky wants to meet with a specific agent of Israeli intelligence, a man who has made a habit of getting his picture in the paper saving the lives of important people."

The flash of a camera illuminated the forecourt like lightning. Navot and Gabriel stood in unison and started toward the basilica. Five minutes later, after descending a long flight of steps, they were seated in the gloom of the Lower Church before the Tomb of St. Francis. Navot spoke in a whisper.

"We tried to explain to Ostrovsky that you weren't free to take a meeting at the moment, but I'm afraid he's not the sort to take no for an answer." He looked at the tomb. "Are the old boy's bones really in there?"

Gabriel shook his head. "The Church keeps the exact location of the remains a carefully guarded secret because of relic hunters."

Navot pondered this piece of information in silence for a moment, then continued with his briefing. "King Saul Boulevard has determined that Boris Ostrovsky is a credible figure. And they're eager to hear what he has to say."

"And they want *me* to meet with him?"

Navot gave a single nod of his big head.

"Let someone else do it, Uzi. I'm on my

honeymoon, remember? Besides, it goes against every convention of tradecraft. We don't agree to the demands of walk-ins. We meet with whom we want under circumstances of our choosing."

"The assassin is lecturing the agent-runner about matters of tradecraft?"

A nun in full habit materialized out of the gloom and pointed toward a sign that forbade talking in the area surrounding the tomb. Gabriel apologized and led Navot into the nave, where a group of Americans were listening intently to a lecture by a cassocked priest. No one appeared to notice the two Israeli spies conversing softly before a stand of votive candles.

"I know it violates all our rules," Navot resumed, "but we want to hear what Ostrovsky has to say. Besides, we're not going to give up control of the environment. You can still decide how and where you'll make the meeting."

"Where is he staying?"

"He's barricaded in a room at the Excelsior. He'll be there until the day after tomorrow; then he's heading back to Russia. He's made it clear he wants no contact from us in Moscow."

Navot drew a photograph from the breast pocket of his blazer and handed it to Gabriel. It showed a balding, overweight man in his early fifties with a florid face.

"We've given him a set of instructions for a surveillance detection run tomorrow afternoon. He's supposed to leave the hotel at one-thirty sharp and visit four destinations: the Spanish Steps, the Trevi Fountain, the Pantheon, and the Piazza Navona. When he gets to Navona, he's supposed to walk around the piazza once, then take a table at Tre Scalini."

"What happens when he gets to Tre Scalini?"

"If he's under watch, we walk away."

"And if he's clean?"

"We'll tell him where to go next."

"And where's that? A safe flat?"

Navot shook his head. "I don't want him near any of our properties. I'd rather do it someplace public — someplace where it will look like you're just two strangers chatting." He hesitated, then added, "Someplace a man with a gun can't follow."

"Ever heard of the Moscow Rules, Uzi?"

"I live by them."

"Perhaps you recall rule three: Assume everyone is potentially under opposition control. It's quite possible we're going to a great deal of trouble to meet with a man who's going to spoon-feed us a pile of Russian shit." Gabriel looked down at the photograph. "Are we sure this man is really Boris Ostrovsky?"

"Moscow Station says it's him."

Gabriel returned the photograph to the envelope and looked around the Lower Church. "In order to get back into the country, I had to make a solemn promise to the Vatican and the Italian services. No operational work of any kind on Italian soil."

"Who says you're going to operate? You're just going to have a conversation."

"With a Russian editor who just lost one of his reporters to a professional assassin in Courchevel." Gabriel shook his head slowly. "I don't know about you, Uzi, but I don't think it's exactly good karma to lie to a pope."

"Shamron is our pope and Shamron wants it done."

Gabriel led Navot from the basilica, and they walked together through the darkened streets, with the *bat leveyha* trailing quietly after them. He didn't like it but he had to admit he was curious about the nature of the message the Russian wanted to deliver. The assignment had one other potential windfall. It could be used as leverage to get Shamron off his back once and for all. As they crossed the Piazza del Commune, he listed his demands.

"I listen to what he has to say, then I file a report and I'm done with it."

"That's it."

"I go back to my farm in Umbria and finish my painting. No more complaints from Shamron. No more warnings about my security."

Navot hesitated, then nodded his head.

"Say it, Uzi. Say it before God, here in the sacred city of Assisi."

"You can go back to Umbria and restore paintings to your heart's content. No more complaints from Shamron. No more warnings from me or anyone else about the legion of terrorists who wish you dead."

"Is Ostrovsky under surveillance by assets from Rome Station?"

"We put him under watch within an hour of the first contact."

"Tell them to back off. Otherwise, you run the risk of inadvertently telegraphing our interest to the Italian security services and anyone else who might be watching him."

"Done."

"I need a watcher I can trust."

"Someone like Eli?"

"Yes, someone like Eli. Where is he?"

"On a dig somewhere near the Dead Sea."

"Get him on the sunrise express out of

Ben-Gurion. Tell him to meet me at Piperno. Tell him to have a bottle of Frascati and a plate of *filetti di baccalà* waiting."

"I love fried cod," Navot said.

"Piperno makes the best *filetti* in Rome. Why don't you join us for lunch?"

"Bella says I have to stay away from fried food." Navot patted his ample midsection. "She says it's very fattening."

5
VILLA DEI FIORI, UMBRIA

To restore an Old Master painting, Gabriel always said, was to surrender oneself body and soul to the canvas and the artist who had produced it. The painting was always the first thing in his thoughts when he woke and the last thing he saw before dropping off to sleep. Even in his dreams, he could not escape it; nor could he ever walk past a restoration in progress without stopping to examine his work.

He switched off the halogen lamps now and climbed the stone steps to the second floor. Chiara was propped on one elbow in bed, leafing distractedly through a thick fashion magazine. Her skin was dark from the Umbrian sun and her auburn hair was moving faintly in the breeze of the open window. A dreadful Italian pop song was issuing from the bedside clock radio; two Italian celebrities were engaged in a deep but silent conversation on the muted television.

Gabriel pointed the remote at the screen and fired.

"I was watching that," she said without looking at him.

"Oh, really? What was it about?"

"Something to do with a man and a woman." She licked her forefinger and elaborately turned the page of her magazine. "Did you boys have a nice time?"

"Where's your gun?"

She lifted the corner of the bedcover and the walnut grip of a Beretta 9mm shone in the light of her reading lamp. Gabriel would have preferred the weapon be more accessible, but he resisted the impulse to chide her. Despite the fact that she had never handled a gun before her recruitment, Chiara routinely outscored him in accuracy on the basement firing range at King Saul Boulevard — a rather remarkable achievement, considering the fact she was the daughter of the chief rabbi of Venice and had spent her youth in the tranquil streets of the city's ancient Jewish Ghetto. Officially, she was still an Italian citizen. Her association with the Office was a secret, as was her marriage to Gabriel. She covered the Beretta again and flipped another page.

"How's Uzi?"

"He and Bella are going to get married."

"Is it serious or just idle talk?"

"You should see the eyeglasses she has him wearing."

"When a man lets a woman choose his eyeglasses, it's only a matter of time before he's standing under a chuppah with his foot on a glass." She looked up and scrutinized him carefully. "Maybe it's time you had your eyes checked, Gabriel. You were squinting last night when you were watching television."

"I was squinting because my eyes were fatigued from working all day."

"You never used to squint. You know, Gabriel, you've reached an age when most men —"

"I don't need glasses, Chiara. And, when I do, I'll be sure to consult you before choosing the frames."

"You look very distinguished when you wear false eyeglasses for cover." She closed her magazine and lowered the volume on the clock radio. "So is that why Uzi came all the way to Italy to see you? To tell you he was getting married?"

"The Sword of Allah has hung a contract around my neck. Shamron is concerned about our security."

"That sounds like something that could have been handled with a phone call, darling. Surely Uzi had more to say than that."

"He wants me to run an errand for him in Rome."

"Really? What sort of errand?"

"It's need-to-know, Chiara."

"Good, Gabriel, because I need to know why you would interrupt our honeymoon to run off on an assignment."

"It's not an assignment. I'll be back tomorrow night."

"What's the job, Gabriel? And don't hide behind silly Office rules and regulations. We've always told each other everything." She paused. "Haven't we?"

Gabriel sat down on the edge of the bed and told her about Boris Ostrovsky and his unorthodox request for an audience.

"And you agreed to this?" She gathered her hair into a bun and patted the bed distractedly for a clasp. "Am I the only one who's considered the possibility that you're walking straight into a trap?"

"It may have crossed my mind."

"Why didn't you just tell them to send a stand-in? Surely Uzi can find someone from Special Ops who looks enough like you to fool a Russian journalist who's never seen you in person before." Greeted by Gabriel's silence, Chiara supplied her own answer. "Because you're curious what this Russian has to say."

"Aren't you?"

"Not enough to interrupt my honeymoon." Chiara gave up trying to find the clasp and allowed her hair to tumble about her shoulders once more. "Uzi and Shamron will always dream up something to keep pulling you back into the Office, Gabriel, but you only get *one* honeymoon."

Gabriel walked over to the closet and took down a small leather overnight bag from the top shelf. Chiara watched him silently as he filled it with a change of clothing. She could see that further debate was futile.

"Did Uzi have a *bat leveyha?*"

"A very pretty one, actually."

"We're all pretty, Gabriel. You middle-aged Office hacks love to go into the field with a pretty girl on your arm."

"Especially when she has a big gun in her handbag."

"Who was it?"

"He said her name was Tamara."

"She is pretty. She's also trouble. Bella better keep an eye on her." Chiara looked at Gabriel packing his bag. "Will you really be back tomorrow night?"

"If everything goes according to plan."

"When was the last time one of your assignments went according to plan?" She took hold of the Beretta and held it out toward him. "Do you need this?"

"I have one in the car."

"Who's going to be watching your back? Not those idiots from Rome Station."

"Eli's flying to Rome in the morning."

"Let me come with you."

"I've already lost one wife to my enemies. I don't want to lose another."

"So what am I supposed to do while you're gone?"

"Make sure no one steals the Poussin. His Holiness will be rather miffed if it vanishes while in my possession." He kissed her and started toward the door. "And whatever you do, don't try to follow me. Uzi put a security detail at the front gate."

"Bastard," she murmured as he started down the steps.

"I heard that, Chiara."

She picked up the remote and pointed it at the television.

"Good."

6
ROME

To call it a safe flat was no longer accurate. Indeed, Gabriel had spent so much time in the pleasant apartment near the top of the Spanish Steps that the lords of Housekeeping, the division of the Office that handled secure accommodations, referred to it as his Rome address. There were two bedrooms, a large, light-filled sitting room, and a spacious terrace that looked west toward the Piazza di Spagna and St. Peter's Basilica. Two years earlier, Gabriel had been standing in the shadow of Michelangelo's dome, at the side of His Holiness Pope Paul VII, when the Vatican was attacked by Islamic terrorists. More than seven hundred people were killed that October afternoon, and the dome of the Basilica had nearly been toppled. At the behest of the CIA and the American president, Gabriel had hunted down and killed the two Saudis who masterminded and financed the operation. The pope's powerful private secretary, Monsignor Luigi Donati, knew of Gabriel's involvement in the killings and tacitly approved. So, too, Gabriel suspected, did the Holy Father himself.

The flat had been fitted with a system capable of recording the time and duration of unwanted entries and intrusions. Even so, Gabriel inserted an old-fashioned telltale between the door and the jamb as he let himself out. It wasn't that he didn't trust the geniuses in the Office's Technical division; he was simply a man of the sixteenth century at heart and clung to antiquated ways when it came to matters of tradecraft and security. Computerized telltales were wonderful devices, but a scrap of paper never failed, and it didn't require an engineer with a Ph.D. from MIT to keep it running.

It had rained during the night, and the pavements of the Via Gregoriana were still damp as Gabriel stepped from the foyer. He turned to the right, toward the Church of the Trinità dei Monti, and descended the Spanish Steps to the piazza, where he drank his first cappuccino of the day. After deciding that his return to Rome had gone unnoticed by the Italian security services, he hiked back up the Spanish Steps and climbed aboard a Piaggio motorbike. Its little four-stroke engine buzzed like an insect as he sped down the graceful sweep of the Via Veneto.

The Excelsior Hotel stood near the end of the street, near the Villa Borghese. Gabriel parked on the Corso d'Italia and locked his helmet in the rear storage compartment. Then he put on a pair of dark wraparound sunglasses and a ball cap and headed back to the Via Veneto on foot. He walked nearly the length of the boulevard to the Piazza Barberini, then crossed over to the opposite side and headed back toward the Villa Borghese. Along the way, he spotted four men he assumed to be plainclothes American security — the U.S. Embassy stood at Via Veneto 121 — but no one who appeared to be an agent of Russian intelligence.

The waiters at Doney were setting the sidewalk tables for lunch. Gabriel went inside and drank a second cappuccino while standing at the bar. Then he walked next door to the Excelsior and lifted the receiver of a house phone near the elevators. When the operator came on the line, he asked to speak to a guest named Boris Ostrovsky and was connected to his room right away. Three rings later, the phone was answered by a man speaking English with a pronounced

Russian accent. When Gabriel asked to speak to someone named "Mr. Donaldson," the Russian-speaking man said there was no one there by that name and immediately hung up.

Gabriel left the connection open for a few seconds and listened for the sound of a transmitter on the line. Hearing nothing suspicious, he hung up and walked to the Galleria Borghese. He spent an hour looking at paintings and checking his tail for signs of surveillance. Then, at 11:45, he climbed aboard the Piaggio motorbike again and set off toward a quiet square at the edge of the old ghetto. The *filetti* and Frascati were waiting when he arrived. And so was Eli Lavon.

"I thought you were supposed to be on your honeymoon."

"Shamron had other ideas."

"You need to learn how to set boundaries."

"I could build a Separation Fence and it still wouldn't stop him."

Eli Lavon smiled and pushed a few strands of wispy hair from his forehead. Despite the warmth of the Roman afternoon, he was wearing a cardigan sweater beneath his crumpled tweed jacket and an ascot at his throat. Even Gabriel, who had known Lavon for more than thirty years, sometimes found it difficult to believe that the brilliant, bookish little archaeologist was actually the finest street surveillance artist the Office had ever produced. His ties to the Office, like Gabriel's, were tenuous at best. He still lectured at the Academy — indeed, no Office recruit ever made it into the field without first spending a few days at Lavon's legendary feet — but these days his primary work address was Jerusalem's Hebrew University, where he taught biblical archaeology and regularly took part in digs around the country.

Their close bond had been formed many years earlier during Operation Wrath of God, the secret Israeli intelligence operation to hunt down and kill the perpetrators of the 1972 Munich Olympics massacre. In the Hebrew-based lexicon of the team, Gabriel was known as an *aleph*. Armed with a .22 caliber Beretta pistol, he had personally assassinated six of the Black September terrorists responsible for Munich, including a man named Wadal Abdel Zwaiter, whom he had killed in the foyer of an apartment building a few miles from where they were seated now. Lavon was an *ayin* — a tracker and surveillance specialist. They had spent three years stalking their prey across Western Europe, killing both at night and in broad daylight, living in fear that, at any moment, they would be arrested by European police and charged as murderers. When they finally returned home, Gabriel's temples were the color of ash and his face was that of a man twenty years his senior. Lavon, who had been exposed to the terrorists for long periods of time with no backup, suffered from innumerable stress disorders, including a notoriously fickle stomach. Gabriel winced inwardly as Lavon took a very large bite of the fish. He knew the little watcher would pay for it later.

"Uzi tells me you're working in the Judean Desert. I hope it wasn't something too important."

"Only one of the most significant archaeological expeditions in Israel in the last twenty years. We've gone back into the Cave of Letters. But instead of being there with my colleagues, sifting through the relics of our ancient past, I'm in Rome with you." Lavon's brown eyes flickered around the piazza. "But, then, we have a bit of history here ourselves, don't we, Gabriel? In a way, this is where it began for the two of us."

"It began in *Munich,* Eli, not Rome."

"I can still smell that damn fig wine he

was carrying when you shot him. Do you remember the wine, Gabriel?"

"I remember, Eli."

"Even now, the smell of figs turns my stomach." Lavon took a bite of the fish. "We're not going to kill anyone today, are we, Gabriel?"

"Not today, Eli. Today, we just talk."

"You have a picture?"

Gabriel removed the photograph from his shirt pocket and placed it on the table. Lavon shoved on a pair of smudged half-moon reading glasses and scrutinized the image carefully.

"These Russians all look the same to me."

"I'm sure they feel the same way about you."

"I know *exactly* how they feel about me. Russians made the lives of my ancestors so miserable that they chose to live beside a malarial swamp in Palestine instead. They supported the creation of Israel to begin with, but in the sixties they threw in their lot with those who were sworn to destroy us. The Russians like to portray themselves as allies of the West in the war against international terrorism, but we should never forget they helped to create international terrorism in the first place. They encour-aged leftist terror groups across Western

Europe in the seventies and eighties, and, of course, they were the patron saints of the PLO. They gave Arafat and his killers all the weapons and explosives they wanted, along with freedom of movement behind the Iron Curtain. Don't forget, Gabriel, the attack on our athletes in Munich was directed from East Berlin."

"Are you finished, Professor?"

Lavon slipped the photo into the breast pocket of his jacket. Gabriel ordered two plates of *spaghetti con carciofi* and briefed Lavon on the assignment as they ate the last of the fish.

"And if he's clean when he gets to Tre Scalini?" Lavon asked. "What happens then?"

"I want you to have a go at him in that fluent Russian of yours. Back him into a corner and see if he breaks."

"And if he insists on talking to you?"

"Then you tell him to visit one more Roman tourist attraction."

"Which one?"

Lavon, after hearing Gabriel's answer, picked at the corner of his napkin in silence for a moment. "It certainly meets your requirements for a public place, Gabriel. But I doubt that your friend His Holiness will be pleased if he ever finds out you used his church for a clandestine meeting."

"It's a basilica, Eli. And His Holiness will never know a thing."

"Unless something goes wrong."

"It's my honeymoon. What could go wrong?"

The waiter appeared with the two plates of pasta. Lavon glanced at his wristwatch.

"Are you sure we have time for lunch?"

"Eat your pasta, Eli. You have a long walk ahead of you."

7
ROME

They finished their lunch at a slightly un-Roman pace and departed the ghetto aboard the Piaggio scooter. Gabriel dropped Lavon near the Excelsior and rode to the Piazza di Spagna, where he took a window table at Caffè Greco. He appeared to be engrossed in his copy of *La Repubblica* as Boris Ostrovsky came strolling along the Via Condotti. Lavon was trailing fifty yards behind. He was still wearing his ascot, which meant he had seen no sign of surveillance.

Gabriel finished his coffee while checking *Lavon's* tail, then paid the check and rode to the Trevi Fountain. He was standing near the figure of Neptune's rearing seahorse when Ostrovsky shouldered his way through the crowd of tourists and stood along the balustrade. The Russian was old enough to have endured the hardships of "developed Socialism" and seemed genuinely offended by the sight of rich Westerners hurling money into a work of art commissioned by the papacy. He dipped his handkerchief into the water and used it to dab the perspiration from his forehead. Then, reluctantly, he dug a single coin from his pocket and flung it into the fountain before turning and walking away. Gabriel glimpsed Lavon as he started after him. He was still wearing his ascot.

The third stop on the itinerary was a slightly shorter walk, but the portly Russian appeared footsore and weary by the time he finally labored up the front steps of the Pantheon. Gabriel was standing at the tomb of Raphael. He watched Ostrovsky stroll once around the interior of the rotunda, then stepped outside onto the portico, where Lavon was leaning against a column.

"What do you think?"

"I think we'd better get him into a chair at Tre Scalini before he passes out."

"Is there anyone following him?"

Lavon shook his head. "Clean as a whistle."

Just then Ostrovsky emerged from the rotunda and headed down the steps toward the Piazza Navona. Lavon gave him a generous head start before setting out after him. Gabriel climbed aboard the Piaggio and headed to the Vatican.

It had been a Roman racetrack once. Indeed, the baroque structures along its elliptical perimeter were built upon the ruins of ancient grandstands. There were no more chariot races and sporting contests in the Piazza Navona, only a never-ending carnival-like atmosphere that made it one of the most popular and crowded squares in all of Rome. For his observation post, Eli Lavon had chosen the Fontana de Moro, where he was pretending to watch a cellist performing Bach's Suite No. 1 in G Major. In reality, his gaze was focused on Boris Ostrovsky, who was settling into a table, fifty yards away, at Tre Scalini. The Russian ordered only a small bottle of mineral water, which the white-jacketed waiter took an eternity to deliver. Lavon took one final look around the square, then walked over and sat down in the empty seat.

"You really should order something more than water, Boris. It's bad manners."

Lavon had spoken in rapid Russian. Ostrovsky responded in the same language.

"I'm a Russian journalist. I don't take beverages in public unless they come with a cap on them."

He regarded Lavon and frowned, as

though he had decided the small man in the crumpled tweed jacket could not possibly be the legendary Israeli agent whom he had read about in the newspapers.

"Who are you?"

"None of your business."

Another frown. "I did everything I was told to do. Now, where is he?"

"Who?"

"The man I want to speak with. The man called Allon."

"What makes you think we would ever let you anywhere near him? No one summons Gabriel Allon. It's always the other way around."

A waiter sauntered over to the table; Lavon, in respectable Italian, ordered two coffees and a plate of *tartufo.* Then he looked again at Ostrovsky. The Russian was perspiring freely now and glancing nervously around the piazza. The front of his shirt was damp and beneath each arm was a dark blossom of sweat.

"Something bothering you, Boris?"

"Something is always bothering me. It's how I stay alive."

"Who are you afraid of?"

"The *siloviki,*" he said.

"The *siloviki?* I'm afraid my Russian isn't that good, Boris."

"Your Russian is very good, my friend, and I'm a bit surprised you haven't heard the word before. It's how we refer to the former KGB men who are now running my country. They do not take kindly to dissent, and that's putting it mildly. If you cross them, they will kill you. They kill in Moscow. They kill in London. And they wouldn't hesitate to kill here" — Ostrovsky looked around the lively piazza — "in the historic center of Rome."

"Relax, Boris. You're clean. No one followed you here."

"How do you know?"

"We're good at what we do."

"They're better, my friend. They've had a lot of practice. They've been at it since the Revolution."

"All the more reason why you're not going anywhere near the man you wish to speak to. Give me the message, Boris, and I'll give it to Allon. It's much safer that way for everyone. It's the way we do things."

"The message I have to deliver is of the utmost gravity. I speak to him and only him."

The waiter appeared with the coffee and chocolate. Lavon waited until he was gone before speaking again.

"I am a good friend of the man in question. I've known him for a long time. If you give me the message, you can be sure it will reach his ears."

"I meet with Allon or I go back to Moscow in the morning and meet with no one at all. The choice is yours." Greeted by silence, the Russian pushed his chair away from the table and stood. "I risked my life coming here. Many of my fellow journalists have been murdered for far less."

"Sit down," Lavon said calmly. "You're making a scene."

Ostrovsky remained standing.

"I said sit down, Boris."

This time, Ostrovsky obeyed. He was a Russian. He was used to taking orders.

"Is this your first time in Rome?" Lavon asked.

Ostrovsky nodded his head.

"Allow me to give you some advice on your next destination."

Lavon leaned forward across the table, as did Ostrovsky. Two minutes later, the Russian journalist was on his feet again, this time heading eastward across the piazza toward the Tiber. Lavon remained at Tre Scalini long enough to make a brief call on his mobile phone. Then he paid the check and started after him.

■ ■ ■ ■

At the heart of St. Peter's Square, flanked by Bernini's colossal Tuscan Colonnade, stands the Egyptian Obelisk. Brought to Rome from Egypt by Emperor Caligula in the year 37, it was moved to its current location in 1586 and raised in a monumental feat of engineering involving one hundred forty horses and forty-seven winches. To protect the Obelisk from terrorists and other modern threats, it is now surrounded by a circle of stubby brown barriers of reinforced concrete. Gabriel sat atop one, wraparound sunglasses in place, as Boris Ostrovsky appeared at the outer edge of the piazza. He watched the Russian's approach, then turned and headed toward the row of magnetometers located near the front of the Basilica. After enduring a brief wait, he passed through them without so much as a ping and started up the sunlit steps toward the Portico.

Of the Basilica's five doors, only the Filarete Door was open. Gabriel allowed himself to be swallowed up by a large band of cheerful Polish pilgrims and was propelled by them into the Atrium. He paused there to exchange his wraparound sunglasses for a pair of horn-rimmed spectacles, then struck out up the center of the vast nave. He was standing before the Papal Altar as Boris Ostrovsky came in from the Portico.

The Russian walked over to the Chapel of the Pietà. After spending just thirty seconds pretending to marvel at Michelangelo's masterpiece, he continued up the right side of the nave and paused again, this time before the Monument to Pope Pius XII. Because of the statue's position, the Russian was temporarily shielded from Gabriel's view. Gabriel looked toward the opposite side of the nave and saw Lavon standing near the entrance of the Vatican Grottoes. Their eyes met briefly; Lavon nodded once. Gabriel took one final look at the soaring Dome, then set off toward the spot where the Russian was waiting for him.

The sculpture of Pius XII is a curious one. The right hand is raised in blessing, but the head is turned a few degrees to the right, a somewhat defensive pose that makes it appear as if the wartime pontiff is attempting to ward off a blow. Even more curious, however, was the scene Gabriel encountered as he entered the enclave where the statue is located. Boris Ostrovsky was on his knees before the pedestal, with his face lifted sharply toward the ceiling and his hands raised to his neck. A few feet away, three African nuns were conversing softly in French, as though there was nothing unusual about the sight of a man kneeling in fervent veneration before the statue of so great a pope.

Gabriel slipped past the nuns and moved quickly to Ostrovsky's side. His eyes were bulging and frozen in terror, and his hands were locked around his own throat, as though he were attempting to strangle himself. He wasn't, of course; he was only trying to breathe. Ostrovsky's affliction wasn't natural. In fact, Gabriel was quite certain the Russian had been poisoned. Somehow, somewhere, an assassin had managed to get to him, despite all their precautions.

Gabriel eased Ostrovsky to the floor and spoke quietly into his ear while attempting to pry loose his hands. The nuns gathered round and began to pray, along with a crowd of curious bystanders. Within thirty seconds, the first officers of the Vigilanza, the Vatican's police force, arrived to investigate. By then, Gabriel was no longer there. He was walking calmly down the steps of the Basilica, with his sunglasses on his face and Eli Lavon at his side. "He was clean,"

Lavon was saying. "I'm telling you, Gabriel, he was clean."

8
VATICAN CITY

It took just one hour for the death in St. Peter's to reach the airwaves of Italy and another hour for the first report to appear in a roundup of European news on the BBC. By eight o'clock, the corpse had a name; by nine, an occupation.

At 9:30 p.m. Rome time, global interest in Ostrovsky's death increased dramatically when a spokesman for the Vatican Press Office issued a terse statement suggesting the Russian journalist appeared to have died as a result of foul play. The announcement ignited a frenzy of activity in newsrooms around the world, it being an otherwise rather slow day, and by midnight there were satellite broadcast trucks lining the Via della Conciliazione from the Tiber to St. Peter's Square. Experts were brought in to analyze every possible angle, real or imagined: experts on the police and security forces of the Vatican; experts on the perils facing Russian journalists; experts on the Basilica itself, which had been sealed off and declared a crime scene. An American cable channel even interviewed the author of a book about Pius XII, before whose statue Ostrovsky had died. The scholar was engaged in idle speculation about a possible link between the dead Russian journalist and the controversial pope as Gabriel parked his motorbike on a quiet side street near the Vatican walls and made his way toward St. Anne's Gate.

A young priest was standing just inside the gate, chatting with a Swiss Guard dressed in a simple blue night uniform. The priest greeted Gabriel with a nod, then turned and escorted him silently up the Via Belvedere. They entered the Apostolic Palace through the San Damaso Courtyard and stepped into a waiting elevator that bore them slowly up to the third floor. Monsignor Luigi Donati, private secretary to His Holiness Pope Paul VII, was waiting in the frescoed loggia. He was six inches taller than Gabriel and blessed with the dark good looks of an Italian film star. His handmade black cassock hung gracefully from his slender frame, and his gold wristwatch glinted in the restrained light as he banished the young priest with a curt wave.

"Please tell me you didn't actually kill a man in my Basilica," Donati murmured after the young priest had receded into the shadows.

"I didn't kill anyone, Luigi."

The monsignor frowned, then handed Gabriel a manila file folder stamped with the insignia of the Vigilanza. Gabriel lifted the cover and saw himself, cradling the dying figure of Boris Ostrovsky. There were other photos beneath: Gabriel walking away as the onlookers gathered round; Gabriel slipping out the Filarete Door; Gabriel at the side of Eli Lavon as they hurried together across St. Peter's Square. He closed the file and held it out toward Donati like an offertory.

"They're yours to keep, Gabriel. Think of them as a souvenir of your visit to the Vatican."

"I assume the Vigilanza has another set?"

Donati gave a slow nod of his head.

"I would be eternally grateful if you would be so kind as to drop those prints in the nearest pontifical shredder."

"I will," Donati said icily. "*After* you tell me everything you know about what transpired here this afternoon."

"I know very little, actually."

"Why don't we start with something

simple, then? For example, what in God's name were you doing there?"

Donati removed a cigarette from his elegant gold case, tapped it impatiently against the cover, then ignited it with an executive gold lighter. There was little clerical in his demeanor; not for the first time, Gabriel had to remind himself that the tall, cassocked figure standing before him was actually a priest. Brilliant, uncompromising, and notoriously short of temper, Donati was one of the most powerful private secretaries in the history of the Roman Catholic Church. He ran the Vatican like a prime minister or CEO of a Fortune 500 company, a management style that had won him few friends behind the walls of the Vatican. The Vatican press corps called him a clerical Rasputin, the true power behind the papal throne, while his legion of enemies in the Roman Curia often referred to him as "the Black Pope," an unflattering reference to Donati's Jesuit past. Their loathing of Donati had diminished some during the past year. After all, there were few men who could say they had actually stepped in front of a bullet meant for the Supreme Pontiff.

"It might be in your interests, Monsignor Donati, to limit your exposure to certain facts surrounding the circumstances of Ostrovsky's death." Gabriel's tone was law-yerly. "Otherwise, you might find yourself in a ticklish situation when the investigators start asking questions."

"I've been in ticklish situations before." Donati blew a stream of smoke toward the high ceiling and gave Gabriel a sideways glance. "We *both* have. Just tell me every-thing you know and let me worry about how to handle the questions from the investiga-tors."

"It's been a long time since I've been to confession, Luigi."

"Try it," Donati said. "It's good for the soul."

Gabriel may have harbored serious doubts about the benefits of confession, but he had none when it came to the trustworthiness of Luigi Donati. Their bond had been forged in secrecy and was drenched in blood, some of it their own. The former Jesuit knew how to keep a secret. He was also skilled at telling the occasional untruth, as long as it was in the service of a noble cause. And so, as they walked the silent halls of the Apostolic Palace together, Gabriel told him everything, beginning with his summons to Assisi and ending with Ostrov-sky's death.

"Do I have to remind you that we had an

agreement? We asked the Italian authorities to allow you to reside in the country under a false identity. We gave you work and accommodations — very pleasant accommodations, I might add. In exchange for this, we asked only that you refrain from any and all work for your former employer."

Gabriel offered an uninspired version of the "Navot defense" — that it was not really an operation, only a conversation. Donati dismissed it with a wave of his hand.

"You gave us your word, Gabriel, and you broke it."

"We had no choice. Ostrovsky said he would only talk to me."

"Then you should have picked somewhere else to meet him other than *my* Basilica. You've laid a potential scandal on our doorstep and that's the last thing we need right now."

"The difficult questions will be directed toward Moscow, not the Vatican."

"Let's hope you're correct. I'm obviously no expert, but it appears Ostrovsky was poisoned by someone." Donati paused. "Someone who apparently didn't want him talking to *you*."

"I concur."

"Because he's a Russian, and because the Russians have a history of this sort of thing, there's bound to be speculation about a Kremlin connection."

"It's already begun, Luigi. A hundred reporters are camped at the edge of St. Peter's Square saying that very thing."

"What do you believe?"

"Ostrovsky told us he was afraid of the *siloviki*. It's the word Russians use to describe the gang of former KGB men who've set up shop inside the Kremlin. He also told us that the information he had concerned a grave threat to the West and to Israel."

"What sort of threat?"

"He didn't get a chance to tell us that."

Donati clasped his hands behind his back thoughtfully and looked down at the marble floor. "For the moment, Ostrovsky's death is a matter for the police and security services of the Vatican, but it is unlikely to remain so. I anticipate pressure will build rather quickly for us to grant the Italian authorities primacy in the investigation. Fortunately, murder is not a common occurrence at the Vatican — except when you come to town, of course. We simply don't have the technical expertise necessary to carry out an inquiry of this complexity, especially if sophisticated poisons or toxins are involved."

"How long before you'll have to let the

Italians take over?"

"If I had to guess, the request will be on my desk by tomorrow. If we refuse, we'll be accused of engaging in a cover-up. The press will spin wild theories about dark forces at play behind the walls of the Vatican. Which brings us back to the photographs of you inside the Basilica at the time of Ostrovsky's death."

"What about them?"

"Dropping the prints into the pontifical shredder is only a temporary solution. As you might expect, the images are stored permanently in the memory of our computers. And don't even think about asking me to delete them. I won't countenance the destruction of evidence — not with the Italians about to take over the case."

"No one is going to recognize me from those images, Luigi. There's only one way the Italians will find out I was here."

"Don't worry, Gabriel. Your secret is safe with us. Three people know of your involvement: the Holy Father, myself, and the Vigilanza detective who's leading our investigation. I've sworn him to secrecy and he's agreed to remain silent. He's what we Italians call an *uomo di fiducia:* a man of trust. He used to work for the Polizia di Stato."

"If it's all right with you, Luigi, I'd like to

have a brief word with the inspector."

"About what?"

"It's possible the security cameras in the Basilica picked up someone other than me."

"Who?"

"The man who killed Boris Ostrovsky, of course."

9
VATICAN CITY

Gabriel did not require an escort to find the Vatican Central Security Office. Unfortunately, he knew the way. It was there, shortly before the attack on St. Peter's Basilica, that he had engaged in a frantic search for evidence of an al-Qaeda infiltrator at the Vatican. Had he been able to start a few minutes sooner, he might have prevented the deadliest single act of Islamic terrorism since 9/11.

Ispettore Mateo Cassani, a trim figure in a well-cut dark suit, was waiting in the reception foyer. He regarded Gabriel with a pair of weary, bloodshot eyes, then extended his hand. "Welcome back, Signore. Come with me, please."

They headed down a narrow corridor and paused briefly in an open doorway. Inside, two uniformed Vigilanza officers were seated before a wall of video monitors. Gabriel quickly scanned the images: St. Anne's

Gate, the Arch of Bells, St. Peter's Square, the San Damaso Courtyard, the Vatican Gardens, the interior of the Basilica.

"This is our main observation room. It also serves as our command center in times of crisis, such as the morning of the attack. Everything is recorded and stored digitally. For all eternity," he added with a tired smile. "Just like the Holy Mother Church."

"I was afraid of that."

"Don't worry, Signore. I know who you are, and I know exactly what you did the day those terrorists attacked this place. The Church lost four cardinals and eight bishops in a matter of seconds. And if it wasn't for you, we might have lost a pope as well."

They left the observation room and entered a cramped office overlooking the darkened Belvedere Courtyard. Cassani sat down before a desktop computer and invited Gabriel to look over his shoulder.

"Monsignor Donati told me you wanted to see every image we had of the dead Russian."

Gabriel nodded. The detective clicked the mouse and the first image appeared, a wide-angle shot of St. Peter's Square, taken from a camera mounted atop the left flank of the Colonnade. The shot advanced at the rate of one frame per second. When the time code in the bottom left portion of the screen reached 15:47:23, Cassani clicked the PAUSE icon and pointed to the top right-hand corner.

"There's Signore Ostrovsky. He enters the square alone and makes his way directly to the security checkpoint outside the Basilica." Cassani glanced at Gabriel. "It's almost as if he was intending to meet someone inside."

"Can you set the shot in motion?" Gabriel asked.

The detective clicked the PLAY icon and Boris Ostrovsky began moving across the square, with Eli Lavon following carefully in his wake. Ninety seconds later, as Ostrovsky was passing between the Obelisk and the left fountain, he slipped out of the range of the camera atop the Colonnade and into the range of another camera mounted near the Loggia of the Blessings. A few seconds later, he was surrounded by a group of tourists. A solitary figure approached from the left side of the image; rather than wait for the group to pass, he shouldered his way through it. The man appeared to bump several members of the group, including Ostrovsky, then headed off toward the entrance of the square.

Gabriel watched the final three minutes of

Boris Ostrovsky's life: his brief wait at the security checkpoint; his passage through the Filarete Door; his stop at the Chapel of the Pietà; his final walk to the Monument to Pius XII. Precisely sixty-seven seconds after his arrival, he fell to his knees before the statue and began clutching his throat. Gabriel appeared twenty-two seconds after that, advancing spiritlike across the screen, one frame per second. The detective appeared moved by the sight of Gabriel lowering the dying Russian carefully to the floor.

"Did he say anything to you?" the detective asked.

"No, nothing. He couldn't speak."

"What were you telling him?"

"I was telling him that it was all right to die. I was telling him he would be going to a better place."

"You are a believer, Signore Allon?"

"Take it back to the shot at fifteen-fifty."

The Vatican detective did as Gabriel requested and for the second time they watched as Ostrovsky advanced toward the Basilica. And as the solitary figure approached him from the left . . .

"Stop it right there," Gabriel said suddenly.

Cassani immediately clicked PAUSE.

"Back it up to the previous frame, please."

The Vatican detective complied with the request.

"Can you enlarge the image?"

"I can," Cassani said, "but the resolution will be poor."

"Do it anyway."

The Vatican detective used the mouse to crop the image to the necessary dimensions, then clicked the ENLARGE icon. The resolution, as promised, was nebulous at best. Even so, Gabriel could clearly see the right hand of the solitary figure wrapped around the upper portion of Boris Ostrovsky's right arm.

"Where's Ostrovsky's body?"

"In our morgue."

"Has anyone examined it yet?"

"I gave it a brief examination to see if there were any signs of physical trauma or wounds. There was nothing."

"If you check again, I suspect you'll find a very small perforation to the skin of his upper arm. It's where the assassin injected him with a Russian poison that paralyzes the respiratory system within minutes. It was developed by the KGB during the Cold War."

"I'll have a look right away."

"There's something I need from you first." Gabriel tapped the screen. "I need to know what time this man entered the square and which direction he went when he left. And I need the five best pictures of him you can find."

He was a professional, and, like all professionals, he had been aware of the cameras. He had lowered his guard just once, at 15:47:33, ten seconds after Boris Ostrovsky was first picked up by Vatican surveillance on the edge of the square. The image had been captured by a camera near the Bronze Doors of the Apostolic Palace. It showed a sturdy-jawed man with wide cheekbones, heavy sunglasses, and thick blond hair. Eli Lavon examined the photograph by the glow of a streetlamp atop the Spanish Steps. Fifty yards away, an Office security team was hastily searching the safe flat for traces of toxins or radioactive material.

"The hair is artificial, but I'd say those cheekbones are real. He's a Russian, Gabriel, and he's not someone I'd ever care to meet in a dark alley." Lavon studied the photo showing the assassin's hand wrapped around Ostrovsky's upper arm. "Poor Boris barely gives him a look after they bump into each other. I don't think he ever knew what hit him."

"He didn't," Gabriel said. "He walked

straight into the Basilica and followed your instructions as though there was nothing out of the ordinary. Even as he was dying, he didn't seem to realize why."

Lavon looked at the photograph of the assassin again. "I stand by what I said as we were leaving the Basilica. Ostrovsky was clean. I didn't see anyone following him. And there's no way I could have missed someone who looks like this."

"Maybe Ostrovsky was clean, but *we* weren't."

"You're suggesting they were watching the watchers?"

"Exactly."

"But how did they know we were going to be there?"

"Ostrovsky's probably been under watch in Moscow for months. When he came to Rome, he made contact with our embassy on an insecure line. Someone from the other side picked up the call, either here in Rome or from a listening post in Moscow. The assassin is a real pro. He knew we wouldn't go near Ostrovsky without sending him on a surveillance detection run. And he did what real pros are trained to do. He ignored the target and watched us instead."

"But how did he get to the Vatican ten minutes *before* Ostrovsky?"

"He must have been following *me.* I missed him, Eli. It's my fault Ostrovsky died a miserable death on the floor of the Basilica."

"It makes sense, but it's not something your average run-of-the-mill Russian gangster could pull off."

"We're not dealing with gangsters. These are professionals."

Lavon handed the photographs back to Gabriel. "Whatever it was Boris intended to tell you, it must have been important. Someone needs to find out who this man is and whom he's working for."

"Yes, someone should."

"I could be wrong, Gabriel, but I think King Saul Boulevard already has a candidate in mind for the job."

Lavon handed him a slip of paper.

"What's this?"

"A message from Shamron."

"What does it say?"

"It says your honeymoon is now officially over."

97

10
BEN-GURION
AIRPORT, ISRAEL

There is a VIP reception room at Ben-Gurion Airport that few people know and where even fewer have set foot. Reached by an unmarked door near passport control, it has walls of Jerusalem limestone, furnishings of black leather, and a permanent odor of burnt coffee and male tension. When Gabriel entered the room the following evening, he found it occupied by a single man. He had settled himself at the edge of his chair, with his legs slightly splayed and his large hands resting atop an olive-wood cane, like a traveler on a rail platform resigned to a long wait. He was dressed, as always, in a pair of pressed khaki trousers and a white oxford cloth shirt with the sleeves rolled up to the elbows. His head was bullet-shaped and bald, except for a monkish fringe of white hair. His ugly wire-framed spectacles magnified a pair of blue eyes that were no longer clear.

"How long have you been sitting there?" Gabriel asked.

"Since the day you returned to Italy," replied Ari Shamron.

Gabriel regarded him carefully.

"Why are you looking at me like that?"

"I'm just wondering why you're not smoking."

"Gilah told me I have to quit — or *else*."

"That's never stopped you before."

"This time she means it."

Gabriel kissed Shamron on the top of the head. "Why didn't you just let someone from Transport pick me up?"

"I was in the neighborhood."

"You live in Tiberias! You're retired now, Ari. You should be spending time with Gilah to make up for all those years when you were never around."

"I'm *never* going to retire!" Shamron thumped the arm of his chair for emphasis. "As for Gilah, she was the one who suggested I come here to wait for you. She told me to get out of the house for a few hours. She said I was underfoot."

Shamron closed his hooded eyes for a moment and gave a ghost of a smile. His loved ones, like his power and influence, had slowly slipped through his fingers. His son was a brigadier general in the IDF's Northern Command and used almost any excuse to avoid spending time with his famous father, as did his daughter, who had finally returned to Israel after spending years abroad. Only Gilah, his long-suffering wife, remained faithfully by his side, but now that Shamron had no formal role in the affairs of state, even Gilah, a woman of infinite patience, found his constant presence a burden. His real family were men like Gabriel, Navot, and Lavon — men whom he had recruited and trained, men who operated by a creed, even spoke a language, written by him. They were the secret guardians of the State, and Ari Shamron was their overbearing, tyrannical father.

"I made a foolish wager a long time ago," Shamron said. "I devoted my life to building and protecting this country and I assumed that my wife and children would forgive my sins of absence and neglect. I was wrong, of course."

"And now you want to inflict the same outcome on my life."

"You're referring to the fact I've interrupted your honeymoon?"

"I am."

"Your wife is still on the Office payroll. She understands the demands of your work. Besides, you've been gone for over a month."

"We agreed my stay in Italy would be indefinite."

"*We* agreed to no such thing, Gabriel. You issued a demand and at the time I was in no position to turn it down — not after what you'd just gone through in London." Shamron squeezed his deeply lined face into a heavy frown. "Do you know what I did for my honeymoon?"

"Of course I know what you did for your honeymoon. The whole country knows what you did for your honeymoon."

Shamron smiled. It was an exaggeration, of course, but only a slight one. Within the corridors and conference rooms of the Israeli intelligence and security services, Ari Shamron was a legend. He had penetrated the courts of kings, stolen the secrets of tyrants, and killed the enemies of Israel, sometimes with his bare hands. His crowning achievement had come on a rainy night in May 1960, in a squalid suburb north of Buenos Aires, when he had leapt from the back of a car and seized Adolf Eichmann, architect of the Holocaust. Even now, Shamron could not go out in public in Israel without being approached by aging survivors who simply wanted to touch the hands that had clamped around the neck of the monster.

"Gilah and I were married in April of 'forty-seven, at the height of the War of Independence. I put my foot on a glass, our friends and family shouted *'Mazel tov,'* then I kissed my new wife and went back to join my Palmach unit."

"They were different times, Ari."

"Not so different. We were fighting for survival then and we fight for survival now." Shamron scrutinized Gabriel for a long moment through his spectacles. "But you already know that, don't you, Gabriel? That explains why you simply didn't ignore my message and return to your villa in Umbria."

"I should have ignored your original summons. Then I wouldn't be back here." He made a show of looking around the dreary furnishings. "Back in this room."

"I wasn't the one who summoned you. Boris Ostrovsky did. Then he had the terrible misfortune of dying in your arms. And now you're going to find out who killed him and why. Under the circumstances, it is the least you can do for him."

Gabriel glanced at his wristwatch. "Did Eli make it in all right?"

They had traveled on separate planes and by different routes. Lavon had taken the direct flight from Fiumicino to Ben-Gurion; Gabriel had flown first to Frankfurt, where he had spent three hours waiting for a connecting flight. He had put the time to good use by walking several miles through Frankfurt's endless terminals, searching his tail for Russian assassins.

"Eli's already inside King Saul Boulevard undergoing a rather unpleasant debriefing. When they're finished with him, they'd like a crack at you as well. As you might expect, Amos is unhappy about the way things turned out in Rome. Given his precarious position, he wants to make certain that *you're* the one who gets the blame rather than him."

Amos Sharret was the director of the Office. Like nearly everyone else at the top of Israel's security and military establishment, he had come under intense criticism for his performance during the most recent war in Lebanon and was now hanging on to the reins of power by his fingernails. Shamron and his allies in the Prime Minister's Office were quietly trying to pry them loose.

"Someone should tell Amos that I'm not interested in his job."

"He wouldn't believe it. Amos sees enemies everywhere. It's a professional affliction." Shamron inched toward the edge of his chair and used his cane to leverage himself upright. "Come," he said. "I'll take you home."

An armored Peugeot limousine was waiting outside in the secure VIP parking area. They climbed into the back and headed toward the Judean Hills.

"There were developments in Rome this evening after you boarded your flight in Frankfurt. The Italian Ministry of Justice sent a letter to the Vatican, formally requesting permission to take over the investigation into Ostrovsky's death. I don't suppose I have to tell you how the Vatican responded."

"Donati agreed immediately."

"Actually, it was the Vatican secretary of state who issued the formal response, but I'm sure your friend the monsignor was whispering into his ear. The Italian police have taken possession of Ostrovsky's body and removed all his luggage and personal effects from his room at the Excelsior. Hazmat teams are now searching the hotel for evidence of poisons and other toxins. As for the Basilica, it's been cordoned off and is being treated as a crime scene. The Ministry of Justice has asked all those who witnessed the death to come forward immediately. I suppose that would include you." Shamron scrutinized Gabriel for a moment. "It seems to me your position vis-à-vis Boris Ostrovsky is somewhat tenuous at the moment."

"Donati has promised to keep my name out of it."

"God knows the Vatican is good at keeping secrets, but surely there are others there who know about your connection to this affair. If one of them wants to embarrass Donati — or us, for that matter — all they have to do is make a quiet phone call to the Polizia di Stato."

"Boris Ostrovsky was killed by a professional Russian assassin in St. Peter's Square." Gabriel removed a manila folder from the side flap of his bag and handed it to Shamron. "And these pictures prove it."

Shamron switched on his overhead reading light and examined the photos. "It's a brazen act, even by Russian standards. Ostrovsky must have known something very important for them to resort to this."

"I take it you have a theory?"

"Unfortunately, we do." Shamron slipped the photos back into the file folder and switched off the lamp. "Our good friends in the Kremlin have been selling sophisticated weapons systems to the rogue regimes of the Middle East at an unprecedented rate. The mullahs of Iran are one of their best customers, but they've also been selling antiaircraft and antitank systems to their old friends in Damascus. We've been picking up reports that the Syrians and the Kremlin are about to close a major deal involving an advanced Russian missile known as the Iskander. It's a road-mobile weapon with a range of one hundred seventy miles, which means Tel Aviv would be well within Syria's range. I don't need to explain the ramifications of that to you."

"It would alter the strategic balance in the Middle East overnight."

Shamron nodded his head slowly. "And unfortunately, given the track record of the Kremlin, it's only one of many unsettling possibilities. The entire region is bristling with rumors of some kind of new deal *some*-where. We've been hammering away at the issue for months. So far, we've been unable to come up with anything we can take to the prime minister. I'm afraid he's beginning to get annoyed."

"It's part of his job description."

"And mine." Shamron smiled humorlessly. "All of this goes to explain why we were so interested in having you meet with Boris Ostrovsky in the first place. And why we would now like you to travel to Russia to find out what he intended to say to you."

"*Me?* I've never set foot in Russia. I don't know the terrain. I don't even speak the language."

"You have something more important than local knowledge and language."

"What's that?"

"A name and a face that the extremely nervous staff of *Moscovsky Gazeta* will recognize."

"Chances are, the Russian security services will recognize it, too."

"We have a plan for that," Shamron said.

The Old Man smiled. He had a plan for everything.

11
JERUSALEM

There were security agents at either end of
Narkiss Street, a quiet, leafy lane in the
heart of Jerusalem, and another standing
watch outside the entrance of the dowdy
little limestone apartment house at Number
16. Gabriel, as he crossed the tiny foyer with
Shamron at his heels, didn't bother checking the postbox. He never received mail,
and the name on the box was false. As far
as the bureaucracy of the State of Israel was
concerned, Gabriel Allon did not exist. He
was no one, he lived nowhere. He was the
eternal wandering Jew.

Uzi Navot was seated on the living-room
couch in Gabriel's apartment, with his feet
propped on the coffee table and an Israeli
diplomatic passport wedged between the
first two fingers of his right hand. He
adopted an expression of bored indifference
as he handed it over for inspection. Gabriel
opened the cover and looked at the photo-

graph. It showed a silver-haired man with a neat gray beard and round eyeglasses. The silver hair was the handiwork of a stylist who worked for Identity. The gray beard, unfortunately, was his own.

"Who's Natan Golani?"

"A midlevel functionary in the Ministry of Culture. He specializes in building artistic bridges between Israel and the rest of the world: peace through art, dance, music, and other pointless endeavors. I'm told Natan is rather handy with a paintbrush himself."

"Has he ever been to Russia?"

"No, but he's about to." Navot removed his feet from the coffee table and sat up. "Six days from now, the deputy minister is scheduled to travel from Jerusalem to Russia for an official visit. We've prevailed upon him to become ill at the last moment."

"And Natan Golani will go in his place?"

"Provided the Russians agree to grant him a visa. The ministry anticipates no problems on that front."

"What's the purpose of his trip?"

Navot reached into his stainless steel attaché case and removed a glossy magazine-sized brochure. He held it aloft for Gabriel to see the cover, then dropped it on the coffee table. Gabriel's eyes focused on a single word: UNESCO.

"Perhaps it escaped your notice, but the United Nations Educational, Scientific and Cultural Organization, better known as UNESCO, has declared this 'the decade for the promotion of a culture of peace and nonviolence for the children of the world.' "

"You're right, Uzi. Somehow I missed that."

"In furtherance of that noble goal, it holds a conference each year to assess progress and discuss new initiatives. This year's conference will be held at the Marble Palace in St. Petersburg."

"How many days of this nonsense do I have to sit through?"

"Three," said Navot. "Your speech is scheduled for day two of the conference. Your remarks will focus on a groundbreaking new program we've instituted to improve cultural ties between Israelis and our Arab neighbors. You will be roundly criticized and, in all likelihood, denounced as an oppressor and an occupier. Many of those in attendance will not hear your remarks, however, because, as is customary, they will walk out of the hall en masse as you mount the rostrum."

"It's better that way, Uzi. I've never really enjoyed speaking to large crowds. What happens next?"

"At the conclusion of the conference, our ambassador to Russia, who happens to be an old friend of yours, will invite you to visit Moscow. If you are fortunate enough to survive the Aeroflot flight, you will check into the Savoy Hotel and sample the cultural delights of the capital. The true purpose of your visit, however, will be to establish contact with one Olga Sukhova. She's one of Russia's best-known and most controversial investigative journalists. She's also the acting editor in chief of *Moskovsky Gazeta.* If there's anyone at the *Gazeta* who knows why Boris Ostrovsky went to Rome, it's Olga."

"Which means she's probably under full-time FSB surveillance. And as a visiting Israeli diplomat, I will be, too."

The Russian Federal Security Service, or FSB, had assumed most of the internal security functions that were once the province of the KGB, including counterintelligence. Though the FSB liked to present itself to the outside world as a modern European security service, it was staffed largely by KGB veterans and even operated from the KGB's notorious old headquarters in Lubyanka Square. Many Russians didn't even bother calling it by its new name. To them, it was still the KGB.

"Obviously," said Navot, "we'll have to be a bit creative."

"How creative?" Gabriel asked warily.

"Nothing more dangerous than a dinner party. Our ambassador has agreed to host a small affair at the official residence while you're in town. The guest list is being drawn up as we speak. It will be an interesting mix of Russian journalists, artists, and opposition figures. Obviously, the ambassador will do his utmost to make certain Olga Sukhova is in attendance."

"What makes you think she'll come? Dinner at the home of the Israeli ambassador is hardly a coveted invitation, even in Moscow."

"Unless it comes attached with a promise of an exclusive scoop of some sort. Then it will be irresistible."

"What sort of exclusive?"

"Let us worry about that."

"And if she comes?"

"Then you will pull her aside for a private conversation within the secure environment of the residence. And you will reveal yourself to her in whatever manner, and in whatever detail, you deem appropriate. And you will prevail upon her to share anything she knows about why Boris Ostrovsky went to Rome to see you."

"What if she doesn't know anything? Or she's too afraid to talk?"

"Then I suppose you'll have to be charming, which, as we all know, comes quite naturally to you. Besides, Gabriel, there *are* worse ways to spend an evening."

Navot reached back into his attaché case and withdrew a file. Gabriel opened the cover and removed Olga Sukhova's photograph. She was an attractive woman in her mid-forties, with sleek Slavic features, ice-blue eyes, and satiny blond hair swept over one shoulder. He closed the file and looked at Shamron, who was standing before a pair of open French doors, twirling his old Zippo lighter between his fingertips. Talk of an operation was clearly testing his newfound commitment not to smoke.

"You'll go to Moscow, Gabriel. You'll have a nice evening with Olga at the embassy, and, at the very least, you'll pick up whatever information you can about why the journalists at the *Gazeta* are being targeted. Then you can go back to your farm in Umbria — back to your wife and your painting."

"And what happens if the FSB doesn't fall for your little ruse?"

"Your diplomatic passport will protect you."

"The Russian mafia and FSB assassins don't bother much with diplomatic niceties. They shoot first and worry about the political fallout later."

"Moscow Station will be watching your back from the moment you land in St. Petersburg," Navot said. "You'll never be out of our reach. And if things start to look dicey, we can always arrange for an official security detail for you."

"What makes you think Moscow Station will ever see it coming, Uzi? A man brushed against Boris Ostrovsky in Rome yesterday afternoon and, before anyone knew what had happened, he was lying dead on the floor of the Basilica."

"So don't let anyone touch you. And whatever you do, don't drink the tea."

"Sound advice, Uzi."

"Your protection isn't your diplomatic passport," Shamron said. "It's the reputation of the Office. The Russians know that if anyone lays a finger on you, we'll declare open season on them and no Russian agent anywhere in the world will ever be safe again."

"A war against the Russian services is the last thing we need now."

"They're selling advanced weaponry to countries and terror groups that wish to exterminate us. We're already at war with them." Shamron slipped the lighter into his pocket. "You have a lot to do in six days, including learning how to speak and act like an employee of the Ministry of Culture. The deputy minister is expecting you in his office tomorrow morning at ten. He'll brief you thoroughly on your *other* mission in Russia. I want you to behave yourself at that conference, Gabriel. It's important you do nothing to make our position at the UN any worse than it already is."

Gabriel stared at the passport photograph and ran a hand absently over his chin. It had been four days since he'd shaved last. He already had a good start on the beard.

"I need to get a message to Chiara. I need to tell her I won't be coming back to Umbria anytime soon."

"She already knows," Shamron said. "If you want, we can bring her here to Jerusalem."

Gabriel closed the passport and shook his head. "Someone needs to keep an eye on the Poussin. Let her stay in Italy until I get back."

He looked up and saw Navot gazing dubiously at him through his spindly modern eyeglasses.

"What's your problem, Uzi?"

"Don't tell me the great Gabriel Allon is afraid to let his beautiful young wife see him with a gray beard."

"Thirty pounds," said Gabriel. "Thirty pounds."

12
ST. PETERSBURG

Pulkovo 2, St. Petersburg's aging international airport, had thus far been spared the wrecking ball of progress. The cracked tarmac was dotted with forlorn-looking Soviet-era planes that seemed no longer capable of flight, and the structure itself looked more like a factory complex or prison than a hub of modern air travel. Gabriel entered the terminal under the bleary-eyed gaze of a boy militiaman and was pointed toward passport control by an information hostess who seemed annoyed by his presence. After being formally admitted into Russia with only a slight delay, he made his way to baggage claim, where he waited the statutory hour for his luggage. Lifting the bag from the clattering carousel, he noticed the zipper was halfway open. He extended the handle and made his way to the men's room, where he was nearly overcome by a cloud of cigarette smoke. Though smoking was strictly forbidden throughout the terminal, Russians apparently did not feel the ban extended to the toilets.

A watcher was standing outside when Gabriel emerged; they walked together to the arrivals hall, where Gabriel was accosted by a large Russian woman wearing a red shirt with UNESCO across her ample breast. She adhered a name tag to his lapel and directed him to a bus waiting outside in the traffic circle. The interior, already crowded with delegates, looked like a miniature version of the General Assembly. Gabriel nodded to a pair of Saudis as he climbed aboard and received only a blank stare in return. He found an unoccupied seat near the rear of the coach, next to a sullen Norwegian who wasted little time before launching into a quiet tirade about Israel's inhumane treatment of the Palestinians. Gabriel listened patiently to the diplomat's remarks, then offered a few carefully rendered counterpoints. By the time the bus was rolling up the traffic-choked Moskovsky Prospekt toward the heart of the city, the Norwegian declared he now had a better understanding of the Israeli predicament. They exchanged cards and promised to continue the discussion over dinner the next time Natan Golani was in Oslo.

A Cuban zealot on the other side of the aisle attempted to continue the debate but was mercifully interrupted by the Russian woman in the red UNESCO shirt, who was now standing at the front of the bus, microphone in hand, playing the role of tour guide. Without the slightest trace of irony in her amplified voice, she pointed out the landmarks along the wide boulevard: the soaring statue of Lenin, with his hand extended, as though he were forever attempting to hail a cab; the stirring monuments to the Great Patriotic War; the towering temples of Soviet central planning and control. She ignored the dilapidated office buildings, the Brezhnev-era apartment blocks collapsing under their own weight, and the storefront shops now brimming with consumer goods the Soviet state could never provide. These were the relics of the grand folly the Soviets had attempted to foist on the rest of the world. Now, in the minds of the New Russians, the murderous crimes of the Bolsheviks were but a way station on the road to an era of Russian greatness. The gulags, the cruelty, the untold millions who were starved to death or "repressed" — they were only unpleasant details. No one had ever been called to account for his actions. No one was ever punished for his sins.

The prolonged ugliness of the Moskovsky Prospekt finally gave way to the imported European elegance of the city center. First stop was the Astoria Hotel, headquarters of First World delegations. Luggage in hand, Natan Golani filed into the ornate lobby along with his new comrades in culture and joined the lengthy queue at the check-in counter. Though capitalism had taken Russia by storm, the concept of customer service had not. Gabriel stood in line for twenty minutes before finally being processed with Soviet warmth by a flaxen-haired woman who made no attempt to conceal her loathing of him. Refusing an indifferent offer of assistance from a bellman, he carried his own bags to his room. He didn't bother searching it; he was playing by the Moscow Rules now. Assume every room is bugged and every telephone call monitored. Assume every person you encounter is under opposition control. And don't look back. You are never completely alone.

And so Natan Golani attached his laptop computer to the complimentary high-speed data port and read his e-mail, knowing full well that the spies of the FSB were reading it, too. And he called his ersatz wife in Tel

Aviv and listened dutifully while she complained about her ersatz mother, knowing full well the FSB was enduring the same tedious monologue. And having dispensed with his affairs, both personal and professional, he changed into casual clothing and plunged into the soft Leningrad evening. He dined surprisingly well at an Italian restaurant next door at the Angleterre and later was tailed by two FSB watchers, whom he nicknamed Igor and Natasha, as he strolled the Neva embankment through the endless dusk of the white nights. In Palace Square, he paused to gaze at a wedding party drinking champagne at the foot of the Alexander Column, and for a moment he allowed himself to think that perhaps it was better to forget the past after all. Then he turned away and started back to the Astoria, with Igor and Natasha trailing silently after him through the midnight sun.

The following morning Natan Golani threw himself into the business of the conference with the determination of a man with much to accomplish in very little time. He was seated at his assigned place in the grand hall of the Marble Palace when the conference commenced and remained there, translation headphones in place, long after many of the other delegates wisely decided that the real business of the gathering was being conducted in the bars of the Western hotels. He did the working lunches and made the rounds of the afternoon cocktail receptions. He did the endless dinners and never once bowed out of the evening entertainment. He spoke French to the French, German to the Germans, Italian to the Italians, and passable Spanish to the many delegations from Latin America. He rubbed shoulders with the Saudis and the Syrians and even managed a polite conversation with an Iranian about the madness of Holocaust denial. He reached an agreement, in principle, for an Israeli chamber orchestra to tour sub-Saharan Africa and arranged for a group of Maori drummers from New Zealand to visit Israel. He could be combative and conciliatory in the span of a few moments. He spoke of new solutions to old problems. He said Israel was determined to build bridges rather than fences. All that was needed, he said to anyone who would listen, was a man of courage on the other side.

He mounted the dais in the grand hall of the Marble Palace at the end of the second day's session and, as Uzi Navot had forecast, many of the delegates immediately walked out. Those who remained found the speech quite unlike anything they had ever heard from an Israeli representative before. The chief of UNESCO declared it "a clarion call for a new paradigm in the Middle East." The French delegate referred to Monsieur Golani as "a true man of culture and the arts." Everyone in attendance agreed that a new wind seemed to be blowing from the Judean Hills.

There was no such wind blowing, however, from the headquarters of the FSB. Their break-in artists searched his hotel room each time he left, and their watchers followed him wherever he went. During the final gala at the Mariinsky Theatre, an attractive female agent flirted shamelessly with him and invited him back to her apartment for an evening of sexual compromise. He politely declined and left the Mariinsky with no company other than Igor and Natasha, who were by now too bored to even bother concealing their presence.

It being his final night in St. Petersburg, he decided to climb the winding steps to the top of St. Isaac's golden dome. The parapet was empty except for a pair of German girls, who were standing at the balustrade, gazing out at the sweeping view of the city. One of the girls handed him a camera and posed dramatically while he snapped her picture. She then thanked him profusely and told him that Olga Sukhova had agreed to attend the embassy dinner. When he returned to his hotel room, he found the message light winking on his telephone. It was the Israeli ambassador, insisting that he come to Moscow. "You have to see the place to believe it, Natan! Billionaires, dirty bankers, and gangsters, all swimming in a sea of oil, caviar, and vodka! We're having a dinner party Thursday night — just a few brave souls who've had the chutzpah to challenge the regime. And don't *think* about trying to say no, because I've already arranged it with your minister."

He erased the message, then dialed Tel Aviv and informed his ersatz wife that he would be staying in Russia longer than expected. She berated him for several minutes, then slammed down the phone in disgust. Gabriel held the receiver to his ear a moment longer and imagined the FSB listeners having a good laugh at his expense.

13
Moscow

On Moscow's Tverskaya Street, the flashy foreign cars of the newly rich jockeyed for position with the boxy Ladas and Zhigulis of the still deprived. The Kremlin's Trinity Tower was nearly lost in a gauzy shroud of exhaust fumes, its famous red star looking sadly like just another advertisement for an imported luxury good. In the bar of the Savoy Hotel, the sharp boys and their bodyguards were drinking cold beer instead of vodka. Their black Bentleys and Range Rovers waited just outside the entrance, engines running for a quick getaway. Conservation of fuel was hardly a priority in Russia these days. Petrol, like nearly everything else, was in plentiful supply.

At 7:30 p.m., Gabriel came down to the lobby dressed in a dark suit and diplomatic silver tie. Stepping from the entrance, he scanned the faces behind the wheels of the parked cars before heading down the hill to the Teatralnyy Prospekt. Atop a low hill loomed the hulking yellow fortress of Lubyanka, headquarters of the FSB. In its shadow was a row of exclusive Western designer boutiques worthy of Rodeo Drive or Madison Avenue. Gabriel could not help but marvel at the striking juxtaposition, even if it was only a bit of pantomime for the pair of watchers who had left the comfort of their air-conditioned car and were now trailing him on foot.

He consulted a hotel street map — needlessly, because his route was well planned in advance — and made his way to a large open-air esplanade at the foot of the Kremlin walls. Passing a row of kiosks selling everything from Soviet hockey jerseys to busts of the murderers Lenin and Stalin, he turned to the left and entered Red Square. The last of the day's pilgrims stood outside the entrance of Lenin's Tomb, sipping Coca-Cola and fanning themselves with tourist brochures and guides to Moscow nightlife. He wondered what drew them here. Was it misplaced faith? Nostalgia for a simpler time? Or did they come merely for morbid reasons? To judge for themselves whether the figure beneath the glass was real or more worthy of a wax museum?

He crossed the square toward the candy-cane domes of St. Basil's Cathedral, then followed the eastern wall of the Kremlin down to the Moscow River. On the opposite bank, at Serafimovicha Street 2, stood the infamous House on the Embankment, the colossal apartment block built by Stalin in 1931 as an exclusive residence for the most elite members of the *nomenklatura*. During the height of the Great Terror, 766 residents, or one-third of its total population, had been murdered, and those "privileged" enough to reside in the house lived in constant fear of the knock at the door. Despite its bloody history, many of the old Soviet elite and their children still lived in the building, and flats now sold for millions of dollars. Little of the exterior had changed except for the roof, which was now crowned by a Stalin-sized revolving advertisement for Mercedes-Benz. The Nazis may have failed in their bid to capture Moscow, but now, sixty years after the war, the flag of German industrial might flew proudly from one of the city's most prestigious landmarks.

Gabriel gave his map another pointless glance as he set out across the Moskvoretsky Bridge. Crimson-and-black banners of the ruling Russian Unity Party hung from the lampposts, swaying drunkenly in the warm breeze. At the opposite end of the bridge, the Russian president smiled disagreeably at Gabriel from a billboard three stories in height. He was scheduled to face the Russian "electorate," such that it was, for the fourth time at the end of the summer. There was little suspense about the outcome; the president had long ago purged Russia of dangerous democratic tendencies, and the officially sanctioned opposition parties were now little more than useful idiots. The smiling man on the billboard was the new tsar in everything but name — and one with imperial ambitions at that.

On the other side of the river lay the pleasant quarter known as Zamoskvoreche. Spared the architectural terror of Stalin's replanning, the district had retained some of the atmosphere of nineteenth-century Moscow. Gabriel walked past flaking imperial houses and onion-domed churches until he came to the walled compound at Bolshaya Ordynka 56. The plaque at the gate read EMBASSY OF ISRAEL in English, Russian, and Hebrew. Gabriel held his credentials up to the fish-eye lens of the camera and heard the electronic dead-bolt locks immediately snap open. As he stepped into the compound, he glanced over his shoulder and saw a man in a car across the street raise a camera and blatantly snap a photograph. Apparently, the FSB knew about the ambassador's dinner party and intended to intimidate the guests as they arrived and departed.

The compound was cramped and drab, with a cluster of featureless buildings standing around a central courtyard. A youthful security guard — who was not a security guard at all but an Office field agent attached to Moscow Station — greeted Gabriel cordially by his cover name and escorted him into the foyer of the small apartment building that housed most of the embassy's personnel. The ambassador was waiting on the top-floor landing as Gabriel stepped off the lift. A polished career diplomat whom Gabriel had seen only in photographs, he threw his arms around Gabriel and gave him two thunderous claps between the shoulder blades that no FSB transmitter could fail to detect. "Natan!" he shouted, as though to a deaf uncle. "My God! Is it really you? You look as though you've been traveling an age. St. Petersburg surely wasn't as bad as all that." He thrust a glass of tepid champagne into Gabriel's hand and cast him adrift. "As usual, Natan, you're the last to arrive. Mingle with the masses. We'll chat later after you've had a chance to say hello to everyone. I want to hear all about your dreadful conference."

Gabriel hoisted his most affable diplomatic smile and, glass in hand, waded into the noisy smoke-filled sitting room.

He met a famous violinist who was now the leader of a ragtag opposition party called the Coalition for a Free Russia.

He met a playwright who had revived the time-tested art of Russian allegory to carefully criticize the new regime.

He met a filmmaker who had recently won a major human rights award in the West for a documentary about the gulag.

He met a woman who had been confined to an insane asylum because she had dared to carry a placard across Red Square calling for democracy in Russia.

He met an unrepentant Bolshevik who thought the only way to save Russia was to restore the dictatorship of the proletariat and burn the oligarchs at the stake.

He met a fossilized dissident from the Brezhnev era who had been raised from the near dead to wage one last futile campaign for Russian freedom.

He met a brave essayist who had been nearly beaten to death by a band of Unity Party Youth.

And finally, ten minutes after his arrival, he introduced himself to a reporter from

Moskovsky Gazeta, who, owing to the murders of two colleagues, had recently been promoted to the post of acting editor in chief. She wore a black sleeveless dress and a silver locket around her neck. The bangles on her wrist clattered like wind chimes as she extended her hand toward Gabriel and gave him a melancholy smile. "How do you do, Mr. Golani," she said primly in English. "My name is Olga Sukhova."

The photograph Uzi Navot had shown him a week earlier in Jerusalem had not done justice to Olga's beauty. With translucent eyes and long, narrow features, she looked to Gabriel like a Russian icon come to life. He was seated at her right during dinner but managed only a few brief exchanges of conversation, largely because the documentary filmmaker monopolized her attention with a shot-by-shot description of his latest work. With no place to take shelter, Gabriel found himself in the clutches of the ancient dissident, who treated him to a lecture on the history of Russian political opposition dating back to the days of the tsars. As the waiters cleared the dessert plates, Olga gave him a sympathetic smile. "I'm afraid I feel a cigarette coming on," she said. "Would you care to join me?"

They rose from the table together under the crestfallen gaze of the filmmaker and stepped onto the ambassador's small terrace. It was empty and in semidarkness; in the distance loomed one of the "the Seven Sisters," the monstrous Stalinist towers that still dominated the Moscow skyline. "Europe's tallest apartment building," she said without enthusiasm. "Everything in Russia has to be the biggest, the tallest, the fastest, or the most valuable. We cannot live as normal people." Her lighter flared. "Is this your first time in Russia, Mr. Golani?"

"Yes," he answered truthfully.

"And what brings you to our country?"

You, he answered truthfully again, but only to himself. Aloud, he said that he had been drafted on short notice to attend the UNESCO conference in St. Petersburg. And for the next several minutes he spoke glowingly of his achievements, until he could see that she was bored. He glanced over his shoulder, into the ambassador's dining room, and saw no movement to indicate that their moment of privacy was about to be interrupted anytime soon.

"We have a common acquaintance," he said. "Actually, we *had* a common acquaintance. I'm afraid he's no longer alive."

She lifted the cigarette to her lips and held

it there as though it were a shield protecting her from harm. "And who might that be?" she asked in her schoolgirl English.

"Boris Ostrovsky," Gabriel said calmly.

Her gaze was blank. The ember of her cigarette was trembling slightly in the half-light. "And how were you acquainted with Boris Ostrovsky?" she asked guardedly.

"I was in St. Peter's Basilica when he was murdered."

He gazed directly into the iconic face, assessing whether the fear he saw there was authentic or a forgery. Deciding it was indeed genuine, he pressed on.

"I was the reason he came to Rome in the first place. I held him while he died."

She folded her arms defensively. "I'm sorry, Mr. Golani, but you are making me extremely uncomfortable."

"Boris wanted to tell me something, Miss Sukhova. He was killed before he could do that. I need to know what it was. And I think you may know the answer."

"I'm afraid you were misled. No one on the staff knew what Boris was doing in Rome."

"We know he had information, Miss Sukhova. Information that was too dangerous to publish here. Information about a threat of some sort. A threat to the West and Israel."

She glanced through the open doorway into the dining room. "I suppose this evening was all staged for my benefit. You wanted to meet me somewhere you thought the FSB wouldn't be listening and so you threw a party on my behalf and lured me here with promises of an exclusive story." She placed her hand suggestively on his forearm and leaned close. Her voice, when she spoke again, was little more than a whisper. "You should know that the FSB is *always* listening, Mr. Golani. In fact, two of the guests your embassy invited here tonight are on the FSB payroll."

She released his arm and moved away. Then her face brightened suddenly, like a lost child glimpsing her mother. Gabriel turned and saw the filmmaker advancing toward them, with two other guests in his wake. Cigarettes were ignited, drinks were fetched, and within a few moments they were all four conversing in rapid Russian as though Mr. Golani was not there. Gabriel was convinced he had overplayed his hand and that Olga was now forever lost to him, but as he turned to leave he felt her hand once more upon his arm.

"The answer is yes," she said.

"I'm sorry?"

"You asked whether I would be willing to give you a tour of Moscow tomorrow. And the answer is yes. Where are you staying?"

"At the Savoy."

"It's the most thoroughly bugged hotel in Moscow." She smiled. "I'll call you in the morning."

14
NOVODEVICHY CEMETERY, MOSCOW

She wanted to take him to a cemetery. To understand Russia today, she said, you must first know her past. And to know her past, you had to walk among her bones.

She telephoned the Savoy the first time at ten and suggested they meet at noon. A short time later she called again to say that, due to an unforeseen complication at the office, she would not be able to meet him until three. Gabriel, playing the role of Natan Golani, spent much of the day touring the Kremlin and the Tretyakov Gallery. Then, at 2:45, he stepped onto the escalator of the Lubyanka Metro station and rode it down into the warm Moscow earth. A train waited in the murky light of the platform; he stepped on board as the doors rattled closed and took hold of the overhead handrail as the carriage lurched forward. His FSB minder had managed to secure the only empty seat. He was fiddling with his iPod, symbol of the New Russian man, while an old babushka in a black headscarf looked on in bewilderment.

They rode six stops to Sportivnaya. The watcher emerged into the hazy sunlight first and went to the left. Gabriel turned to the right and entered a chaotic outdoor market of wobbly kiosks and trestle tables piled high with cheap goods from the former republics of central Asia. At the opposite end of the market a band of Unity Party Youth was chanting slogans and handing out election leaflets. One of them, a not-so-youthful man in his early thirties, was trailing a few steps behind Gabriel as he arrived at the entrance of the Novodevichy Cemetery.

On the other side of the gate stood a small redbrick flower shop. Olga Sukhova was waiting outside the doorway, a bouquet of carnations in her arms. "Your timing is impeccable, Mr. Golani." She kissed Gabriel formally on both cheeks and smiled warmly. "Come with me. I think you're going to find this fascinating."

She led him up a shaded footpath lined with tall elm and spruce. The graves were on either side: small plots surrounded by iron fences; tall sculpted monuments; redbrick niche walls covered in pale moss. The atmosphere was parklike and tranquil, a reprieve from the chaos of the city. For a moment, Gabriel was almost able to forget they were being followed.

"The cemetery used to be inside the Novodevichy Convent, but at the turn of the last century the Church decided that there were too many burials taking place inside the monastery's walls so they created this place." She spoke to him in English, at tour guide level, loudly enough so that those around them could hear. "It's the closest thing we have to a national cemetery — other than the Kremlin wall, of course. Playwrights and poets, monsters and murderers: they all lie together here in Novodevichy. One can only imagine what they talk about at night when the gates are closed and the visitors all leave." She stopped before a tall gray monument with a pile of wilted red roses at its base. "Do you like Chekhov, Mr. Golani?"

"Who doesn't?"

"He was one of the first to be buried here." She took him by the elbow. "Come, I'll show you some more."

They drifted slowly together along a footpath strewn with fallen leaves. On a parallel pathway, the watcher who had been handing out leaflets in the market was now feigning excessive interest in the grave of a renowned Russian mathematician. A few feet away stood a woman with a beige anorak tied around her waist. In her right hand was a digital camera, pointed directly at Gabriel and Olga.

"You were followed here." She gave him a sideways glance. "But, then, I suppose you already know that, don't you, Mr. Golani? Or should I call you Mr. Allon?"

"My name is Natan Golani. I work for the Israeli Ministry of Culture."

"Forgive me, Mr. Golani."

She managed a smile. She was dressed casually in a snug-fitting black pullover and a pair of blue jeans. Her pale hair was pulled straight back from her forehead and secured by a clasp at the nape of her neck. Her suede boots made her appear taller than she had the previous evening. Their heels tapped rhythmically along the pavement as they walked slowly past the graves.

The musicians Rostropovich and Rubinstein . . .

The writers Gogol and Bulgakov . . .

The Party giants Khrushchev and Kosygin . . .

Kaganovich, the Stalinist monster who murdered millions during the madness of collectivization . . .

Molotov, signer of the secret pact that condemned Europe to war and the Jews of Poland to annihilation . . .

"There's no place quite like this to see the striking contradictions of our history. Great beauty lies side by side with the incomprehensible. These men gave us everything, and when they were gone we were left with nothing: factories that produced goods no one wanted, an ideology that was tired and bankrupt. All of it set to beautiful words and music."

Gabriel looked at the bouquet of flowers in her arms. "Who are those for?"

She stopped before a small plot with a low, unadorned stone monument. "Dmitri Sukhova, my grandfather. He was a playwright and a filmmaker. Had he lived in another time, under a different regime, he might have been great. Instead, he was drafted to make cheap Party propaganda for the masses. He made the people believe in the myth of Soviet greatness. His reward was to be buried here, among true Russian genius."

She crouched next to the grave and brushed pine needles from the plaque.

"You have his name," Gabriel said. "You're not married?"

She shook her head and placed the flowers gently on the grave. "I'm afraid I've yet to find a countryman suitable for marriage and procreation. If they have any money, the first thing they do is buy themselves a mistress. Go into any trendy sushi restaurant in Moscow and you'll see the pretty young girls lined up at the bar, waiting for a man to sweep them off their feet. But not just any man. They want a New Russian man. A man with money and connections. A man who winters in Zermatt and Courchevel and summers in the South of France. A man who will give them jewelry and foreign cars. I prefer to spend my summers at my grandfather's dacha. I grow radishes and carrots there. I still believe in my country. I don't need to vacation in the exclusive playgrounds of Western Europe to be a contented, self-fulfilled New Russian woman."

She had been speaking to the grave. Now she turned her head and looked over her shoulder at Gabriel.

"You must think I'm terribly foolish."

"Why foolish?"

"Because I pretend to be a journalist in a country where there is no longer true journalism. Because I want democracy in a country that has never known it — and, in all likelihood, never will."

She stood upright and brushed the dust

from her palms. "To understand Russia today, you must understand the trauma of the nineties. Everything we had, everything we had been told, was swept away. We went from superpower to basket case overnight. Our people lost their life's savings, not just once but over and over again. Russians are a paternalistic people. They believe in the Orthodox Church, the State, the Tsar. They associate democracy with chaos. Our president and the *siloviki* understand this. They use words like 'managed democracy' and 'State capitalism,' but they're just euphemisms for something more sinister: fascism. We have lurched from the ideology of Lenin to the ideology of Mussolini in a decade. We should not be surprised by this. Look around you, Mr. Golani. The history of Russia is nothing but a series of convulsions. We cannot live as normal people. We never will."

She looked past him, into a darkened corner of the cemetery. "They're watching us very closely. Hold my arm, please, Mr. Golani. It is better if the FSB believes you are attracted to me."

He did as she asked. "Perhaps fascism is too strong a word," he said.

"What term would you apply to our system?"

"A corporate state," Gabriel replied without conviction.

"I'm afraid that is a euphemism worthy of the Kremlin. Yes, our people are now free to make and spend money, but the State still picks the winners and the losers. Our leaders speak of regaining lost empires. They use our oil and gas to bully and intimidate our neighbors. They have all but eliminated the opposition and an independent press, and those who dare to protest are beaten openly in the streets. Our children are being coerced into joining Party youth organizations. They are taught that America and the Jews want to control the world — that America and the Jews want to steal Russia's wealth and resources. I don't know about you, Mr. Golani, but I get nervous when young minds are trained to hate. The inevitable comparisons to another time and place are uncomfortable, to say the least."

She stopped beneath a towering spruce tree and turned to face him.

"You are an Ashkenazi Jew?" she asked.

He nodded.

"Your family came from Russia originally?"

"Germany," he said. "My grandparents were from Berlin."

"Did they survive the war?"

143

He shook his head and, once again, told her the truth. "They were murdered at Auschwitz. My mother was young enough to work and she managed to survive. She died several years ago."

"I wonder what your mother would have said about a leader who fills young minds with paranoid fantasies about others plotting to steal what is rightly theirs. Would she have called it the ideology of a corporate state or would she have used a more sinister term?"

"Point taken, Miss Sukhova."

"Forgive my tone, Mr. Golani. I am an old-fashioned Russian woman who likes to grow radishes and carrots in the garden of her grandfather's broken-down dacha. I believe in my Russia, and I want no more acts of evil committed in my name. Neither did Boris Ostrovsky. That is why he wanted to talk to you. And that is why he was murdered."

"Why did he go to Rome, Olga? What did he want to tell me?"

She reached up and touched his cheek with her fingertip. "Perhaps you should kiss me now, Mr. Golani. It is better if the FSB is under the impression we intend to become lovers."

15
MOSCOW

They drove to the Old Arbat in her car, an ancient pea soup green Lada with a dangling front bumper. She knew a place where they could talk: a Georgian restaurant with stone grottoes and faux streams and waiters in native dress. It was loud, she assured him. *Bedlam.* "The owner looks a little too much like Stalin for some people." She pointed out the window at another one of the Seven Sisters. "The Ukraina Hotel."

"World's biggest?"

"We cannot live as normal people."

She left the car in a flagrantly illegal space near Arbat Square and they walked to the restaurant through the fading late-afternoon light. She had been right about the owner — he looked like a wax figure of Stalin come to life — and about the noise as well. Gabriel had to lean across the table a few degrees to hear her speak. She was talking about an anonymous tip the *Gazeta* had received before the New Year. A tip from a source whose name she could never divulge . . .

"This source told us that an arms dealer with close ties to the Kremlin and our president was about to conclude a major deal that would put some very dangerous weapons into the hands of some very dangerous people."

"What kind of people?"

"The kind you have been fighting your entire life, Mr. Golani. The kind who have vowed to destroy your country and the West. The kind who fly airplanes into buildings and set off bombs in crowded markets."

"Al-Qaeda?"

"Or one of its affiliates."

"What type of weapons?"

"We don't know."

"Are they conventional?"

"We don't know."

"Chemical or biological?"

"We don't know."

"But you can't rule it out?"

"We can't rule *anything* out, Mr. Golani. For all we know, the weapons could be radiological or even *nuclear.*" She was silent for a moment, then managed a cautious smile, as if embarrassed by an awkward pause in the conversation. "Perhaps it would be better if I simply told you what I *do* know."

She was now gazing at him intently. Gabriel heard a commotion to his left and glanced over his shoulder. Stalin was seating a group of people at the neighboring table: two aging mobsters and their high-priced professional dates. Olga took note of them as well and continued speaking.

"The source who provided us with the initial tip about the sale is impeccable and assured us that the information was accurate. But we couldn't print a story based on a single source. You see, unlike many of our competitors, the *Gazeta* has a reputation for thoroughness and accuracy. We've been sued many times by people who didn't like what we wrote about them but we've never lost, not even in the kangaroo courts of Russia."

"So you started asking questions?"

"We're reporters, Mr. Golani. That's what we do. Our investigation unearthed a few intriguing bits but nothing specific and nothing we could publish. We decided to send one of our reporters to Courchevel to follow the arms dealer in question. The dealer owns a chalet there. A rather *large* chalet, actually."

"The reporter was Aleksandr Lubin?"

She nodded her head slowly. "I assume you know the details from the news accounts. Aleksandr was murdered within a few hours of his arrival. Obviously, it was a warning to the rest of the *Gazeta* staff to back off. I'm afraid it had the opposite effect, though. We took Aleksandr's murder as confirmation the story was true."

"And so you kept digging?"

"Carefully. But, yes, we kept digging. We were able to uncover much about the arms dealer's operations in general, but were never able to pin down the specifics of a deal. Finally, the matter was taken out of our hands entirely. Quite unexpectedly, the owner of the *Gazeta* decided to sell the magazine. I'm afraid he didn't reach the decision on his own; he was pressured into the sale by the Kremlin and the FSB. Our new owner is a man with no experience in journalism whatsoever, and his first move was to appoint a publisher with even less. The publisher announced that he was no longer interested in hard news or investigative journalism. The *Gazeta* was now going to focus on celebrity news, the arts, and life in the New Russia. He then held a meeting with Boris Ostrovsky to review upcoming stories. Guess which story he killed first?"

"An investigation into a possible deal

between a Russian arms trafficker and al-Qaeda."

"Exactly."

"I assume the time of the sale wasn't a coincidence."

"No, it wasn't. Our new owner is an associate of the arms dealer. In all likelihood, it was the arms dealer who put up all the money. Rather remarkable, don't you think, Mr. Golani? Only in Russia."

She reached into her handbag and withdrew a pack of cigarettes and a lighter. "Do you mind?"

Gabriel shook his head, and glanced around the restaurant. One of the mobsters had his hand on the bare thigh of his date, but there were no signs of any watchers. Olga lit her cigarette and placed the pack and lighter on the table.

"The sale of the magazine presented us with a terrible dilemma. We believed the story about the missile sale to be true, but we now had no place to publish it. Nor could we continue to investigate the story inside Russia. We decided on another course of action. We decided to make our findings known to the West through a trusted figure inside Israeli intelligence."

"Why me? Why not walk over to the U.S. Embassy and tell the CIA station chief?"

"It is no longer wise for members of the opposition or the press to meet with American officials, especially those who also happen to work for the CIA. Besides, Boris always admired the secret intelligence service of Israel. And he was especially fond of a certain agent who recently got his picture in the paper for saving the life of the daughter of the American ambassador to London."

"And so he decided to leave the country and contact us in Rome?"

"In keeping with the new mission of the *Gazeta,* he told our publisher he wanted to do a piece about Russians at play in the Eternal City. After he arrived in Rome, he made contact with your embassy and requested a meeting. Obviously, the arms dealer and his security service were watching. I suspect they're watching now."

"Who is he? Who is the arms dealer?"

She said a name, then picked up the wine list and opened the cover.

"Let's have something to drink, shall we, Mr. Golani? Do you prefer red or white?"

Stalin brought the wine. It was Georgian, bloodred, and very rough. Gabriel's thoughts were now elsewhere. He was thinking of the name Olga Sukhova had just

150

spoken. It was familiar to him, of course. Everyone in the trade had heard the name Ivan Kharkov.

"How much do you know about him, Mr. Golani?"

"The basics. Former KGB turned Russian oligarch. Passes himself off as a legitimate investor and international businessman. Lives mainly in London and France."

"Those *are* the basics. May I give you a more thorough version of the story?"

Gabriel nodded his head. Olga braced herself on her elbows and held the wineglass near her face with both hands. Between them, a candle flickered in a red bowl. It added blush to her pale cheeks.

"He was a child of Soviet privilege, our Ivan. His father was high-ranking KGB. *Very* high-ranking. In fact, when he retired, he was the chief of the First Main Directorate, the foreign espionage division. Ivan spent a good part of his childhood abroad. He was permitted to travel, while ordinary Soviet citizens were kept prisoner in their own country. He had blue jeans and Rolling Stones records, while ordinary Soviet teenagers had Communist propaganda and Komsomol weekends in the country. In the days of shortages, when the workers were forced to eat seaweed and whale meat, he and his family had fresh veal and caviar."

She drank some of the wine. At the front entrance, Stalin was negotiating with two male customers over a table. One of them had been at the cemetery. Olga seemed not to notice.

"Like all the children of Party elite, he was automatically granted a place at an elite university. In Ivan's case, it was Moscow State. After graduation, he was admitted directly into the ranks of the KGB. Despite his fluency in English and German, he was not deemed suitable material for a life as a foreign spy, so he was assigned to the Fifth Main Directorate. Do you know about the Fifth Main Directorate, Mr. Golani?"

"It was responsible for internal security functions: border control, dissidents, artists and writers."

"Don't forget the *refuseniks,* Mr. Golani. The Fifth Directorate was also responsible for persecuting Jews. Rumor has it Ivan was very diligent in that regard."

Stalin was now seating the two men at a table near the center of the restaurant, well out of earshot.

"Ivan benefited from the magic hand of his famous father and was promoted rapidly through the ranks of the directorate. Then came Gorbachev and glasnost and perestroika, and overnight everything in our country changed. The Party loosened the reins on central planning and allowed young entrepreneurs — in some cases the very dissidents whom Ivan and the Fifth Directorate were monitoring — to start cooperatives and private banks. Against all odds, many of these young entrepreneurs actually started to make money. This didn't sit well with our secret overlords at Lubyanka. They were used to picking society's winners and losers. A free marketplace threatened to upset the old order. And, of course, if there was money to be made, they wanted what was rightly theirs. They decided they had no option but to go into business for themselves. They needed an energetic young man of their own, a young man who knew the ways of Western capitalism. A young man who had been permitted to read the forbidden books."

"Ivan Kharkov."

She raised her glass in salutation to his correct answer. "With the blessing of his masters at Lubyanka, Ivan was allowed to leave the KGB and start a bank. He was given a single dank room in an old Moscow office building, a telephone, and an American-made personal computer, something most of us had never seen. Once again, the magic hand was laid upon Ivan's shoulder and within months his new bank was raking in millions of dollars in profit, almost all of it due to State business. Then the Soviet Union crumbled, and we entered the roaring nineties period of gangster capitalism, shock therapy, and instant privatization. When the State-owned enterprises of the Soviet Union were auctioned off to the highest bidder, Ivan gobbled up some of the most lucrative assets and factories. When Moscow real estate could be purchased for a song and a promise, Ivan snatched up some of the gems. During the period of hyperinflation, Ivan and his patrons at Lubyanka Square made fortunes in currency speculation — fortunes that inevitably found their way into secret bank accounts in Zurich and Geneva. Ivan never had any illusions about the reason for his astonishing success. He had been helped by the magic hand of the KGB, and he was very good at keeping the magic hand filled with money."

A waiter appeared and began laying small dishes of Georgian appetizers on the table. Olga explained the contents of each; then, when the waiter was gone, she resumed her lecture.

"One of the State assets Ivan scooped up

in the early nineties was a fleet of cargo planes and container vessels. They didn't cost him much, since at the time most of the planes were sinking into the ground at airfields around the country and the ships were turning to rust in dry dock. Ivan bought the facilities and the personnel necessary to get the fleet up and running again, and within a few months he had one of the most valuable properties in Russia: a company capable of moving goods in and out of the country, no questions asked. Before long, Ivan's ships and planes were filled with lucrative cargo bound for troubled foreign lands."

"Russian weapons," said Gabriel.

Olga nodded. "And not just AK-47s and RPG-7s, though they are a substantial part of his operation. Ivan deals in the big-ticket items, too: tanks, antiaircraft batteries, attack helicopters, even the occasional frigate or out-of-date MiG. He hides now behind a respectable veneer as one of Moscow's most prominent real estate developers and investors. He owns a palace in Knightsbridge, a villa in the South of France, and the chalet in Courchevel. He buys paintings, antique furniture, and even a share of an English football team. He's a regular at Kremlin functions and is very close to the president and the *siloviki.* But beneath it all, he's nothing but a gunrunner and a thug. As our American friends like to say, he's a full-service operation. He has inventory and the cargo ships and transport planes to deliver it. If necessary, he can even provide financing through his banking operations. He's renowned for his ability to get weapons to their destination quickly, sometimes overnight, just like DHL and Federal Express."

"If we're going to find out whether Ivan has really made a deal with al-Qaeda, we have to get inside his network. And to get inside Ivan's network, we need the name of your original source."

"You can't have it, Mr. Golani. Two people are already dead. I'm afraid the matter is closed." She looked down at her menu. "We should eat something, Mr. Golani. It's better if the FSB thinks we're actually hungry."

For the remainder of dinner, Olga did not mention Ivan Kharkov and his missiles. Instead, she spoke of books recently read, films recently viewed, and the coming election. When the check came, they engaged in a playful tussle, male chivalry versus Russian hospitality, and chivalry prevailed. It was still light out; they walked directly to her car, arm in arm for the benefit of any spectators. The old Lada wouldn't turn over at first, but it finally rattled into life with a puff of silver-blue smoke. "Built by the finest Soviet craftsmen during the last years of developed socialism," she said. "At least we don't have to remove our wipers anymore."

She turned up the radio very loud and embraced him without passion. "Would you be so kind as to see me to my door, Mr. Golani? I'm afraid my building isn't as safe as it once was."

"It would be my pleasure."

"It's not far from here. Ten minutes at most. There's a Metro stop nearby. You can —"

Gabriel placed a finger to her lips and told her to drive.

16
MOSCOW

It is said that Moscow is not truly a city but a collection of villages. This was one of them, thought Gabriel, as he walked at Olga's side. And it was a village with serious problems. Here a band of alcoholics swilling beer and tots of vodka. Here a pack of drug addicts sharing a pipe and a tube of glue. Here a squadron of skateboard punks terrorizing a trio of old babushkas out for an evening stroll. Presiding over it all was an immense portrait of the Russian president with his arm raised in the fashion of Lenin. Across the top, in red lettering, was the Party's ubiquitous slogan: FORWARD AS ONE!

Her building was known as K-9, but the local English-speaking wits called it the House of Dogs. Built in the footprint of an H, it had thirty-two floors, six entrances, and a large transmission tower on the roof with blinking red warning lights. An identical twin stood on one side, an ugly stepsister on the other. It was not a home, thought Gabriel, but a storage facility for people.

"Which doorway is yours?"

"Entrance C."

"Pick another."

"But I always go through C."

"That's why I want you to pick another."

They entered through a doorway marked B and struck out down a long corridor with a cracked linoleum floor. Every other light was out, and from behind the closed doors came the sounds and odors of too many people living too closely together. Arriving at the elevators, Olga stabbed at the call button and gazed at the ceiling. A minute elapsed. Then another.

"It's not working."

"How often does it break down?"

"Once a week. Sometimes twice."

"What floor do you live on?"

"The *eleventh*."

"Where are the stairs?"

With a glance, she indicated around the corner. Gabriel led her into a dimly lit stairwell that smelled of stale beer, urine, and vaguely of disinfectant. "I'm afraid progress has come slowly to Russian stairwells," she said. "Believe it or not, it used to be much worse."

Gabriel mounted the first step and started upward, with Olga at his heels. For the first four floors, they were alone, but on the fifth they encountered two girls sharing a cigarette and on the seventh two boys sharing a syringe. On the eighth-floor landing, Gabriel had to slow for a moment to scrape a condom from the bottom of his shoe, and on the tenth he walked through shards of broken glass.

By the time they reached the eleventh-floor landing, Olga was breathing heavily. Gabriel reached out for the latch, but before he could touch it, the door flew away from him as though it had been hurled open by a blast wave. He pushed Olga into the corner and managed to step clear of the threshold as the first rounds tore the dank air. Olga began to scream but Gabriel scarcely noticed. He was now pressed against the wall of the stairwell. He felt no fear, only a sense of profound disappointment. Someone was about to die. And it wasn't going to be him.

The gun was a P-9 Gurza with a suppressor screwed into the barrel. It was a professional's weapon, though the same could not be said for the dolt who was wielding it.

Perhaps it was overconfidence on the part of the assassin, Gabriel would think later, or perhaps the men who had hired him had neglected to point out that one of the targets was a professional himself. Whatever the case, the gunman blundered through the doorway with the weapon exposed in his outstretched hands. Gabriel seized hold of it and pointed it safely toward the ceiling as he drove the man against the wall. The gun discharged harmlessly twice before Gabriel was able to deliver two vicious knees to the gunman's groin, followed by a crushing elbow to the temple. Though the final blow was almost certainly lethal, Gabriel left nothing to chance. After prying the Gurza from the gunman's now-limp hand, he fired two shots into his skull, the ultimate professional insult.

Amateurs, he knew from experience, tended to kill in pairs, which explained his rather calm reaction to the sound of crackling glass rising up the stairwell. He pulled Olga out of the line of fire and was standing at the top of the stairs as the second man came round the corner. Gabriel put him down as if he were a target on a training range: three tightly grouped shots to the center of the body, one to the head for style points.

He stood motionless for a few seconds, until he was certain there were no more assassins, then turned around. Olga was cowering on the floor, next to the first man Gabriel had killed. Like the one at the bottom of the stairs, his head was covered by a black balaclava. Gabriel tore it off, revealing a lifeless face with a dark beard.

"He's Chechen," Olga said.

"You're sure?"

Before Olga could answer, she leaned over the edge of the stairs and was violently sick. Gabriel held her hand as she convulsed. In the distance, he could hear the first sirens of the police.

"They'll be here any minute, Olga. We're never going to see each other again. You must give me the name. Tell me your source before it's too late."

17
Moscow

The first officers to arrive were members of a Moscow City Militia public security unit, the proletariat of the city's vast police and intelligence apparatus. The ranking officer was a stubble-chinned sergeant who spoke only Russian. He took a brief statement from Olga, whom he appeared to know by reputation, then turned his attention to the dead gunmen. "Chechen gangsters," he declared with disgust. He gathered a few more facts, including the name and nationality of Miss Sukhova's foreign friend, and radioed the information to headquarters. At the end of the call, he ordered his colleagues not to disturb the scene and confiscated Gabriel's diplomatic passport, hardly an encouraging sign.

The next officers to appear were members of the GUOP, the special unit that handles cases related to organized crime and contract killings, one of Moscow's most lucrative industries. The team leader wore blue jeans, a black leather jacket, and a pair of wraparound sunglasses backward on his shaved head. He called himself Markov. No rank. No first name. Just Markov. Gabriel instantly recognized the type. Markov was the sort who walked the delicate line between criminal and cop. He could have gone either way, and, at various times during his career, he probably had.

He examined the corpses and agreed with the sergeant's findings that they were probably Chechen contract killers. But unlike the younger man, he spoke a bit of English. His first questions were directed not at the famous reporter from the *Gazeta* but at Gabriel. He seemed most interested in hearing how a middle-aged Israeli diplomat from the Ministry of Culture had managed to disarm a professional assassin, shoot him twice in the head, and then kill his partner. Listening to Gabriel's account, his expression was one of open skepticism. He scrutinized Gabriel's passport carefully, then slipped it into his coat pocket and said they would have to continue this conversation at headquarters.

"I must protest," Gabriel said.

"I understand," said Markov sadly.

For reasons never made clear, Gabriel was

164

handcuffed and taken by unmarked car to a busy Militia headquarters. There, he was led into the central processing area and placed on a wooden bench, next to a weathered man in his sixties who had been roughed up and robbed by street toughs. An hour passed; Gabriel finally walked over to the duty officer and asked for permission to phone his embassy. The duty officer translated Gabriel's request to his colleagues, who immediately erupted into uproarious laughter. "They want money," the elderly man said when Gabriel returned to the bench. "You cannot leave until you pay them what they want." Gabriel managed a brief smile. If only it were that simple.

Shortly after 1 a.m., Markov reappeared. He ordered Gabriel to stand, removed the handcuffs, and led him into an interrogation room. Gabriel's possessions — his billfold, diplomatic passport, wristwatch, and mobile — were laid out neatly on a table. Markov picked up the phone and made a show of calling up the directory of recent calls.

"You dialed your embassy before the first Militia officers arrived."

"That's correct."

"What did you say to them?"

"That I had been attacked and that the police were going to be involved."

"You didn't mention this when I questioned you at the apartment house."

"It's standard procedure to contact the embassy immediately in a situation like this."

"Are you often in situations like this?"

Gabriel ignored the question. "I am a diplomat of the State of Israel, entitled to every and all diplomatic protection and immunity. I assume an officer of your rank and position would realize that my first responsibility is to contact my embassy and report what has transpired."

"Did you *report* that you killed two men?"

"No."

"Did this detail slip your mind? Or did you neglect to tell them this for other reasons?"

"We are instructed to keep telephone communications brief in all situations. I'm sure you understand."

"Who's *we*, Mr. Golani?"

"The ministry."

"I see."

Gabriel thought he could see a trace of a smile.

"I want to see a representative of my embassy immediately."

"Unfortunately, due to the special circumstances of your case, we're going to have to detain you a little longer."

Gabriel focused on a single word: *detain.*

"What special circumstances?"

Markov led Gabriel silently out of the room. This time, he was locked in a fetid holding cell with a pair of bloodied drunks and three anorexic prostitutes, one of whom immediately propositioned him. Gabriel found a relatively clean spot along one wall and lowered himself cautiously to the concrete floor. "You have to pay them," the prostitute explained. "Consider yourself lucky. I have to give them something else."

Several hours crawled past with no more contact from Markov — precisely how many Gabriel did not know, because he had no watch and there was no clock visible from the holding cell. The drunks passed the time debating Pushkin; the three prostitutes slept against the opposite wall, one leaning against the next, like dress-up dolls on a little girl's shelf. Gabriel sat with his arms wrapped around his shins and his forehead to his knees. He shut out the sounds around him — the slamming of doors, the shouting of orders, the cries of a man being beaten — and kept his thoughts focused only on Olga Sukhova. Was she somewhere in this building with him, he wondered, or had she been taken elsewhere due to the "special circumstances" of her case? Was she even alive or had she suffered the same fate as her colleagues Aleksandr Lubin and Boris Ostrovsky? As for the name Olga had spoken to him in the stairwell of the House of Dogs, he pushed it to a far corner of his memory and concealed it beneath a layer of gesso and base paint.

"It was Elena . . . Elena was the one who told me about the sale."

Elena who? Gabriel thought now. *Elena where? Elena nobody . . .*

Finally, one sound managed to penetrate his defenses: the sound of Markov's approaching footsteps. The grim expression on his face suggested an ominous turn in events.

"Responsibility for your case has been transferred to another department."

"Which department is that?"

"Get on your feet, then face the wall and place your hands behind your back."

"You're not going to shoot me here in front of all these witnesses, are you, Markov?"

"Don't tempt me."

Gabriel did as instructed. A pair of uniformed officers entered the cell, reattached the handcuffs, and led him outside to a waiting car. It sped through a maze of side streets before finally turning onto a broad, empty prospekt. Gabriel's destination now lay directly ahead, a floodlit fortress of yellow stone looming atop the low hill. *Elena who?* he thought. *Elena where? Elena nobody . . .*

18
FSB Headquarters, Moscow

The iron gates of Lubyanka swung slowly open to receive him. In the center of a large interior courtyard, four bored-looking officers stood silently in the darkness. They extracted Gabriel from the backseat with a swiftness that spoke of much experience in such matters and propelled him across the cobblestones into the building. The stairwell was conveniently located a few steps from the entrance foyer. On the precipice of the first step, Gabriel was given a firm shove between the shoulder blades. He tumbled helplessly downward, somersaulting once, and came to rest on the next landing. A knifelike jab to the kidney blinded him with pain that ran the length of his body. A well-aimed kick to the abdomen left him unable to speak or breathe.

They propped him upright again and flung him like war dead down the next flight. This time, the fall itself inflicted damage sufficient enough so that they did not have to further exert themselves with needless kicks or punches. After placing him on his feet again, they dragged him into a dark corridor. To Gabriel, it seemed to stretch an eternity. To the gulags of Siberia, he thought. To the killing fields outside Moscow where Stalin sentenced his victims to "seven grams of lead," his favorite punishment for disloyalty, real or imagined.

He had expected a period of isolation in a cell where Lubyanka's blood-soaked history could chip away at his resistance. Instead, he was taken directly to an interrogation room and forced into a chair before a rectangular table of pale wood. Seated on the other side was a man in a gray suit with a pallor to match. He wore a neat little goatee and round, wire-framed spectacles. Whether or not he was trying to look like Lenin, the resemblance was unmistakable. He was several years younger than Gabriel — mid-forties, perhaps — and recently divorced, judging by the indentation on the ring finger of his right hand. Educated. Intelligent. A worthy opponent. A lawyer in another life, though it was unclear whether he was a defense attorney or prosecutor. A man of words rather than violence. Gabriel considered himself lucky. Given his loca-

171

tion, and the available options, he could have done far worse.

"Are you injured?" the man asked in English, as though he did not care much about the answer.

"I am a diplomat of the State of Israel."

"So I'm told. You might find this difficult to believe, but I am here to help you. You may call me Sergei. It is a pseudonym, of course. Just like the pseudonym that appears in your passport."

"You have no legal right to hold me."

"I'm afraid I do. You killed two citizens of Russia this evening."

"Because they tried to kill *me*. I demand to speak to a representative of my embassy."

"In due time, Mr. —" He made a vast show of consulting Gabriel's passport. "Ah, here it is. Mr. Golani." He tossed the passport onto the table. "Come now, Mr. Golani, we are both professionals. Surely we can handle this rather embarrassing situation in a professional manner."

"I've given a complete statement to the Militia."

"I'm afraid your statement raises many more questions than it answers."

"What else do you need to know?"

He produced a thick file; then, from the file, a photograph. It showed Gabriel, five

172

days earlier, walking through the terminal of Pulkovo 2 Airport in St. Petersburg.

"What I need to *know,* Mr. Golani, is exactly what you are doing in Russia. And don't try to mislead me. If you do, I will become very angry. And that is the last thing you want."

They went through it once; then they went through it again. The sudden illness of the deputy minister. Natan Golani's hasty recruitment as a stand-in. The meetings and the speeches. The receptions and the dinners. Each contact, formal or casual, was duly noted, including the woman who had tried to seduce him during the final gala at the Mariinsky Theatre. Despite the fact the room was surely fitted with a recording system, the interrogator documented each answer in a small notebook. Gabriel couldn't help but admire his technique. Had their roles been reversed, he would have done precisely the same thing.

"You were originally scheduled to return to Tel Aviv the morning after the UNESCO conference concluded."

"That's correct."

"But you abruptly decided to extend your stay in Russia and travel to Moscow instead." He lay a small hand atop the file, as if to remind Gabriel of its presence. "Why did you do this, Mr. Golani?"

"Our ambassador here is an old friend. He suggested I come to Moscow for a day or two."

"For what purpose?"

"To see him, of course — and to see Moscow."

"What did he say to you exactly, your friend the ambassador?"

"He said I had to see Moscow to believe it. He said it was filled with billionaires, dirty bankers, and Russian gangsters. He said it was a boomtown. He said something about a sea of oil, caviar, and vodka."

"Did he mention a dinner party?" He tapped the file with the tip of his index finger. "The dinner party that took place at the Israeli Embassy last evening?"

"I believe he did."

"Think carefully, Mr. Golani."

"I'm sure he mentioned it."

"What did he say about it — *exactly,* Mr. Golani?"

"He said there would be some people from the opposition there."

"Is that how he described the invited guests? As members of the *opposition?*"

"Actually, I think he referred to them as 'brave souls' who've had the chutzpah to challenge the regime."

"And why did your ambassador feel it was necessary to throw such a party? Was it his intention to meddle in the internal affairs of the Russian Federation?"

"I can assure you no meddling took place. It was just dinner and pleasant conversation."

"Who was in attendance?"

"Why don't you ask the agents who were watching the embassy that night? They photographed everyone who entered the compound, including me. Look in your file. I'm sure it's there."

The interrogator smiled. "Who was in attendance, Mr. Golani?"

Gabriel listed the names to the best of his recollection. The last name he recited was Olga Sukhova.

"Was that the first time you and Miss Sukhova had met?"

"Yes."

"Did you know her by reputation?"

"No, I'd never heard her name."

"You're certain of that?"

"Absolutely."

"You seem to have hit it off quite well."

"We were seated next to each other at dinner. We had a pleasant conversation."

"Did you discuss the recent murders of

her colleagues?"

"The topic might have come up. I can't remember."

"What *do* you remember, Mr. Golani?"

"We talked about Palestine and the Middle East. We talked about the war in Iraq. We talked about Russia."

"What about Russia?"

"Politics, of course — the coming election."

"What did Miss Sukhova say about the election?"

"She said Russian politics are nothing more than professional wrestling. She said the winners and losers are chosen in advance. That the campaign itself is much sound and fury, signifying nothing. She said the president and the Russian Unity Party will win in a landslide and claim another sweeping mandate. The only question is, how many votes will they feel compelled to steal in order to achieve their goals."

"The Russian Federation is a democracy. Miss Sukhova's political commentary, while entertaining and provocative, is slanderous and completely false."

The interrogator turned to a fresh page of his notebook.

"Did you and Miss Sukhova spend any time alone at the party?"

"Olga said she needed a cigarette. She invited me to join her."

"There were no cigarettes among your possessions tonight."

"That's hardly surprising, given the fact that I don't smoke."

"But you joined her in any case?"

"Yes."

"Because you wanted to have a word alone with her in a place where no one could overhear?"

"Because I was attracted to her — and, yes, because I wanted to have a word alone with her in a place no one else could hear."

"Where did you go?"

"The terrace."

"How long were you alone?"

"A minute or two, no more."

"What did you discuss?"

"I asked if I could see her again. If she would be willing to give me a tour of Moscow."

"Did you also tell her you were a married man?"

"We'd already discussed that."

"At dinner?"

"Yes."

"Whose idea was it to visit Novodevichy?"

"Hers."

"Why did she select this place?"

"She said that to understand Russia today you had to walk among her bones."

"Did you travel to the cemetery together?"

"No, I met her there."

"How did you travel? By taxi?"

"I took the Metro."

"Who arrived first?"

"Olga was waiting at the gates when I got there."

"And you entered the cemetery together?"

"Of course."

"Which grave did you visit first?"

"It was Chekhov's."

"Are you certain?"

"Yes."

"Describe it for me."

Gabriel closed his eyes, as if trying to summon an image of the gravestone, but instead he heard the voice of Olga whispering softly into his ear. *You mustn't give them her name,* she was saying. *If Ivan discovers it was Elena who betrayed him, he'll kill her.*

19
FSB HEADQUARTERS, MOSCOW

They forged on together — for how long, Gabriel could only guess. At times, they wandered through unexplored territory. At others, they retraced their steps over familiar ground. Trivial inconsistencies were pounced upon as proof of treachery, minor lapses in memory as proof of deceit. There is a strange paradox to an interrogation: it can often impart more information to the subject than to the officer posing the questions. Gabriel had concluded that his opponent was but a small cog in a much larger machine. His questions, like Russia's campaign politics, were much sound and fury signifying nothing. Gabriel's real enemies resided elsewhere. Since he was supposed to be dead by now, his very presence in Lubyanka was something of an inconvenience for them. One factor would determine whether he survived the night: Did they have the power to reach into the basement of Lubyanka and kill him?

The interrogator's final questions were posed with the bored air of a traffic cop recording the details of a minor accident. He jotted the responses in his notebook, then closed the cover and regarded Gabriel through his little spectacles.

"I find it interesting that, after killing the two Chechen gangsters, you did not become ill. I take it you've killed before, Mr. Golani?"

"Like all Israeli men, I had to serve in the IDF. I fought in Sinai in 'seventy-three and in Lebanon in 'eighty-two."

"So you've killed many innocent Arabs?"

"Yes, many."

"You are a Zionist oppressor of innocent Palestinians?"

"An unrepentant one."

"You are not who you say you are, Mr. Golani. Your diplomatic passport is false, as is the name written in it. The sooner you confess your crimes, the better."

The interrogator placed the cap on his pen and screwed it slowly into place. It must have been a signal, for the door flew open and the four handlers burst into the room. They took him down another flight of stairs and placed him in a cell no larger than a broom closet. It stank of damp and feces. If there were other prisoners nearby, he could not tell, for when the windowless door was closed, the silence, like the darkness, was absolute.

He placed his cheek against the cold floor and closed his eyes. Olga Sukhova appeared in the form of an icon, head tilted to one side, hands folded in prayer. *If you are fortunate enough to make it out of Russia alive, don't even think about trying to make contact with her. She's surrounded by bodyguards every minute of the day. Ivan sees everything. Ivan hears everything. Ivan is a monster.*

He was sweating one minute and shivering violently the next. His kidney throbbed with pain, and he could not draw a proper breath because of the bruising to his ribs. During one intense period of cold, he groped the interior of the cell to see if they had left him a blanket but found only four slick walls instead.

He closed his eyes and slept. In his dreams, he walked through the streets of his past and encountered many of the men he had killed. They were pale and bloodless, with bullet holes in their hearts and faces. Chiara appeared, dressed in her wedding gown, and told him it was time to come back to Umbria. Olga mopped the sweat from his forehead and laid a bouquet of dead carnations at a grave in the Novodevichy Cemetery. The engraving on the headstone was in Hebrew instead of Cyrillic. It read: GABRIEL ALLON . . .

He woke finally to the sight of flashlights blazing in his face. The men holding them lifted him to his feet and frog-marched him up several flights of steps. Gabriel tried to count, but soon gave up. Five? Ten? Twenty? He couldn't be sure. Using his head as a battering ram, they burst through a doorway, into the cold night air. For a moment, he was blinded by the sudden darkness. He feared they were about to hurl him from the roof — Lubyanka had a long history of such unfortunate *accidents* — but then his eyes adjusted and he could see they were only in the courtyard instead.

Sergei the interrogator was standing next to a black van, dressed in a fresh gray suit. He opened the rear doors, and, with a few terse words in Russian, ordered the handlers to put Gabriel inside. His hands were freed briefly, only to be restrained again a few seconds later to a steel loop in the ceiling. Then the doors closed with a deafening thud and the van lurched forward over the cobblestones.

Where now? he thought. Exile or death?

He was alone again. He reckoned it was before midnight because Moscow's traffic was still moving at a fever pitch. He heard no sirens to indicate they were under escort, and the driver appeared to be obeying traffic rules, such as they were. At one long stop, he heard the sound of laughter, and he thought of Solzhenitsyn. *The vans . . .* That was how the KGB had moved the inhabitants of the Gulag Archipelago — at night, in ordinary-looking vans, invisible to the souls around them, trapped in a parallel world of the damned.

Sheremetyevo 2 Airport lay north of the city center, a journey of about forty-five minutes when the traffic was at its most reasonable. Gabriel had allowed himself to hope it was their destination, but that hope dissolved after an hour in the back of the van. The quality of the roads, deplorable even in Moscow, deteriorated by degrees the farther they moved away from Lubyanka. Each pothole sent shock waves of pain through his bruised body, and he had to cling to the steel loop to avoid being thrown from his bench. It was impossible to guess in which direction they were traveling. He could not tell whether they were heading west, toward civilization and enlightenment, or east, into the cruel heart of the Russian interior. Twice the van stopped and twice Gabriel could hear Russian voices raised in anger. He supposed even an unmarked FSB van had trouble moving through the countryside without being shaken down by *banditi* and traffic cops looking for bribes.

The third time the van stopped, the doors swung open and a handler entered the compartment. He unlocked the handcuffs and motioned for Gabriel to get out. A car had pulled up behind them; the interrogator was standing in the glow of the parking lamps, stroking his little beard as though deciding on a suitable place to carry out an execution. Then Gabriel noticed his suitcase lying in a puddle of mud, next to the ziplock bag containing his possessions. The interrogator nudged the bag toward Gabriel with the toe of his shoe and pointed toward a smudge of yellow light on the horizon.

"The Ukrainian border. They're expecting you."

"Where's Olga?"

"I suggest you get moving before we change our minds, Mr. *Allon*. And don't come back to Russia again. If you do, we will kill you. And we won't rely on a pair of Chechen idiots to do the job for us."

Gabriel collected his belongings and started toward the border. He waited for the crack of a pistol and the bullet in his spine, but he heard nothing but the sound of the cars turning around and starting back to Moscow. With their headlights gone, the heavy darkness swallowed him. He kept his eyes focused on the yellow light and walked on. And, for a moment, Olga was walking beside him. *Her life is now in your hands,* she reminded him. *Ivan kills anyone who gets in his way. And if he ever finds out his own wife was my source, he won't hesitate to kill her, too.*

■ ■ ■ ■

PART TWO
THE RECRUITMENT

■ ■ ■ ■

20
BEN-GURION AIRPORT, ISRAEL

"Wake up, Mr. Golani. You're almost home."

Gabriel opened his eyes slowly and gazed out the window of the first-class cabin. The lights of the Coastal Plain lay in a glittering arc along the edge of the Mediterranean, like a strand of jewels painted by the hand of Van Dyck.

He turned his head a few degrees and looked at the man who had awakened him. He was twenty years younger than Gabriel, with eyes the color of granite and a fine-boned, bloodless face. The diplomatic passport in his blazer pocket identified him as Baruch Goldstein of the Israeli Ministry of Foreign Affairs. His real name was Mikhail Abramov. Bodyguard jobs were not exactly Mikhail's specialty. A former member of the Sayeret Metkal special forces, he had joined the Office after assassinating the top terrorist masterminds of Hamas and

Islamic Jihad. He had one other attribute that had made him the perfect candidate to escort Gabriel out of Eastern Europe and back to Israel. Mikhail had been born in Moscow to a pair of dissident scientists and spoke fluent Russian.

They had been traveling together for the better part of a day. After crossing the border, Gabriel had surrendered himself to a waiting team of Ukrainian SBU officers. The SBU men had taken him to Kiev and handed him over to Mikhail and two other Office security men. From Kiev, they had driven to Warsaw and boarded the El Al flight. Even on the plane, Shamron had taken no chances with Gabriel's safety. Half of the first-class cabin crew were Office agents, and, before takeoff, the entire aircraft had been carefully searched for radioactive material and other toxins. Gabriel's food and drink had been kept in a separate sealed container. The meal had been prepared by Shamron's wife, Gilah. "It's the Office version of glatt kosher," Mikhail had said. "Sanctified under Jewish law and guaranteed to be free of Russian poison."

Gabriel tried to sit up, but his kidney began to throb again. He closed his eyes and waited for the pain to subside. Mikhail, a nervous flier by nature, was now drumming on his tray table with his fingertip.

"You're giving me a headache, Mikhail."

Mikhail's finger went still. "Did you manage to get any rest?"

"Not much."

"You should have watched your step on those KGB stairs."

"It's called the FSB now, Mikhail. Haven't you read the papers lately? The KGB doesn't exist anymore."

"Where did you ever get that idea? They were KGB when I was growing up in Moscow and they're KGB now." He glanced at his watch. "We'll be on the ground in a few minutes. A reception team will be waiting for you on the tarmac. After you finish delivering your report, you can sleep for a month."

"Unless my report makes that impossible."

"Bad?"

"Something tells me you'll know soon enough, Mikhail."

An electronic ping sounded over the cabin's audio system. Mikhail looked up at the flashing SEAT BELT sign and tapped Gabriel on the forearm. "You'd better buckle up. You wouldn't want the flight attendant to get angry with you."

Gabriel followed Mikhail's gaze and saw Chiara making her way slowly down the aisle. Dressed in a flattering blue El Al uniform, she was sternly reminding passengers to straighten their seat backs and stow their tray tables. Mikhail swallowed the last of his beer and absently handed her the empty bottle.

"The service on this flight was dreadful, don't you think?"

"Even by El Al standards," Gabriel agreed.

"I think we should institute a training program immediately."

"Now, that's the kind of thinking that's going to get you a job in the executive suite of King Saul Boulevard."

"Maybe I should volunteer to teach it."

"And work with our girls? You'd be safer going back to Gaza and chasing Hamas terrorists."

Gabriel leaned back against the headrest and closed his eyes.

"You sure you're all right, Gabriel?"

"Just a touch of Lubyanka hangover."

"Who could blame you?" Mikhail was silent for a moment. "The KGB kept my father there for six months when I was a kid. Did I ever tell you that?"

He hadn't, but Gabriel had read Mikhail's personnel file.

"After six months in Lubyanka, they declared my father mentally ill and sent him away to a psychiatric hospital for treatment. It was all a sham, of course. No one ever got better in a Soviet psychiatric hospital — the hospitals were just another arm of the gulag. My father was lucky, though. Eventually, he got out, and we were able to come to Israel. But he was never the same after being locked away in that asylum."

Just then the cabin shuddered with the impact of a hard landing. From the depths of economy class arose a desultory patter of applause. It was a tradition for flights landing in Israel, and, for the first time, Gabriel was tempted to join in. Instead, he sat silently while the plane taxied toward the terminal and, unlike the rest of his fellow countrymen, waited until the SEAT BELT sign was extinguished before rising to his feet and collecting his bag from the overhead bin.

Chiara was now standing at the cabin door. She anonymously bade Gabriel a pleasant evening and warned him to watch his step as he followed Mikhail and the two other security agents down the stairs of the Jetway. Upon reaching the tarmac, Mikhail and the others turned to the right and filed into the motorized lounges, along with the rest of the passengers. Gabriel headed in the opposite direction, toward the waiting Peugeot limousine, and climbed into the backseat. Shamron examined the dark reddish blue bruise along Gabriel's cheek.

"I suppose you don't look *too* bad for someone who survived Lubyanka. How was it?"

"The rooms were on the small side, but the furnishings were quite lovely."

"Perhaps it would have been better if you'd found some other way of dealing with those Chechens besides killing them."

"I considered shooting the guns out of their hands, Ari, but that sort of thing really only works in the movies."

"I'm glad to see you emerged from your ordeal with your fatalistic sense of humor intact. A team of debriefers is waiting for you at King Saul Boulevard. I'm afraid you have a long night ahead of you."

"I'd rather go back to Lubyanka than face the debriefers tonight."

Shamron gave Gabriel a paternalistic pat on the shoulder.

"I'll take you home, Gabriel. We'll talk on the way."

21
JERUSALEM

They still had much ground to cover when they arrived at Gabriel's apartment in Narkiss Street. Despite the fact it was after midnight, Shamron invited himself upstairs for coffee. Gabriel hesitated before inserting his key into the lock.

"Go ahead," Shamron said calmly. "We've already swept it."

"I think I like fighting Arab terrorists better than Russians."

"Unfortunately, we don't always have the luxury of choosing our enemies."

Gabriel entered the apartment first and switched on the lights. Everything was exactly as he had left it a week earlier, including the half-drunk cup of coffee he had left in the kitchen sink on the way out the door. He poured the now-moldy remnants down the drain, then spooned coffee into the French press and placed a kettle of water on the stove to boil. When he went into the sitting room, he found Shamron with a cigarette between his lips and a cocked lighter poised before it. "You don't get to take up smoking again just because I got thrown into Lubyanka. Besides, if Chiara smells smoke in here when she comes home I'll never hear the end of it."

"So you'll blame it on me."

"I blame everything on you. The impact has been diluted by overuse."

Shamron extinguished the lighter and laid the cigarette on the coffee table, where it would be easily accessible for a sneak attack at a moment when Gabriel's back was turned.

"I should have left you in Russia," Shamron muttered.

"How *did* you get me out?"

"When it became clear to our ambassador and Moscow Station chief that the FSB had no intention of respecting your diplomatic passport, we decided to go on offense. Shin Bet regularly monitors the movements of Russian Embassy employees. As it turned out, four of them were drinking heavily in the bar of the Sheraton Hotel."

"How surprising."

"A mile from the hotel, they were pulled over for what appeared to be a routine traffic stop. It wasn't, of course."

"So you kidnapped four Russian diplomats and held them hostage in order to coerce them into releasing me."

"We Israelites invented tit for tat. Besides, they weren't just diplomats. Two of them were known intelligence officers of the SVR."

When the KGB was disbanded and reorganized, the directorate that conducted espionage activities abroad became a separate agency known as the Foreign Intelligence Service, or SVR. Like the FSB, the SVR was merely KGB with a new name and a pretty wrapper.

"When we received confirmation from the Ukrainians that you'd made it safely across the border, we released them from custody. They've been quietly recalled to Moscow for consultations. With a bit of luck, they'll stay there forever."

The teakettle screamed. Gabriel went into the kitchen and removed it from the stove, then switched on the television while he saw to the coffee. It was tuned to the BBC; a gray-haired reporter was standing before the domes of St. Basil's Cathedral bellowing about the possible motives behind the attempt on Olga Sukhova's life. None of his theories were even remotely close to the truth, but they were delivered with an authority that only a British accent can bestow. Shamron, who was now standing at Gabriel's shoulder, seemed to find the report vaguely amusing. He viewed the news media only as a source of entertainment or as a weapon to be wielded against his enemies.

"As you can see, the Russians are being rather circumspect about exactly what transpired inside that apartment building. They've acknowledged Olga was the target of an attack, but they've released few other details about the incident. Nothing about the identity of the gunmen. Nothing about the man who saved her life."

"Where is she now?"

"Back in her apartment, surrounded by private security guards and brave Western reporters like our friend from the BBC. She's as safe as one can be in Russia, which is to say not terribly safe at all. Eventually, she might want to consider a new life in the West." His eyes settled on Gabriel. "Is she as good as she appears or is it possible she's something else entirely?"

"Are you asking whether she's been turned by the FSB and was blowing smoke in my face?"

"That is precisely what I'm asking."

"She's golden, Ari. She's a gift from the

intelligence gods."

"I'm just wondering why she asked you to take her home. I'm wondering whether it's possible she led you into that stairwell to be killed."

"Or maybe that wasn't Olga Sukhova at all. Maybe it was Ivan Kharkov in a clever disguise."

"I'm paid to think dark thoughts, Gabriel. And so are you."

"I saw her reaction to the shooting. She's the real thing, Ari. And she agreed to help us at great risk to herself. Remember, I was allowed to leave. Olga is still in Moscow. If the Kremlin wants her dead, they'll kill her. And there's nothing those security guards and brave reporters can do to protect her."

They sat down at the kitchen table. The BBC had moved on from Russia and was now showing footage of a fatal bomb blast in a Baghdad market. Gabriel aimed the remote at the screen and, frowning, pressed the MUTE button. Shamron fiddled with the French press for a moment before appealing to Gabriel for assistance. He occupied his spare time by restoring antique radios and clocks yet even the most basic kitchen appliances were beyond his capabilities. Coffeemakers, blenders, toasters: these items were a mystery to him. Gilah often joked that her husband, if left to his own devices, would find a way to starve to death in a house filled with food.

"How much do we have on Ivan Kharkov?" Gabriel asked.

"Plenty," said Shamron. "Ivan's been active in Lebanon for years. He makes regular deliveries to Hezbollah, but he also sells weapons to the more radical Palestinian and Islamist factions operating inside the refugee camps."

"What kind of weapons?"

"The usual. Grenades, mortars, RPGs, AK-47s — and bullets, of course. *Lots* of bullets. But during our war with Hezbollah, the Kharkov network arranged for a special shipment of armor-piercing antitank weapons. We lost several tank crews because of them. We dispatched the foreign minister to Moscow to protest, all to no avail, of course."

"Which means Ivan Kharkov has an established track record of selling weapons directly to terrorist organizations."

"Without question. RPGs and AK-47s we can deal with. But our friend Ivan has the connections to lay his hands on the most dangerous weapons in the world. Chemical. Biological. Even nuclear weapons aren't out of the question. We know that agents of al-

Qaeda have been scouring the remnants of the old Soviet Union for years looking for nuclear material or even a fully functioning nuclear device. Maybe they've finally found someone willing to sell it to them."

Shamron spooned sugar into his coffee and stirred it slowly. "The Americans might have better insight into the situation. They've been watching Ivan closely for years." He gave a sardonic smile. "The Americans love to monitor problems but do nothing about them."

"They'll have to do something about him now."

Shamron nodded in agreement. "It's my recommendation we dump this in their lap as soon as possible and wash our hands of the affair. I want you to go to Washington and see your friend Adrian Carter. Tell him everything you learned in Moscow. Give them Elena Kharkov. Then get on the next plane to Umbria and finish your honeymoon. And don't ever accuse me of failing to live up to my word again."

Gabriel stared at the silent television but made no response.

"You disagree with my recommendation?" Shamron asked.

"What do you think Adrian Carter and the Americans are going to do with this information?"

"I suspect they'll go cap in hand to the Kremlin and plead with the Russian president to block the sale."

"And he'll tell the Americans that Ivan is a legitimate businessman with no ties to the illegal international arms trade. He'll dismiss the intelligence as an anti-Russian slur spread by Jewish provocateurs who are conspiring to keep Russia backward and weak." Gabriel shook his head slowly. "Going to the Russians and appealing for help is the last thing we should be doing. We should regard the Russian president and his intelligence services as adversaries and act accordingly."

"So what exactly are you suggesting?"

"That we have a quiet word with Elena Kharkov and see if she knows more than she told Olga Sukhova."

"Just because she trusted Olga Sukhova once doesn't mean she'll trust an intelligence service of a foreign country. And remember, two Russian journalists have lost their lives because of her actions. I don't suspect she's going to be terribly receptive to an approach."

"She spends the majority of her time in London, Ari. We can get to her."

"And so can Ivan. She's surrounded by

his security goons night and day. They're all former members of the Alpha Group and OMON. All her contacts and communications are probably monitored. What do you intend to do? Invite her to tea? Call her on her cell phone? Drop her an e-mail?"

"I'm working on that part."

"Just know Ivan is three steps ahead of you. There's been a leak from somewhere in his network and he knows it. His private security service is going to be on high alert. Any approach to his wife is going to set off alarm bells. One misstep and you could get her killed."

"So we'll just have to do it quietly."

"We?"

"This isn't something we can do alone, Ari. We need the assistance of the Americans."

Shamron frowned. As a rule, he didn't like joint operations and was uncomfortable with Gabriel's close ties to the CIA. His generation had lived by a simple axiom known as *kachol lavan,* or "blue and white." They did things for themselves and did not rely on others to help them with their problems. It was an attitude borne from the experience of the Holocaust, when most of the world had stood by silently while the Jews were fed to the fires. It had bred in men like Shamron a reluctance — indeed, a fear — of operating with others.

"I seem to remember a conversation we had a few days ago during which you berated me for interrupting your honeymoon. Now you want to run an open-ended operation against Ivan Kharkov?"

"Let's just say I have a personal stake in the outcome of the case."

Shamron sipped his coffee. "Something tells me your new wife isn't going to be pleased with you."

"She's Office. She'll understand."

"Just don't let her anywhere near Ivan," Shamron said. "Ivan likes to break pretty things."

22
JERUSALEM

"Is this some sort of sick fantasy of yours, Gabriel? Watching a stewardess remove her clothing?"

"I've never really been attracted to girls in uniform. And they're called flight attendants now, Chiara. A woman in your line of work should know that."

"You could have at least flirted with me a little bit. All men flirt with flight attendants, don't they?"

"I didn't want to blow your cover. You seemed to be having enough trouble as it was."

"I don't know how they can wear these uniforms. Help me with my zipper."

"With pleasure."

She turned around and pulled aside her hair. Gabriel lowered the zipper and kissed the nape of her neck.

"Your beard tickles."

"I'll shave."

She turned around and kissed him. "Leave it for now. It makes you look very distinguished."

"I think it makes me look like Abraham." He sat on the edge of the bed and watched Chiara wriggle out of the dress. "This is certainly better than spending another night in Lubyanka."

"I should hope so."

"You were supposed to be keeping an eye on the Poussin. Please tell me you didn't leave it unguarded."

"Monsignor Donati took it back to the Vatican."

"I was afraid you were going to say that. How long do I have before he gives it to one of the butchers from the Vatican's restoration department?"

"The end of September." She reached behind her back and loosened the clasp on her brassiere. "Is there any food in this house? I'm famished."

"You didn't eat anything on the flight?"

"We were too busy. How was Gilah's chicken?"

"Delicious."

"It looked a lot better than the food we were serving."

"Is that what you were doing?"

"Was I that bad?"

"Let's just say the first-class passengers were less than pleased by the level of service. If that flight had lasted another hour, you would have had an intifada on your hands."

"They didn't give us adequate training to accomplish our mission. Besides, Jewish girls shouldn't be flight attendants."

"Israel is the great equalizer, Chiara. It's good for Jews to be flight attendants and farmers and garbagemen."

"I'll tell Uzi to keep that in mind the next time he's handing out field assignments."

She gathered up her clothing. "I need to take a shower. I smell like bad food and other people's cologne."

"Welcome to the glamorous world of air travel."

She leaned down and kissed him again. "Maybe you *should* shave after all, Gabriel. I really can't make love to a man who looks like Abraham."

"He fathered Isaac at a very old age."

"With help from God. I'm afraid you're on your own tonight." She touched the bruise on his cheek. "Did they hurt you?"

"Not really. We spent most of the night playing gin rummy and swapping stories about the good old days before the Wall came down."

"You're upset about something. I can

always tell when you're upset. You make terrible jokes to cover it up."

"I'm upset because it appears a Russian arms trafficker named Ivan Kharkov is planning to sell some very dangerous weapons to al-Qaeda. And because the woman who risked her life to tell us about it is now in very serious danger." He hesitated, then added, "And because it's going to be a while before we can resume our honeymoon in Umbria."

"You're not thinking about going back to Russia?"

"Just Washington."

She stroked his beard and said, "Have a nice trip, Abraham."

Then she walked into the bathroom and slammed the door behind her.

She's Office, he told himself. *She'll understand.*

Eventually.

23
GEORGETOWN

The CIA sent a plane for him, a Gulfstream G500, with leather club chairs, in-flight action movies, and a galley stocked with a vast amount of unwholesome snack food. It touched down at Andrews Air Force Base in the equatorial heat of midday and was met in a secure hangar by a pair of Agency security agents. Gabriel recognized them; they were the same two officers who had dragged him against his will to CIA Headquarters during his last visit to Washington. He feared a return engagement now but was pleasantly surprised when their destination turned out to be a graceful redbrick town house in the 3300 block of N Street in Georgetown. Waiting in the entrance hall was a man of retirement age, dressed in a navy blue blazer and crumpled gabardine trousers. He had the tousled thinning hair of a university professor and a mustache that had gone out of fashion with disco music, Crock-Pots, and the nuclear freeze. "Gabriel," said Adrian Carter as he extended his hand. "So good of you to come."

"You're looking well, Adrian."

"And you're still a terrible liar." He looked at Gabriel's face and frowned. "I assume that lovely bruise on your cheek is a souvenir of your night in Lubyanka?"

"I wanted to bring you something, but the gift shop was closed."

Carter gave a faint smile and took Gabriel by the elbow. "I thought you might be hungry after your travels. I've arranged for some lunch. How was the flight, by the way?"

"It was very considerate of you to send your plane on such short notice."

"That one isn't mine," Carter said without elaboration.

"Air Guantánamo?"

"And points in between."

"So that explains the handcuffs and the hypodermics."

"It beats having to listen to them talk. Your average jihadi makes a damn lousy traveling companion."

They entered the living room. It was a formal Georgetown salon, rectangular and high-ceilinged, with French doors overlooking a small terrace. The furnishings were costly but in poor taste, the sort of pieces one finds in the hospitality suite of a luxury business hotel. The impression was made complete by the catered buffet-style meal that had been laid upon the sideboard. All that was missing was a pretty young hostess to offer Gabriel a glass of mediocre chardonnay.

Carter wandered over to the buffet and selected a ham sandwich and a ginger ale. Gabriel drew a cup of black coffee from a silver pump-action thermos and sat in a wing chair next to the French doors. Carter sat down next to him and balanced his plate on his knees.

"Shamron tells me Ivan has been a bad boy again. Give me everything you've got. And don't spare me any of the details." He cracked open his soft drink. "I happen to love stories about Ivan. They serve as helpful reminders that there are some people in this world who will do absolutely anything for money."

It wasn't long after Gabriel began his briefing that Carter seemed to lose his appetite. He placed his partially eaten sandwich on the table next to his chair and sat motionless as a statue, with his legs crossed and his hands bunched thoughtfully beneath his chin. It had been Gabriel's experience that any decent spy was at his core a good listener. It came naturally to Carter, like his gift for languages, his ability to blend into his surroundings, and his humility. Little about Carter's clinical demeanor suggested that he was one of the most powerful members of Washington's intelligence establishment — or that before his ascension to the rarified atmosphere of Langley's seventh floor, where he served as director of the CIA's national clandestine service, he had been a field man of the highest reputation. Most mistook him for a therapist of some sort. When one thought of Adrian Carter, one pictured a man enduring confessions of affairs and inadequacies, not tales of terrorists and Russian arms dealers.

"I wish I could say your story sounded like the ravings of an angry wife," Carter said. "But I'm afraid it dovetails nicely with some rather alarming intelligence we've been picking up over the past few months."

"What sort of intelligence?"

"Chatter," said Carter. "More to the point, a specific phrase that has popped several times over the past few weeks — so many times, in fact, that our analysts at the National Counterterrorism Center are no longer willing to dismiss it as mere coincidence."

"What's the phrase?"

"The arrows of Allah. We've seen it about a half-dozen times now, most recently on the computer of a jihadi who was arrested by our friend Lars Mortensen in Copenhagen. You remember Lars, don't you, Gabriel?"

"With considerable fondness," Gabriel replied.

"Mortensen and his technicians at the Danish PET found the phrase in an old e-mail that the suspect had tried to delete. The e-mail said something about 'the arrows of Allah piercing the hearts of the infidels,' or sentiments to that effect."

"What's the suspect's name?"

"Marwan Abbas. He's a Jordanian now residing in the largely immigrant quarter of Copenhagen known as Nørrebro — a quarter you know quite well, if I'm not mistaken. Mortensen says Abbas is a member of Hizb ut-Tahrir, the radical Islamist political movement. The Jordanian GID told us he was also an associate of Abu Musab al-Zarqawi, may he rest in peace."

"If I were you, Adrian, I'd send that Gulfstream of yours to Copenhagen to take possession of Marwan for a private chat."

"I'm afraid Mortensen is in no position to play ball with us at the moment. PET and the Danish government still have bruised feelings over our actions during the Halton affair. I suppose, in hindsight, we should have signed the guestbook on the way into Denmark. We told the Danes about our presence on their soil *after* the fact. It's going to take a while for them to forgive us our sins."

"Mortensen will come around eventually. The Danes need you. So do the rest of the Europeans. In a world gone mad, America is still the last best hope."

"I hope you're right, Gabriel. It's become popular in Washington these days to think that the threat of terrorism has receded — or that we can somehow live with the occasional loss of national monuments and American life. But when the next attack comes — and I do mean *when,* Gabriel — those same freethinkers will be the first to fault the Agency for failing to stop it. We can't do it without the cooperation of the Europeans. And *you,* of course. You're our secret servant, aren't you, Gabriel? You're the one who does the jobs we're unwilling, or unable, to do for ourselves. I'm afraid Ivan falls into that category."

Gabriel recalled the words Shamron had spoken the previous evening in Jerusalem: *The Americans love to monitor problems but do nothing about them . . .*

"Ivan's main stomping ground is Africa," Carter said. "But he's made lucrative forays into the Middle East and Latin America as well. In the good old days, when the Agency and the KGB played the various factions of the Third World against one another for our own amusement, we were judicious with the flow of arms. We wanted the killing to remain at morally acceptable levels. But Ivan tore up the old rule book, and he's torn up many of the world's poorest places in the process. He's willing to provide the dictators, the warlords, and the guerrilla fighters with whatever they want, and, in turn, they're willing to pay him whatever he asks. He's a vulture, our Ivan. He preys on the suffering of others and makes millions in the process. He's responsible for more death and destruction than all the Islamic terrorists of the world combined. And now he trots around the playgrounds of Russia and Europe, safe in the knowledge that we can't lay a finger on him."

"Why didn't you ever go after him?"

"We tried during the nineties. We noticed that much of the Third World was burning, and we started asking ourselves a single question: Who was pouring the gasoline on the flames? The Agency started tracking the movement of suspicious cargo planes around Africa and the Middle East. NSA started listening to telephone and radio conversations. Before long, we had a good idea where all the weapons were coming from."

"Ivan Kharkov."

Carter nodded. "We established a working group at NSC to come up with a strategy for dealing with the Kharkov network. Since he had violated no American laws, our options were extremely limited. We started looking for a country to issue an indictment but got no takers. By the end of the millennium, the situation was so bad we even considered using a novel concept known as extraordinary rendition to get Ivan's operatives off the streets. It came to nothing, of course. When the administration left town, the Kharkov network was still in business. And when the new crowd settled into the White House, they barely had time to figure out where the bathrooms were before they were hit with 9/11. Suddenly, Ivan Kharkov didn't seem so important anymore."

"Because you needed Russia's help in the fight against al-Qaeda."

"Exactly," said Carter. "Ivan is former KGB. He has powerful benefactors. To be fair, even if we *had* pressed the Kremlin on

216

the Kharkov issue, it probably wouldn't have done any good. On paper, there are no legal or financial ties between Ivan Kharkov the legitimate oligarch and Ivan Kharkov the international arms trafficker. Ivan is a master of the corporate front and the offshore account. The network is completely quarantined."

Carter fished a pipe and a pouch of tobacco from the flap pocket of his jacket. "There's something else we need to keep in mind: Ivan has a long track record of selling his wares to unsavory elements in the Middle East. He sold weapons to Gadhafi. He smuggled arms to Saddam in violation of UN sanctions. He armed Islamic radicals in Somalia and Sudan. He even sold weapons to the *Taliban*."

"Don't forget Hezbollah," said Gabriel.

"How could we forget our good friends at Hezbollah?" Carter methodically loaded tobacco into the bowl of his pipe. "In a perfect world, I suppose we would go to the Russian president and ask him for help. But this world is far from perfect, and the current president of Russia is anything but a trustworthy ally. He's a dangerous man. He wants his empire back. He wants to be a superpower again. He wants to challenge American supremacy around the globe, especially in the Middle East. He's sitting atop a sea of oil and natural gas, and he's willing to use it as a weapon. And the last thing he's going to do is intervene on our behalf against a protected oligarch by the name of Ivan Kharkov. I lived through the end of the first Cold War. We're not there yet, but we're definitely heading in that direction. I'm certain of *one* thing, though. If we're going to track down those weapons, we're going to have to do it *without* Russia's help."

"I prefer it that way, Adrian. We Jews have a long history of dealing with Russians."

"So how do you suggest we proceed?"

"I want to arrange a meeting with Elena Kharkov."

Carter raised an eyebrow. "I suggest you proceed carefully, Gabriel. Otherwise, you might get her killed."

"Thank you, Adrian. That really hadn't occurred to me."

"Forgive me," said Carter. "How can I help?"

"I need every scrap of intelligence you have on Ivan's network. And I mean *all* of it, Adrian — especially NSA intercepts of Ivan's telephone communications. And don't just give me the transcripts. I need to get inside his head. And to get inside his head, I need to hear his voice."

"You're talking about a great deal of *highly* classified material. It can't be turned over to an officer of a foreign intelligence service on a whim, even you. I have to run it through channels. It could take weeks to get approval, if at all."

"Those weapons could be heading toward America's shores as we speak, Adrian."

"I'll see what I can do to expedite matters."

"No, Adrian, you *must* expedite matters. Otherwise, I'm going to pick up that phone over there and call my friend at the White House. I still have that number you gave me in Copenhagen, the one that rings directly in the Oval Office."

"You wouldn't."

"In a heartbeat."

"I'll get the material released to you within twenty-four hours. What else do you need?"

"A Russian speaker."

"Believe it or not, we've still got a few of those."

"Actually, I have one in mind. I need you to get him into the country right away."

"Who is it?"

Gabriel told him the name.

"Done," said Carter. "Where do you intend to set up shop? At your embassy?"

"I've never been fond of embassies." Gabriel looked around the room. "This will do quite nicely. But do me a favor, Adrian. Ask your techs to come over here and remove all the cameras and microphones. I don't want your bloodhounds watching me while I shower."

24
GEORGETOWN

It took Adrian Carter the better part of the next morning to secure the authorization necessary to release the Kharkov files into Gabriel's custody. Then several additional hours elapsed while they were gathered, sorted, and purged of anything remotely embarrassing to the Central Intelligence Agency or the government of the United States. Finally, at seven that evening, the material was delivered to the house on N Street by an unmarked Agency van. Carter stopped by to supervise the load in and to secure Gabriel's signature on a draconian release form. Hastily drafted by a CIA lawyer, it threatened criminal prosecution and many other forms of punishment if Gabriel shared the documents or their contents with anyone else.

"This document is ridiculous, Adrian. How can I operate without *sharing* the intelligence?"

"Just sign it," Carter said. "It doesn't mean what it says. It's just the lawyers being lawyers."

Gabriel scribbled his name in Hebrew across the bottom of the form and handed it to Eli Lavon, who had just arrived from Tel Aviv. Lavon signed it without protest and gave it back to Adrian Carter.

"No one is allowed in or out of the house while this material is on the premises. And that includes you two. Don't think about trying to sneak out, because I've got a team of watchers on N Street and another in the alley."

When Carter departed, they divided up the files and retreated to separate quarters. Gabriel took several boxes of Agency cables, along with the data assembled by the now-defunct NSC task force, and settled into the library. Eli Lavon took everything from NSA — the transcripts and the original recordings — and set up shop in the drawing room.

For the remainder of the evening, and late into the night, they were treated to the sound of Ivan Kharkov's voice. Ivan the banker and Ivan the builder. Ivan the real estate mogul and Ivan the international investor. Ivan the very emblem of a Russia resurgent. They listened while he negotiated with the mayor of Moscow over a prime piece of riverfront property where he wished to develop an American-style shopping mall. They listened while he coerced a fellow Russian businessman into surrendering his share of a lucrative Bentley dealership located near the Kremlin walls. They listened while he threatened to castrate the owner of a London moving company over damage to his mansion in Belgravia incurred during the delivery of a Bösendorfer piano. And they listened to a rather tense conversation with an underling called Valery who was having difficulty obtaining the clearance for a large shipment of medical equipment to Sierra Leone. The equipment must have been urgently needed, for, twenty minutes later, NSA intercepted a second call to Valery, during which Ivan said the papers were now in order and that the flight could proceed to Freetown without delay.

When not tending to his far-flung business empire, Ivan juggled his many women. There was Yekatarina, the supermodel whom he kept for personal viewing in an apartment in Paris. There was Tatyana, the Aeroflot flight attendant who saw to his needs each time their paths happened to intersect. And there was poor Ludmila, who had come to London looking for a way out of her dreary Siberian village and had found Ivan instead. She had believed Ivan's lies and, when cast aside, had threatened to tell Elena everything. Another man might have tried to defuse the situation with expensive gifts or money. But not Ivan. Ivan threatened to have her killed. And then he threatened to kill her parents in Russia as well.

Occasionally, they would be granted a reprieve from Ivan by the voice of Elena. Though not an official target of NSA surveillance, she became ensnared in NSA's net each time she used one of Ivan's phones. She was silk to Ivan's steel, decency to Ivan's decadence. She had everything money could buy but seemed to want nothing more than a husband with an ounce of integrity. She raised their two children without Ivan's help and, for the most part, passed her days free of Ivan's boorish company. Ivan bought her large houses and gave her endless piles of money to fill them with expensive things. In return, she was permitted to ask nothing of his business or personal affairs. With the help of NSA's satellites, Gabriel and Lavon became privy to Ivan's many lies. When Ivan told Elena he was in Geneva for a meeting with his Swiss bankers, Gabriel and Lavon knew he was actually in Paris partaking in the delights of Yekatarina. And when Ivan told Elena he was in Düsseldorf meeting with a German industrialist, Gabriel and Lavon knew he was actually in Frankfurt helping Tatyana pass a long layover in an airport hotel room. Lavon's loathing of him grew with each passing hour. "Lots of women make deals with the Devil," he said. "But poor Elena was foolish enough to actually marry him."

An hour before dawn, Gabriel was reading an excruciatingly dull cable by the CIA station chief in Angola when Lavon poked his head in the door.

"I think you need to come and listen to something."

Gabriel set aside the cable and followed Lavon into the drawing room. The anonymous air of a hotel hospitality suite had been replaced by that of a university common room on the night before a final exam. Lavon sat down before a laptop computer and, with a click of the mouse, played a series of fourteen intercepts, each featuring the voice of Elena Kharkov. None required translation because in each conversation she was speaking fluent English and addressing the same man. The last intercept was only two months old. Gabriel listened to it three times, then looked at Lavon and smiled.

"What do you think?" Lavon asked.

"I think you may have just found a way for us to talk to Ivan's wife."

25
GEORGETOWN

"She's obsessed with Mary Cassatt."

"Is that one of Ivan's girlfriends?"

"She's a painter, Adrian. An Impressionist painter. A rather good one, actually."

"Forgive me, Gabriel. I've been somewhat busy since 9/11. I can give you chapter and verse on the one hundred most dangerous terrorists in the world, but I can't tell you the title of the last movie I saw."

"You need to get out more, Adrian."

"Tell that to al-Qaeda."

They were walking along the dirt-and-gravel towpath at the edge of the Chesapeake and Ohio Canal. It was early morning, but the sun had yet to burn its way through the layer of gauzy gray cloud that had settled over Washington during the night. On their left, the wide green waters of the Potomac River flowed listlessly toward Georgetown, while, on their right, warring motorists sped toward the same destination along Canal Road. Gabriel wore faded jeans and a plain white pullover; Carter, a nylon tracksuit and a pair of pristine running shoes.

"I take it Mary Cassatt was French?"

"American, actually. She moved to Paris in 1865 and eventually fell under the spell of the Impressionists. Her specialty was tender portraits of women and children — intriguing, since she was unmarried and childless herself. Her work is a bit too sentimental for my taste, but it's extremely popular among a certain type of collector."

"Like Elena Kharkov?"

Gabriel nodded. "Based on what we heard in the NSA intercepts, she owns at least six Cassatts already and is in the market for more. She's on a first-name basis with every significant dealer in Paris, London, and New York. She's also got excellent contacts at the big auction houses, including the director of the Impressionist and Modern Art department at Christie's in London."

"Know him?"

"In another life."

"I take it you're planning to renew your professional relationship?"

"One step at a time, Adrian."

Carter walked in silence for a moment, with his hands clasped behind his back and his eyes cast downward. "I had a chance to peruse her file. Elena's an interesting woman, to say the least. She's a Leningrad girl. Did you notice that, Gabriel?"

"Yes, Adrian, I did notice that."

"Her father was a Party muckety-muck. Worked for Gosplan, the central planning bureaucracy that oversaw the Rube Goldberg contraption once known as the Soviet economy. She went to Leningrad State University and was supposed to be an economist like her father. But apparently she had a change of heart and decided to study languages and art instead. It seems she was working at the Hermitage when she met Ivan. One wonders what she saw in him."

"They had similar backgrounds. Both were children of the elite."

"There's a big difference between Gosplan and the KGB."

Gabriel heard footfalls and looked up to see a floppy-haired runner bounding toward them with headphones over his ears. He envied those innocent souls who could go out in public deprived of a vital sense. When they were alone again, Carter asked, "How do you intend to play this?"

"After listening to those intercepts, I'm convinced that if a painting by Mary Cassatt were to come quietly onto the market Elena Kharkov would jump at the opportunity to have a look."

"And you would be standing next to it when she did?"

"Or one of my associates. Someone with a pleasing demeanor and a deep passion for the paintings of Mary Cassatt. Someone who won't make Elena's bodyguards nervous."

Carter absently patted his right pocket, as if looking for his pipe. "Should I assume this encounter would take place on British soil?"

"You should."

"That means you're going to have to bring the British into the picture. Ivan and his entourage are under full-time MI5 surveillance whenever they're in London. I suspect our British cousins will be more than willing to cooperate. The British have been pressing us to do something about Ivan for years."

Twenty yards ahead, a young woman was being pulled along the towpath by a panting Siberian husky. Gabriel, whose fear of dogs was legendary in the trade, deftly switched places with Carter and watched with a certain professional satisfaction as the dog pressed its dripping muzzle against the leg of Carter's tracksuit.

"This agent with a pleasing demeanor and a deep passion for Mary Cassatt," Carter said as he wiped away the spittle. "Do you have someone in mind for the job yet?"

"I'm inclined to use a woman. She would have to be able to pass as an American or a Brit. We have several suitable candidates but none with any real expertise when it comes to art. Which means I'd have to start from scratch to get them ready."

"That's a shame. After all, the clock is ticking."

"Yes, Adrian, I realize that."

"As you may recall, we have someone who might fit the bill. She has a Ph.D. in art history from Harvard and she's done a job like this before. She's even operated with your service on a couple of occasions, which means she understands your rather archaic Hebrew-based lexicon."

"It might be complicated, Adrian."

"Because she's secretly in love with you." Carter glanced at Gabriel to see his reaction but received only a blank stare in return. "She's a big girl, Gabriel. And thanks to you, she's a true professional now."

"Where is she?"

"Still at the Counterterrorism Center at Langley, which means she's technically under my control. If you want her, she's yours."

"Poor choice of words, Adrian."

"I was speaking in a professional sense, of course."

Gabriel walked in silence for a moment. "Obviously, she's perfect for the job. But are you sure she's ready to go back into the field?"

"She worked with you during the Halton affair."

"As a liaison only. This operation would require sending her undercover again."

"I'm given regular updates on her progress. The Agency psychiatrist we assigned to her says she's coming along nicely. Personnel says she's had no problems adapting to her new cover identity, and her superiors at the CTC have given her extremely high marks."

"Not surprising, Adrian. She's a star. God only knows why your recruiters rejected her in the first place."

"They thought she was too independent — and maybe a bit too intelligent. We're not like you, Gabriel. We like our case officers to think *inside* the box."

"And you wonder why your most talented operatives are working for private contractors now."

"Spare me the critique, Gabriel. Do you want to use her or not?"

"I'll know after I talk to her."

"She comes on duty in the CTC at noon."

"Langley?" Gabriel shook his head. "I want to see her somewhere the Agency isn't listening."

"That narrows our options considerably." Carter made a show of careful consideration. "How about Dumbarton Oaks? The gardens, at noon."

"Just make sure she's alone."

Carter smiled sadly. "Thanks to you, Gabriel, she never goes anywhere alone. And she probably never will."

26

DUMBARTON OAKS, GEORGETOWN

The sun managed to burn through the veil of haze by midmorning, and by the time Gabriel presented himself at the entrance of Dumbarton Oaks it had grown appallingly hot. He purchased an admission ticket from a man in a little booth and was handed a glossy brochure. He consulted it frequently while he strolled past the elaborate arbors, trellises, and ornamental pools. A few minutes after noon, he made his way to a distant corner of the gardens, where he found an attractive woman in her early thirties seated primly on a wooden bench, a paperback book open in her lap, lilies of the valley at her feet. She wore a simple cotton sundress and sandals. Her blond hair had grown out since he had seen her last; her alabaster skin was beginning to turn red from the intense sun. She looked up sharply as Gabriel approached, but her face remained oddly expressionless, as if it had been rendered by the hand of Mary Cassatt.

"Were you able to spot Adrian's watchers?" asked Sarah Bancroft.

He kissed her cheek and led her toward the shade of a nearby trellis. "A nearsighted probationer fresh out of the academy could have spotted Adrian's watchers."

"Let's hear it."

"Woman with the sunhat, man with the plaid Bermuda shorts, the couple wearing matching 'I Love New York' shirts."

"Very good. But you missed the two boys in the dark sedan on R Street."

"I didn't miss them. They might as well have just waved hello to me as I came inside."

They sat down together, but even in the shade there was little relief from the heavy wet heat. Sarah pushed her sunglasses into her hair and brushed a trickle of perspiration from her cheek. Gabriel gazed at her in profile while her eyes flickered restlessly around the gardens. The daughter of a wealthy Citibank executive, Sarah Bancroft had spent much of her childhood in Europe, where she had acquired a Continental education along with a handful of Continental languages and impeccable Continental manners. She had returned to America to attend Dartmouth, and later, after spending a year studying at the prestigious Courtauld Institute of Art in London, became the youngest woman ever to earn a Ph.D. in art history at Harvard. While finishing her dissertation, she began dating a young lawyer named Ben Callahan, who had the misfortune of boarding United Airlines Flight 175 on the morning of September 11, 2001. He managed to make one telephone call before the plane plunged into the South Tower of the World Trade Center. That call was to Sarah. Gabriel had given her the chance that Langley had denied her: to fight back against the murderers. With Carter's blessing, and with the help of a lost Van Gogh, he had inserted her into the entourage of a Saudi billionaire named Zizi al-Bakari and ordered her to find the terrorist mastermind lurking within it. She had been lucky to survive. Her life had never been the same since.

"I was afraid you wouldn't come," he said.

"Why ever would you think that? Because in the midst of a very tense operation, I committed the terribly unprofessional act of confessing my true feelings for you?"

"That was one reason."

"You don't have to worry about that, Gabriel. I'm over you now." She looked at him and smiled. "Is it my imagination or do you seem a little disappointed?"

"No, Sarah, I'm not disappointed."

"Of course you are. The question is, do you really want *me* tagging along on another operation?"

"Why wouldn't I?"

"Because your lovely new Italian bride might not approve." She adjusted the thin straps of her sundress. It clung to her breasts in a way that could cause even the most faithful eye to wander. "You know, for a man of your many gifts, your knowledge of women is shockingly deficient."

"I make up for it in other ways."

"With your unfailingly pleasant demeanor?"

"For starters."

She gazed at him for a moment as though he were a dull student. "The last person Chiara wants to see in the field again is *me.*"

"You were a guest at our wedding."

"One of the worst days of my life. And that's saying something, because I've had some pretty terrible days."

"But you're over me now?"

"Not even a flicker of interest."

A pair of Japanese tourists approached and, in a combination of broken English and halting gestures, asked Sarah to take their photograph. She agreed, much to Gabriel's displeasure.

"Are you out of your mind?"

"What have I done now?"

"What if there had been a bomb in that camera?"

"Who would put a bomb in a camera?"

"*We* would."

"If it was so dangerous, then why did you let me do it?"

"Because they were obviously harmless Japanese tourists."

"How did you know that?"

"I can tell."

"Just by looking at them?"

"Yes, I can tell just by looking at them."

She laughed. "You'd better be careful, Gabriel. Otherwise, you might make me fall in love with you again."

"And we can't have that."

"No, we can't."

Gabriel gazed across the gardens and asked how much Carter had told her.

"Only that you're going after Ivan Kharkov."

"Know much about him?"

"He's not formally under the purview of the CTC, but he probably should be. We went to war in Iraq, in part, because we feared that Saddam might be willing to supply the terrorists with sophisticated weaponry or even weapons of mass destruction. But the terrorists don't have to go to a state like Iraq to get their weapons. They can go to a nonstate actor like Ivan instead. For the right amount of money, he'll sell them whatever they want and route it to them through one of his customers in Africa or Latin America."

"You've obviously learned your craft well."

"I was well trained." She crossed one leg over the other and smoothed the wrinkles from her sundress. "What do you need me to do this time?"

"Memorize the CIA's files on Ivan and his network, and read everything you can about Mary Cassatt. Adrian will tell you the rest."

"Kharkov and Cassatt? Only a Gabriel Allon operation could feature a combination like that." She lowered her sunglasses. "Should I assume you'll need me to go undercover again?"

"Yes, you should." A silence fell between them, heavy as the midday heat. "If you don't want to do it, Sarah, just tell me. God knows, you've done more than enough already."

She looked at him and smiled. It was a brave smile, thought Gabriel. The kind that didn't quite extend to the rest of the face. "And miss all the fun?" She fanned herself dramatically with her book. "Besides, I'd do just about anything to get out of here for a few days. I can't stand Washington in the summer."

27
LONDON

Number 7 Mornington Terrace was a sooty postwar apartment block overlooking the rail tracks of Euston Station. When Gabriel rang the bell of Apartment 5C, the door opened a few inches and a pair of gray eyes regarded him coolly over the chain. They didn't look pleased to see him. They rarely did.

Free of the chain, the door swung open a more hospitable distance. Gabriel stepped inside and took stock of his surroundings: a dreary little bed-sit, with a cracked linoleum floor and flea market furnishings. The man waiting inside looked as though he had wandered into the flat by mistake. He wore a pin-striped suit, a Burberry raincoat, and cuff links the size of shillings. His hair had been blond once; now it had the cast of pewter. It gave him the appearance of a model in a magazine advertisement for fine cognac, or an actor in a soap opera, the older millionaire type who puts himself about with younger women.

Graham Seymour didn't have time to pursue women. As deputy director of MI5, the British Security Service, he had more than enough work on his desk to keep him occupied. His country was now home to several thousand Islamic extremists with known terrorist connections. And just to keep things interesting, Russian espionage activities in London were now at levels not seen since the end of the Cold War. Those activities included the 2006 murder of Aleksandr Litvinenko, a former FSB agent and Kremlin critic who had been poisoned with a dose of highly radioactive polonium-210, an act of nuclear terrorism carried out by the FSB in the heart of the British capital.

Seymour must have arrived just before Gabriel because the shoulders of his coat were still beaded with raindrops. He tossed it wearily over the back of a chair and held out his hand. The palm was facing up.

"Let's not do this again, Graham."

"Hand it over."

Gabriel exhaled heavily and surrendered his passport. Seymour opened the cover and frowned.

"Martin Stonehill. Place of birth: Hamburg, Germany."

"I'm a naturalized American citizen."

"So that explains the accent." Seymour handed the passport back to Gabriel. "Is this a gift from your friend the president or the handiwork of your little band of forgers at King Saul Boulevard?"

"Adrian was kind enough to let me borrow it. Traveling is hard enough these days without doing it on an Israeli passport bearing the name Gabriel Allon." He slipped the passport back into his coat pocket and looked around the room. "Do you use this for all your high-level liaison meetings, Graham, or is this palace reserved for Israeli visitors?"

"Don't get your nose bent out of shape, Gabriel. I'm afraid it was all we could find on short notice. Besides, you were the one who refused to come to Thames House."

Thames House was MI5's riverfront headquarters near Lambeth Bridge.

"I really like what you've done with the place, Graham."

"It's been in the family for years. We use it mainly as a crash pad and for debriefing sources and penetration agents."

"What sort of penetration agents?"

"The sort that we slip into potential terrorist cells."

"In that case, I'm surprised you were able to squeeze me in."

"I'm afraid it does get its fair share of use."

"Any of your sources picking up any whispers about Russian arms headed this way?"

"I put that question to the Joint Terrorism Analysis Centre last night after talking to Adrian. The Americans aren't the only ones who've been hearing chatter about the arrows of Allah. We've intercepted references to them as well."

In the galley kitchen, an electric teakettle began to spew steam. Gabriel walked over to the window and peered out at a passing West Coast Main Line train while Seymour saw to the tea. He returned with two cups, plain for Gabriel, milk and sugar for himself. "I'm afraid the housekeepers neglected to stock the pantry with digestive biscuits," he said morosely. "It's bad enough they left shelf milk instead of fresh, but failure to leave a package of McVitie's is a firing offense, in my humble opinion."

"I can run down to the corner market if you'd like, Graham."

"I'll survive." Seymour lowered himself hesitantly onto the couch and placed his mug on a scratched coffee table. "Adrian gave me the basics of what you picked up in

Moscow. Why don't you fill me in on the rest?"

Gabriel told Seymour everything, beginning with the murder of Boris Ostrovsky in Rome and ending with his interrogation and deportation from Russia. Seymour, who did nothing more dangerous these days than change his own ink cartridges, was suitably impressed.

"My, my, but you *do* manage to get around. And to think you accomplished all that with only three dead bodies. That's something of an accomplishment for you." Seymour blew thoughtfully into his tea. "So what are you proposing? You want to pull Elena Kharkov aside for a private chat about her husband's operations? Easier said than done, I'm afraid. Elena doesn't put a toe outside her Knightsbridge mansion without a full complement of very nasty bodyguards. No one talks to Elena without talking to Ivan first."

"Actually, that's not exactly true. There's someone in London she talks to on a regular basis — someone who might be willing to help, considering the gravity of the situation."

"He's a British citizen, I take it?"

"Quite."

"Is he honestly employed?"

"I suppose that depends on your point of view. He's an art dealer."

"Where does he work?"

Gabriel told him.

"Oh, dear. This could be a bit ticklish."

"That's why I'm here, Graham. I wouldn't dream of operating in London without consulting you first."

"Spare me."

"I think we should have a little look under his fingernails before we make any approach. The art world is filled with a lot of shady characters. One can never be too careful."

"*We?* No, Gabriel, *we* won't go anywhere near him. The Security Service will handle this matter with the utmost discretion and a proper Home Office warrant."

"How soon can you start?"

"Seventy-two hours should suffice."

"I'll have a man on him by lunch," Seymour said. "I propose we meet once a day to review the watch reports."

"Agreed."

"We can do it here if you like."

"Surely you jest."

"Your choice, then."

"St. James's Park. Six o'clock. The benches on the north side of Duck Island."

Graham Seymour frowned. "I'll bring the bread crumbs."

28
LONDON

In the aftermath, when the archivists and analysts of a dozen different services and agencies were picking over the scorched bones of the affair, all would be puzzled by the fact that Gabriel's primary target during those first tenuous days of the operation was not Ivan Kharkov or his beautiful wife, Elena, but Alistair Leach, director of Impressionist and Modern Art at the august Christie's auction house, Number 8 King Street, St. James's, London. They took no joy in it; he was a good and decent man who became ensnared in the affair through no fault of his own, other than his serendipitous proximity to evil. Adrian Carter would later refer to him as "our own little cautionary tale." Few lives are lived without a trace of sin, and fewer still can stand up to the scrutiny of an MI5 telephone tap and a full-time complement of MI5 watchers. There, by the grace of God, Carter would say, went us all.

Any intelligence officer with a modicum of conscience knows it can be a disquieting experience to rifle through the drawers of a man's life, but Seymour, who had more scruples than most, made certain it was done with the gentlest hand possible. His listeners eavesdropped on Leach's telephone conversations with a forgiving ear, his watchers stalked their quarry from a respectable distance, and his burrowers dug through Leach's phone records, bank statements, and credit card bills with the utmost sensitivity. Only the room transmitters caused them to squirm — the transmitters that, at Gabriel's insistence, had been hidden in Leach's Kentish Town residence. It did not take long for the bugs to reveal why Leach spent so little time there. The listeners began referring to his wife, Abigail, only as "the Beast."

Unbeknownst to Graham Seymour and MI5, Gabriel had taken up quiet residence during this phase of the affair in an Office safe flat in Bayswater Road. He used the lull in the operation to catch up on his rest and to heal his bruised body. He slept late, usually until nine or ten, and then spent the remainder of his mornings dawdling over coffee and the newspapers. After lunch, he would leave the flat and take long walks around central London. Though he was careful to alter his routes, he visited the same three destinations each day: the Israeli Embassy in Old Court Road, the American Embassy in Grosvenor Square, and Duck Island in St. James's Park. Graham Seymour appeared promptly at six o'clock the first two evenings, but on the third he arrived forty-five minutes later, muttering something about his director-general being in a snit. He immediately opened his stainless steel attaché and handed Gabriel a photograph. It showed Alistair Leach strolling the pavements of Piccadilly with a spinsterish woman at his side.

"Who is she?"

"Rosemary Gibbons. She's an administrator in the Old Master Paintings department at Sotheby's. For obvious reasons, both personal and professional, they keep their relationship highly secret. As far as we can tell, it's strictly platonic. To tell you the truth, my watchers are actually rooting for poor Alistair to take it to the next step. Abigail is an absolute fiend, and his two children can't bear the sight of him."

"Where are they now?"

"The wife and children?"

"Leach and Rosemary," Gabriel answered

250

impatiently.

"A little wine bar in Jermyn Street. Quiet table in the far corner. Very cozy."

"You'll get me a picture, won't you, Graham? A little something to keep in my back pocket in case he digs in his heels?"

Seymour ran a hand through his gray locks, then nodded.

"I'd like to move on him tomorrow," Gabriel said. "What's his schedule like?"

"Appointments all morning at Christie's, then he's attending a meeting of something called the Raphael Club. We have a researcher checking it out."

"You can tell your researcher to stand down, Graham. I can assure you the members of the Raphael Club pose no threat to anyone except themselves."

"What is it?"

"A monthly gathering of art dealers, auctioneers, and curators. They do nothing more seditious than drink far too much wine and bemoan the shifting fortunes of their trade."

"Shall we do it before the meeting or after?"

"*After,* Graham. Definitely after."

"You don't happen to know where and when these gentlemen gather, do you?"

"Green's Restaurant. One o'clock."

29
ST. JAMES'S, LONDON

The members of the little-known but much-maligned Raphael Club began trickling into the enchanted premises of Green's Restaurant and Oyster Bar, Duke Street, St. James's, shortly before one the following afternoon. Oliver Dimbleby, a lecherous independent dealer from Bury Street, arrived early, but then Oliver always liked to have a gin or two at the bar alone, just to get the mood right. The unscrupulous Roddy Hutchinson came next, followed by Jeremy Crabbe, the tweedy director of Old Master Paintings from Bonhams. A few minutes later came a pair of curators, one from the Tate and another from the National. Then, at one sharp, Julian Isherwood, the Raphael Club's founder and beating heart, came teetering up the front steps, looking hungover as usual.

By 1:20, the guest of honor — at least in the estimation of Gabriel and Graham Seymour, who were sitting across the street from Green's in the back of an MI5 surveillance van — had not yet arrived. Seymour telephoned the MI5 listeners and asked whether there was any recent activity on Leach's work line or his mobile. "It's the Beast," explained the listener. "She's giving him a list of errands he's to run on the way home from work." At 1:32, the listener called back again to say that Leach's line was now inactive, and, at 1:34, a surveillance team in King Street reported that he had just left Christie's in "a highly agitated state." Gabriel spotted him as he rounded the corner, a reedlike figure with rosy patches on his cheeks and two wiry tufts of hair above his ears that flapped like gray wings as he walked. A team inside Green's reported that Leach had joined the proceedings and that the white Burgundy was now flowing.

The luncheon was three hours and fifteen minutes in length, which was slightly longer than usual, but then it was June and June was a rather slow time of the year for all of them. The final wine count was four bottles of Sancerre, four bottles of a Provençal rosé, and three more bottles of an excellent Montrachet. The bill, when it finally arrived, caused something of a commotion, but this, too, was Raphael ritual. Estimated at "somewhere north of fifteen hundred pounds" by the team inside the restaurant, it was collected by means of a passed plate, with Oliver Dimbleby, tubbiest of the club's members, cracking the whip. As usual, Jeremy Crabbe was short of cash and was granted a bridge loan by Julian Isherwood. Alistair Leach tossed a couple hundred quid onto the plate as it passed beneath his nose and he finished his last glass of wine. The interior team would later report that he had the look of a man who seemed to know his world was about to change, and not necessarily for the better.

They clustered briefly outside in Duke Street before going their separate ways. Alistair Leach lingered a moment with Julian Isherwood, then turned and started back toward Christie's. He would get no farther than the corner of Duke and King streets, for it was there that Graham Seymour had chosen to make the scoop. The task was handled by a young operative named Nigel Whitcombe, who had a face like a parson and the grip of a blacksmith. Leach offered only token resistance as he was led by the elbow toward a waiting MI5 Rover.

"Mind telling me what this is all about?"

he asked meekly as the car pulled away from the curb.

"I'd love to tell you more, Alistair, but I'm afraid I'm just the delivery boy."

"It's not a long drive, is it? I'm afraid you caught me at a delicate moment. A little too much wine at lunch. That damn Oliver Dimbleby. He's trouble, Oliver. Always was. Always will be. He's the one you should be picking up."

"Perhaps another time." Whitcombe's smile was like balm. "Do try to relax, Alistair. You're not in any trouble. We just need to borrow some of your connections and expertise."

"Any idea how long we'll be?"

"I suppose that depends on you."

"I'll need to call Abigail if we're going to be late. She's a worrier, you know."

Yes, thought Whitcombe. *We know all about Abigail.*

They had debated over where to take him next. Graham Seymour had recommended the imposing formality of Thames House, but Gabriel, who had a field man's aversion to all things Headquarters, successfully lobbied for something cozier and less official. And so it was that, twenty minutes after he was plucked from King Street, Alistair

Leach was shown into the drawing room of a hastily leased mews house not far from Sloane Square. It was a pleasant room with good books on the shelves and good whiskey on the trolley. The blinds were partially open and the agreeable light of late afternoon was filtering through the slits and making striped patterns along the wood flooring. Graham Seymour was slowly pacing in order to better showcase his English scale, his English good looks, and his perfectly tailored English suit. Gabriel, who had not yet been invited to join the proceedings, was seated before a television monitor in an upstairs bedroom. He had two MI5 technicians for company, one called Marlowe and the other called Mapes. Inside the Service, they were better known as M&M Audio and Video.

Whitcombe instructed Leach to sit on the couch, then sat next to him. On the coffee table was a single sheet of paper. Graham Seymour drew a pen from his pocket and held it toward Leach like a loaded gun.

"Be a love, Alistair, and sign that for me. It's a copy of the Official Secrets Act. You needn't bother reading it, since the wording isn't terribly important. Rest assured, it gives us the right to lock you away in the Tower and lop off your head if you ever breathe a word of what is about to transpire here. You're not to talk about it with anyone. Not with your colleagues. Not with Abigail or your children. And not with any other friend or acquaintance with whom you might share the occasional intimacy."

Leach looked up sharply, and for an instant Gabriel feared that Seymour had played his ace when a jack would have done the trick. Then Leach looked at Whitcombe, who nodded gravely.

"What have I done?" Leach asked, pen to the document. "Short-changed Inland Revenue? Misbehaved on the Tube? Said something nasty about the current occupant of Number Ten?"

"You're fortunate enough to have been born in a free country," said Seymour. "You can say anything you like — within certain limits, of course. You're here not because of your own actions but because of your association with a man who is a threat to British national security. A rather serious threat, actually."

"Where's *here?*" Leach looked around the room, then at Seymour. "And who are *we?*"

"The *here* is not important. This is all temporary. As for the *we*, that's a bit more permanent. We're from the Security Service, sometimes referred to as MI5. I'm Charles." He nodded toward Whitcombe. "This is my colleague, Gerald."

"And this *association* of mine who's a threat to national security? Who might that be? My newsagent? The bloke who brings us coffee at the office?"

"It's one of your clients, actually."

"I'm afraid one encounters all sorts in a business like mine and not all of them are candidates for sainthood."

"The client I'm talking about need never apply for admission to God's heavenly kingdom, Alistair. He's not your average robber baron or hedge fund thief. He's been pouring weapons into the most volatile corners of the Third World for years. And it now appears he's about to conclude a transaction that could make the London bombings seem like child's play."

"He's an arms dealer? Is that what you're saying?"

"That's exactly what I'm saying. They're an unscrupulous lot by definition. This man is the worst of the worst."

"Does he have a name?"

"You don't get to know his name yet — not until you've agreed to help us."

"But what can *I* do? I sell paintings."

"We're asking you to make a telephone

call, Alistair. Nothing more. For that telephone call, you will be handsomely compensated. More important, we are giving you the opportunity to help defend your country and your fellow citizens of the world from an enemy that thinks nothing of slaughtering innocents." Seymour stopped walking. His eyes were concealed by shadow. "Shall I go on or should we run you home to Abigail and pretend this encounter never took place?"

Leach, at the second mention of his wife's name, shifted uneasily in his seat. He looked at Whitcombe, like a witness looking to his lawyer for counsel. Whitcombe gave an almost imperceptible nod of his head, as if imploring Leach to join their crusade.

"Go on," said Leach to no one in particular.

Seymour resumed his slow pacing. "Because the threat is international, our effort to counter it is international as well. You are about to meet an officer from the intelligence service of another country, a country allied with our own in the struggle against terrorism and global Islamic extremism. What's more, it is quite possible you will recognize this gentleman from your professional life. The document you signed covers your contact with this man as well as us."

"Please tell me he isn't a bloody American."

"Worse, I'm afraid."

"The only thing worse than an American is an Israeli."

Whitcombe gave Leach an admonitory tap on the side of the knee.

"Have I put my foot in it?" Leach asked.

"I'm afraid so," said Seymour.

"You won't say anything to him, will you? They *do* tend to get their back up at even the slightest insult."

Seymour gave a ghost of a smile. "It will be our little secret."

30
CHELSEA, LONDON

Gabriel entered the drawing room and, without a word, lowered himself into the armchair opposite Leach.

"Dear heavens, you're —"

"I'm no one," said Gabriel, finishing the sentence for him. "You don't know me. You've never seen me before in your life. You've never heard my name. You've never seen my face. Are we clear, Alistair?"

Leach looked at Seymour and appealed for assistance. "Are you going to stand there and do nothing? For Christ's sake! The man just threatened me."

"He did nothing of the sort," Seymour said. "Now, answer his question."

"But I *do* know his name. I know *both* his names. He's Mario Delvecchio. He used to clean pictures for juicy Julian Isherwood. He was the best. Painted like an angel and could authenticate a work simply by running his fingers over the brushstrokes. Then he broke our hearts. You see, the entire time he was cleaning for Julian, he was killing on behalf of the Israeli secret service."

"I'm afraid you have me confused with someone else, Alistair."

"That's not what *The Times* says. According to *The Times,* you were one of the gunmen who killed those poor sods in front of Westminster Abbey on Christmas morning."

" 'Those poor sods,' as you call them, were hardened terrorists who were about to commit an act of mass murder. As for the affiliation of the men who killed them, the official record states that they were attached to the SO19 division of the Metropolitan Police."

"*The Times* had your picture, though, didn't it?"

"Even a newspaper as reputable as *The Times* occasionally makes a mistake," said Graham Seymour.

Gabriel silently handed Leach a single sheet of paper.

"Read this."

"What is it?"

"A transcript of a phone conversation."

"Whose telephone conversation?"

"*Read* it, Alistair."

Leach did as instructed, then looked up at Gabriel in anger.

262

"Where did you get this?"

"It's not important."

"Tell me where you got this or this conversation is over."

Gabriel capitulated. In recruitments, Shamron always said, it was sometimes necessary to accept small defeats in order to secure ultimate victory.

"It was given to us by the Americans."

"The Americans? Why in God's name are the Americans tapping my phones?"

"Don't be grandiose," Seymour interjected. "They're not tapping *your* telephones. They're tapping *hers.*"

"Are you trying to tell me Elena Kharkov is an arms dealer?"

"Ivan Kharkov is the arms dealer," Gabriel said pedantically. "Elena just gets caught when she happens to place a call from one of the phones they're monitoring. On that day, she was calling you from her home in Knightsbridge. Look at the transcript, Alistair. Refresh your memory, if you need to."

"I don't need to refresh anything. I remember the conversation quite clearly. The Americans have no right to record these calls and store them away in their supercomputers. It's like opening someone else's mail. It's unseemly."

"If it makes you feel any better, no one bothered to read it — until I came along. But let's put all that aside and focus on what's important. You were talking to her about a painting that day — a painting by Mary Cassatt, to be precise."

"Elena has a thing for Cassatt. An obsession, really. Buys anything that comes on the market. I thought I'd managed to pry loose a painting for her from a minor collector — a picture called *Two Children on a Beach* that Cassatt painted in 1884 while convalescing from a case of bronchitis. The collector kept us hanging for several weeks before finally telling me that he wasn't ready to sell. I placed a call to Elena and got her machine. She called me back and I gave her the bad news."

"You've seen it?"

"The painting? Yes, it's quite lovely, actually."

"Did you ever tell Elena the name of the owner?"

"You know better than to ask that, Signore Delvecchio."

Gabriel looked at Graham Seymour, who had wandered over to the shelves and was pulling down books for inspection. "Who is he, Alistair? And don't try to hide behind some claim of dealer-client privilege."

"Can't do it," said Leach obstinately. "Owner wishes to remain anonymous."

Nigel Whitcombe made a church steeple with his fingertips and pressed it thoughtfully against his lips, as if pondering the morality of Leach's refusal to answer.

"And if the owner was aware of the stakes involved? I suspect he — or *she,* if that's the case — might actually relish the chance to help us. I suspect the owner is a patriot, Alistair." A pause. "Just like you."

The official recording of the interrogation would contain no evidence of what transpired next, for there would be no sound for the microphones to capture. It was a hand. The hand that Whitcombe placed gently upon Leach's shoulder, as though he were petitioning him to reclaim his lost faith.

"Boothby," Leach said, as if the name had popped suddenly into his memory. "Sir John Boothby. Lives in a big Edwardian pile on a couple hundred acres in the Cotswolds. Never worked a day in his life, as far as I can tell. The father worked for your lot. Rumor has it he had a wonderful war."

Seymour twisted his head around. "You're not talking about Basil Boothby, are you?"

"That's him. Ruthless bastard, from what I hear."

265

"Basil Boothby was one of the legends of the Service. He was involved in our deception program during the Second World War. Ran captured German spies back to their masters in Berlin. And, yes, he *was* a ruthless bastard. But there are times when one has to be. These are such times, Alistair."

"I'm wondering whether there's a chance Sir John might have had a change of heart," Gabriel said. "I'm wondering whether it might be time to have another go at him."

"He's not going to sell that painting — at least, not to Elena Kharkov."

"Why not?"

"Because in a moment of professional indiscretion, I may have mentioned that the prospective buyer was the wife of a Russian oligarch. Boothby's father spent the final years of his career battling KGB spies. The old man didn't hold with the Russians. Neither does Sir John."

"Sounds like a patriot to me," said Graham Seymour.

"I might use another word to describe him," Leach muttered. "Elena Kharkov would have paid a premium for that painting. Two million pounds, maybe a bit more. He would have been wise to take the deal. From what I hear, Sir John is not exactly flush with funds at the moment."

"Perhaps we can convince him to see the error of his ways."

"Good luck. But remember, if that Cassatt changes hands, I get my cut."

"How much are you getting these days, Alistair?" asked Gabriel.

Leach smiled. "You have your secrets, Signore Delvecchio. And I have mine."

31
GLOUCESTERSHIRE, ENGLAND

Havermore, the ancestral home of the Boothby clan, lay five miles to the northwest of the picturesque Cotswold Hills market town of Chipping Camden. At its zenith, the estate had sprawled over eight hundred acres of rolling pastures and wooded hills and had employed several dozen men and women from the surrounding villages. Its fortunes had dwindled in recent years, along with those of the family that owned it. All but a hundred acres had been sold off, and the manor house, a honey-colored limestone monstrosity, had fallen into a state of rather alarming disrepair. As for the staff, it now consisted of a single farmhand called Old George Merrywood and a plump housekeeper named Mrs. Lillian Devlin.

She greeted Gabriel and Graham Seymour early the next afternoon and informed them Sir John was eagerly awaiting their arrival. They found him standing before an easel in a patch of overgrown grass called the East Meadow, flailing away at a dreadful landscape. Boothby and Graham Seymour shook hands cordially and regarded each other for a moment in silence. They were of similar size and shape, though John Boothby was several years older and several inches bigger around the middle. He wore Wellington boots and a tan smock. His thick gray hair and tangled eyebrows gave him the appearance of a bottlebrush come to life.

"This is an associate of mine," Seymour said, his hand resting on Gabriel's shoulder. "He's a fellow traveler, Sir John. He works for an intelligence service in the Middle East whose interests occasionally intersect with our own."

"So you're an Israeli then," said Boothby, shaking Gabriel's hand.

"I'm afraid so," replied Gabriel contritely.

"No apologies necessary around here, my dear fellow. I have no quarrel with Israelis — *or* Jews, for that matter. We Europeans dropped you into the swamp, didn't we? And now we condemn you for daring to stand your ground." He released Gabriel's hand. "Do I get to know your name or are names off-limits?"

"His name is Gabriel, Sir John. Gabriel Allon."

Boothby gave a wry smile. "I thought it was you. An honor, Mr. Allon." He returned to the easel and looked morosely at the painting. "Bloody awful, isn't it? I can never seem to get the trees right."

"May I?" asked Gabriel.

"Do you paint, too?"

"When I get the chance."

Boothby handed him the brush. Gabriel worked on the painting for thirty seconds, then stepped aside.

"Good Lord! But that's bloody *marvelous.* You're obviously a man of considerable talent." He took Gabriel by the arm. "Let's go up to the house, shall we? Mrs. Devlin has made a roast."

They ate outside on the terrace beneath an umbrella that gave their faces the sepia coloring of an old photograph. Gabriel remained largely silent during the meal while Graham Seymour talked at length about Boothby's father and his work during the Second War. Gabriel was left with the impression that Boothby the Younger did not necessarily enjoy hearing about his father — that he had spent his life living in the shadow of Basil Boothby's wartime exploits and wished to be taken seriously in his own right. Gabriel could only imagine what it was like to be the son of a great man. His own father had been killed during the Six-Day War and Gabriel's memories of him were now fragmentary at best: a pair of intelligent brown eyes, a pleasant voice that was never raised in anger, a strong pair of hands that never struck him. The last time he had seen his father was the night before the war started, a figure dressed in olive green rushing off to join his army unit. Gabriel often wondered whether that memory was the source of Shamron's hold over him, the memory of a father answering the call to defend his country and his people. A father whom he never saw again.

Gabriel formed one other impression of Boothby during the meal: that he had the natural patience of a good spy. It wasn't until Mrs. Devlin served the coffee that he finally asked why Seymour and his friend from Israel had come all the way to Havermore to see him. But when Seymour commenced a somewhat meandering explanation, Boothby's patience wore thin.

"Come, come, Graham. We're all men of the world here, and I'm practically a member of the family. If you want me to sign a copy of the Official Secrets Act, I'll find the pen myself. But please spare me the bullshit." He looked at Gabriel. "You Israelis are known for your bluntness. Be blunt, for God's sake."

"We've picked up intelligence that a Russian arms dealer named Ivan Kharkov may be about to sell some very dangerous weapons to the terrorists of al-Qaeda. Is that blunt enough for you, Sir John?"

"Quite." He scratched his gray head and made a show of thought. "*Kharkov?* Why do I know that name?"

"Because his wife wants to buy *Two Children on a Beach* by Mary Cassatt."

"Ah, yes. I remember now. The wife's name is Elena, isn't it? She's represented by Alistair Leach at Christie's." He grimaced. "Appropriate name for an art dealer, don't you think? *Leach.* Especially when you see the size of his commissions. Good Lord, but they're absolutely *criminal.*"

"Is it true that you told Alistair you wouldn't sell the painting to Elena because she's Russian?"

"Of course it's true!"

"Would you care to tell us why?"

"Because they're monsters, aren't they? Look what they did to that poor chap in St. Peter's a few weeks ago. Look at the way they're bullying and blackmailing their

272

neighbors. If the Russians want a new Cold War, then I say we give them one." He sat back in his chair. "Listen, gentlemen, perhaps I'm not as foxy or devious as my old father was, but what *exactly* are you asking me to do?"

"I need to arrange a meeting with Elena Kharkov." Gabriel paused a moment and looked around at the landscape. "And I'd like to do it *here,* at Havermore."

"Why do you need to meet with Elena Kharkov?"

Graham Seymour cleared his throat judiciously. "I'm afraid we're not at liberty to discuss that with you, Sir John."

"Then I'm afraid I can't help you, Graham."

Seymour looked at Gabriel and nodded his head.

"We have strong reason to believe Mrs. Kharkov is aware of her husband's plans and does not approve," Gabriel said. "And we also believe she may be receptive to a quiet approach."

"A recruitment? Is that what you're suggesting? You want to ask Elena Kharkov to betray her husband — *here,* in my home?"

"It's perfect, actually."

"I must say, I'm rather intrigued by the

idea. Who's going to make the actual pass at her?"

"Your American niece."

"But I don't *have* an American niece."

"You do now."

"And what about *me?*"

"I suppose we could get a stand-in," Seymour said. "One of our older officers, or perhaps even someone who's retired. Heaven knows, we have many fine officers who would leap at the chance to come out of retirement and take part in a novel operation like this." Seymour lapsed into silence. "I suppose there is *one* other alternative, Sir John. *You* could play the role yourself. Your father was one of the greatest deceivers in history. He helped fool the Germans into thinking we were coming at Calais in Normandy. Deception is in your genes."

"And what happens if Ivan Kharkov ever finds out? I'll end up like that poor bloke, Litvinenko, dying an agonizing death in University College Hospital with my hair falling out."

"We'll make certain Ivan never gets anywhere near you. And the fact that you were never married and have no children makes our job much easier."

"What about Old George and Mrs. Devlin?"

"We'll have to deceive them, of course. You might have to let them go."

"Can't do that. Old George worked for my father. And Mrs. Devlin has been with me for nearly thirty years. We'll just have to work around them."

"So you'll do it, then?"

Boothby nodded. "If you gentlemen truly believe I'm up to the job, then it would be my honor to join you."

"Excellent," said Seymour. "That leaves only the small matter of the painting itself. If Elena Kharkov wants to buy it, we have no choice but to sell it to her."

Boothby brought his hand down on the table hard enough to rattle the china and the crystal. "Under no circumstances am I selling that painting to the wife of a Russian arms dealer."

Gabriel patted his lips with his napkin. "There is another possible solution — something your father would have enjoyed."

"What's that?"

"A deception, of course."

They hiked up the grand central staircase beneath yellowed portraits of Boothbys dead and gone. The nursery was in semi-darkness when they entered; Boothby pushed open the heavy curtains, allowing the golden Cotswold light to stream through the tall, mullioned windows. It fell upon two matching children's beds, two matching children's dressers, two matching hand-painted toy chests, and *Two Children on a Beach* by Mary Cassatt.

"My father bought it in Paris between the wars. Didn't pay much for it, as I recall. By then, Madame Cassatt had fallen out of fashion. My mother and sisters adored it, but, to be honest, I never much cared for it."

Gabriel walked over to the painting and stood before it in silence, right hand to his chin, head tilted slightly to one side. Then he licked three fingers of his right hand and scrubbed away the surface grime from the chubby knee of one of the children. Boothby frowned.

"I say, Gabriel. I hope you know what you're doing."

Gabriel took two steps back from the painting and calculated its dimensions.

"Looks like thirty-eight by twenty-nine."

"Actually, if memory serves, it's thirty-eight and three-quarters by twenty-nine and a quarter. You obviously have quite an eye."

Gabriel gave no indication he had heard the compliment. "I'm going to need a place to work for a few days. Somewhere quiet.

Somewhere I'm not going to be disturbed."

"There's an old gamekeeper's cottage at the north end of the property. I did a bit of renovation a few years back. Usually, it's rented this time of year, but it's vacant for the next several weeks. The entire second floor was converted into a studio. I think you'll find it to your liking."

"Please tell Mrs. Devlin that I'll see to my own cleaning. And tell Old George not to come snooping around." Gabriel resumed his appraisal of the Cassatt, one hand pressed to his chin, head tilted slightly to one side. "I don't like people watching me while I work."

32
GLOUCESTERSHIRE, ENGLAND

The following morning, Gabriel gave MI5 an operational shopping list the likes of which it had never seen. Whitcombe, who had developed something of a professional infatuation with the legendary operative from Israel, volunteered to fill it. His first stop was L. Cornelissen & Son in Great Russell Street, where he collected a large order of brushes, pigment, medium, ground, and varnish. Next, it was up to Camden Town for a pair of easels, then over to Earl's Court for three commercial-grade halogen lamps. His final two stops were just a few doors apart in Bury Street: Arnold Wiggins & Sons, where he ordered a lovely carved frame in the French style, and Dimbleby Fine Arts, where he purchased a work by a largely unknown French landscapist. Painted outside Paris in 1884, its dimensions were 29 inches by 38 inches.

By afternoon, the painting and the supplies were at Havermore, and Gabriel was soon at work in the second-floor studio of the old gamekeeper's cottage. Though advances in modern technology gave him considerable advantages over the great copyists of the past, he confined himself largely to the tried-and-true methods of the Old Masters. After subjecting the Cassatt to a surface examination, he snapped more than a hundred detail photographs and taped them to the walls of the studio. Then he covered the painting with a translucent paper and carefully traced the image beneath. When the sketch was complete, he removed it and made several thousand tiny perforations along the lines he had just drawn. He then transferred the tracing to the second canvas — which had been stripped bare and covered in a fresh ground — and carefully sprinkled charcoal powder over the surface. A moment later, when he removed the paper, a ghost image of *Two Children on a Beach* appeared on the surface.

A copyist of lesser gifts might have produced two or three drafts of the painting before attempting the final version, but Gabriel felt no need to practice, nor was he possessed with an abundance of time. He placed the easels side by side, with Cassatt's original on the left, and immediately prepared his first palette. He worked slowly for the first few days, but as he grew more accustomed to Cassatt's style, he was able to apply the paint to the canvas with increasing confidence and swiftness. Sometimes he had the sensation she was standing at his shoulder, carefully guiding his hand. Usually, she appeared to him alone, in a floor-length dress and ladylike bonnet, but occasionally she would bring along her mentors — Degas, Renoir, and Pissarro — to instruct him on the finer points of palette and brushwork.

Though the painting consumed most of Gabriel's attention, Ivan and Elena Kharkov were never far from his thoughts. NSA redoubled its efforts to intercept all of Ivan's electronic communications, and Adrian Carter arranged for a man from London Station to make regular trips to Havermore to share the take. As a child of the KGB, Ivan had always been careful on the telephone and remained so now. He spent those days largely sequestered in his walled mansion in Zhukovka, the restricted secret city of the oligarchs west of Moscow. Only once did he venture outside the country: a day trip to Paris to spend a few hours with Yekatarina, his supermodel mistress. He phoned Elena three times from Yekatarina's bed to say that his business meetings were going splendidly. One of the calls came while she was dining with two companions at the exclusive Café Pushkin, and the moment was captured by an Office watcher with a miniature camera. Gabriel couldn't help but be struck by the melancholy expression on her face, especially when compared to the outward gaiety of her two companions. He tacked the picture to the wall of his make-shift studio and called it *Three Ladies in a Moscow Café.*

One salient operational fact eluded Gabriel: the precise date Ivan and Elena were planning to leave Moscow and return to Knightsbridge. As he labored alone before the canvas, he became gripped by a fear he was about to throw an elaborate party that no one would attend. It was an irrational notion; Ivan Kharkov tolerated his native country only in small doses and it was only a matter of time before he would be overcome by the urge to leave it once more. Finally, an MI5 team monitoring the Kharkov mansion in Rutland Gate witnessed the delivery of a large consignment of vodka, champagne, and French wine — strong evidence, they argued, of Ivan's impending return. The next day, NSA intercepted a telephone call from Ivan to

Arkady Medvedev, the chief of his personal security and intelligence service. Buried within a lengthy discussion about the activities of a Russian rival was the nugget of intelligence for which Gabriel had been so anxiously waiting: Ivan was coming to London in a week for what he described as a round of important business meetings. After leaving London, he would travel to the South of France to take up residence at Villa Soleil, his sumptuous summer palace overlooking the Mediterranean Sea near Saint-Tropez.

That evening, Gabriel ate dinner while standing before the canvas. Shortly after nine, he heard the sound of car tires crunching over the gravel drive and an engine note that was unfamiliar to him. He walked over to the window and peered down as a tall woman with pale blond hair emerged with a single bag slung over her shoulder. She came upstairs to the studio and stood at his shoulder while he worked.

"Would you like to tell me why you're forging a Cassatt?" asked Sarah Bancroft.

"The owner won't sell me the original."

"What happens when it's finished?"

"You're going to sell it to Elena Kharkov."

"Ask a silly question." She leaned forward and scrutinized the canvas. "Watch your brushwork on the hands, Gabriel. It's a bit too impasto."

"My brushwork, as usual, is flawless."

"How foolish of me to suggest otherwise." She smothered an elaborate yawn. "I'm running on fumes."

"You can sleep here tonight, but tomorrow, you're moving up to the main house. Uncle John is expecting you."

"What's he like?"

"I wouldn't want to spoil the surprise."

"If you need any more advice, don't hesitate to wake me."

"I think I can manage on my own."

"You sure about that?"

"I'm sure."

Sarah kissed his cheek and slipped silently through the doorway. Gabriel pressed the PLAY button on a small portable stereo and stood motionless while the first notes of *La Bohème* filled the room. Then he tapped his brush against the palette and painted alone until midnight.

Sir John Boothby was introduced to his American niece, an attractive young woman now using the name Sarah Crawford, over breakfast the following morning. Gabriel swiftly sketched the missing chapters of their long and cordial relationship. Though

Sarah's mother, now deceased, had been foolish enough to marry a Wall Street banker, she had made certain her daughter maintained strong connections to England, which is why Sarah had spent summers at Havermore, and why she still made an annual pilgrimage to the estate now that she was in her thirties. As a young girl, she had stayed in the nursery and formed a deep bond with *Two Children on a Beach.* Therefore, it would be natural for Sarah to show Elena Kharkov the painting rather than her uncle, who had never really cared for it. The Cassatt would be viewed "in situ," meaning that Sarah would be required to escort Elena to the upstairs to see it, thus leaving her ample time for a quiet but unmistakable approach. Uncle John's task would be to assist in the separation of Elena from her bodyguards. Gabriel estimated they would have ten minutes. Any more than that, he reckoned, and the bodyguards would start getting jumpy. And jumpy Russian bodyguards were the last thing they needed.

With Sarah's arrival, the pace of the preparations increased dramatically. M&M Audio and Video rolled into Havermore, disguised as local electricians, and installed cameras and microphones around the house and the grounds. They also created a make-shift command post in the hayloft of the barn, where the feeds could be monitored and recorded. Sarah spent her mornings "reacquainting" herself with a home she knew well and cherished deeply. She spent many pleasant hours with her uncle, familiarizing herself with the vast old manor house, and led herself on long walks around the estate with Punch and Judy, Boothby's poorly behaved Pembroke Welsh corgis, trotting at her heels. Old George Merrywood invariably stopped her for a chat. His local Gloucestershire accent was so broad that even Sarah, who had spent much time in England, could barely understand a word he said. Mrs. Devlin pronounced her "simply the most delightful American I've ever met." She knew nothing of Sarah's alleged blood relationship to her employer — indeed, she had been told by Sir John that Sarah was the daughter of an American friend and had recently gone through a nasty divorce. *Poor lamb,* thought Mrs. Devlin one afternoon as she watched Sarah emerge from the dappled light of the North Wood with the dogs at her heels. *What idiot would ever let a girl like that slip through his fingers?*

In the evenings, Sarah would wander out to the gamekeeper's cottage to discuss the real purpose of her stay at Havermore, which was the recruitment of Elena Kharkov. Gabriel would lecture her while he stood before his easel. At first, he spoke about the craft in general terms, but as the date of Elena's arrival drew nearer, his briefings took on a decidedly more pointed tone. "Remember, Sarah, two people are already dead because of her. You can't push too hard. You can't force the issue. Just open the door and let her walk through it. If she does, get as much information as you can about Ivan's deal and try to arrange a second meeting. Whatever you do, don't let the first encounter last longer than ten minutes. You can be sure the bodyguards will be watching the clock. And they report *every*thing to Ivan."

The following morning, Graham Seymour called from Thames House to say that Ivan Kharkov's plane — a Boeing Business Jet, tail number N7287IK — had just filed a flight plan and was due to arrive at Stansted Airport north of London at 4:30 p.m. After hanging up the phone, Gabriel applied the final touches of paint to his ersatz version of *Two Children on a Beach* by Mary Cassatt. Three hours later, he removed the canvas from its stretcher and carried it downstairs to the kitchen, where he placed it in a 350-degree oven. Sarah found him there twenty minutes later, leaning nonchalantly against the counter, coffee mug in hand.

"What's that smell?"

Gabriel glanced down at the oven. Sarah peered through the window, then looked up in alarm.

"Why are you baking the Cassatt?"

Just then the kitchen timer chimed softly. Gabriel removed the canvas from the oven and allowed it to cool slightly, then laid it faceup on the table. With Sarah watching, he took hold of the canvas at the top and bottom and pulled it firmly over the edge of the table, downward toward the floor. Then he gave the painting a quarter turn and dragged it hard against the edge of the table a second time. He examined the surface for a moment, then, satisfied, held it up for Sarah to see. Earlier that morning, the paint had been smooth and pristine. Now the combination of heat and pressure had left the surface covered by a fine webbing of fissures and cracks.

"Amazing," she whispered.

"It's not amazing," he said. "It's craquelure."

Whistling tunelessly to himself, he carried the canvas upstairs to his studio, placed it back on the original stretcher, and covered the painting with a thin coat of yellow-tinted varnish. When the varnish had dried, he summoned Sarah and John Boothby to the studio and asked them to choose which canvas was the original, and which was the forgery. After several minutes of careful comparison and consultation, both agreed that the painting on the right was the original, and the one on the left was the forgery.

"You're absolutely sure?" Gabriel asked.

After another round of consultation, two heads nodded in unison. Gabriel removed the painting on the right from its easel and mounted it in the new frame that had just arrived from Arnold Wiggins & Sons. Sarah and John Boothby, humiliated over being duped, carried the forgery up to the main house and hung it in the nursery. Gabriel climbed into the back of an MI5 car and, with Nigel Whitcombe at his side, headed back to London. The operation was in Alistair Leach's hands now. But, then, it always had been.

33
THAMES HOUSE, LONDON

Gabriel knew that discretion came naturally to those who work the highlands of the art trade, but even Gabriel was surprised by the extent to which Alistair Leach had remained faithful to his vow of silence. Indeed, after more than a week of relentless digging and observation MI5 had found no trace of evidence to suggest he had broken discipline in any way — nothing in his phone calls, nothing in his e-mail or faxes, and nothing in his personal contacts. He had even allowed things to cool with Rosemary Gibbons, his lady friend from Sotheby's. Whitcombe, who had been appointed Leach's guardian and confessor, explained why during a final preoperational dinner. "It's not that Alistair's no longer fond of her," he said. "He's chivalrous, our Alistair. He knows we're watching him and he's trying to protect her. It's quite possible he's the last decent man left in the whole of

London — present company excluded, of course." Gabriel gave Whitcombe a check for one hundred thousand pounds and a brief script. "Tell him not to blow his lines, Nigel. Tell him expectations couldn't be higher."

Leach's star turn was to occur during a matinee performance but was no less significant because of it. For this phase of the operation, Graham Seymour insisted on using Thames House as a command post, and Gabriel, having no other choice, reluctantly agreed. The ops room was a hushed chamber of blinking monitors and twinkling lights, staffed by earnest-looking young men and women whose faces reflected the rainbow racial quilt of modern Britain. Gabriel wore a guest pass that read BLACKBURN: USA. It fooled no one.

At 2:17 p.m., he was informed by Graham Seymour that the stage was now set and the performance ready to commence. Gabriel made one final check of the video monitors and, with several MI5 officers watching expectantly, nodded his head. Seymour leaned forward into a microphone and ordered the curtain to be raised.

He was conservatively dressed and possessed a churchman's forgiving smile. His card identified him as Jonathan Owens, associate editor of something called the Cambridge Online Journal of Contemporary Art. He claimed to have an appointment. Try as she might, the receptionist in the lobby of Christie's could find no record of it in her logbook.

"Would it be too much trouble to actually ring him?" the handsome young man asked through a benedictory smile. "I'm sure he's just forgotten to notify you."

"I'm sure you're right," said the receptionist. "Give me a moment, please."

She picked up the receiver of her impressive multiline telephone and punched in a four-digit extension. *"Owens,"* she said, repeating the name for the third time. *"Jonathan* Owens . . . Cambridge Online Journal of Contemporary Art. Youngish chap . . . Yes, that's him, Mr. Leach . . . Quite lovely manners."

She hung up the phone and handed the young visitor a temporary guest identification badge, which he affixed to the lapel of his suit jacket.

"Third floor, dear. Turn left after you come off the lift."

He stepped away from the receptionist's desk and, after clearing a security checkpoint, boarded a waiting elevator. Alistair

Leach was waiting in the doorway of his office. He regarded his visitor with a somewhat baleful expression, as though he were a debt collector, which, to some degree, he was.

"What can I do for you, Mr. *Owens?*"

Nigel Whitcombe closed the door and handed Leach the script.

"Think you can do it cold, Alistair, or do you want to run through it a time or two?"

"I do this for a living. I think I can manage it on my own."

"You're sure, Alistair? We have a lot of time and money invested in this. It's important you not stumble over your delivery."

Leach lifted the receiver of his telephone and dialed the number from memory. Ten seconds later, in the opinion of young Nigel Whitcombe, Gabriel's operation truly took flight.

"Elena, darling. It's Alistair Leach from Christie's. Am I catching you at a perfectly dreadful time?"

He hadn't, of course. In fact, at the moment her mobile rang, Elena Kharkov was having tea with her seven-year-old twins, Anna and Nikolai, at the café atop Harrods department store. She had arrived there after taking the children for a boat ride on the Serpentine in Hyde Park — an idyllic scene that might have been painted by Mary Cassatt herself were it not for the fact that Mrs. Kharkov and her children were shadowed the entire time by two additional boats filled with Russian bodyguards. They were with her now, seated at an adjacent table, next to several veiled Saudi women and their African servants. The telephone itself was in a rather smart Italian leather handbag; withdrawing it, she appeared to recognize the number in the caller ID screen and was already smiling when she lifted the phone to her ear. The conversation that followed was forty-nine seconds in length and was intercepted at multiple transmission points and by multiple services, including the U.S. National Security Agency, Britain's GCHQ, and even by the Russian eavesdropping service, which made nothing of it. Gabriel and Graham Seymour listened to it live by means of a direct tap on Leach's line at Christie's. When the connection went dead, Gabriel looked at one of the technicians — Marlowe or Mapes, he could never be certain which was which — and asked him to play it again.

"Elena, darling, it's Alistair Leach. Am I catching you at a perfectly dreadful time?"

"Of course not, Alistair. What can I do for you?"

"Actually, darling, it's what I can do for you. I'm pleased to say that I have some extremely interesting news about our mutual friend, Madame Cassatt."

"What sort of news?"

"It seems our man may have had a change of heart. He rang me this morning to say he's interested in discussing a sale. Shall I call you later or would you like to hear the rest now?"

"Don't be a tease, Alistair! Tell me everything."

"He says he's had a chance to reconsider. He's says if the price is right, he'll let it go."

"How much does he want for it?"

"In the neighborhood of two and a half, but you might be able to do a bit better than that. Between us, Elena, his finances aren't what they once were."

"I'm not going to take advantage of him."

"Of course you are, darling. You're the one with the money."

"Are you sure about the attribution and the provenance?"

"Signed, dated, and airtight."

"When can I see it?"

"That's completely up to you."

"Tomorrow, Alistair. Definitely tomorrow."

"I'll have to check to see if he's free, but I

suspect he'll be able to squeeze you in. His funds aren't unlimited, but time is something he has in plentiful supply."

"Can you reach him now?"

"I'll try, love. Shall I call you back this afternoon or would you rather it wait till morning?"

"Call me right away! Ciao, Alistair!"

The technician clicked the PAUSE icon. Graham Seymour looked at Gabriel and smiled.

"Congratulations, Gabriel. Looks like you've managed to get your hooks in her."

"How long is it going to take her to get from Knightsbridge to Havermore?"

"The way those Russians drive? No more than two hours door to door."

"And you're sure about Ivan's schedule?"

"You've heard the intercepts yourself."

"Humor me, Graham."

"He's got a delegation of City investment bankers coming to Rutland Gate for lunch at one. Then he's got a four o'clock conference call with Zurich. He'll be tied up all afternoon."

A voice crackled over the monitors. It was one of the watchers at Harrods. Elena had asked for the check. The bodyguards were setting a perimeter. Departure imminent.

"Call her back," Gabriel said. "Tell her to

come at four. Tell her not to be late."

"Shall we do it now or should we make her wait?"

"She has enough stress in her life, don't you think?"

Seymour snatched up the phone and dialed.

Whitcombe's mobile purred. He listened in silence for a moment, then looked at Alistair Leach.

"The reviews are in, Alistair. Looks like we've got a smash hit on our hands."

"What now?"

Whitcombe answered. Leach pressed the REDIAL button and waited for Elena's voice to come back on the line.

It was 5:30 that same evening when Mrs. Devlin entered the library at Havermore, bearing a silver tray with a glass of whiskey in the center of it. Sir John was reading the *Telegraph*. He always read the *Telegraph* at this time of day; like most idle men, he kept to a strict regime. He took a single sip of the whiskey and watched while Mrs. Devlin began straightening the books and papers on his desk. "*Leave* it, Lillian," he said. "Whenever you clean my library, I spend the next week searching for my things."

"If you've nothing else for me, Sir John, I'll be going home now. Your dinner's in the oven."

"What are we having tonight?"

"Rack of lamb."

"Divine," he murmured.

Mrs. Devlin bade him a good evening and started toward the door. Boothby lowered his newspaper. "Oh, Lillian?"

"Yes, Sir John?"

"We'll be having a visitor tomorrow afternoon."

"*More* visitors, Sir John?"

"I'm afraid so. She won't be staying long. She's just going to have a look at the painting in the nursery."

The painting in the nursery . . . The painting that spent a week in the gamekeeper's cottage, in the possession of the man whose presence she had been told to say nothing about.

"I see," she said. "Shall I make a batch of scones?"

"She's not exactly a *scone* person, if you catch my meaning."

"I'm not sure I do, Sir John."

"She's a *Russian,* Lillian. A very well-to-do Russian. I doubt she'll be staying for tea. With a bit of luck, she'll have a very quick look and be on her way."

Mrs. Devlin remained rooted in the doorway.

"Something bothering you, Lillian?"

"May I speak bluntly, Sir John?"

"You usually do."

"Is there something going on at Havermore that you're not telling me?"

"Many things, I suppose. You'll have to be a bit more specific."

"The odd man in the gamekeeper's cottage. The lovely young girl who claims to be the daughter of your American friend. The men doing the electrical work all through the house. Old George is convinced they're up to no good in the barn!"

"Old George sees conspiracies everywhere, Lillian."

"And now you're thinking about selling that beautiful painting to a *Russian?* Your poor father, may he rest in peace, would be spinning in his grave."

"I need the money, Lillian. *We* need the money."

She tugged skeptically on the drawstring of her apron. "I'm not sure I believe you, Sir John. I think something important is going on in this house. Something to do with secrets, just like when your father was alive."

Boothby gave her a conspiratorial look over his whiskey. "The Russians will be arriving at four o'clock sharp, Lillian." He paused. "If you would rather not be here —"

"I'll be here, Sir John," she said quickly.

"What about Old George?"

"Perhaps we should give him the afternoon off, sir."

"Perhaps we should."

34
HAVERMORE,
GLOUCESTERSHIRE

The limousines passed the concealed check-point on the Station Road at 3:45: two custom Mercedes-Benz S65s with blacked-out windows, riding low and heavy with bulletproof glass and armor. They flashed down the terraced High Street of Chipping Camden, past the quaint shops and the old limestone St. James' Church, and roared out of town again on Dyers Lane. One shopkeeper timed the run at sixteen seconds, shortest visit to Chipping Camden in recorded history.

At the once-grand estate known as Havermore, there was no visible evidence to suggest that anyone was aware of the cars' rapid approach. Mrs. Devlin was in the kitchen, where, in contravention of Sir John's direct orders, she was putting the final touches on a tray of fresh scones, strawberry jam, and Cotswold clotted cream. Sir John was unaware of her rebellion, for he was sequestered in the library, pondering serious and weighty matters. As for the attractive young woman known to them as Sarah Crawford, she was coming up the footpath from the East Meadow wearing a pair of green Wellington boots, with Punch and Judy watching her back like tiny tan bodyguards.

Only in the hayloft of the tumbledown barn were there hints that something truly out of the ordinary was about to take place. Four men were there, seated before a bank of video and audio monitors. Two of the men were young, scruffy technicians. The third was a tall figure of authority who looked as though he had stepped out of a magazine advertisement. The fourth had short dark hair with ash-colored temples. His eyes were fixed on a video image of the young woman, who was in the process of removing her Wellingtons in the mudroom and changing into a pair of sensible black flats. She entered the kitchen and playfully dipped a finger into Mrs. Devlin's fresh cream, then passed through a pair of double doors and made her way into the entrance hall. There, standing before a long mirror, she smoothed the front of her white blouse and pale yellow pedal pushers and adjusted the sweater knotted with feigned casualness round her shoulders. She wore only a hint of blush on her alabaster cheeks and cat-eyed spectacles instead of contact lenses. *Your beauty must pose no challenge to Elena's,* the man with ash-colored temples had told her. *Elena's not used to finishing second at anything.*

At precisely 4:04, the pair of armored Mercedes limousines turned through the gates of Havermore and started up the long drive. The men in the hayloft saw them first, followed by Sir John, whose library window gave him a superb outpost from which to monitor their approach. Sarah, from her position in the entrance hall, could not see the cars but heard them a few seconds later as they came prowling into the gravel fore-court. Two powerful engines went silent; several doors opened and six young body-guards with faces of chiseled marble emerged. The men in the hayloft knew their names. Three were Oleg, Yuri, and Gennady: Elena Kharkov's permanent detail. The other three were Vadim, Vasily, and Viktor: "the three V's," as they were known to Kharkov watchers the world over. Their presence at Havermore was curious, since they served almost exclusively as Ivan's prae-torian guard.

Having established a loose perimeter around the lead Mercedes, two of the guards opened the rear doors. Elena Kharkov emerged from the driver's side, a radiant flash of lustrous dark hair and green silk. From the passenger side came a sturdy figure, well dressed, with hair the color of steel. For a few seconds, the men in the hayloft mistook him for a seventh security man. Then, as he turned his face toward the cameras, they realized he was no bodyguard. He was the man who was supposed to be on a conference call with Zurich. The man who was not supposed to be here.

The men in the hayloft attempted to warn Sarah — they had hidden a tiny audio speaker in the entrance hall for just such a contingency — but she had already opened Havermore's impressive door and was stepping into the forecourt. Punch and Judy scampered past her ankles and shot across the gravel like a pair of honey-colored torpedoes. By some natural instinct, they advanced directly toward the most authoritative-looking member of the entourage. The three V's formed a wall in front of their target: Ivan Kharkov.

He was standing calmly behind them, an expression of mild bemusement on the heavy features of his face. Sarah used a moment of mock anger at the dogs to help conceal the shock of seeing the monster face to face for the first time. She seized the dogs by the collars and gave them each a firm shove on the hindquarters toward the house. By the time she turned around again, a small crack opened between Vadim and Viktor. She extended her hand through it toward Ivan and managed a smile. "I'm afraid herding instincts take over when they see a large group of people," she heard herself say. "I'm Sarah Crawford."

Ivan's right hand rose from the seam of his trousers. It looked, thought Sarah, like a manicured mallet. It gave her hand a testing squeeze and quickly released it.

"You're an American," he pointed out.

And you forgot to tell me your name, she thought.

"Actually, I'm only half American."

"Which half?"

"The self-centered half, according to my uncle. This is his home. I'm just visiting."

"From America?"

"Yes."

"Where do you live in America?"

"Washington, D.C. And you?"

"I like to think of myself as a citizen of the world, Miss Crawford."

A citizen of the world, perhaps, but exposure to the West had yet to buff away the last traces of KGB English. It was surprisingly fluent but still flecked with the intonation of a Radio Moscow propagandist. He was proud of his English, thought Sarah, just like he was proud of his armored limousines, his bodyguards, his handmade suit, his three-thousand-dollar necktie, and the rich aftershave that hung round him like a vaporous cloud. No amount of Western clothing and cologne could conceal his Russianness, though. It was etched in the sturdy forehead, the almond-shaped eyes, and the angular cheekbones. Nor could it hide the fact that he was a KGB hood who had stumbled into a mountain of money.

Almost as an afterthought, he lifted his left hand and, with his eyes still fixed on Sarah, said, "My wife." She was standing several feet away, surrounded by her own palace guard. She was taller than Ivan by an inch or two and held herself with the erect carriage of a dancer. Her skin was pale, her eyes liquid green, her hair black. She wore it long and allowed it to fall loosely about her shoulders. As for the prospect of Sarah's beauty posing a challenge to Elena's, there was little chance of that, for at forty-six years, seven months and nineteen days, she was still a strikingly attractive woman. She took a step forward and extended her hand. "It's a pleasure to meet you, Sarah. I'm

Elena Kharkov." Her accent, unlike Ivan's, was authentic and rich, and completely beguiling. "I believe Alistair told you I would be coming alone. My husband decided to join me at the last minute."

A husband who still has no name, Sarah thought.

"Actually, Alistair told me a *woman* would be coming alone. He didn't give me a name. He was very discreet, Mrs. Kharkov."

"And we trust that you will be discreet as well," Ivan said. "It is important for people such as ourselves to conduct our acquisitions and business transactions with a certain amount of privacy."

"You may rest assured my uncle feels precisely the same way, Mr. Kharkov."

As if on cue, Boothby emerged, with Punch and Judy now swirling noisily at his feet. "Did my ears deceive me," he trumpeted, "or is it true that the great Ivan Kharkov has come to Havermore? That dolt from Christie's told me to expect a VIP, but no one of your stature." He took Ivan's hand in his own and pumped it vigorously. "It is indeed an *honor* to have you here, Mr. Kharkov. I *do* admire your accomplishments. I knew you were a man of many interests, but I never knew art was one of them."

Ivan's stony face broke briefly into something approaching a genuine smile. Ivan, they knew, was vulnerable to flattery, from pretty young girls, and even from tattered English landed gentry.

"Actually, my wife is the expert when it comes to art," he said. "I just felt like getting out of London for a few hours."

"Oh, yes, of course. Can't stand London any longer, what with the traffic and the terrorism. Go there now to see the odd play or hear a bit of music at Covent Garden, but I'd choose the Cotswold Hills over Kensington any day of the week. Too expensive in London, these days. Too many people such as yourself buying everything up. No insult intended, of course."

"None taken."

"Do you have a country estate yet or just your London residence?"

"Just the house in Knightsbridge at the moment."

Boothby gestured toward the façade of Havermore. "This has been in my family for five generations. I'd love to give you a tour while our two art experts have a look at the painting."

A glance passed between Ivan and Elena: coded, secure, inscrutable to an outsider. She murmured a few words in Russian; Ivan responded by looking at Boothby and giving a single nod of his sturdy head. "I'd love a tour," he said. "But we'll have to make it brief. I'm afraid my wife tends to make decisions quickly."

"Brilliant!" said Boothby. "Allow me to show you the grounds."

He lifted his hand and started toward the East Meadow. Ivan, after a brief hesitation, followed after him, with the three V's flying close behind in tight formation. Boothby looked at the bodyguards and politely objected.

"I say, but is that really necessary? I can assure you, Mr. Kharkov, that you have no enemies here. The most dangerous things at Havermore are the dogs and my martinis."

Ivan glanced once again at Elena, then spoke a few words in Russian to the bodyguards in a baritone murmur. When he started toward the meadow a second time, the guards remained motionless. Elena watched her husband's departure in silence, then looked at Sarah.

"I'm sorry about the security, Miss Crawford. I would do almost anything to be rid of them, but Ivan insists they stay by my side wherever I go. I imagine that it must seem very exciting to be surrounded by men in dark suits. I can assure you it is not."

Sarah was momentarily taken aback by the intimacy of her words. They constituted a betrayal. A small one, thought Sarah, but a betrayal nonetheless. "A woman in your position can't be too careful," she said. "But I can assure you that you are among friends here."

Boothby and Ivan disappeared around the corner of the house. Sarah placed her hand gently on Elena's arm.

"Would you like to see my uncle's Cassatt, Mrs. Kharkov?"

"I would *love* to see your uncle's Cassatt, Miss Crawford."

When they started toward the portico, the bodyguards remained motionless.

"You know, Mrs. Kharkov, I really think it's best we see the painting alone. I've always found Cassatt to be a painter *of* women *for* women. Most men don't understand her."

"I couldn't agree more. And I'll let you in on a little secret."

"What's that?"

"Ivan loathes her."

In the hayloft of the barn, the four men standing before the video monitors moved for the first time in three minutes.

"Looks like Uncle John just saved our

309

asses," said Graham Seymour.

"His father would be very proud."

"Ivan's not the world's most patient man. I suspect you'll have five minutes with Elena at most."

"I'd kill for five minutes."

"Let's hope there's no killing today, Gabriel. Ivan's the one with all the guns."

The two women climbed the central staircase together and paused on the landing to admire a Madonna and Child.

"Is that actually a Veronese?" Elena asked.

"Depends on whom you ask. My uncle's ancestors did the Grand Tour of Italy in the nineteenth century and came home with a boat-load of paintings. Some were quite lovely. Some of them were just copies made by lesser artists. I've always thought this one was among the best."

"It's beautiful."

"The Cassatt is still in the nursery. My uncle thought you would enjoy seeing it in its original setting."

Sarah took Elena carefully by the arm and led her down the hall. The key was resting on the woodwork above the door. Standing on tiptoe, Sarah removed it, then raised a finger to her lips in a gesture of mock conspiracy.

"Don't tell anyone where we keep the key."

Elena smiled. "It will be our little secret."

"Ivan's starting to get restless."

"I can see that, Graham."

"She's burned three minutes already."

"Yes, I can see that, too."

"She should have done it on the staircase."

"She knows what she's doing."

"I hope to God you're right."

So do I, thought Gabriel.

Elena entered the room first. Sarah closed the door halfway, then walked over to the window and pushed open the curtains. The golden light fell upon two matching beds, two matching dressers, two matching hand-painted toy chests, and *Two Children on a Beach* by Gabriel Allon. Elena covered her mouth with her hands and gasped.

"It's glorious," she said. "I must have it."

Sarah allowed a silence to fall between them. She lowered herself onto the end of the bed nearest the window and, with her eyes cast downward toward the floor, absently ran her hand over the Winnie the Pooh spread. Seeing her reaction, Elena said, "My God, I'm so sorry. You must think I'm terribly spoiled."

"Not at all, Mrs. Kharkov." Sarah made a show of looking around the nursery. "I spent every summer in this room when I was a little girl. That painting was the first thing I saw in the morning and the last thing I saw at night before my mother switched off the lights. The house just won't feel the same without it."

"I can't take it from you, then."

"You must," Sarah said. "My uncle has to sell it. Trust me, Mrs. Kharkov, if you don't buy it, someone else will. I want it to go to someone who loves it as much as I do. Someone like *you,*" she added.

Elena turned her gaze from Sarah and looked at the painting once more. "I'd like to have a closer look at it before I make a final decision. Would you help me take it down from the wall, please?"

"Of course."

Sarah rose to her feet and, passing before the window, glanced downward toward the meadow. Boothby and Ivan were still there, Boothby with his arm extended toward some landmark in the distance, Ivan with his patience clearly at an ebb. She walked over to the painting and, with Elena's help, lifted it from its hooks and laid it flat upon the second bed. Elena then drew a magnifying glass and a small Maglite flashlight from her handbag. First she used the magnifying glass to examine the signature in the bottom left corner of the painting. Then she switched on the Maglite and played the beam over the surface. Her examination lasted three minutes. When it had ended, she switched off the Maglite and slipped it back into her handbag.

"This painting is an obvious forgery," she said.

She regarded Sarah's face carefully for a moment as if she realized Sarah was a forgery, too.

"Please tell me who you are, Miss Crawford."

Sarah opened her mouth to respond, but before she could speak, the door swung open and Ivan appeared in the threshold, with Boothby at his shoulder. Ivan stared at Elena for a moment, then his gaze settled on Sarah.

"Is something wrong?" he asked.

It was Elena who answered. "Nothing's wrong, Ivan. Miss Crawford was just telling me how much the painting means to her and she became understandably emotional."

"Perhaps they've had a change of heart."

"No, Mr. Kharkov," Sarah said. "I'm afraid we have no choice but to part with it. The painting belongs to your wife now — if she wants it, of course."

"Well, Elena?" Ivan asked impatiently. "Do you want it or not?"

Elena ran her fingers over the faces of the children, then looked at Sarah. "It's one of the most extraordinary Cassatts I've ever seen." She turned around and looked at Ivan. "I must have it, my love. Please pay them whatever they ask."

35

LONDON

Precisely how Ivan Kharkov had managed to slip past the vaunted watchers of MI5 was never determined to anyone's satisfaction. There were recriminations and post-mortems. Regrettable letters were inserted into personnel files. Demerits were handed out. Gabriel paid little attention to the fallout, for by then he was wrestling with weightier matters. By paying two and a half million dollars for a painting she knew to be a worthless forgery, Elena had clearly shown herself to be receptive to a second approach. Which was why Adrian Carter boarded his Gulfstream jet and came to London.

"Sounds as if you had an interesting afternoon in the Cotswolds, Gabriel. I'm only sorry I wasn't there to see it. How did Sarah hold up when confronted with the monster in the flesh?"

"As one would expect. Sarah is very

talented."

They were seated together on Gabriel's bench in St. James's Park. Carter wore the traveling attire of the American businessman: blue blazer, blue button-down, tan chinos. His oxblood penny loafers were dull for want of polish. He needed a shave.

"How do you think Elena was able to tell the painting wasn't real?"

"She owns several other Cassatts, which means she spends a great deal of time around them. She knows how they look, but, perhaps more important, how they *feel*. After enough time, one develops an instinct about these things, a certain sense of touch. Elena's instincts must have told her that the painting was a forgery."

"But did her instincts also tell her that Sarah Crawford was a forgery as well?"

"Without question."

"Where's the painting now?"

"Still at Havermore. Elena's shippers are coming to collect it. She told Alistair Leach she intends to hang it in the children's room at Villa Soleil."

A group of Croatian schoolgirls approached the bench and, in halting English, asked for directions to Buckingham Palace. Carter pointed absently toward the west. When the girls were gone, he and Gabriel rose in unison and set out along the Horse Guards Road.

"I take it Saint-Tropez is now in your travel plans as well?"

"It's not what it once was, Adrian, but it's still the only place to be in August."

"You can't set up shop there without first getting your ticket punched by the French services. And, knowing the French, they're going to want in on the fun. They're understandably angry with Ivan. His weapons have spread a great deal of death and destruction in parts of Africa where the *Tricolore* used to fly and where the French still wield considerable influence."

"They can't have in, Adrian. The circle of knowledge is already too wide on this operation for my comfort. And if it widens again, the chances of Ivan and the FSB getting wind of it increase substantially."

"We're back on speaking terms with the French, and your friend the president would like to keep it that way. Which means that you're not to take any action on French soil that might bring yet another euro shit storm down upon our heads. We have to go on the record with the French, just the way we did with Graham Seymour and the Brits. Who knows? Perhaps something good might come of it. A new golden age in Franco-

Israeli relations."

"Let's not get carried away," Gabriel said. "The French aren't likely to be pleased with my terms."

"Let's hear them."

"Unlike the Brits, the French will be granted no formal role. In fact, it is my wish that they do nothing more than stay out of the way. That means shutting down any surveillance operations they might be running on Ivan. Saint-Tropez is a village, which means we're going to be working in close proximity to Ivan and his security gorillas. If they see a bunch of French agents, alarm bells will go off."

"What do you need from us?"

"Continued coverage of all of Ivan's communications. Make sure someone is sitting on the account twenty-four hours a day — someone who can actually speak Russian. If Ivan calls Arkady Medvedev and tells him to put a watch on Elena's tail, I would obviously need to know. And if Elena makes a reservation for lunch or dinner, I would need to know about that, too."

"Message received. What else?"

"I'm thinking about giving Sarah Crawford a Russian-American boyfriend. I can do Russian-Israeli on short notice, but not Russian-American." Gabriel handed Carter an envelope. "He'll need a full set of identification, of course, but he'll also need a cover story that can stand up to the scrutiny of Ivan and his security service."

They came to Great George Street. Carter paused in front of a newsstand and frowned at the morning papers. Osama bin Laden had released a new videotape, warning of a coming wave of attacks against the Crusaders and the Jews. It might have been dismissed by the professionals of Western intelligence as yet another empty threat had the statement not contained four critical words: the arrows of Allah.

"He's promising the autumn is going to be bloody," Carter said. "The fact that he was specific about the timing is noteworthy in itself. It's almost as if he's telling us there's nothing we can do to stop it. On deep background, we're telling the media that we see nothing new or unusual in the tape. Privately, we're shitting bricks. The system is blinking red again, Gabriel. They're overdue for another attack against an American target, and we know they want to hit us again before the president leaves office. Expert opinion is convinced this plot may be the one. All of which means you have a limited amount of time."

"How limited?"

"End of August, I'd say. Then we raise the terror warning to red and go on war footing."

"The moment you do, we lose any chance of getting to Elena."

"Better to lose Elena than live through another 9/11. Or *worse.*"

They were walking toward the river along Great George Street. Gabriel looked to his right and saw the North Tower of Westminster Abbey aglow in the bright sunshine. The Caravaggio image flashed in his memory again: the man with a gun in hand, firing bullets into the face of a fallen terrorist. Carter had been standing a few yards away that morning, but now his thoughts were clearly focused on the unpleasant meeting he was about to conduct on the other side of the English Channel.

"You know, Gabriel, you get the easy job. All you have to do is convince Elena to betray her husband. I have to go hat in hand to the Frogs and beg them to give you and your team the run of the Riviera."

"Be charming, Adrian. I hear the French like that."

"Care to join me for the negotiations?"

"I'm not sure that's a wise idea. We have a somewhat testy relationship."

"So I've heard." Carter was silent for a

moment. "Is there any chance of amending your demands to allow the French some sort of operational role?"

"None."

"You have to give them *something,* Gabriel. They're not going to agree otherwise."

"Tell them they can cook for us. That's the one thing they do well."

"Be reasonable."

Gabriel stopped walking. "Tell them that if we manage to block Ivan's sale, we'll be happy to make sure all the credit goes to the French president and his intelligence services."

"You know something?" Carter said. "That might actually work."

The conference convened in Paris two days later, at a gated government guesthouse off the Avenue Victor Hugo. Carter had pleaded with the French to keep the guest list short. They had not. The chief of the DST, the French internal security service, was there, along with his counterpart from the more glamorous DGSE, the French foreign intelligence service. There was a senior man from the Police Nationale and his overlord from the Ministry of the Interior. There was a mysterious figure from military intelligence and, in a troubling sign that politics might play a role in French decision making, there was the president's national security adviser, who had to be dragged to the gathering against his will from his château in the Loire Valley. And then there were the nameless bureaucrats, functionaries, factotums, note-takers, and food tasters who came and went with hushed abandon. Each one, Carter knew, represented a potential leak. He recalled Gabriel's warnings about an ever-widening circle of knowledge and wondered how long they had until Ivan learned of the plot against him.

The setting was intensely formal, the furnishings preposterously French. The talks themselves were conducted in a vast mirrored dining room, at a table the size of an aircraft carrier. Carter sat alone on one flank, behind a little brass nameplate that read THOMAS APPLEBY, FEDERAL BUREAU OF INVESTIGATION — a mere formality since he was known to the French and was held by them in considerable regard despite the many sins of his service. The opening notes were cordial, as Carter anticipated they would be. He raised a glass of rather good French wine to the renewal of Franco-American cooperation. He endured a rather tedious briefing about what Paris knew of Ivan's activities in the former

French colonies of sub-Saharan Africa. And he suffered through a rather odious lecture by the national security adviser over the failure of Washington to do anything about Ivan until now. He was tempted to lash back — tempted to chastise his newfound allies for pouring their own weapons into the most combustible corners of the planet — but he knew discretion was the better part of valor. And so he nodded at the appropriate times and conceded the appropriate points, all the while waiting for his opportunity to seize the initiative.

It came after dinner, when they retired to the cool of the garden for coffee and the inevitable cigarette. There were moments at any such gathering when the participants ceased to be citizens of their own land and instead banded together as only brothers of the secret world can do. This, Carter knew, was one of those moments. And so with only the faint murmur of distant traffic to disturb the stately silence, he quietly placed Gabriel's demands before them — though Gabriel's name, like Ivan's and Elena's, was not uttered in the insecurity of the open air. The French were appalled, of course, and insulted, which is the role the French play best. Carter cajoled and Carter pleaded. Carter flattered and Carter appealed to their better angels. And last, Carter played Gabriel's trump card. It worked, just as Gabriel had known it would, and by dawn they had a draft agreement ready for signature. They called it the Treaty of Paris. Adrian Carter would later think of it as one of his finest hours.

36
SAINT-TROPEZ, FRANCE

The village of Saint-Tropez lies at the far western end of the Côte d'Azur, at the base of the French *département* known as the Var. It was nothing but a sleepy fishing port when, in 1956, it was the setting for a film called *And God Created Woman,* starring Brigitte Bardot. Nearly overnight, Saint-Tropez became one of the most popular resorts in the world, an exclusive playground for the fashionable, the elite, and other assorted euro millionaires. Though it had fallen from grace in the eighties and nineties, it had seen a revival of late. The actors and rock stars had returned, along with the models and the rich playboys who pursued them. Even Bardot herself had started coming back again. Much to the horror of the French and longtime habitués, it had also been discovered by newly rich invaders from the East: the Russians.

The town itself is surprisingly small. Its

two primary features are the Old Port, which in summer is filled with luxury yachts instead of fishing boats, and the Place Carnot, a large, dusty esplanade that once each week hosts a bustling outdoor market and where local men still pass summer days playing *pétanque* and drinking pastis. The streets between the port and the square are little more than medieval passageways. In the height of summer, they are jammed with tourists and pedestrians, which makes driving in the *centre ville* of Saint-Tropez nearly impossible. Just outside the town center lies a labyrinth of towering hedgerows and narrow lanes, leading to some of the world's most popular beaches and expensive homes.

In the hills above the coast are a number of *villages perchés,* where it is almost possible to imagine Saint-Tropez does not exist. One such village is Gassin. Small and quaint, it is known mainly for its ancient windmills — the Moulins de Paillas — and for its stunning views of the distant sea. A mile or so beyond the windmills is an old stone farmhouse with pale blue shutters and a large swimming pool. The local rental agency described it as a steal at thirty thousand euros a week; a man with a German passport and money to burn took it for the remainder of the summer. He then informed the agent he wanted no cooks, no maid service, no gardeners, and no inter-ruptions of any kind. He claimed to be a filmmaker at work on an important project. When the agent asked the man what type of film it would be, he mumbled something about a period piece and showed the agent to the door.

The other members of the filmmaker's "crew" trickled into the villa like scouts returning to base after a long time behind enemy lines. They traveled under false names and with false passports in their pockets, but all had one thing in common. They had sailed under Gabriel's star before and leapt at the chance to do so again — even if the journey was to take place in August, when most would have preferred to be on holiday with their families.

First came Gabriel's two Russian speak-ers, Eli Lavon and Mikhail Abramov. Next it was a man with short black hair and pockmarked cheeks named Yaakov Ross-man, a battle-hardened case officer and agent-runner from the Arab Affairs Depart-ment of Shin Bet. Then Yossi Gavish, a tall, balding intellectual from the Office's Re-search division who had read classics at Oxford and still spoke Hebrew with a pronounced British accent.

Finally, this rather motley, all-male troupe was graced by the presence of two women. The first had sandstone-colored hair and childbearing hips: Rimona Stern, an army major who served in Israel's crack military intelligence service and who also happened to be Shamron's niece by marriage. The second was dark-haired and carried herself with the quiet air of early widowhood: Dina Sarid, a veritable encyclopedia of terrorism from the Office's History division who could recite the time, place, and casualty count of every act of violence ever committed against the State of Israel. Dina knew the horrors of terrorism personally. She had been standing in Tel Aviv's Dizengoff Square in October 1994 when a Hamas terrorist detonated his suicide belt aboard a Number 5 bus. Twenty-one people were killed, including Dina's mother and two of her sisters. Dina herself had been seriously wounded and still walked with a slight limp.

For the next several days, the lives of Gabriel and his team stood in stark contrast to those of the man and woman they were pursuing. While Ivan and Elena Kharkov entertained wildly at their palace on the Baie de Cavalaire, Gabriel and his team rented three cars and several motor scooters of different makes and colors. And while Ivan and Elena Kharkov lunched elegantly in the Old Port, Gabriel and his team took delivery of a large consignment of weaponry, listening devices, cameras, and secure communications gear. And while Elena and Ivan Kharkov cruised the waters of the Golfe de Saint-Tropez aboard *October,* Ivan's 263-foot motor yacht, Gabriel and his team hid miniature cameras with secure transmitters near the gates of Villa Soleil. And while Ivan and Elena dined lavishly at Villa Romana, a hedonistic and scandalously expensive restaurant adored by Russians, Gabriel and his team dined at home and plotted a meeting they hoped to conduct at the earliest date.

The first step toward creating the circumstances of that meeting occurred when Mikhail climbed into a red Audi convertible with a new American passport in his pocket and drove to the Côte d'Azur International Airport in Nice. There, he met an attractive young American woman arriving on a flight from London Heathrow: Sarah Crawford of Washington, D.C., lately of the Havermore estate, Gloucestershire, England. Two hours later, they checked into their suite at the Château de la Messardière, a luxury five-star hotel located a few minutes from the *centre ville.* The bellman who showed the young couple to an ocean-view room reported to his colleagues that they could barely keep their hands off one another. The next morning, while the guests were partaking of a buffet breakfast, the chambermaids found their king-size bed in a shambles.

They drifted through the same world but along distinctly parallel planes. When Elena and the children chose to remain cloistered at the Villa Soleil, Sarah and her lover would spend the day poolside at the Messardière — or "the Mess," as they referred to it privately. And when Elena and the children chose to spend the day frolicking in the gentle surf of Tahiti Beach, Sarah and her lover would be stretched out on the sands of the Plage de Pampelonne instead. And if Elena chose to do a bit of late-afternoon shopping on the rue Gambetta, Sarah and her lover could be found strolling past the storefronts of the rue Georges Clemenceau or having a quiet drink in one of the bars on the Place Carnot. And at night, when Elena and Ivan dined at Villa Romana or one of the other Russian haunts, Sarah and her lover would dine quietly at the Mess —

in close proximity to their room, lest the urge to ravage each other grow too strong to resist.

It proceeded in this seemingly direction-less fashion until the early afternoon of the fourth day, when Elena decided the time had finally come to have lunch at Grand Joseph, her favorite restaurant in Saint-Tropez. She reserved early — a requirement in August, even for the wife of an oligarch — and although she did not know it, her call was intercepted by an NSA spy satellite floating high overhead. Due to a minor traffic accident on the D61, she and the children arrived at the restaurant seventeen minutes late, accompanied, as usual, by a team of four bodyguards. Jean-Luc, the maître d', greeted Elena effusively with kisses on both cheeks before conveying the party to their tables along the creamy white banquette. Elena took a seat with her back turned discreetly to the room, while her bodyguards settled at each end of the table. They took only scant notice of the postcard that arrived with her bottle of rosé, though it sent a jolt of fear the length of Elena's body. She concealed it with a look of mild displeasure, then picked up the card and read the handwritten note scribbled on the back:

Elena,
I hope you're enjoying the Cassatt.
May we join you?

Sarah

37
SAINT-TROPEZ, FRANCE

Wineglass in hand, Mikhail at her side, Sarah gazed calmly across the crowded dining room toward Elena's long back. The postcard was still in Elena's grasp. She was gazing down at it with an air of mild curiosity, as was Oleg, her chief bodyguard. She laid the postcard on the tablecloth and turned slowly around to survey the room. Twice, her gaze passed over Sarah with no visible sign of recognition. Elena Kharkov was a child of Leningrad, Sarah thought. A child of the Party. She knew how to scan a room for watchers before making a meeting. She knew how to play the game by the Moscow Rules.

On its third sweep over the room, her gaze finally settled on Sarah's face. She lifted the postcard dramatically and opened her mouth wide in a show of surprise. The smile was forced and illuminated with artificial light, but her bodyguards could not see it.

Then, before they could react, she was suddenly on her feet and flowing across the dining room, her hips swiveling as she maneuvered between the tightly packed tables, her white skirt swirling around her suntanned thighs. Sarah stood to greet her; Elena kissed her formally on each cheek and pressed her mouth to Sarah's ear. The right ear, Sarah noted. The one her bodyguards couldn't see. "I can't believe it's really you! What a wonderful surprise!" Then, in a quiet voice that caused a cavernous ache in Sarah's abdomen: "You'll be careful, won't you? My husband is a very dangerous man."

Elena released her tense grip on Sarah and looked at Mikhail, who had risen to his feet and was standing silently at his chair. She appraised him carefully, as though he were a painting propped on a viewing easel, then extended a bejeweled hand while Sarah saw to the introduction.

"This is my very good friend, Michael Danilov. Michael and I work in the same office in Washington. If any of our colleagues found out we were here together, there would be a terrible scandal."

"So we share another secret? Just like the hiding place for the key to the nursery?" She was still clinging to Mikhail's hand. "It's a pleasure to meet you, Michael."

"The pleasure is mine, Mrs. Kharkov. I've been an admirer of your husband's success for some time. When Sarah told me that she'd met you, I was extremely envious."

Hearing Mikhail's accent, Elena's face took on an expression of surprise. It was contrived, Sarah thought, just as her smile had been a moment earlier. "You're a Russian," she said, not as a question but as a statement of fact.

"Actually, I'm an American citizen now, but, yes, I was born in Moscow. My family moved to the States not long after the fall of communism."

"How fascinating." Elena looked at Sarah. "You never told me you had a Russian boyfriend."

"It's not exactly the sort of personal information one reveals during a business transaction. Besides, Michael is my secret Russian boyfriend. Michael doesn't really exist."

"I love conspiracies," Elena said. "Please, you must join me for lunch."

"Are you sure it's not an imposition?"

"Are *you* sure you want to have lunch with my children?"

"We would love to have lunch with your children."

"Then it's settled."

Elena summoned Jean-Luc with an imperious wave of her hand and, in French, asked him to add another table to the banquette so her friends could join her. There followed much frowning and pouting of lips, then a lengthy explanation of how the tables were too closely aligned already for him to possibly add another. The only solution, he ventured cautiously, was for Mrs. Kharkov's *two* friends to trade places with *two* of Mrs. Kharkov's entourage. This time it was Oleg, the chief of her detail, who was summoned. Like Jean-Luc before him, he offered resistance. It was overcome by a few tense words that, had they not been spoken in colloquial Russian, would have scandalized the entire room.

The exchange of places was swiftly carried out. Two of the bodyguards were soon sulking at the far end of the table, one with a mobile phone pressed to his ear. Sarah tried not to think about whom he was calling. Instead, she kept her gaze focused on the children. They were miniature versions of their parents: Nikolai, fair and compact; Anna, lanky and dark. "You should see photographs of Ivan and me when we were their age," Elena said, as if reading Sarah's thoughts. "It's even more shocking."

"It's as if you produced exact duplicates."

"We did, right down to the shape of their toes."

"And their dispositions?"

"Anna is much more independent than I was as a child. I was always clinging to my mother's apron. Anna lives in her own world. My Anna likes time to herself."

"And Nikolai?"

Elena was silent for a moment, as if deciding whether to answer the question with evasion or honesty. She chose the latter. "My precious Nikolai is much sweeter than his father. Ivan accuses me of babying him too much. Ivan's father was distant and authoritarian, and I'm afraid Ivan is as well. Russian men don't always make the best fathers. Unfortunately, it is a cultural trait they pass on to their sons." She looked at Mikhail and, in Russian, asked: "Wouldn't you agree, Michael?"

"My father was a mathematician," he replied, also in Russian. "His head was too filled with numbers to think much about his son. But he was gentle as a lamb, and he never touched alcohol."

"Then you should consider yourself extremely lucky. A weakness for alcohol is another trait our men tend to pass on to their sons." She raised her wineglass and spoke in English again. "Although I must confess I have a certain weakness for cold rosé on a warm summer day, especially the rosé that comes from the vineyards around Saint-Tropez."

"A weakness I share myself," Sarah said, raising her glass.

"Are you staying here in Saint-Tropez?"

"Just outside," said Sarah. "At the Château de la Messardière."

"I hear it's very popular with Russians."

"Let's just say that no one expressed any surprise at my accent there," Mikhail replied.

"I hope our countrymen are behaving themselves."

"For the most part. But I'm afraid there was *one* minor incident at the pool involving a middle-aged Moscow businessman and his extremely young girlfriend."

"What sort of incident?"

Mikhail made a show of thought. "I suppose uncontrolled lust would be the best way to describe it in polite company."

"I hear there's a great deal of that going around," Elena said. "We Russians love it here in France, but I'm not so sure the French love us in return. Some of my countrymen don't know how to conduct themselves in polite company yet. They like to drink vodka instead of wine. And they like to flaunt their pretty young mistresses."

"The French like anyone with money and power," said Mikhail. "And, at the moment, the Russians have both."

"Now, if we could only learn some manners." Elena turned her gaze from Mikhail to Sarah. "By the way, the answer to your question is yes."

Sarah was momentarily confused. Elena tapped the postcard with her fingertip. "The Cassatt," she said. "I *am* enjoying it. In fact, I'm enjoying it a great deal. I'm not sure whether you know this, Sarah, but I own six other paintings by Madame Cassatt. I know her work extremely well. I think this one might actually be my favorite."

"I'm glad you feel that way. It takes away some of the sting of losing it."

"Has it been hard for you?"

"The first night was hard. And the first morning was even worse."

"Then you must come see it again. It's here, you know."

"We wouldn't want to impose."

"Not at all. In fact, I insist that you come tomorrow. You'll have lunch and a swim." Then, almost as an afterthought, she added: "And you can see the painting, of course."

A waiter appeared and placed a plate of *steak haché avec pomme frites* in front of each child. Elena instructed Sarah and Mikhail to have a look at the menu and was opening her own when her mobile phone began to chime. She drew it from her handbag and looked at the display screen before lifting the cover. The conversation that followed was brief and conducted in Russian. When it was over, she closed the phone with a snap and placed it carefully on the table before her. Then she looked at Sarah and treated her to another smile filled with false light.

"Ivan was planning to take his yacht out to sea this afternoon but he's decided to join us for lunch instead. He's just over in the harbor. He'll be here in a minute or two."

"How lovely," said Sarah.

Elena closed her menu and shot a glance at the bodyguards. "Yes," she said. "Ivan can be very thoughtful when he wants to be."

38
SAINT-TROPEZ,
FRANCE

The "arrival," as it would become known in the lexicon of the operation, took place precisely forty-seven seconds after Elena laid her mobile phone upon the white tablecloth. Though Ivan had been standing just three hundred yards away at the moment he placed the call, he came by armored Mercedes rather than on foot, lest one of his enemies was lurking amid the sea of humanity shuffling listlessly along the quays of the Old Port. The car roared into the Place de l'Hôtel de Ville at high speed and stopped abruptly a few feet from Grand Joseph's entrance. Ivan waited in the backseat another fifteen seconds, long enough to ignite a murmur of intense speculation inside the restaurant as to his identity, nationality, and profession. Then he emerged in an aggressive blur, like a prizefighter charging from his corner to finish off a hapless opponent. Once inside the restaurant, he paused again in the entranceway, this time to survey the room and to allow the room to survey him in return. He wore loose-fitting trousers of black linen and a shirt of luminous white cotton. His iron hair shone with a fresh coat of oil, and around his thick left wrist was a gold watch the size of a sundial. It glittered like plundered treasure as he strode over to the table.

He did not sit down immediately; instead, he stood for a moment at Elena's back and placed his huge hands proprietarily around the base of her neck. The faces of Nikolai and Anna brightened with the unexpected appearance of their father, and Ivan's face softened momentarily in response. He said something to them in Russian that made the children both burst into laughter and caused Mikhail to smile. Ivan appeared to make a mental note of this. Then his gaze flashed over the table like a searchlight over an open field, before coming to rest on Sarah. The last time Ivan had seen her, she had been cloaked in Gabriel's dowdy clothing. Now she wore a thin peach-colored sundress that hung from her body in a way that created the impression of veiled nudity. Ivan admired her unabashedly, as though he were contemplating adding her to his collection. Sarah extended her hand, more as a defense mechanism than a sign of friendship, but Ivan ignored it and kissed her cheek instead. His sandpaper skin smelled of coconut butter and another woman.

"Saint-Tropez obviously agrees with you, Sarah. Is this your first time here?"

"Actually, I've been coming to Saint-Tropez since I was a little girl."

"You have an uncle here, too?"

"Ivan!" snapped Elena.

"No uncles." Sarah smiled. "Just a long-time love affair with the South of France."

Ivan frowned. He didn't like to be reminded of the fact that anyone, especially a young Western woman, had ever been anywhere or done anything before him.

"Why didn't you mention you were coming here last month? We could have made arrangements to get together."

"I didn't realize you spent time here."

"Really? It was in all the papers. My home used to be owned by a member of the British royal family. When I acquired it, the London papers went into something of a frenzy."

"I somehow missed it."

Once again, Sarah was struck by the flat quality of Ivan's English. It was like being addressed by an announcer on the English-language service of Radio Moscow. He glanced at Mikhail, then looked at Sarah again.

"Aren't you going to introduce me to your friend?" he asked.

Mikhail rose and held out his hand. "My name is Michael Danilov. Sarah and I work together in Washington."

Ivan took the proffered hand and gave it a bone-crushing squeeze. "Michael? What kind of name is that for a Russian?"

"The kind that makes me sound less like a boy from Moscow and more like an American."

"To hell with the Americans," Ivan declared.

"I'm afraid you're in the presence of one."

"Perhaps we can do something to change that. I assume your real name is Mikhail?"

"Yes, of course."

"Then Mikhail you shall be, at least for the remainder of the afternoon." He seized the arm of a passing waiter. "More wine for the women, please. And a bottle of vodka for me and my new friend, *Mikhail.*"

He enthroned himself on the luminous white banquette, with Sarah to his right and Mikhail directly opposite. With his left hand, he was pouring icy vodka into Mikhail's glass as though it were truth serum. His right arm was flung along the back of the banquette. The fine cotton of his shirt was brushing against Sarah's bare shoulders.

"So you and Sarah are friends?" he asked Mikhail.

"Yes, we are."

"What kind of friends?"

Once again Elena objected to Ivan's forwardness and once again Ivan ignored her. Mikhail stoically drained his glass of vodka and, with a sly Russian nod of the head, implied that he and Sarah were very good friends indeed.

"You came to Saint-Tropez together?" Ivan asked, refilling the empty glass.

"Yes."

"You're staying together?"

"We are," Mikhail answered. Then Elena added helpfully: "At the Château de la Messardière."

"You like it there? The staff is looking after you?"

"It's lovely."

"You should come stay with us at Villa Soleil. We have a guesthouse. Actually, we have three guesthouses, but who's counting?"

You're counting, Sarah thought, but she said politely: "That's very kind of you to make such a generous offer, Mr. Kharkov, but we really couldn't impose. Besides, we paid for our room in advance."

"It's only money," Ivan said with the dismissive tone of a man who has far too much of it. He tried to pour more vodka into Mikhail's glass, but Mikhail covered it with his hand.

"I've had quite enough, thanks. Two's my limit."

Ivan acted as though he had not heard him and doled out a third. The interrogation resumed.

"I assume you live in Washington, too?"

"A few blocks from the Capitol."

"Do you and Sarah live together?"

"Ivan!"

"No, Mr. Kharkov. We only work together."

"And where is that?"

"At the Dillard Center for Democracy. It's a nonprofit group that attempts to promote democracy around the world. Sarah runs our sub-Saharan Africa initiative. I do the computers."

"I believe I've heard of this organization. You poked your nose into the affairs of Russia a few years ago."

"We have a very active program in Eastern Europe," Sarah said. "But our Russia initia-

346

tive was closed down by your president. He wasn't terribly fond of us."

"He was right to close you down. Why is it you Americans feel the need to push democracy down the throats of the rest of the world?"

"You don't believe in democracy, Mr. Kharkov?"

"Democracy is fine for those who wish to be democratic, Sarah. But there are some countries that simply don't want democracy. And there are others where the ground has not been sufficiently fertilized for democracy to take root. Iraq is a fine example. You went into Iraq in the name of establishing a democracy in the heart of the Muslim world, a noble goal, but the people were not ready for it."

"And Russia?" she asked.

"We *are* a democracy, Sarah. Our parliament is elected. So is our president."

"Your system allows for no viable opposition, and, without a viable opposition, there can be no democracy."

"Perhaps not your kind of democracy. But it is a democracy that works for Russia. And Russia must be allowed to manage its own affairs without the rest of the world looking over our shoulder and criticizing our every move. Would you rather we return to the chaos of the nineties, when Yeltsin placed our future in the hands of American economic and political advisers? Is this what you and your friends wish to inflict on us?"

Elena cautiously suggested a change of subject. "Ivan has many friends in the Russian government," she explained. "He takes it rather personally when they're criticized."

"I meant no disrespect, Mr. Kharkov. And I think you raise interesting points."

"But not valid ones?"

"It is my hope, and the hope of the Dillard Center, that Russia should one day be a *true* democracy rather than a managed one."

"The day of Russian democracy has already arrived, Sarah. But my wife is correct, as usual. We should change the subject." He looked at Mikhail. "Why did your family leave Russia?"

"My father felt we would have more opportunities in America than Moscow."

"Your father was a dissident?"

"Actually, he was a member of the Party. He was a teacher."

"And did he find his opportunities?"

"He taught high school mathematics in New York. That's where I grew up."

"A schoolteacher? He went all the way to America to become a schoolteacher?

What kind of man forsakes his own country to teach school in another? You should undo your father's folly by coming back to Russia. You wouldn't recognize Moscow. We need talented people like you to help build our country's future. Perhaps I could find a position for you in my own organization."

"I'm quite happy where I am, but thank you for the offer."

"But you haven't heard it yet."

Ivan smiled. It was as pleasant as a sudden crack in a frozen lake. Once again, Elena offered apologia.

"You'll have to forgive my husband's reaction. He isn't used to people saying no to him." Then to Ivan: "You can try again tomorrow, darling. Sarah and Michael are coming to the villa for the afternoon."

"Wonderful," he said. "I'll send a car to collect you from your hotel."

"We have a car," Mikhail countered. "I'm sure we can find our way."

"Don't be silly. I'll send a proper car to collect you."

Ivan opened his menu and insisted everyone else do the same. Then he leaned close to Sarah, so that his chest was pressing against her bare shoulder.

"Have the lobster-and-mango spring rolls

to start," he said. "I promise, your life will never be the same again."

39
GASSIN, FRANCE

At the old stone villa outside Gassin, dinner that evening had been a hasty affair: baguettes and cheese, a green salad, roasted chickens from the local charcuterie. Their ransacked bones lay scattered over the outdoor table like carrion, along with a heel of bread and three empty bottles of mineral water. At one end of the table lay a tourist brochure advertising deep-sea fishing trips in a sea now empty of fish. It might have looked like ordinary refuse were it not for the brief message, hastily scribbled over a photograph of a young boy holding a tuna twice his size. It had been written by Mikhail and passed to Yaakov, in a classic maneuver, in the Place Carnot. Gabriel was gazing at it now as if trying to rewrite it through the sheer force of his will. Eli Lavon was gazing at Gabriel, his chin resting in his palm, like a grandmaster pleading with a lesser opponent to either move or capitulate.

"Maybe it's the travel arrangements that bother me most," Lavon said finally in an attempt to prod Gabriel into action. "Maybe I'm not comfortable with the fact that Ivan won't let them come in their own car."

"Maybe he's just a control freak." Gabriel's tone was ambivalent, as if he were expressing a possible explanation rather than a firmly held opinion. "Maybe he doesn't want strange cars on his property. Strange cars can contain strange electronic equipment. Sometimes, strange cars can even contain bombs."

"Or maybe he wants to take them on a surveillance detection run before he lets them onto the property. Or maybe he'll just skip the professional niceties and kill them immediately instead."

"He's not going to kill them, Eli."

"Of course not," said Lavon sarcastically. "Ivan wouldn't lay a finger on them. After all, it's not as if he didn't kill a meddlesome reporter in broad daylight in St. Peter's Basilica." He held up a single sheet of paper, a printout of an NSA intercept. "Five minutes after Ivan left that restaurant, he was on the phone to Arkady Medvedev, the chief of his private security service, telling him to run a background check on Mikhail's father and the Dillard Center."

"And when he does, he'll find that Mikhail's father was indeed a teacher who immigrated to America in the early nineties. And he'll find that the Dillard Center occupies a small suite of offices on Massachusetts Avenue in Washington."

"Ivan knows about cover stories, and he certainly knows about CIA front organizations. The KGB was far better at it than Langley ever was. The Russians had a network of fronts all around the globe, some of them run by Ivan's father, no doubt. Ivan drank KGB tradecraft with his mother's milk. It's in his DNA."

"If Ivan had qualms about Sarah and Mikhail, he wouldn't let them come close to him. He'd push them away. And he'd make it clear to Elena that they were strictly off-limits."

"No, he wouldn't. Ivan's KGB. If he suspected Sarah and Mikhail weren't kosher, he'd play it *exactly* like this. He'd put a team of watchers on them. He'd slip a bug in their hotel room to make sure they're really who they say they are. And he'd invite them to lunch to try to find out how much they know about his network."

Gabriel, with his silence, conceded the point.

"Cancel lunch," said Lavon. "Arrange

another bump."

"If we cancel, Ivan will know something's not right. And there's no way he'll believe that another chance encounter is only a co-incidence. We've flirted long enough. Elena's clearly interested. It's time to start talking about consummating the relationship. And the only way we can talk is by going to lunch at Ivan's house."

Lavon picked up a chicken bone and searched it for a scrap of meat. "Do I need to remind you whom Sarah works for? And do I also need to remind you that Adrian Carter might not agree with your decision to send her in there tomorrow?"

"Sarah might work for Langley, but she belongs to us. And as for a decision about what to do, I haven't made one yet."

"What are you going to do, Gabriel?"

"I'm going to sit here for a while and think about it."

Lavon tossed the bone onto the pile and placed his chin in his palm.

"I'll help."

40
SAINT-TROPEZ, FRANCE

Next day, the heat arrived. It came from the south on a scalding wind, fierce, dry, and filled with grit. The pedestrians who ventured into the *centre ville* clung to the false cool of the shadows, while on the coastline, from the Baie de Pampelonne down to Cap Cartaya, beachgoers huddled motionless beneath their parasols or sat simmering in the shallows. A few deranged souls stretched themselves prostrate upon the broiling sands; by late morning, they looked like casualties of a desert battle. At noon, the local radio reported that it was officially the hottest day ever recorded in Saint-Tropez. All agreed the Americans were to blame.

Villa Soleil, Ivan Kharkov's estate on the Baie de Cavalaire, seemed to have been spared the full force of the heat's fury. Immediately behind its twelve-foot walls lay a vast circular drive where nymphs frolicked in splashing fountains and flowers erupted

355

in gardens groomed to hotel brochure perfection. The villa itself stood hard against the rocky coastline, imposing its own beauty upon the remarkable landscape. It was more palace than home, an endless series of loggias, marble corridors, statuary halls, and cavernous sitting rooms where white curtains billowed and snapped like mainsails in the constant breeze. Each wing of the house seemed to have its own unique view of the sea. And each view, thought Sarah, was more breathtaking than the last.

They finally came upon Elena at the end of a long, cool colonnade with a checkerboard marble floor. She wore a strapless top and a floor-length wrap that shimmered with each breath of wind. Ivan stood next to her, a glass of wine sweating in his grasp. Once again, he was wearing black and white, as if to illustrate the fact that he was a man of contradictions. This time, however, the colors of his outfit were reversed: black shirt, white trousers. As they greeted each other with the casualness of an old friendship renewed, his enormous wristwatch caught the rays of the sun and reflected them into Sarah's eyes. Before treating her to a damp kiss and a blast of his rich aftershave, he placed his wineglass carelessly on the plinth of a statue. It was female, nude, and Greek. For the moment, Sarah thought spitefully, it was the world's most expensive coaster.

It was immediately clear that Elena's invitation to a quiet lunch and swim had been transformed by Ivan into a more extravagant affair. On the terrace below the colonnade, a table had been set for twenty-four. Several pretty young girls were already cavorting in a pool the size of a small bay, watched over by a dozen middle-aged Russians lounging about on chaises and divans. Ivan introduced his guests as if they were simply more of his possessions. There was a man who did something with nickel, another who traded in timber, and one, with a face like a fox, who ran a personal and corporate security firm in Geneva. The girls in the pool he introduced collectively, as though they had no names, only a purpose. One of them was Yekatarina, Ivan's supermodel mistress, a gaunt, pouty child of nineteen, all arms, legs, and breasts, colored to caramel perfection. She gazed hard at Sarah, as though she were a potential rival, then leapt into the pool like a dolphin and disappeared beneath the surface.

Sarah and Mikhail settled themselves between the wife of the nickel magnate, who looked deeply bored, and the timber trader, who was genial but dull. Ivan and Elena returned to the colonnade, where more guests were arriving in boisterous packs. They came down the steps in waves, like revolutionaries storming the Winter Palace, and with each new group the volume and intensity of the party seemed to rise a notch. Several frosted bottles of vodka appeared; dance music pulsated from invisible speakers. On the terrace, a second table was set for lunch, then a third. The vast pool soon took on the appearance of just another of Ivan's fountains, as nubile nymphs were groped and tossed about by fat millionaires and muscled bodyguards. Elena moved effortlessly from group to group, kissing cheeks and refreshing drinks, but Ivan remained aloof, gazing upon the merriment as though it were a performance arranged for his own private amusement.

It was nearly three o'clock by the time he summoned them all to lunch. By Sarah's count, the guests now numbered seventy in all, but from Ivan's kitchens miraculously emerged more than enough food to feed a party twice as large. She sat next to Mikhail at Ivan's end of the table, where they were well within his sphere of influence and the scent of his cologne. It was a gluttonous affair; Ivan ate heavily but without pleasure, stabbing punitively at his food, his thoughts remote. At the end of the meal, his mood improved when Anna and Nikolai appeared, along with Sonia, their Russian nanny. The children sat together on his lap, imprisoned in his massive arms. "These two are my world," he said directly to Sarah. "If anything ever happened to them . . ." His voice trailed off, as if he were suddenly at a loss for words. Then he added menacingly: "God help the man who ever harms my children."

It was an oddly gloomy note on which to end lunch, though the rest of Ivan's guests seemed to think nothing of it as they rose from the table and filed down the steps to the pool for a final swim. Ivan released his grip on the children and seized Mikhail's wrist as he stood. "Don't go so quickly," he said. "You promised to give me a chance to convince you to come home to Russia and work for me."

"I'm not sure I remember that promise."

"But I remember it quite clearly and that's all that matters." He stood and smiled charmingly at Sarah. "I can be rather persuasive. If I were you, I would begin planning a move to Moscow."

He guided Mikhail to a distant corner of the terrace and sat with him in the shade of a cupola. Sarah looked at Elena. The children were now seated on her lap, in a pose as tender as Ivan's was fierce.

"You look like a painting by Mary Cassatt."

"I'll take that as a compliment."

Elena kissed Anna's cheek and whispered something to the child that caused her to smile and nod. Then she whispered something to Nikolai, with the same result.

"Are you saying naughty things about me?" Sarah asked playfully.

"The children think you're very pretty."

"Please tell the children I think they're very pretty as well."

"They were also wondering whether you would like to see their room. It contains a new painting, and they're very anxious for you to see it."

"Please tell the children that I would like nothing more."

"Come, then," said Elena. "The children will show us the way."

They flitted in and out of the colonnade like starlings and hop-scotched along the checkerboard marble floor. Ascending the sweeping main staircase, Nikolai pretended to be a ferocious Russian bear and Sarah pretended to be terribly afraid in return. At the top of the stairs, Anna took hold of

Sarah's hand and pulled her down a glorious corridor filled with buttery light. It ended at the children's room, which was not a room at all but an elaborate suite. *Two Children on a Beach* hung in the entrance foyer, next to a similarly sized portrait of a young dancer by Degas. Elena Kharkov, student of art history and former employee of the Hermitage Museum in Leningrad, slipped effortlessly into tour guide mode.

"They knew each other well quite well, Cassatt and Degas. In fact, Degas had a profound influence on her work. I thought it was appropriate they be together." She looked at Sarah and gave a faint smile. "Until two weeks ago, I was certain the Degas was actually painted by Degas. Now I'm not so sure."

Elena sent the children off to play. In their absence, a heavy silence fell over the foyer. The two women stood several feet apart, Elena before the Degas, Sarah before the Cassatt. Overhead, a camera peered down at them like a gargoyle.

"Who are you?" Elena asked, her eyes straight ahead. "And why are you in my home?"

Sarah glanced up at the camera.

"Don't be frightened," said Elena. "Ivan is watching but not listening. I told him long ago I would never live in a house filled with microphones. And he swore to me he would never install them."

"And you trust him?"

"On this matter, yes. Remember, microphones would pick up *everyone's* voice, including Ivan's. And their signals can also be intercepted by law enforcement agencies and intelligence services." She paused. "I would have thought you would be aware of that. Who are you? And who do you work for?"

Sarah stared straight ahead at Gabriel's immaculate brushstrokes. *Under no circumstances are you to tell her your real name or occupation when you're on hostile territory,* he had said. *Your cover is everything. Wear it like body armor, especially when you're on Ivan's turf.*

"My name is Sarah Crawford. I work for the Dillard Center for Democracy in Washington. We met for the first time in the Cotswolds, when you purchased this painting by Mary Cassatt from my uncle."

"Quickly, Sarah. We haven't much time."

"I'm a friend, Elena. A very good friend. I'm here to help you finish what you started. You have something you want to tell us about your husband. I'm here to listen."

Elena was silent for a moment. "He's

362

quite fond of you, Sarah. Was it always your intention to seduce my husband?"

"I assure you, Elena, your husband has absolutely no interest in me."

"How can you be so certain?"

"Because he's brought his mistress into your house."

Elena's head turned sharply toward Sarah. "Who is she?"

"Yekatarina."

"It's not possible. She's a child."

"That *child* is staying in a suite at the Carlton Hotel. Ivan is paying her bills."

"How do you know this?"

"We know, Elena. We know everything."

"You're lying to me. You're trying to —"

"We're not trying to do anything but help you. And the only lies we tell are the ones necessary to deceive Ivan. We haven't lied to you, Elena, and we never will."

"How do you know he's seeing her?"

"Because we follow him. And we listen to him. Did you see those pearls she was wearing today?"

Elena gave an almost imperceptible nod.

"He gave those pearls to her in June when he went to Paris. You remember his trip to Paris, don't you, Elena? You were in Moscow. Ivan said he needed to go for business. It was a lie, of course. He went there to see

Yekatarina. He called you three times while he was in her apartment. You took the third call while you were having lunch with friends at Café Pushkin. We have a photograph if you'd like to see it."

Elena was forced to absorb this news of her husband's treachery with a tranquil smile — Ivan's cameras were watching. Sarah was tempted to spare her the rest. She didn't, more out of loathing for Ivan than any other reason.

"Yekatarina thinks she's the only one, but she's not. There's a flight attendant called Tatyana. And there was a girl in London named Ludmila. I'm afraid Ivan treated her very badly. Eventually, he treats them all badly."

Elena's eyes filled with tears.

"You mustn't cry, Elena. Ivan might be watching us. You have to smile while I tell you these awful things."

Elena went to Sarah's side, and their shoulders touched. Sarah could feel her trembling. Whether it was with grief or fear, she could not tell.

"How long have you been watching me?"

"It's not important, Elena. It's only important that you finish what you started."

Elena laughed softly to herself, as though she found Sarah's remark mildly amusing.

Her gaze swept over the surface of the painting while her fingertips explored the texture of the faux craquelure.

"You had no right to pry into my private life."

"We had no choice."

Elena lapsed into silence. Sarah, for the moment, was listening to another voice.

Place the sales contract carefully before her and lay the pen next to it. But don't pressure her into signing. She has to reach the decision on her own. Otherwise, she's no use to us.

"He wasn't always like this," Elena said finally. "Even when he worked for the KGB. You might find this hard to believe, Sarah, but Ivan was really quite charming when I first met him."

"I don't find it hard to believe at all. He's still quite charming."

"When he wants to be." She was still touching the craquelure. "When I first met Ivan, he told me he worked in some dreary Soviet agricultural office. A few weeks later, after we'd fallen in love, he told me the truth. I almost didn't believe him. I couldn't imagine this considerate, somewhat shy young man was actually locking dissidents away in mental hospitals and the gulag."

"What happened?"

"The money happened. The money changed everything. It's changed Russia, too. Money is the new KGB in Russia. Money controls our lives. And the pursuit of money prevents us from questioning the actions of our so-called democratic government."

Elena reached toward the face of one of the children, the little boy, and stroked the cracks on his cheek.

"Whoever did this is quite good," she said. "I assume you know him?"

"Very well, actually." A silence, then: "Would you like to meet him?"

"Who is he?"

"It's not important. It's only important that you agree to see him. He's trying to save innocent lives. He needs your help."

Elena's finger moved to the face of the other child. "How will we do it? Ivan sees everything."

"I'm afraid we're going to need to tell a small lie."

"What kind of small lie?"

"I want you to spend the rest of the afternoon flirting with Mikhail," Sarah said. "Mikhail will tell you everything you need to know."

Sarah's BlackBerry had one feature not

available on over-the-counter models: the ability to encode and "squirt" data messages to a nearby receiver in less than a thousandth of a second. The message she transmitted early that evening was greeted with much celebration at the villa in Gassin. Gabriel immediately sent word to the Operations Desk at King Saul Boulevard and the Global Ops Center at CIA Headquarters in Langley. Then he gathered his team and began putting the final touches on the next phase of the operation. The small lie they were going to tell Ivan. The small lie to cover the much bigger one.

41
SAINT-TROPEZ,
FRANCE

The storms had come down from the Maritime Alps after midnight and laid siege to Ivan Kharkov's fortress on the Baie de Cavalaire. Elena Kharkov had not been awakened by the violent weather. Having endured two sleepless nights already, she had taken twice her normal dose of sedative. Now, she woke grudgingly and in stages, like a diver rising to the surface from a great depth. She lay motionless for some time, eyes closed, head throbbing, unable to recall her dreams. Finally, she reached blindly toward Ivan's side of the bed and her hand caressed the warm supple form of a young girl. For an instant, she feared Ivan had been so audacious as to bring Yekatarina into their bed. Then she opened her eyes and saw it was only Anna. The child was wearing Ivan's gold reading glasses and was scribbling with Ivan's gold fountain pen on the back of some important business documents. Elena smiled in spite of her headache.

"Tell Maria to bring me a café au lait. A very *large* café au lait."

"I'm very busy. I'm working, just like Papa."

"Get me a coffee, Anna, or I'll beat you severely."

"But you never beat me, Mama."

"It's never too late to start."

Anna scribbled stubbornly away.

"Please, Anna, I'm begging. Mama's not feeling well."

The child exhaled heavily; then, in a gesture that mimicked her father to perfection, she flung the papers and pen onto the nightstand in mock anger and threw aside the blanket. As she started to climb out of bed, Elena reached out suddenly and drew her tightly to her body.

"I thought you wanted coffee."

"I do. But I want to hold you for a minute first."

"What's wrong, Mama? You seem sad."

"I just love you very much."

"Does that make you sad?"

"Sometimes." Elena kissed Anna's cheek. "Go, now. And don't come back without coffee."

She closed her eyes again and listened to

the patter of Anna's bare feet receding. A gust of cool wind moved in the curtains and made shadows dance and play for her on the walls of the bedroom. Like all the rooms of the house, it was far too large for familial or marital intimacy, and now, alone in the cavernous space, Elena felt a prisoner to its vastness. She pulled the blankets tightly to her chin, creating a small space for herself, and thought of Leningrad before the fall. As a child of a senior Communist Party official, she had lived a life of Soviet privilege — a life of special stores, plentiful food and clothing, and trips abroad to other Warsaw Pact countries. Yet nothing in her charmed upbringing could have prepared her for the extravagance of life with Ivan. Homes such as this did not exist, she had been told as a child, not only by the Soviet system but by an orthodox father who kept faith with communism even when it was clear the emperor truly had no clothes. Elena realized now that she had been lied to her entire life, first by her father and now by her husband. Ivan liked to pretend this grand palace by the sea was a reward for his capitalist ingenuity and hard work. In truth, it had been acquired through corruption and connections to the old order. And it was awash in blood. Some nights, in her dreams, she saw the blood. It flowed in rivers along the endless marble corridors and spilled like waterfalls down the grand staircases. The blood shed by men wielding Ivan's weapons. The blood of children forced to fight in Ivan's wars.

Anna reappeared, a breakfast tray balanced precariously in her hands. She placed it on the bed next to Elena and took great pleasure in pointing out its contents: a bowl of café au lait, two slices of toasted baguette, butter, fresh strawberry preserves, copies of the *Financial Times* and the *Herald Tribune.* Then she kissed Elena's cheek and departed. Elena quickly drank half the coffee, hoping the caffeine would act as an antidote to her headache, and devoured the first slice of the toast. For some reason, she was unusually hungry. A glance at the clock on her bedside table told her why. It was nearly noon.

She slowly finished the rest of the coffee while her headache gradually receded. With its departure, she was granted a sudden clarity of vision. She thought of the woman she knew as Sarah Crawford. And of Mikhail. And of the man who had painted such a beautiful forgery of *Two Children on a Beach* by Mary Cassatt. She did not know precisely who they were; she only knew that she had no choice but to join them. For the innocent who might die, she told herself now. For Russia. For herself.

For the children . . .

Another gust of wind stirred the long curtains. This time, it brought the sound of Ivan's voice. Elena wrapped herself in a silk robe and walked onto the terrace overlooking the swimming pool and the sea. Ivan was supervising the cleanup of the storm damage, barking orders at the groundskeepers like the foreman of a chain gang. Elena slipped back inside before he could see her and quickly entered the large sunlit chamber he used as his informal upstairs office. Though the rules of their marriage were largely unspoken, this room, like all of Ivan's offices, was a forbidden zone for both Elena and the children. He had been there already that morning; it was evident in the stench of cologne that hung on the air and the morning headlines from Moscow scrolling across the screen of the computer. Two identical mobile phones lay on the leather blotter, power lights winking. In violation of all marital decrees, spoken and unspoken, she picked up one of the phones and clicked to the directory of the ten most recently dialed numbers. One number appeared three times: *3064006.* With another click of a button, she dialed it again now. Ten seconds later, a female voice in French answered: "Good morning. Carlton Hotel. How may I direct your call?"

"Yekatarina Mazurov."

"One moment, please."

Then, two rings later, another female voice: younger than the first, Russian instead of French.

"Ivan, darling, is that you? I thought you would never call. Can I come with you on the trip, or is Elena going to be with you? Ivan . . . What's wrong . . . Answer me, Ivan . . ."

Elena calmly terminated the call. Then, from behind her, came another voice: Russian, male, taut with quiet rage.

"What are you doing in here?"

She spun round, telephone still in her hand, and saw Ivan standing in the doorway.

"I told my mother I would call her this morning."

He walked over and removed the phone from her grasp, then reached into the pocket of his trousers and handed her another. "Use this one," he ordered without explanation.

"What difference does it make which phone I use?"

Ignoring her question, he inspected the surface of the desk to see if anything else had been disturbed. "You slept late," he said, as if pointing out something Elena hadn't considered. "I don't know how you managed to sleep through all that thunder and lightning."

"I wasn't feeling well."

"You look well this morning."

"I'm a bit better, thank you."

"Aren't you going to call her?"

"Who?"

"Your mother."

Ivan was a veteran of such games and far too quick for her. Elena felt a sudden need for time and space. She slipped past him and carried the phone back to bed.

"What are you doing?"

She held up the phone. "Calling my mother."

"But you should be getting dressed. Everyone's meeting us in the Old Port at twelve-thirty."

"For what?" she asked, feigning ignorance.

"We're spending the afternoon on the boat. I told you yesterday."

"I'm sorry, Ivan. It must have slipped my mind."

"So what are you doing back in bed? We have to leave in a few minutes."

"Who have you invited?"

He rattled off a few names, all Russian, all male.

"I'm not sure I'm up to it, Ivan. If it's all right with you, I'll stay with the children. Besides, you and your friends will have more fun if I'm not there."

He didn't bother to protest. Instead, he consulted his gold wristwatch, as if checking to see if there was still time to reach Yekatarina. Elena resisted the impulse to inform him that she was eagerly awaiting his call.

"What are you going to do with yourself all day?" he inquired casually, as if her answer didn't much concern him.

"I'm going to lie in bed and read the newspapers. Then, if I'm feeling well enough, I'll take the children into town. It's market day, Ivan. You know how much the children love the market."

The market: Ivan's vision of hell on earth. He made one final indifferent attempt to change her mind before retiring to his private bathroom suite to shave and shower. Ten minutes later, freshly clothed and scented, he headed downstairs. Elena, still in bed, switched on the television and scrolled through the channels to the closed-circuit shot from the security cameras at the front gate. Ivan must have been anticipating a dangerous day on the waters off the Côte d'Azur because he was carrying his full package of security: a driver and two body-guards in his own car, plus a second car filled with four other men. Elena glimpsed him one final time as he climbed into the back of his car. He was talking on his mobile phone and wearing the smile he reserved for Yekatarina.

She switched off the television and, using her last perfidious vision as motivation, swung her feet to the floor. *Don't stop now,* she told herself. *If you stop, you'll never find the courage to start again. And whatever you do, don't look back. You're never alone.* Those final words were not her own. They had been spoken by the man she knew as Mikhail. The man who would soon become her lover.

Elena heard his instructions now, soft but assured, as she took the final banal steps toward betrayal. She bathed in her swimming pool-sized Jacuzzi tub, singing softly to herself, something she normally did not do. She took great care applying her makeup and appeared to struggle finding a hairstyle she deemed suitable. Her wardrobe seemed to be the source of similar vacillation, for she tried on and discarded a half-dozen outfits before settling on a simple cream-colored Dior dress that Ivan had purchased out of guilt during his last trip to Paris. The rejects she flung onto the bed, just as Michael had instructed. Evidence of romantic indecision, he had called it. Visible proof of her desire to look attractive for her lover.

Finally, at one o'clock, Elena informed Sonia and the children that she would be going to town for a few hours. Then she ordered Oleg to prepare a car and security detail. The traffic on the way into Saint-Tropez was deplorable as usual; she occupied her time by telephoning her mother in Moscow. Oleg, who was seated next to her in the backseat, made no attempt to conceal the fact he was eavesdropping, and Elena made no effort to modulate the volume of her voice. When the call was over, she switched off the phone and dropped it into her handbag. As she climbed out of the car on the Avenue du Marechal, she hung the bag over her left shoulder, just as she had been told to do. Right shoulder meant that she'd had a change of heart. Left shoulder meant she was ready to join them.

She entered the Place Carnot at the southeast corner and, with Oleg and Gennady trailing a few paces behind, started into the crowded outdoor market. In the clothing section, she bought matching cashmere sweaters for Ivan and Nikolai and a pair of sandals for Anna to replace the ones she had left behind during their last visit to Pampelonne Beach. She gave the parcels to Oleg to carry, then headed toward the food stalls in the center of the square, where she paused to watch a man with a grizzled face preparing ratatouille in the largest pan she had ever seen. A young woman with dark hair materialized briefly at her side; she murmured a few words in English, then melted once more into the crowds.

Elena purchased a half kilo of the ratatouille and handed the container to Gennady, then continued diagonally across the square, toward the Boulevard Louis Blanc. An Audi convertible, bright red, was parked on the corner. Michael was behind the wheel, face tilted toward the sun, dreadful American music blaring from the stereo. Elena tossed her handbag onto the passenger seat and quickly climbed inside. As the car shot forward, she kept her eyes straight ahead. Had she looked over her shoulder, she would have seen Oleg, red-faced, screaming into his cell phone. And Gennady, the younger of the two, chasing

after them on foot, the ratatouille still in his
hand.

42
SAINT-TROPEZ, FRANCE

"Who are you?"

"Michael Danilov. Sarah's friend from Washington. Your husband calls me Mikhail. You can call me Mikhail, too."

"I want to know your *real* name."

"It is my real name."

"Where do you work?"

"You already know where I work. I work with Sarah, at the Dillard Center for Democracy."

"Where are you taking me?"

"Somewhere we can be alone."

"We don't have much time. You can be sure Ivan is already looking for us."

"Try not to think about Ivan. For now, there's no one but us."

"The bodyguards saw you. They're going to tell Ivan it was you and Ivan won't rest until you're dead."

"Your husband isn't going to kill me, Elena."

"You don't know my husband. He kills people all the time."

"I know your husband very well. And he never kills for love. Only money."

43
THE MASSIF DES MAURES, FRANCE

They headed inland, up a winding road, into the highlands of the Massif des Maures. He drove very fast but without anxiety or visible exertion. His left hand lay lightly atop the steering wheel while his right worked the stick shift with liquid smoothness. He was no computer technician, Elena thought. She had spent enough time in the company of elite soldiers to realize when she was in the presence of a fellow traveler. She took comfort in this. She realized she had simply traded one set of bodyguards for another.

The terrain grew more rugged with each passing mile. To their right lay a dense forest of pine and eucalyptus; to their left, a bottomless green gorge. They flashed through villages with names she did not recognize. And she thought how terrible it was she had never been here until now. And she vowed that one day, when this was over, she would bring the children here without their bodyguards for a picnic.

The children . . .

It had been a mistake to think of them now. She wanted to phone Sonia and make certain they were safe. She wanted to scream at this strange man called Mikhail to turn the car around. Instead, she focused on the wind in her hair and the warm sunlight on her skin. A married woman who is about to give herself to a another man does not destroy the ache of sexual anticipation by telephoning her children. She thinks only of the moment, and to hell with the consequences.

They entered another village with a single street shaded by plane trees. A Rubenesque girl sat astride a burgundy motor scooter outside a *tabac,* her face shielded by a helmet and dark visor. She flicked her headlamp twice as they approached and entered the road ahead of them. They followed her for another mile, then turned together into a dirt track lined with twisted Van Gogh olive trees, their silver-green leaves shimmering like coins in the gentle breeze. At the end of the track was an open wooden gate and, beyond the gate, the courtyard of a tiny stucco villa. Mikhail switched off the engine.

"Remember how it looks, Elena. It's important you're able to recall small details. Ivan will expect that when he questions you."

"Where are we?"

"Somewhere in the mountains. You're not exactly sure. We were attracted to one another from the moment we met at Grand Joseph. Ivan didn't notice because he was thinking about Yekatarina. You were vulnerable; I could see that. I just had to think of some way to get you alone. I knew a hotel wouldn't do, so I took the liberty of renting this place from a local estate agent for the week."

He removed the keys from the ignition.

"You did everything the way we asked? You dialed Yekatarina's room at the Carlton? You left clothes all over your room for Ivan and the housekeepers to see?"

"I did everything."

"Then you have nothing to worry about. You'll tell Ivan that you've suspected he was being unfaithful for years. You'll tell him you've had suspicions about Yekatarina for a long time and that these suspicions were confirmed by the numbers you found on his mobile phone. You'll tell him I made a pass at you the afternoon we came to the villa. That you were so angry and hurt that you were unable to resist. You'll tell him you wanted to punish him and that the only way was to give your body to another man. He's going to be furious, of course, but he'll have no reason to doubt the veracity of your story since he knows he is guilty of the sins you accuse him of committing. Sleeping with me was a crime of passion and anger, something Ivan understands all too well. In due time, he'll forgive you."

"He might forgive me but not you."

"I'm none of your concern. In fact, you will soon hate me for the trouble I've caused you. As far as you're concerned, I can look after myself."

"Can you?"

"Quite well, actually." He opened the door. "Time to go inside, Elena. There's someone inside who's very anxious to meet you."

It was the antithesis of Villa Soleil, a small, tidy space of white-washed walls, terra-cotta floors, and rustic Provençal furniture. Seated at a rough-hewn wood table was a man of indeterminate age and nationality, with a long nose that looked as though it had been carved with a chisel and the greenest eyes Elena had ever seen. He rose slowly to his feet as she approached and extended his hand without speaking. Mikhail handled the introductions.

"Meet the man who painted your Cassatt, Elena. I am about to commit the grave professional sin of telling you his real name, which is Gabriel Allon. He wants you to know it, because he admires you deeply and does not wish to lie to you. You are in the presence of royalty, Elena — at least as far as the inhabitants of our world are concerned. I'll leave you to your business."

Mikhail withdrew. Gabriel looked at Elena in silence for a moment, then, with a glance, invited her to sit. He retook his seat on the opposite side of the table and folded his hands before him. They were dark and smooth, with slender, articulate fingers. The hands of a musician, thought Elena. The hands of an artist.

"I would like to begin by thanking you," he said.

"For what?"

"For having the courage to come forward."

"What are you talking about?"

"We're here because of you, Elena. We're here because you summoned us."

"But I didn't summon you. I didn't *summon* anyone."

"Of course you did. You summoned us with Olga Sukhova. And with Aleksandr Lubin. And with Boris Ostrovsky. Whether you realized it or not, Elena, you sent them to us. But you only gave them a part of the story. Now you have to tell us the rest."

There was something in his accent she could not quite place. He was a polyglot, she decided. A man without roots. A man who had lived many places. A man with many names.

"Who do you work for?"

"I am employed by a small agency answerable only to the prime minister of the State of Israel. But there are other countries involved as well. Your husband's actions have caused an international crisis. And the response to this crisis has been international as well."

"Is Sarah an Israeli, too?"

"Only in spirit. Sarah is an American. She works for the Central Intelligence Agency."

"And Mikhail?"

"As you can probably tell by Mikhail's perfect Russian, he was born in Moscow. He left when he was a young boy and moved to Israel. He left Russia because of men like your husband. And now your husband is planning to sell very dangerous weapons to people who are sworn to destroy us.'

"How much do you know?"

"Very little, unfortunately. Otherwise, we wouldn't have upended your life by bringing you here today. We only know that your husband has entered into a deal with the Devil. He's killed two people to keep that deal a secret. And others will surely die as well, unless you help us." He reached out and took her by the hand. "Will you help us, Elena?"

"What do you want from me?"

"I want you to finish what you started when you arranged to meet with your old friend Olga Sukhova. I want you to tell me the rest of the story."

Five miles due east of Saint-Tropez, the rocky headland known as the Pointe de l'Ay juts defiantly into the Mediterranean Sea. At the base of the point lies a small beach of fine sand, often overlooked because it is absent any boutiques, clubs, or restaurants. The girl with shoulder-length dark hair and scars on her leg had taken great care in choosing her spot, selecting an isolated patch of sand near the rocks with an unobstructed view out to sea. There, shielded from the sun by a parasol, she had passed a pleasant if solitary afternoon, now sipping from a plastic bottle of mineral water, now delving into the pages of a worn paperback novel, now peering out to sea through a pair of miniature Zeiss binoculars toward the enormous private motor yacht called *October* adrift on the calm waters some three miles offshore.

At 3:15, she noticed something in the ship's movements that made her sit up a bit straighter. She watched it another moment to make certain her initial impression was correct, then lowered the glasses and removed a BlackBerry PDA from her canvas beach bag. The message was brief; the transmission, lightning fast. Two minutes later, after complying with a request for confirmation, she placed the device back into her beach bag and peered out to sea again. The yacht had completed its turn and was now making for Saint-Tropez like a frigate steaming toward battle. *Party's over a bit early,* the girl thought as she traded the glasses for her paperback novel. *And on such a lovely day.*

44

THE MASSIF DES
MAURES, FRANCE

Elena began by setting the scene, as much for her own benefit as for his. It was autumn, she said. November. *Mid*-November, she added for the sake of clarity. She and Ivan were staying at their country dacha north of Moscow, a palace of pine and glass built atop the remains of a smaller dacha that had been given to Ivan's father by Soviet leader Leonid Brezhnev. It was snowing heavily. A good Russian snow, like falling ash from a volcanic eruption.

"Ivan received a phone call late in the evening. After hanging up, he told me some business associates would be coming to the house in a few hours for an important meeting. He didn't identify these business associates and I knew far better than to ask. For the rest of the evening, he was on edge. Anxious. Pacing. Cursing the Russian weather. I knew the signs. I'd seen my husband in moods like this before. Ivan always gets very excited before a big dance."

"Dance?"

"Forgive me, Mr. Allon. Dance is one of the code words he and his men use when discussing arms transactions. 'We have to make final arrangements for the *dance.*' 'We have to book a hall for the *dance.*' 'We have to hire a band for the *dance.*' 'How many chairs will we need for the *dance?*' 'How many bottles of vodka?' 'How much caviar?' 'How many loaves of black bread?' I'm not sure who they think they're deceiving with this nonsense but it certainly isn't me."

"And did Ivan's visitors actually come that evening?"

"Technically, it was the next morning. Two-thirty in the morning, to be exact."

"You saw them?"

"Yes, I saw them."

"Describe the scene for me. Carefully, Elena. The smallest details can be important."

"There were eight of them in all, plus a team of Ivan's bodyguards. Arkady Medvedev was there as well. Arkady is the chief of my husband's personal security service. The bodyguards have a joke about Arkady. They say Arkady is Ivan on his worst day."

"Where was the delegation from?"

"They were from Africa. Sub-Saharan Africa." She managed a smile. "Sarah's area of expertise."

"Which country?"

"I couldn't say."

"Did you meet them?"

"I'm *never* allowed to meet them."

"Had you ever seen any of them before?"

"No, just different versions of them. They're all the same, really. They speak different languages. They fly different flags. They fight for different causes. But in the end they're all the same."

"Where were you while they were in the dacha?"

"Upstairs in our bedroom."

"Were you ever able to hear their voices?"

"Sometimes. Their leader was a giant of a man. He was a baritone. His voice made the walls vibrate. He had a laugh like thunder."

"You're a linguist, Elena. If they spoke another European language, what would it be?"

"French. Most definitely French. It had that lilt, you know?"

They drank first, she said. There was always drinking involved when Ivan was planning a dance. By the time the hard bargaining began, the guests were well lubricated, and Ivan made no effort to control the volume of their voices, especially the voice of their baritone leader. Elena began to hear words and terms she recognized: AKs. RPGs. Mortars. Specific types of ammunition. Helicopter gunships. Tanks.

"Before long they were arguing about money. The prices of specific weapons and systems. Commissions. Bribes. Shipping and handling. I knew enough about my husband's business dealings to realize they were discussing a *major* arms deal — most likely with an African nation that was under international embargo. You see, Mr. Allon, these are the men who come to my husband, men who cannot purchase arms legally on the open market. That's why Ivan is so successful. He fills a very specific need. And that's why the poorest nations on earth pay vastly inflated prices for the weaponry they use to slaughter each other."

"How big a deal are we talking about?"

"The kind that is measured in *hundreds* of millions of dollars." She paused, then said, "Why do you think Ivan didn't bat an eye when I asked him for two and a half million dollars for your worthless Cassatt?"

"How long did these men stay in your home?"

"Until early the next morning. When they

finally left, Ivan came upstairs to our room. He was soaring. I'd seen him in moods like that, too. It was bloodlust. He crawled into bed and practically raped me. He needed a body to pillage. *Any* body. He settled for mine."

"When did you realize this deal was different?"

"Two nights later."

"What happened?"

"I answered a phone I shouldn't have answered. And I listened long after I should have hung up. Simple as that."

"You were still at the dacha?"

"No, we'd left the dacha by then and had returned to Zhukovka."

"Who was on the line?"

"Arkady Medvedev."

"Why was he calling?"

"There was a problem with final arrangements for the big dance."

"What sort of trouble?"

"Big trouble. Merchandise-gone-astray trouble."

Ivan had a tradition after big transactions. The blowout, he called it. A night on the town for the clients, all expenses paid, the bigger the deal, the bigger the party. Drinks in the hottest bars. Dinner in the trendiest restaurants. A nightcap with the most beautiful young girls Moscow had to offer. And a team of Ivan's bodyguards serving as chaperones to make sure there was no trouble. The blowout with the African delegation was a rampage. It began at six in the evening and went straight through till nine the next night, when they finally crawled back to their beds at the Ukraina Hotel and passed out.

"It's one of the reasons Ivan has so many repeat customers. He always treats them well. No delays, no missing stock, no rusty bullets. The dictators and the warlords hate rusty bullets. They say Ivan's stock is always top drawer, just like Ivan's parties."

The post-transaction blowouts served another purpose beyond building customer loyalty. They allowed Ivan and his security service to gather intelligence on clients at moments when their defenses were compromised by alcohol and other recreational pursuits. Given the size of the deal with the African delegation, Arkady Medvedev went along for the ride himself. Within five minutes of dumping the Africans at the Ukraina, he was on the phone to Ivan.

"Arkady is former KGB. Just like Ivan. He's normally a very cool customer. But not that night. He was agitated. It was obvious he'd picked up something he wasn't happy about. I should have hung up, but I couldn't bring myself to take the telephone from my ear. So I covered the mouthpiece with my hand and held my breath. I don't think I took a single breath for five minutes. I thought my heart was going to burst through my skin."

"Why didn't Ivan know you were on the line?"

"I suppose we picked up separate extensions at the same moment. It was luck. Stupid, dumb luck. If it hadn't happened, I wouldn't be here now. Neither would you."

"What did Arkady tell Ivan?"

"He told him that the Africans were planning to resell some of the supplies from the *big dance* at a substantial markup to a third party. And this *third party* wasn't the usual sort of African rebel rabble." She lowered her voice and furrowed her brow in an attempt to give a masculine cast to her face. " 'They are the worst of the worst, Ivan,' " she said, imitating Arkady's voice. " 'They are the sort who fly airplanes into buildings and blow up backpacks on European subways, Ivan. The ones who kill women and children, Ivan. The head choppers. The throat slitters.' "

"Al-Qaeda?"

"He never used that name but I knew who he was talking about. He said it was essential that they cancel that portion of the deal because the merchandise in question was too dangerous to be placed in the hands of just anyone. There could be blowback, he said. Blowback for Russia. Blowback for Ivan and his network."

"How did Ivan react?"

"My husband shared none of Arkady's alarm. Quite the opposite. The merchandise in question was the most lucrative part of the overall deal. Instead of taking that portion of the deal off the table, Ivan insisted that, in light of the new information, they had to renegotiate the entire package. If the Africans were planning to resell at a substantial markup, then Ivan wanted his cut. In addition, there was the potential for more money to be earned on shipping and handling. 'Why let the Africans deliver the weapons?' he asked. 'We can deliver them ourselves and make a few hundred thousand in the process.' It's how Ivan earns much of his money. He has his own cargo fleet. He can put weapons on the ground anywhere in the world. All he needs is an airstrip."

"Did Ivan ever suspect you'd eavesdropped on the call?"

"He never did or said anything to make

me think so."

"Was there another meeting with the Africans?"

"They came to our house in Zhukovka the next evening, after they'd had a chance to sober up. It wasn't as cordial as the first gathering. There was a great deal of shouting, mostly by Ivan. My husband doesn't like double dealings. It brings out the worst in him. He told the Africans he knew all about their plans. He told them that unless they agreed to give him his fair share of the deal, the merchandise was off the table. The baritone giant screamed back for a while but eventually buckled to Ivan's demands for more money. The next night, before they flew home, there was another blowout to celebrate the *new* deal. All sins had been forgiven."

"The merchandise in question — how did they refer to it?"

"They called them needles. In Russian, the word needle is *igla.* I believe the Western designation for this weapon system is SA-18. It's a shoulder-launch antiaircraft weapon. Though I'm not an expert in matters such as these, it is my understanding that the SA-18 is highly accurate and extremely effective."

"It's one of the most dangerous antiair-

398

craft weapons in the world. But are you sure, Elena? Are you *sure* they used the word *igla?*"

"Absolutely. I'm also certain that my husband didn't care whether hundreds, or perhaps even thousands, of innocent people might die because of these weapons. He was only concerned that he get his cut of the action. What was I supposed to do with knowledge such as this? How could I sit silently and do nothing?"

"So what did you do?"

"What *could* I do? Could I go to the police? We Russians don't go to the police. We Russians *avoid* the police. Go to the FSB? My husband *is* the FSB. His network operates under the protection and the blessing of the FSB. If I had gone to the FSB, Ivan would have heard about it five minutes later. And my children would have grown up without a mother."

Her words hung there for a moment, an unnecessary reminder of the consequences of the game they were playing.

"Since it was impossible for me to go to the Russian authorities, I had to find some other way of telling the world what my husband was planning to do. I needed someone I could trust. Someone who could expose his secrets without revealing the fact that I was the source of the information. I knew such a person; I'd studied languages with her at Leningrad State. After the fall of communism, she'd become a famous reporter in Moscow. I believe you're familiar with her work."

Though Gabriel had pledged fidelity to Elena, he had been less than forthright about one aspect of the debriefing: he was not the only one listening. Thanks to a pair of small, concealed microphones and a secure satellite link, their conversation was being beamed live to four points around the globe: King Saul Boulevard in Tel Aviv, the headquarters of both MI5 and MI6 in London, and the CIA's Global Ops Center in Langley, Virginia. Adrian Carter was in his usual seat, the one reserved for the director of the national clandestine service. Known for his tranquil, detached demeanor in times of crisis, Carter appeared somewhat bored by the transmission, as though he were listening to a dull program on the radio. That changed, however, when Elena uttered the word *igla*. As a Russian speaker, Carter did not need to wait for Elena's translation to understand the significance of the word. Nor did he bother to listen to the rest of her explanation before picking up the extension of a hotline that rang only on the desk of the director. "The arrows of Allah are real," Carter said. "Someone needs to tell the White House. *Now.*"

45
THE MASSIF DES
MAURES, FRANCE

They adjourned to the terrace. It was small, cluttered with potted herbs and flowers, and shaded by a pair of umbrella pine. An ancient olive grove spilled into a small gorge, and on the opposite hillside stood two tiny villas that looked as though they had been rendered by the hand of Cézanne. Somewhere in the distance, a child was crying hysterically for its mother. Elena did her best to ignore it while she told Gabriel the rest of the story. Her quiet lunch with Olga Sukhova. The nightmare of Aleksandr Lubin's murder in Courchevel. The near breakdown she had suffered after Boris Ostrovsky's death in St. Peter's Basilica.

"I shut myself off from the outside world. I stopped watching television. I stopped reading the newspaper. I was afraid — afraid that I would learn an airplane had been shot down, or another journalist had been murdered because of me. Eventually, as time went by, I was able to convince myself it had never actually happened. There *were* no missiles, I told myself. There was no delegation of warlords who had come to my home to buy weapons from my husband. There was no secret plan to divert a portion of the consignment to the terrorists of al-Qaeda. In fact, there were no terrorists at all. It had all been a bad dream. A misunderstanding of some sort. A hoax. Then I got a telephone call from my friend Alistair Leach about a painting by Mary Cassatt. And here I am."

On the other side of the ravine, the child was still wailing. "Won't *someone* help that poor thing?" She looked at Gabriel. "Do you have children, Mr. Allon?"

He hesitated, then answered truthfully. "I had a son," he said quietly. "A terrorist put a bomb in my car. He was angry at me because I killed his brother. It exploded while my wife and son were inside."

"And your wife?"

"She survived." He gazed silently across the gorge for a moment. "It might have been better if she hadn't. It took me a few seconds to get her out of the car. She was burned very badly in the fire."

"My God, I'm so sorry. I shouldn't —"

"It's all right, Elena. It was a long time ago."

"Did it happen in Israel?"

"No, not in Israel. It was in Vienna. Not far from the cathedral."

On the other side of the ravine, the child fell silent. Gabriel seemed not to notice, for all his considerable concentration was now focused on the task of opening a bottle of rosé. He filled a single glass and handed it to Elena.

"Drink some. It's important you have wine on your breath when you go home. Ivan will expect that."

She raised the glass to her lips and watched the pine trees moving in the faint breeze.

"How did this happen? How did we end up together in this place, you and I?"

"You were brought here by a telephone you shouldn't have answered. I was brought here by Boris Ostrovsky. I was the reason he went to Rome. He was trying to tell me about Ivan. He died in my arms before he could deliver his message. That's why I had to go to Moscow to meet with Olga."

"Were you with her when the assassins tried to kill her?"

He nodded his head.

"How were you able to escape that stairwell without being killed?"

"Perhaps another time, Elena. Drink some of your wine. You need to be a bit tipsy when you go home."

She obeyed, then asked, "So, in the words of Lenin, glorious agent of the Revolution and father of the Soviet Union, what is to be done? What are we going to do about the missiles my husband has placed in the hands of murderers?"

"You've given us a tremendous amount of information. If we're lucky — *very* lucky — we might be able to find them before the terrorists are able to carry out an attack. It will be difficult, but we'll try."

"Try? What do you mean? You *have* to stop them."

"It's not that easy, Elena. There's so much we don't know. Which country in Africa was your husband dealing with? Have the missiles been shipped? Have they already reached the hands of the terrorists? Is it already too late?"

His questions had been rhetorical but Elena reacted as though they had been directed toward her.

"I'm sorry," she said. "I feel like such a fool."

"Whatever for?"

"I thought that by simply telling you about

the deal, you would have enough information to find the weapons before they could be used. But what have I accomplished? Two people are dead. My friend is a prisoner in her Moscow apartment. And my husband's missiles are still out there somewhere."

"I didn't say it was impossible, Elena. Only that it was going to be difficult."

"What else do you need?"

"A paper trail would help."

"What does that mean?"

"End-user certificates. Invoices. Shipping records. Transit documents. Banking records. Wire transfers. Anything we can lay our hands on to track the sale or the flow of the merchandise."

She was silent for a moment. Her voice, when finally she spoke, was barely audible over the sound of the wind moving in the treetops.

"I think I know where that information might be," she said.

Gabriel looked at her. "Where, Elena?"

"In Moscow."

"Is it somewhere we can get to it?"

"Not you. I would have to do it for you. And I would have to do it alone."

"My husband is a devout Stalinist. It is not

something he generally acknowledges, even in Russia."

Elena drank a bit of the rosé, then held it up to the fading sunlight to examine the color.

"His love of Stalin has influenced his real estate purchases. Zhukovka, the area where we now live outside Moscow, was actually a restricted dacha village once, reserved for only the most senior Party officials and a few special scientists and musicians. Ivan's father was never senior enough in rank to earn a dacha in Zhukovka, and Ivan was always deeply resentful of this. After the fall of the Soviet Union, when it became possible for anyone with enough money to acquire property there, he bought a plot of land that had been owned by Stalin's daughter. He also bought a large apartment in the House on the Embankment. He uses it as a pied-à-terre and keeps a private office there. I also assume he uses it as a place to take his lovers. I've been only a few times. It's filled with ghosts, that building. The residents say that if you listen carefully at night, you can still hear the screaming."

She looked at Gabriel for a moment in silence.

"Do you know the building I'm talking about, Mr. Allon? The House on the Embankment?"

"The big building on Serafimovicha Street with the Mercedes-Benz star on top. It was built for the most senior members of the *nomenklatura* in the early thirties. During the Great Terror, Stalin turned it into a house of horror."

"You've obviously done your homework." She peered into the wineglass. "Stalin murdered nearly eight hundred residents of that building, including the man who lived in my husband's apartment. He was a senior official in the Foreign Ministry. Stalin's henchmen suspected him of being a spy for the Germans, and for that he was taken to the killing fields of Butovo and shot. No one really knows how many of Stalin's victims are buried out there. A few years ago, the government turned the property over to the Orthodox Church, and they've been carefully searching for the remains ever since. There is no sadder place in Russia than Butovo, Mr. Allon. Widows and orphans filing past the trenches, wondering where their husbands and fathers might lie. We mourn Stalin's victims in Butovo while men like my husband pay millions for their flats in the House on the Embankment. Only in Russia."

"Where's the flat?"

"On the ninth floor, overlooking the Kremlin. He and Arkady keep a guard on duty there twenty-four hours a day. The doors to Ivan's office have a wood veneer, but underneath they're bombproof steel. There's a keypad entrance with a biometric fingerprint scanner. Only three people have the code and fingerprint clearance: Ivan, Arkady, and me. Inside the office is a password-protected computer. There's also another vault, same keypad and biometric scanner, same password and procedure. All my husband's secrets are in that vault. They're stored on disks with KGB encryption software."

"Are you allowed to enter his office?"

"Under normal circumstances, only when I'm with Ivan. But, in an emergency, I can enter alone."

"What kind of an emergency?"

"The kind that could happen if Ivan ever fell out of favor with the men who sit across the river in the Kremlin. Under such a scenario, he always assumed that he and Arkady would be arrested together. It would then be up to me, he said, to make certain the files hidden in that vault never fell into the wrong hands."

"Are you supposed to remove them?"

She shook her head. "The interior of the

vault is lined with explosives. Ivan showed me where the detonator button was hidden and taught me how to arm and fire it. He assured me the explosives had been carefully calibrated: just enough to destroy the contents of the safe without causing any other damage."

"What's the password?"

"He uses the numeric version of Stalin's birthday: December 21, 1879. But the password alone is useless. You need my thumb as well. And don't think about trying to create something that will fool the scanner. The guard will never open the door to someone he doesn't recognize. I'm the only one who can get inside that apartment, and I'm the only one who can get inside the vault."

Gabriel stood and walked to the low stone parapet at the edge of the terrace. "There's no way for you to take those disks without Ivan's finding out. And if he does, he'll kill you — just the way he killed Aleksandr Lubin and Boris Ostrovsky."

"He won't be able to kill me if he can't find me. And he won't be able to find me if you and your friends do a good job of hiding me away." She paused for a moment to allow her words to have their full impact. "And the children, of course. You would have to think of some way to get my children away from Ivan."

Gabriel turned slowly around. "Do you understand what you're saying?"

"I believe that during the Cold War we referred to such operations as defections."

"Your life as you know it will be over, Elena. You'll lose the houses. You'll lose the money. You'll lose your Cassatts. No more winters in Courchevel. No more summers in Saint-Tropez. No more endless shopping excursions in Knightsbridge. You'll never be able to set foot in Russia again. And you'll spend the rest of your life hiding from Ivan. Think carefully, Elena. Are you really willing to give up everything in order to help us?" '

"What am I giving up, exactly? I'm married to a man who has sold a cache of missiles to al-Qaeda and has killed two journalists in order to keep it a secret. A man who holds me in such contempt that he thinks nothing of bringing his mistress into my home. My life is a lie. All I have are my children. I'll get you those disks and defect to the West. All you have to do is get my children away from Ivan. Just promise me that nothing will happen to them."

She reached out and took hold of his wrist. His skin was ablaze, as though he

411

were suffering from a fever.

"Surely a man who can forge a painting by Mary Cassatt, or arrange a meeting like this, can think of some way of getting my children away from their father."

"You were able to see through my forgery."

"That's because I'm good."

"You'll have to be more than good to fool Ivan. You'll have to be perfect. And if you're not, you could end up dead."

"I'm a Leningrad girl. I grew up in a Party family. I know how to beat them at their own game. I know the rules." She squeezed his wrist and looked directly into his eyes. "You just have to think of some way to get me back to Moscow that won't make Ivan suspicious."

"And then we have to get you out again. *And* get the children."

"That, too."

He added more wine to her glass and sat down next to her.

"I hear your mother hasn't been well."

"How did you hear that?"

"Because we've been listening to your telephone conversations. *All* of them."

"She had a dizzy spell last week. She's been begging me to come to see her."

"Perhaps you should. After all, it seems to me a woman in your position might actually want to spend some time with your mother, given everything your husband has put you through."

"Yes, I think I might."

"Can your mother be trusted?"

"She absolutely loathes Ivan. Nothing would make her happier than for me to leave him."

"She's in Moscow now?"

Elena nodded. "We brought her there after my father died. Ivan bought her a lovely apartment in a new building on the Kutuzovsky Prospekt, which she resents terribly."

Gabriel placed a hand thoughtfully against his chin and tilted his head slightly to one side.

"I'm going to need a letter. It will have to be in your own hand. It will also have to contain enough personal information about you and your family to let your mother know for certain that you wrote it."

"And then?"

"Mikhail is going to take you home to your husband. And you're going to do your best to forget this conversation ever happened."

At that same moment, in a darkened operations room at King Saul Boulevard in Tel Aviv, Ari Shamron removed a pair of headphones and cast a lethal glance at Uzi Navot.

"Tell me something, Uzi. When did I authorize a defection?"

"I'm not sure you ever did, boss."

"Send the lad a message. Tell him to be in Paris by tomorrow night. Tell him I'd like a word."

46
The Massif des Maures, France

"What did you think of him?"

The voice had spoken to her in Russian. Elena turned around quickly and saw Mikhail standing in the open French doors, hands in his pockets, sunglasses propped on his forehead.

"He's remarkable," she said. "Where did he go?"

Mikhail acted as though he had not heard the question.

"You can trust him, Elena. You can trust him with your life. And with the lives of your children." He held out his hand. "I need to show you a few things before we leave."

Elena followed him back into the villa. In her absence, the rustic wooden table had been laid with a lovers' banquet. Mikhail's voice, when he spoke, had a bedroom intimacy.

"We had lunch, Elena. It was waiting on

the table just like this when we arrived. Remember it, Elena. Remember exactly how it looked."

"When did we eat? Before or after?"

"Before," he said with a slight smile of admiration. "You were nervous at first. You weren't sure you wanted to go through with it. We relaxed. We ate some good food. We drank some good wine. The rosé did the trick." He lifted the bottle from the ice bucket. "It's from Bandol. Very cold. Just the way you like it." He poured a glass and held it out to her. "Drink a bit more, Elena. It's important you have wine on your breath when you go home."

She accepted the glass and raised it to her lips.

"There's something else you need to see," Mikhail said. "Come with me, please."

He led her into the larger of the villa's two bedrooms and instructed her to sit on the unmade bed. At his command, she took a mental photograph of the room's contents. The chipped dresser. The wicker rocking chair. The threadbare curtains over the single window. The pair of faded Monet prints tacked up on either side of the bathroom door.

"I was a perfect gentleman. I was every-thing you could have hoped for and more. I was unselfish. I saw to your every need. We made love twice. I wanted to make love a third time, but it was getting late and you were tired."

"I hope I didn't disappoint you."

"On the contrary."

He stepped into the bathroom and switched on the light, then motioned for her. There was scarcely enough room for the two of them. Their shoulders brushed as he spoke.

"You showered when we were done. That's why you don't smell like you've been making love. Please do it now, Elena. We need to get you home to your husband."

"Do what now?"

"Take a shower, of course."

"A real shower?"

"Yes."

"But we haven't *really* made love."

"Of course we have. Two times, in fact. I wanted to do it a third time, but it was getting late. Get in the shower, Elena. Wet your hair a little. Smudge your makeup. Scrub your face hard so you look like you've been kissed. And use soap. It's important you go home smelling of strange soap."

Mikhail opened the taps and slipped silently out of the room. Elena removed her clothing and stepped naked into the water.

47
SAINT-TROPEZ,
FRANCE

It was the part of the day that Jean-Luc liked best: the truce between lunch and dinner, when he treated himself to a pastis and calmly prepared the battle plan for the evening. Running his eye down the reservation sheet, he could see it was going to be an arduous night: an American rapper with an entourage of ten, a disgraced French politician and his new child bride, an oil sheikh from one of the emirates — Dubai or Abu Dhabi, Jean-Luc could never remember — and a shady Italian businessman who had gone to ground in Saint-Tropez because he was under indictment in Milan. For the moment, though, the dining room of Grand Joseph was a tranquil sea of linen, crystal, and silver, undisturbed, except for the pair of Spanish waifs drinking quietly at the far end of the bar. And the red Audi convertible parked directly outside the entrance, in violation of a long-standing city ordinance, not to mention countless edicts handed down by Joseph himself.

Jean-Luc drank from his glass of pastis and took a closer look at the two occupants of the car. The man behind the wheel was in his early thirties and was wearing an obligatory pair of Italian sunglasses. He was attractive in a vaguely Slavic way and appeared quite pleased with himself. Next to him was a woman, several years older but no less attractive. Her dark hair was done up in a haphazard bun. Her dress looked slept in. Lovers, concluded Jean-Luc. No doubt about it. What's more, he was certain he'd seen them in the restaurant quite recently. The names would come to him eventually. They always did. Jean-Luc had that kind of memory.

The couple talked for a moment longer before finally giving each other a kiss that put to rest any lingering doubt over how they had spent their afternoon. It was the final kiss, apparently, for a moment later the woman was standing alone on the sunlit cobbles of the square and the Audi was speeding off like a getaway car leaving the scene of a crime. The woman watched it disappear around the corner, then turned and headed toward Joseph's entrance. It was then Jean-Luc realized that she was none other than Elena Kharkov, wife of Ivan Kharkov, Russian oligarch and party boy. But where were her bodyguards? And why was her hair mussed and her dress wrinkled? And why in God's name was she kissing another man in a red Audi in the middle of the Place de l'Hôtel de Ville?

She entered a moment later, her hips swinging a little more jauntily than usual, her handbag dangling from her left shoulder. *"Bonsoir, Jean-Luc,"* she sang, as though there was nothing out of the ordinary, and Jean-Luc sang *"Bonsoir"* in return, as though he hadn't seen her giving mouth-to-mouth to blondie boy not thirty seconds earlier. She set the bag on the bar and yanked open the zipper, then withdrew her mobile and reluctantly dialed a number. After murmuring a few words in Russian, she closed the phone with an angry snap.

"Can I get you anything, Elena?" Jean-Luc asked.

"A bit of Sancerre would be nice. And a cigarette if you have one."

"I can do the Sancerre but not the cigarette. It's the new law. No more smoking in France."

"What's the world coming to, Jean-Luc?"

"Hard to say." He scrutinized her over his

pastis. "You all right, Elena?"

"Never better. But I could really use that wine."

Jean-Luc spilled a generous measure of Sancerre into a glass, twice the usual pour, and placed it on the bar in front of her. She was raising it to her lips when two black Mercedes sedans screeched to a stop in the square. She glanced over her shoulder, frowned, and dropped a twenty on the bar.

"Thanks anyway, Jean-Luc."

"It's on the house, Elena."

She rose to her feet and swung her bag over her shoulder, then blew him a kiss and headed defiantly toward the door, like a freedom fighter mounting a guillotine. As she stepped outside into the sunlight, the rear door of the first car was flung open by some immense force within and a thick arm pulled her roughly inside. The cars then lurched forward in unison and vanished in a black blur. Jean-Luc watched them go, then looked down at the bar and saw that Elena had neglected to take the money. He slipped it into his pocket and raised his glass in a silent toast to her bravery. *To the women,* he thought. *Russia's last hope.*

The prolonged and unexplained absence of the guest known as Michael Danilov had caused the most acute crisis the Château de la Messardière had seen all summer. Search parties had been sent forth, bushes had been rustled, authorities had been notified. Yet as he drove into the forecourt of the hotel that evening, it was clear by his expression he had no clue of the distress he had caused. He handed his keys to the valet and strode into the marble lobby, where his lover, the much-distressed Sarah Crawford, waited anxiously. Those who witnessed the blow would later attest to the purity of its sound. It was delivered by her right hand and connected squarely with his left cheek. Because it was rendered without warning or verbal preamble, it caught the recipient and witnesses by complete surprise — all but the two Russian security men, employees of one Ivan Kharkov, who were drinking vodka in the far corner of the lobby bar.

The blond man made no effort at apology or reconciliation. Instead, he climbed back into the red Audi and headed at great speed to his favorite outdoor bar in the Old Port, where he contemplated the tangled state of his affairs over several frigid bottles of Kronenbourg. He never saw the Russians coming; even if he had, he was by then in no condition to do much about it. Their assault, like Sarah's, commenced without warning or preamble, though the damage it inflicted was far more severe. When it was over, a waiter helped him to his feet and made an ice pack for his wounds. A gendarme strolled over to see what the fuss was about; he took a statement and wondered if the victim wanted to press charges. "What can you do to them?" the blond man responded. "They're Russians."

He spent another hour at the bar, drinking quite well on the house, then climbed back into the red Audi and returned to the hotel. Entering his room, he found his clothing flung across the floor and a lipstick epithet scrawled across the bathroom mirror. He remained at the hotel for one more day, licking his numerous wounds, then climbed into his car at midnight and sped off to a destination unknown. Management was quite pleased to see him leave.

PART THREE
THE DEFECTION

48
PARIS

The 7:28 p.m. TGV train from Marseilles eased into the Gare de Lyon ten minutes ahead of schedule. Gabriel did not find this surprising; unionized French drivers could always shave a bit of time off the journey when they wanted to get home early. Crossing the deserted arrivals hall with his overnight bag in hand, he gazed up at the soaring arched ceiling. Three years earlier, the historic Paris landmark had been severely damaged by a suicide bomber. It might have been reduced to rubble had Gabriel not managed to kill two other terrorists before they could detonate their explosives, an act of heroism that had briefly made him the most wanted man in all of France.

A dozen taxis were waiting in the circular drive outside the station; Gabriel walked to the Boulevard Diderot and hailed one there instead. The address he gave the driver was several blocks away from his true destination, which was a small apartment house on a quiet street near the Bois de Boulogne. Confident he had not been followed, he presented himself at the door and pressed the call button for Apartment 4B. The locks opened instantly; Gabriel mounted the stairs and climbed swiftly upward, his suede loafers silent upon the worn runner. Reaching the fourth-floor landing, he found the door of the apartment ajar and the unmistakable scent of Turkish tobacco on the air. He placed his fingertip against the door and gave it a gentle push, just enough to send it gliding inward on its oiled hinges.

It had been two years since he had set foot in the safe flat, yet nothing had changed: the same drab furniture, the same stained carpeting, the same blackout curtains over the windows. Adrian Carter and Uzi Navot were gazing at him curiously from their seats at the cheap dinette set, as though they had just shared a private joke they did not want him to overhear. A few seconds later, Ari Shamron came marching through the kitchen door, a cup and saucer balanced in his hand, his ugly spectacles propped on his bald head like goggles. He was wearing his usual uniform, khaki trousers and a white oxford cloth shirt with the sleeves rolled up to the elbow. Something about being back in the field always did wonders for Shamron's appearance — even if the "field" was a comfortable apartment in the sixteenth arrondissement of Paris — and he looked fitter than he had in some time.

He paused for a moment to glare at Gabriel, then continued into the sitting room, where a cigarette was smoldering in an ashtray on the coffee table. Gabriel arrived a few seconds sooner than Shamron and hastily stabbed it out.

"What do you think you're doing?" Shamron asked.

"You're not supposed to be smoking."

"How can I quit smoking when my most accomplished operative is planning to go to war with Russia?" He placed his cup and saucer on the coffee table and angrily prowled the room. "You were authorized to arrange a meeting with Elena Kharkov and, if possible, to debrief her on what she knew about her husband's illicit arms dealing. You performed that task admirably. Indeed, your operation was in keeping with the best traditions of your service. But in the end, you vastly overstepped your authority. You had no right to discuss a break-in operation in the heart of Moscow. Nor were you authorized to enter into an agreement to secure the defection of Elena Kharkov. In fact, you had no right to even *discuss* the subject of defection with her."

"What was I supposed to do, Ari? Tell her thanks but no thanks? Tell her we really weren't interested after all in getting our hands on her husband's most precious secrets?"

"No, Gabriel, but you could have at least *consulted* your superiors first."

"There wasn't time to consult my superiors. Ivan was tearing Saint-Tropez to pieces looking for her."

"And what do you think he's going to do if you take Elena and the children away from him? Raise the white flag of surrender and roll up his networks?" Shamron answered his own question with a slow shake of his bald head. "Ivan Kharkov is a powerful man with powerful friends. Even if you somehow manage to get Elena and those computer disks — and, in my humble opinion, that remains an open question — Ivan will retaliate and retaliate hard. Diplomats will be expelled en masse. Already testy political relations between Russia and the West will go into the deep freeze. And there could be financial repercussions as well — repercussions the West does not need in a time of global economic uncertainty."

"Diplomatic *sanctions?* When was the last time the great Ari Shamron ever let the threat of diplomatic sanctions deter him from doing what was right?"

"More times than you'll ever know. But I'm not concerned only with the diplomatic fallout. Ivan Kharkov has proven himself to be a man of violence and he'll lash back at us with violence if you steal his wife and children. He has access to the most dangerous weapons systems in the world, along with nuclear, biological, and chemical agents. It doesn't take a devious mind to concoct a scenario under which Ivan and his former KGB hoods could put those weapons in the hands of our enemies."

"They already are," Gabriel said. "We wouldn't be here otherwise."

"And if they sprinkle a few vials of polonium around Tel Aviv? And if a few thousand innocent people die as a result? What would you say then?"

"I would say that it's our job to make sure that never happens. And I would remind you of your own words: that our decisions should never be based on fear but what is in the long-term security interests of the State of Israel. Surely you're not suggesting that it isn't in our interests to take down Ivan Kharkov? He has more blood on his hands than Hezbollah, Hamas, and al-Qaeda combined. And he's been operating his little shop of horrors with the full blessing, cooperation, and protection of the Kremlin. I say we let the Russians impose their diplomatic sanctions. And then we hit back, hard enough so that it hurts."

Shamron stuck a cigarette into the corner of his mouth and ignited it with his old Zippo lighter. Gabriel glanced at Navot and Carter. Their eyes were averted, like accidental witnesses to a public marital spat.

"Is it your intention to personally reignite the Cold War?" Shamron blew a stream of smoke toward the ceiling. "Because that is exactly what you're asking for."

"The Russians have already done that. And if Ivan Kharkov wants to get in line with the rest of the psychotics who wish to do us harm, then let him."

"Ivan will come after more than just Israel. He'll come after *you* and everything you hold dear." For Adrian Carter's benefit, they had been speaking English. Now Shamron switched to Hebrew and lowered his voice a few decibels. "Is that really what you want at this stage of your life, my son? Another determined enemy who wishes you dead?"

"I can look after myself."

"And what about your new wife? Can you look after her, too? Every second of every day?" Shamron gazed theatrically around the room. "Isn't this where you brought Leah after the bombing of the Gare de Lyon?" Greeted by Gabriel's silence, Shamron pressed his case. "The Palestinians were able to get to your wife not once but twice, Gabriel — first in Vienna, then fifteen years later at the psychiatric hospital where you'd tucked her away in England. They were good, the Palestinians, but they're children compared to the Russians. I suggest you keep that in mind before you declare a shooting war against Ivan Kharkov."

Shamron placed the cigarette in the ashtray, confident he had prevailed, and picked up his cup and saucer. In his large, liver-spotted hands, they looked like pieces of a child's toy tea set.

"What about Eichmann?" Gabriel asked quietly. He had spoken in Hebrew, though at the mention of the murderer's name Adrian Carter's head perked up a bit, like a student roused from a slumber during a dull lecture.

"What *about* Eichmann?" Shamron asked stubbornly in return.

"Did you consider the diplomatic consequences before plucking him from that bus stop in Argentina?"

"Of course we did. In fact, we debated long and hard about whether or not to take him. We were afraid the world would condemn us as criminals and kidnappers. We were afraid there would be severe fallout that our young and vulnerable state wasn't prepared to withstand."

"But, in the end, you took that bastard down. You did it because it was the right thing to do, Ari. Because it was the *just* thing to do."

"We *did* it because we had no other choice, Gabriel. If we'd requested extradition, the Argentines would have refused and tipped off Eichmann. And then we would have lost him forever."

"Because the police and security services were protecting him?"

"Correct."

"Just like the FSB and the Kremlin are protecting Ivan."

"Ivan Kharkov isn't Adolf Eichmann. I shouldn't think I'd need to explain the difference to you. I lost most of my family to Eichmann and the Nazis. So did you. Your mother spent the war in Birkenau and she bore Birkenau's scars until the day she died. You bear them now."

"Tell that to the thousands who've died in

the wars that have been stoked by Ivan's guns."

"I'll let you in on a little secret, Gabriel. If Ivan were to stop selling the warlords guns today, someone else would do it for him tomorrow." Shamron lifted his hand toward Carter. "Who knows? Perhaps it will be your good friend Adrian. He and his government poured weapons into the Third World whenever it suited their needs. And we've been known to sell to some pretty atrocious customers ourselves."

"Congratulations, Ari."

"For what?"

"Achieving a new personal low," Gabriel said. "You have just compared our country to the worst man in the world in order to win an argument."

Gabriel could see that Shamron's resistance was beginning to weaken. He decided to press his advantage before the old warrior could reinforce his defenses.

"I'm doing this, Ari, but I can't do it without your support." He paused, then added, "Or your help."

"Who's stooping to personal lows now?"

"I learned from the master."

Shamron tamped out his cigarette and regarded Gabriel through the remnants of the smoke. "Have you given any thought to where you're going to put her?"

"I was thinking about letting her move into the apartment in Narkiss Street with Chiara and me, but we really don't have enough room for her *and* the children."

Shamron, by his dour expression, let it be known he didn't find the remark even faintly amusing. "Resettling Elena Kharkov in Israel is completely out of the question. When Russia finally permitted its Jews to immigrate to Israel, a large number of non-Jewish Russians slipped into the country with them, including several serious organized crime figures. You can be certain that any number of these fine fellow countrymen of yours would be more than willing to kill Elena on Ivan's behalf."

"I never contemplated keeping her in Israel, Ari. She would have to go to America."

"Drop her in Adrian's lap? Is that your solution? We're not talking about resettling some KGB colonel who's used to living on government wages. Elena Kharkov is an extremely wealthy woman. She's grown accustomed to a lifestyle few of us can even contemplate. She'll become a problem. Most defectors eventually do."

Shamron looked to Adrian Carter for affirmation, but Carter knew better than to inject himself into the middle of a family quarrel and maintained a mandarin silence. Shamron removed his glasses and absently polished them against his shirtfront.

"At the moment, the long-term emotional well-being of Elena and her children is the least of your problems. The first thing you have to do is devise some way of getting her back into Russia, *alone,* without Ivan becoming suspicious."

Gabriel dropped an envelope on the coffee table.

"What's that?" Shamron asked.

"Elena's ticket home to Moscow."

Shamron slipped on his spectacles and removed the letter from the envelope. He had no trouble reading it; Russian was one of his many languages. When he had finished, he inserted the letter back into the envelope, carefully, as though trying not to leave fingerprints.

"It's not a bad start, Gabriel, but what about the rest of it? How are you going to get her into that apartment without Ivan's private security service sounding the alarm? And how are you going to get her out of the country safely after she's stolen those disks? And how are you going to keep Ivan occupied while you kidnap his children?"

Gabriel smiled. "We're going to steal his

airplane."

Shamron dropped Elena's letter on the coffee table.

"Keep talking, my son."

It did not take long for Shamron to fall under Gabriel's spell. He sat motionless in his chair, his hooded eyes half closed, his thick arms folded across his chest. Adrian Carter sat next to him, his face still an inscrutable blank mask. Unable to protect himself from the encroachment of Shamron's smoke, he had decided to fill the room with some of his own and was now puffing rhythmically on a pipe that reeked of burning leaves and wet dog. Gabriel and Navot sat side by side on the couch like troubled youth. Navot was rubbing the raw spot on the bridge of his nose where Bella's spectacles pinched him.

At the conclusion of Gabriel's briefing, it was Carter who spoke first. He did so after banging his pipe on the edge of the ashtray, like a judge trying to bring an unruly court to order. "I've never regarded myself as having any particular insights into the French, but, based on our last meeting, I'm confident they'll play ball with you." He cast an apologetic glance at Shamron, who loathed the use of American sports metaphors when discussing sensitive operational details. "French law gives the security services wide latitude, especially when dealing with foreigners. And the French have never been adverse to bending those laws a little bit more when it suits their purposes."

"I don't like operating with the French services," Shamron said. "They annoy me."

"I volunteer to take the point on this one, Ari. Thanks to Gabriel, the French and I have something of a relationship."

Shamron's eyes moved to Gabriel. "I don't suppose I have to ask who's going to serve as Elena's chaperone."

"She won't do it unless I go with her."

"Why did I know that was going to be your answer?"

Carter was slowly reloading his pipe. "He can go in on his American passport. The Russians wouldn't dare to touch him."

"I suppose that depends on what sort of Russians you're talking about, Adrian. There are all different sorts. First you have your run-of-the-mill FSB thugs like the ones Gabriel encountered in Lubyanka. Then there are the private thugs who work for people like Ivan. I doubt very much that they'll be intimidated by a passport, even an American one."

Shamron's gaze moved from Carter to

Gabriel.

"Do I need to remind you, Gabriel, that your friend Sergei made it clear that they knew exactly who you were and what would happen if you ever set foot in Russia again?"

"I'm just going along for the ride. It's Elena's show. All she has to do is walk into the House on the Embankment, grab Ivan's files, and walk out again."

"What could possibly go wrong with a plan like that?" Shamron asked sardonically of no one in particular. "How many of your brave associates do you intend to take along with you on this venture?"

Gabriel recited a list of names. "We can send them in as El Al crew and cabin staff. Then we'll all fly out of Moscow together when it's over."

Adrian Carter was puffing on his freshly loaded pipe and nodding his head slowly. Shamron had settled once more into his Buddha-like pose and was staring at Navot, who was staring back at him in return.

"We'll need the approval of the prime minister," Shamron said.

"The prime minister will do whatever you tell him to do," said Gabriel. "He always does."

"And God help us all if we create another scandal for him." Shamron's gaze flickered from Navot to Gabriel and back again. "Would you boys like to handle this yourselves or would you like adult supervision? I've actually done this a time or two."

"We'd love your help," Navot said. "But are you sure Gilah won't mind?"

"Gilah?" Shamron shrugged his shoulders. "I think Gilah could use a few days to herself. You might find this hard to believe, but I'm not the easiest person to live with."

Gabriel and Navot immediately began to laugh. Adrian Carter bit hard on the stem of his pipe in a bid to stifle the impulse to join them, but after a few seconds he was doubled over as well. "Enjoy yourselves at my expense," Shamron murmured. "But one day you'll be old, too."

49
PARIS

The serious planning began the following morning when Adrian Carter returned to the gated government guesthouse off the Avenue Victor Hugo. As Carter anticipated, the negotiations went smoothly, and by that evening the DST, the French internal security service, had taken formal control of the Kharkov watch. Gabriel's troops, exhausted after nearly two weeks of constant duty, immediately departed for Paris — all but Dina Sarid, who remained at the villa in Gassin to serve as Gabriel's eyes and ears in the south.

It soon became clear to the DST, and to nearly everyone else in Saint-Tropez for that matter, that a pall had descended over the Villa Soleil. There were no more parties by the vast swimming pool, no more drunken day trips aboard *October,* and the name "Kharkov" did not grace the reservation sheets of Saint-Tropez's exclusive restaurants. Indeed, for the first three days of the French watch Ivan and Elena were not seen at all. Only the children, Anna and Nikolai, ventured beyond the villa's walls, once to attend a carnival on the outskirts of town and a second time to visit Pampelonne Beach, where they spent two miserable hours in the company of Sonia and their sunburned Russian bodyguards before demanding to be taken home again.

Because the DST was operating on home soil, they were highly attuned to the gossip swirling through the bars and cafés. According to one rumor, Ivan was planning to put the villa up for sale and then put to sea to heal his wounded pride. According to another, he was planning to subject Elena to a Russian divorce and leave her begging for kopeks in the Moscow Metro. There was a rumor he had beaten her black-and-blue. A rumor he'd drugged her and shipped her off to Siberia. There was even a rumor he had killed her with his bare hands and dumped her body high in the Maritime Alps. All such speculation was put to rest, however, when Elena was spotted strolling along the rue Gambetta at sunset, absent any signs of physical or emotional trauma. Ivan did not accompany her, though a large contingent of bodyguards did. One DST watcher described the security detail as "presidential" in size and intensity.

At the little apartment in the sixteenth arrondissement of Paris, the events in the south were taken as confirmation that the phase of the operation known as "the small lie to cover the big lie" had worked to perfection. Unbeknownst to the neighbors, the flat was by then a beehive of hushed activity. There were surveillance photos and watch reports taped to the walls, a large-scale map of Moscow with flags and stickpins and routes marked in red, and a grease board covered in Gabriel's stylish left-handed Hebrew script. Early in the preparation, Shamron seemed content to play the role of éminence grise. But as time drew short, and his patience thin, he began to assert himself in ways that might have bred resentment in men other than Gabriel and Uzi Navot. They were like sons to Shamron and were therefore accustomed to his bellicose outbursts. They listened when other officers might have covered their ears and took advice others might have discarded for no reason other than pride. But more than anything, thought Adrian Carter, they seemed to cherish the opportunity to be in the field one more time with the legend. So did Carter himself.

For the most part, they remained prisoners of the flat, but once each day Gabriel would take Shamron outside to walk the footpaths of the Bois de Boulogne. By then, the cruelest heat of the summer had passed, and those August afternoons in Paris were soft and fine. Gabriel pleaded with Shamron not to smoke, but to no avail. Nor could he convince him to relinquish, even for a few moments, his obsession with every detail of the operation. Alone in the park, he would say things to Gabriel he dared not say in front of Navot or the other members of the team. His nagging concerns. His unanswered questions and unresolved doubts. Even his fears. On their final outing together, Shamron was moody and distracted. In the Bagatelle Gardens, he spoke words Gabriel had never heard the night before an operation, words warning of the possibility of failure.

"You must prepare yourself for the prospect she won't come out of that building. Give her the allotted time, plus a five-minute grace period. But if she doesn't come out, it means she's been caught. And if she's caught, you can be sure Arkady Medvedev and his goons will start looking for accomplices. If, heaven forbid, she falls into their hands, there's nothing we can do

445

for her. Don't even think about going into that building after her. Your first responsibility is to yourself and your team."

Gabriel walked in silence, hands in the pockets of his jeans, eyes on the move. Shamron talked on, his voice like the beating of distant drums. "Ivan and his allies in the FSB let you walk out of Russia alive once, but you can be sure it won't happen again. Play by the Moscow Rules, and don't forget the Eleventh Commandment. Thou shalt not get caught, Gabriel, even if it means leaving Elena Kharkov behind. If she doesn't come out of that building in time, you have to leave. Do you understand me?"

"I understand."

Shamron stopped walking and seized Gabriel's face in both hands with unexpected force. "I destroyed your life once, Gabriel, and I won't allow it to happen again. If something goes wrong, get to the airport and get on that plane."

They walked back to the apartment in silence through the fading late-afternoon light. Gabriel glanced at his wristwatch. It was nearly five o'clock. The operation was about to commence. And not even Shamron could stop it now.

50
MOSCOW

It was a few minutes after seven in Moscow when the house telephone in Svetlana Federov's apartment on the Kutuzovsky Prospekt rattled softly. She was seated in her living room at the time, watching yet another televised speech by the Russian president, and was pleased by the interruption. She silenced him with the click of a button on her remote — *God, if it were only that easy* — and slowly lifted the receiver to her ear. The voice on the other end of the line was instantly familiar: Pavel, the loathsome evening concierge. It seemed she had a visitor. "A *gentleman* caller," added Pavel, his voice full of insinuation.

"Does he have a name?"

"Calls himself Feliks."

"Russian?"

"If he is, he hasn't lived here in a long time."

"What does he want?"

"Says he has a message. Says he's a friend of your daughter."

I don't have a daughter, she thought spitefully. *The woman I used to call my daughter has left me to die alone in Moscow while she cavorts around Europe with her oligarch husband.* She was being overly dramatic, of course, but at her age she was entitled.

"What's he look like?"

"A pile of old clothes. But he has flowers and chocolates. Godiva chocolates, Svetlana. Your favorite."

"He's not a mobster or a rapist, is he, Pavel?"

"I shouldn't think so."

"Send him up, then."

"He's on his way."

"*Wait,* Pavel."

"What's wrong?"

She looked down at her shabby old housecoat.

"Ask him to wait five minutes. Then send him up."

She hung up the phone. *Flowers and chocolates . . .* He might look like a pile of discarded laundry, but apparently he was still a gentleman.

She went into the kitchen and looked for something suitable to serve. There were no pastries or cakes in the pantry, only a tin of

English tea biscuits, a souvenir from her last dreadful trip to London to see Elena. She arranged a dozen biscuits neatly on a plate and laid the plate on the sitting-room table. In the bedroom, she quickly exchanged her housecoat for a summery frock. Standing before the mirror, she coaxed her brittle gray hair into appropriate condition and stared sadly at her face. There was nothing to be done about that. *Too many years,* she thought. *Too much heartache.*

She was leaving her room when she heard the ping of the bell. Opening the door, she was greeted by the sight of an odd-looking little man in his early sixties, with a head of wispy hair and the small, quick eyes of a terrier. His clothing, as advertised, was rumpled, but appeared to have been chosen with considerable care. There was something old-fashioned about him. Something by-gone. He looked as though he could have stepped from an old black-and-white movie, she thought, or from a St. Petersburg coffeehouse during the days of revolution. His manners were as dated as his appearance. His Russian, though fluent, sounded as if it had not been used in many years. He certainly wasn't a Muscovite; in fact, she doubted whether he was a Russian at all. If someone were to put her on the spot, she would have said he was a Jew. Not that she had anything against the Jews. It was possible she was a little Jewish herself.

"I do hope I'm not catching you at an inconvenient time," he said.

"I was just watching television. The president was making an important speech."

"Oh, really? What was he talking about?"

"I'm not sure. They're all the same."

The visitor handed her the flowers and the chocolates. "I took the liberty. I know how you adore truffles."

"How did you know that?"

"Elena told me, of course. Elena has told me a great deal about you."

"How do you know my daughter?"

"I'm a friend, Mrs. Federov. A trusted friend."

"She sent you here?"

"That's correct."

"For what reason?"

"To discuss something important with you." He lowered his voice. "Something concerning the well-being of Elena and the children."

"Are they in some sort of danger?"

"It would really be better if we spoke in private, Mrs. Federov. The matter is of the utmost sensitivity."

She regarded him suspiciously for a long

moment before finally stepping to one side. He moved past her without a sound, his footsteps silent on the tiled hall. *Like he was floating,* she thought with a shiver as she chained the door. *Like a ghost.*

51
GENEVA

It is said that travelers who approach
Geneva by train from Zurich are frequently
so overcome by its beauty that they hurl
their return tickets out the window and vow
never to leave again. Arriving by car from
Paris, and in the middle of a lifeless August
night, Gabriel felt no such compulsion.
He had always found Geneva to be a charming yet intensely boring city. Once a place
of Calvinistic fervor, finance was the city's
only religion now, and the bankers and
moneymen were its new priests and arch-
bishops.

His hotel, the Métropole, was near the
lake, just across the street from the Jardin
Anglais. The night manager, a diminutive
man of immaculate dress and expressionless
features, handed over an electronic key and
informed him that his wife had already
checked in and was upstairs awaiting his arrival. He found her seated in a wingback

chair in the window, with her long legs propped on the sill and her gaze focused on the Jet d'Eau, the towering water fountain in the center of the lake. Her El Al uniform, crisp and starched, hung from the rod in the closet. Candlelight reflected softly in the silver-domed warmers of a room service table set for two. Gabriel lifted a bottle of frigid Chasselas from the ice bucket and poured himself a glass.

"I expected you an hour ago."

"The traffic leaving Paris was miserable. What's for dinner?"

"Chicken Kiev," she said without a trace of irony in her voice. Her eyes were still trained on the fountain, which was now red from the colored spotlights. "The butter's probably congealed by now."

Gabriel placed his hand atop one of the warmers. "It's fine. Can I pour you some wine?"

"I shouldn't. I have a four o'clock call. I'm working the morning flight from Geneva to Ben-Gurion, then the afternoon flight from Ben-Gurion to Moscow." She looked at him for the first time. "You know, I think it's possible El Al flight attendants might actually get less sleep than Office agents."

"No one gets less sleep than an Office agent." He poured her a glass of the wine.

"Have a little. They say it's good for the heart."

She accepted the glass and raised it in Gabriel's direction. "Happy anniversary, darling. We were married five months ago today." She took a drink of the wine. "So much for our honeymoon in Italy."

"Five months isn't really an anniversary, Chiara."

"Of course it is, you dolt."

She looked out at the fountain again.

"Are you angry with me because I'm late for dinner, Chiara, or is something else bothering you?"

"I'm angry with you because I don't feel like going to Moscow tomorrow."

"Then don't go."

She shot an annoyed look at him, then turned her gaze toward the lake again.

"Ari gave you numerous opportunities to extricate yourself from this affair, but you chose to press on. Usually, it's the other way around. Usually, Shamron's the one doing the pushing and you're the one digging in your heels. Why now, Gabriel? After everything you've been through, after all the fighting and the killing, why would you prefer to do a job like this rather than hide out in a secluded villa in Umbria with me?"

"It's not fair to put it in those terms, Chiara."

"Of course it is. You told me it was going to be a simple job. You were going to meet with a Russian journalist in Rome, listen to what he had to say, and that was going to be the end of it."

"It would have been the end of it, if he hadn't been murdered."

"So you're doing this for Boris Ostrovsky? You're risking your life, and Elena's, because you feel guilty over his death?"

"I'm doing this because we need to find those missiles."

"You're *doing* this, Gabriel, because you want to destroy Ivan."

"Of course I want to destroy Ivan."

"Well, at least you're being honest. Just make sure you don't destroy yourself in the process. If you take his wife and children, he's going to pursue them to the ends of the earth. And us, too. If we're very lucky, this operation might be over in forty-eight hours. But your war with Ivan will just be getting started."

"We should eat, Chiara. After all, it's our anniversary."

She looked at her wristwatch. "It's too late to eat. That butter will go straight to my hips."

"I was planning a similar maneuver myself."

"Promises, promises." She drank some more of the wine. "Did you enjoy working with Sarah again?"

"You're not going to start that again, are you?"

"Let the record show, your honor, that the witness refused to answer the question."

"Yes, Chiara, I did enjoy working with Sarah again. She performed her job admirably and with great professionalism."

"And does she still adore you?"

"Sarah knows I'm unavailable. And the only person she adores more than me is you."

"So you admit it?"

"Admit what?"

"That she adores you."

"Oh, for God's sake. Yes, Sarah had feelings for me once, feelings that surfaced in the middle of a very dangerous operation. I don't happen to share those feelings because I'm quite madly in love with you. I proved that to you, I *hope,* by marrying you — in spectacular fashion, I might add. If memory serves, Sarah was in attendance."

"She was probably hoping you were going to leave me stranded at the chuppah."

"Chiara." He took her face in his hands

and kissed her mouth. Her lips were cool and tasted of the Chasselas. "This will all be over in forty-eight hours. Then we can go back to Italy, and no one, not even Ivan, will be able to find us there."

"No one but Shamron." She kissed him again. "I thought you were planning a maneuver that had something to do with my hips."

"You have a very long day tomorrow."

"Put the table outside in the hall, Gabriel. I can't make love in a room that smells like Chicken Kiev."

Afterward, she slept in his arms, her body restless, her mind troubled by dreams. Gabriel did not sleep; Gabriel never slept the night before an operation. At 3:59, he called the front desk to say a wake-up call would not be necessary, and gently woke Chiara with kisses on the back of her neck. She made love to him one final time, pleading with him throughout to send someone else to Moscow in his place. At five o'clock, she left the room in her crisp El Al uniform and headed downstairs to the lobby, where Rimona and Yaakov were waiting along with the rest of the crew. Gabriel watched from his window as they climbed into a shuttle bus for the ride to the airport and remained there long after they had gone. His gaze was focused on the storm clouds gathering over the distant mountain peaks. His thoughts, however, were elsewhere. He was thinking of an old woman in a Moscow apartment reaching for a telephone, with Eli Lavon, the man she knew only as Feliks, calmly reminding her of her lines.

52
VILLA SOLEIL, FRANCE

They had arrived at an uneasy truce. It had taken seventy-two hours. Seventy-two hours of screaming. Seventy-two hours of threats of malicious divorce. Seventy-two hours of on-and-off interrogation. Like all those who have been betrayed, he demanded to be told the details. She had resisted at first, but under Ivan's withering assault she had eventually surrendered. She paid the information out slowly, inch by inch. The drive into the hills. The lunch that had been waiting on the table. The wine. The little bedroom with its tacky Monet prints. Her baptismal shower. Ivan had demanded to know how many times they had made love. "Twice," she confessed. "He wanted to do it a third time but I told him I had to be going."

Mikhail's predictions had proven accurate; Ivan's rage, while immense, had subsided quickly once he realized he had brought the mess upon himself. He sent a team of bodyguards to Cannes to eject Yekatarina from her suite at the Carlton Hotel, then began to deluge Elena with apologies, promises, diamonds, and gold. Elena appeared to accept the acts of contrition and made several of her own. The matter was now closed, they declared jointly over dinner at Villa Romana. Life could resume as normal.

Many of Ivan's gestures were surely hollow. Many others were not. He spent less time talking on his mobile phone and more time with the children. He kept his Russian friends at bay and canceled a large birthday party he had been planning to throw for a business associate whom Elena did not like. He brought her coffee each morning and read the papers in bed instead of rushing into his office to work. And when her mother called that morning at seven o'clock, he did not grimace the way he usually did but handed Elena the phone with genuine concern on his face. The conversation that followed was brief. Elena hung up the phone and looked at Ivan in distress.

"What's wrong?" he asked.

"She's very sick again, darling. She needs me to come right away."

■ ■ ■ ■

In Moscow, Svetlana Federov gently returned the receiver to its cradle and looked at the man she knew as Feliks.

"She says she'll be here later this evening."

"And Ivan?"

"He wanted to come with her, but Elena convinced him to stay in France with the children. He was kind enough to let her borrow his airplane."

"Did she happen to say what time she was departing?"

"She's leaving Nice airport at eleven o'clock, provided there are no problems with the plane, of course."

He smiled and withdrew a small device from the breast pocket of his rumpled jacket. It had a tiny screen and lots of buttons, like a miniature typewriter. Svetlana Federov had seen such devices before. She did not know what they were called, only that they were usually carried by the sort of men she did not like. He typed something rapidly with his agile little thumbs and returned the device to his pocket. Then he looked at his watch.

"Knowing your son-in-law, he'll have you and your building under surveillance within the hour. Do you remember what you're supposed to say if anyone asks about me?"

"I'm to tell them that you were a con artist — a thief who had come to swindle an old woman out of her money."

"There really are a lot of unscrupulous characters in the world."

"Yes," she said. "One can never be too careful."

In the aftermath of the most recent terrorist attacks in London, many improvements in security and operational capabilities had been made to the American Embassy in Grosvenor Square, some the public could see, many others they could not. Among those that fell into the second category was a sparkling new operations center, located in a bunkerlike annex beneath the square itself. At precisely 6:04 a.m. London time, Eli Lavon's message was handed to Adrian Carter with funereal silence by a young CIA factotum. Carter, after reading it, handed it to Shamron, who in turn handed it to Graham Seymour. "Looks like we're on," said Seymour. "I suppose you'd better cue the Frogs."

Carter activated a secure line to Paris with the press of a button and brought the receiver to his ear. "*Bonjour,* gentlemen. The

462

ball is now heading toward your side of the court. Do try to enjoy yourselves."

This time there was no indecision in her grooming. Elena bathed hastily, expended little effort on her hair and makeup, and dressed in a rather simple but comfortable Chanel pantsuit. She put on more jewelry than she might otherwise have worn on such an occasion and slipped several more expensive pieces into her handbag. Finally, she placed two additional changes of clothing in an overnight bag and took several thousand dollars' worth of euros and rubles from the wall safe. She knew that Ivan would not find this suspicious; Ivan always encouraged her to carry a substantial amount of cash when traveling alone.

She took a final look around the room and started downstairs with as much detachment as she could summon. Sonia and the children had gathered to see her off; she held the children for longer than she should have and ordered them with mock sternness to behave for their father. Ivan was not a witness to their farewell; he was standing outside in the drive, scowling impatiently at his wristwatch. Elena kissed each child one final time, then climbed into the back of the Mercedes with Ivan. She glanced once over her shoulder as the car shot forward and saw the children weeping hysterically. Then the car passed through the security gate and they disappeared from sight.

Word of Ivan and Elena Kharkov's departure from Villa Soleil arrived at the operations room in London at 7:13 a.m. local time. Gabriel was informed of the development five minutes later. One hour after receiving the message, he informed the front desk that he was checking out of his room and that his stay, while far too brief, had been lovely. His rented Renault was waiting for him by the time he stepped outside. He climbed behind the wheel and headed for the airport.

53
NICE, FRANCE

Ivan was preoccupied during the drive, and
for that Elena was grateful. He passed the
journey alternately talking on his mobile or
staring silently out his window, his thick
fingers drumming on the center console.
Because they were moving against the
morning beach traffic, they proceeded
without delay: around the Golfe de Saint-
Tropez to Saint-Maxime, inland on the D25
to the *autoroute,* then eastward on the *autoroute* toward Nice. As they sped through
the northern fringes of Cannes, Elena found
herself thinking about Ivan and Yekatarina
making love in their suite at the Carlton.
Ivan must have been thinking the same
thing, because he took hold of her hand and
said he was sorry for everything that had
happened. Elena heard herself say she was
sorry, too. Then she looked out her window
at the hills rising toward the Alps and began
counting the minutes until she would be

free of him.

The exit for the Côte d'Azur International Airport appeared fifteen minutes later. By then, Ivan had received another phone call and was engaged in a heated conversation with an associate in London. He was still on the phone, five minutes later, as they walked into the air-conditioned office of Riviera Flight Services, the airport's fixed base operator. Standing behind the pristine white counter was a man in his mid-thirties with receding blond hair. He wore navy blue trousers and a white short-sleeved shirt with epaulets. Ivan kept him waiting another two minutes while he concluded the call to London. "Kharkov," he said finally. "Leaving for Moscow at eleven."

The young man hoisted a bureaucrat's troubled smile. "That's not going to be possible, Monsieur Kharkov. I'm afraid there's a rather serious problem with your aircraft."

Elena dug a fingernail into her palm and looked down at her shoes.

"What sort of problem?" asked Ivan.

"A paperwork problem," answered the young man. "Your crew has been unable to produce two very important documents: an RVSM authorization letter and a Stage Three certificate. The DGAC will not allow

466

your plane to depart without them."

The DGAC was the Direction Générale de l'Aviation Civile, the French equivalent of the Federal Aviation Administration.

"This is outrageous!" snapped Ivan. "I've taken off from this airport dozens of times in that same aircraft and I've *never* been required to produce those documents before."

"I understand your frustration, Monsieur Kharkov, but I'm afraid rules are rules. Unless your crew can produce an RVSM authorization and Stage Three certificate, your aircraft isn't going anywhere."

"Is there some sort of fine I can pay?"

"Perhaps eventually, but not now."

"I want to speak to your superior."

"I'm the most senior man on duty."

"Get someone from the DGAC on the phone."

"The DGAC has made its position clear on this matter. They will have nothing further to say until they see those documents."

"We have an emergency in Moscow. My wife's mother is very ill. She has to get there right away."

"Then I would suggest that your crew do their utmost to find those documents. In the meantime, your wife might consider flying commercial."

"Commercial?" Ivan brought his palm down on the counter. "My wife can't fly commercial. We have security issues to consider. It's simply not possible."

"Then I doubt very much that she'll be going to Moscow today, Monsieur."

Elena moved cautiously to the counter. "My mother is expecting me, Ivan. I can't disappoint her. I'll just fly commercial."

The clerk gestured toward his computer. "I can check departure times and seat availability, if you would like."

Ivan frowned, then nodded his head. The clerk sat down at the computer and punched a few keys. A moment later, he pulled his lips downward into a frown and shook his head slowly.

"I'm afraid there are no seats available on any direct flights between Nice and Moscow today. As you probably know, Monsieur Kharkov, we have many Russian visitors this time of year." He tapped a few more keys. "But there is one other option."

"What's that?"

"There's a Swiss International Air Lines flight departing in an hour for Geneva. Assuming it arrives on time, Madame Kharkov can then catch the two p.m. Swissair flight from Geneva to Moscow. It's scheduled to arrive at Sheremetyevo at eight o'clock this evening."

Ivan looked at Elena. "It's a very long travel day. Why don't you wait until I get the paperwork straightened out?"

"I've already told my mother I was coming tonight. I don't want to disappoint her, darling. You heard her voice."

Ivan looked at the clerk. "I need three first-class seats: one for my wife and two for her bodyguards."

A few more taps at the keyboard. Another slow shake of the head.

"There's only one first-class seat available on each flight and nothing in economy. But I can assure you Madame Kharkov will be perfectly safe. If you would prefer, I can arrange a VIP escort with airport security."

"Which terminal does Swissair depart from?"

"Terminal One." The clerk picked up the telephone. "I'll let them know you're on the way."

The young man behind the counter did not work for Riviera Flight Services but was in fact a junior case officer employed by the French internal security service. As for the telephone call he placed after Ivan and Elena's departure, it was not to the offices of Swissair but to his superior, who was sitting in the back of an ersatz service van just outside. Upon receiving the call, the officer in the van alerted regional headquarters in Nice, which, in turn, flashed word to the operations room in London. The news arrived on Gabriel's PDA while he was pretending to look at Rolex watches in an airport duty-free shop. He left the shop empty-handed and wandered slowly toward his gate.

Elena tried to leave him at the curb, but Ivan, in a sudden rush of gallantry, would hear none of it. He stood with her on the endless line at the ticket counter and argued with the poor agent over the details of her itinerary. He bought a small gift for her mother, and made Elena swear to call him the minute she landed in Moscow. And finally, as Elena was preparing to pass through security, he apologized once again for the damage he had done to their marriage. She kissed him one final time and, upon reaching the other side, turned to wave good-bye. Ivan was already walking away, bodyguards at his side, telephone pressed to his ear.

For the next half hour, she reveled in the mundane. She located her gate. She drank a café crème at a crowded bar. She bought a stack of newspapers and magazines. But mainly she just walked. For the first time in many years, Elena was *alone*. Not truly alone, she thought, for surely someone was watching her, but free of the cloying presence of Ivan's bodyguards, at least for a few hours. Soon she would be free of them forever. She just had to run one small errand in Moscow first. She couldn't help but smile at the irony of it. She had to go to Russia to set herself free. She did this not only for herself, she thought, but for her country. She was Russia's conscience. Russia's savior.

Nervous about missing her flight, she presented herself at the gate ten minutes earlier than necessary and waited patiently for the command to board. Her seatmate was a sunburned Swiss gnome, who passed the short flight frowning at numbers. Lunch was a wilted sandwich and a bottle of warm mineral water; Elena ate everything on her tray and thanked the bewildered air hostess profusely for her kind service.

It was nearly 1:30 by the time the plane touched down in Geneva. Stepping from the Jetway, she heard an announcement saying that Swissair Flight 1338 to Moscow was in final boarding. She arrived at her

next gate with five minutes to spare and accepted a glass of champagne from the chief
bursar as she settled into her first-class seat.
This time her seatmate was a man in his
mid-fifties with thick gray hair and the
tinted eyeglasses of someone who suffered
from light sensitivity. He was writing in a
leather portfolio as she sat down and seemed
to take no notice of her. As the plane was
climbing rapidly over the Alps, he tore a
single sheet of paper from the portfolio and
placed it on her lap. It was a tiny pen-and-
ink copy of *Two Children on a Beach* by
Mary Cassatt. Elena turned and looked at
him in disbelief.

"Good afternoon, Elena," said Gabriel.
"It's so good to see you again."

54
MOSCOW

Arkady Medvedev's was a uniquely Russian story. A former breaker of dissident heads from the Fifth Main Directorate of the KGB, he had been going to seed in the shattered remnants of his former service when, in 1994, he received a telephone call from an old underling named Ivan Kharkov. Ivan had a proposition: he wanted Medvedev to construct and oversee a private security service to protect his family and his burgeoning global financial empire. Medvedev accepted the offer without bothering to ask the salary. He knew enough about business in the newly capitalistic Russia to realize that a salary — at least the one listed on an employment contract — didn't much matter.

For fifteen years, Arkady Medvedev had served Ivan well, and Ivan had been more than generous in return. Arkady Medvedev's base earnings now stood at more than one million dollars a year, not bad for a former secret policeman who hadn't had two rubles to rub together after the fall of communism. But the money was only part of his compensation package. There was a generous expense account and clothing allowance. There was a Bentley automobile, apartments in London, the South of France, and the exclusive Sparrow Hills of Moscow. And then there were the women — women like Oxana, a twenty-three-year-old beauty from the provinces whom Medvedev had plucked from a sushi bar two weeks earlier. She had been living at his apartment ever since, in varying states of undress.

If there was one drawback to working for Ivan, it was his knack for telephoning at the absolutely worst moments. True to form, the call came just as Medvedev and Oxana were about to jointly scale a summit of pleasure. Medvedev reached for the phone, bathed in sweat, and brought the receiver reluctantly to his ear. The conversation that followed, though brief, thoroughly spoiled the mood. When the call was over, Oxana resumed where she had left off, but for Medvedev it was no good. She finally collapsed forward onto his chest and sunk her teeth into his ear in frustration.

"You're tired of me already?"

"Of course not."

"So what's the problem, Arkady?"

The *problem,* he thought, was Elena Kharkov. She was arriving in Moscow that evening for an emergency visit. Ivan was suspicious about her motives. Ivan wanted her under full-time watch. Ivan wanted no more stunts like the one in Saint-Tropez. And neither did Arkady Medvedev. He looked at Oxana and told her to get dressed. Five minutes later, as she was slipping out of his apartment, he snatched up the phone again and started moving his teams into place.

Elena ordered white wine; Gabriel, black coffee. They both decided to try the ravioli with wild mushroom reduction. Elena took a single bite and nibbled on her bread instead.

"You don't like the food?" Gabriel asked.

"It's not very good."

"It's actually much better than the usual fare. When was the last time you flew commercial?"

"It's been a while." She gazed out the window. "I suppose I'm a little like Russia itself. I went from having almost nothing to having almost everything. We Russians lurch from one extreme to the other. We never seem to get it just right."

She turned and looked at him.

"May I speak honestly without hurting your feelings?"

"If you must."

"You look quite ridiculous in that disguise. I like you much better with your short hair. And those glasses . . ." She shook her head. "They're atrocious. You shouldn't wear tinted lenses. They hide the color of your eyes."

"I'm afraid that's the point, Elena."

She brushed a strand of hair from her face and asked where she was to be hidden after the defection. Her tone was casual, as though she were making polite conversation with a complete stranger. Gabriel answered in the same manner.

"On Sunday night, instead of boarding your flight back to Geneva and Nice, you're going to board a plane to Tel Aviv. Your stay in Israel will be brief, a day or two at most."

"And then?"

"The Americans have assumed responsibility for your resettlement. It's a bigger country with far more places to hide than Israel. The man who is in charge of the case is a friend of mine. I'd trust him with my life, Elena, and I know he'll take very good care of you and the children. But I'm afraid it won't be anything like the lifestyle to which you've become accustomed."

"Thank God for that."

"You might think that now, but it's going to be a rude awakening. You should anticipate that Ivan will file for divorce in a Russian court. Because you won't be able to appear to contest the case, he'll be able to divorce you in absentia and leave you and the children penniless." He paused. "Unless we can lay our hands on a bit of his money in the next two days."

"I don't want any of Ivan's money. It's blood money."

"Then do it for your children, Elena."

She looked at the sketch he had given her — the two children on a beach. "I have access to joint accounts in London and Moscow," she said softly. "But if I make any large withdrawals, Ivan will know about it."

"He didn't salt away any funds in Switzerland for a rainy day?"

"There's a safe-deposit box in Zurich where he usually keeps a couple of million in cash. You would have to empty it out for me before Ivan has a chance to put a freeze on it."

"Do you know the number and password?"

She nodded her head.

"Give them to me, Elena — for the children."

She recited them slowly, then looked at him curiously.

"Don't you want to write them down?"

"It's not necessary."

"You have a spy's memory, just like Ivan."

She picked at her food without appetite.

"I must say, your performance today was quite extraordinary. You should have seen Ivan's face when he was informed his plane couldn't take off." She looked at him. "I assume you have the next act well choreographed, too?"

"We do, but all the choreography in the world isn't worth a damn if the performer can't pull it off." A pause. "Last chance to bow out, Elena. And no hard feelings if you do."

"I'm going to finish what I started," she said. "For Aleksandr Lubin. For Boris Ostrovsky. And for Olga."

Gabriel signaled the flight attendant and asked her to remove their food. Then he placed his briefcase on the tray table and opened the combination locks. He removed four items: a small plastic spray bottle, a device that looked like an ordinary MP3 player, a second rectangular device with a short USB connector cord, and a boarding pass for El Al Flight 1612, departing Moscow for Tel Aviv at 6:15 p.m. on Sunday.

"As you can probably tell by now, Elena, timing is everything. We've put together a schedule for your final hours in Moscow and it is important you adhere to it rigorously. Pay close attention to everything I tell you. We have a lot of ground to cover and very little time."

The flight touched down at Sheremetyevo punctually at 8:05 p.m. Elena left the plane first and walked a few paces ahead through the terminal, with her handbag over her left shoulder and her overnight bag rolling along the cracked floor at her side. Arriving at passport control, Gabriel joined a line for unwanted foreigners, and by the time he was finally admitted into the country Elena was gone. Outside the terminal, he joined another endless line, this one for a taxi. He eventually climbed into the back of a rattling Lada, driven by a juvenile in mirrored sunglasses. Uzi Navot climbed into the car behind him.

"Where are you going?" asked Gabriel's driver.

"Ritz-Carlton Hotel."

"Your first time in Moscow?"

"Yes."

"Some music?"

"No, I have a terrible headache."

"How about a girl instead?"

"The hotel would be just fine, thank you."

"Suit yourself."

"How old are you?"

"Fifteen."

"Are you sure you can drive?"

"No problem."

"Is this car actually going to make it to the Ritz?"

"No problem."

"It's getting dark out. Are you sure you need those sunglasses?"

"They make me look like I have money. Everyone with money in Moscow wears sunglasses at night."

"I'll try to remember that."

"It's true."

"Can this car go any faster? I'd like to get to the Ritz sometime tonight."

"No problem."

Word of Gabriel and Elena's arrival in Moscow reached the operations center in Grosvenor Square at 6:19 p.m. local time. Graham Seymour stood up from his chair and rubbed the kinks out of his lower back.

"Nothing more to be done from here tonight. What say we adjourn to the Grill

Room of the Dorchester for a celebratory supper? My service is buying."

"I don't believe in mid-operation celebrations," Shamron said. "Especially when I have three of my best operatives on the ground in Moscow and three more on the way."

Carter placed a hand on Shamron's shoulder. "Come on, Ari. There's nothing you can do now except sit there all night and worry yourself to death."

"Which is exactly what I intend to do."

Carter frowned and looked at Graham Seymour. "We can't leave him here alone. He's barely housebroken."

"How would you feel about Indian takeaway?"

"Tell them to take it easy on the spices. My stomach isn't what it used to be."

55
Moscow

With just one week remaining until election day, there was no escaping the face of the Russian president. It hung from every signpost and government building in the city center. It stared from the front pages of every Kremlin-friendly newspaper and flashed across the newscasts of the Kremlin-controlled television networks. It was carried aloft by roving bands of Unity Party Youth and floated godlike over the city on the side of a hot-air balloon. The president himself acted as though he were waging a real election campaign rather than a carefully scripted folly. He spent the morning campaigning in a Potemkin village in the countryside before returning to Moscow for a massive afternoon rally at Dinamo Stadium. It was, according to Radio Moscow, the largest political rally in modern Russian history.

The Kremlin had allowed two other candidates the privilege of contesting the election, but most Russians could not recall their names, and even the foreign press had long ago stopped covering them. The Coalition for a Free Russia, the only real organized opposition force in the country, had no candidate but plenty of courage. As the president was addressing the throng in Dinamo Stadium, they gathered in Arbat Square for a counterrally. By the time the police and their plainclothes helpers had finished with them, one hundred members of Free Russia were in custody and another hundred were in the hospital. Evidence of the bloody melee was still strewn about the square late that afternoon as Gabriel, dressed in a dark corduroy flat cap and Barbour raincoat, headed down the Boulevard Ring toward the river.

The Cathedral of Christ the Savior rose before him, its five golden onion domes dull against the heavy gray sky. The original cathedral had been dynamited by Kaganovich in 1931 on orders from Stalin, supposedly because it blocked the view from the windows of his Kremlin apartment. In its place the Bolsheviks had attempted to erect a massive government skyscraper called the Palace of Soviets, but the riverside soil proved unsuitable for such a building and the construction site flooded repeatedly. Eventually, Stalin and his engineers surrendered to the inevitable and turned the land into a public swimming pool — the world's largest, of course.

Rebuilt after the fall of communism at enormous public expense, the cathedral was now one of Moscow's most popular tourist attractions. Gabriel decided to skip it and made his way directly to the river instead. Three men were standing separately along the embankment, gazing across the water toward a vast apartment building with a Mercedes-Benz star revolving slowly atop the roof. Gabriel walked past them without a word. One by one, the men turned and followed after him.

Upon closer inspection, it was not a single building but three: a massive trapezium facing the riverfront, with two L-shaped appendages running several hundred yards inland. On the opposite side of Serafimovicha Street was a melancholy patch of brown grass and wilted trees known as Bolotnaya Square. Gabriel was seated on a nearby bench next to a fountain when Uzi Navot, Yaakov Rossman, and Eli Lavon came over the bridge. Navot sat next to him, while Lavon and Yaakov went to the edge of the fountain. Lavon was chattering away in Russian like a movie extra in a cocktail party scene. Yaakov was looking at the ground and smoking a cigarette.

"When did Yaakov take up smoking again?" asked Gabriel.

"Last night. He's nervous."

"He's spent his career operating in the West Bank and Gaza and he's nervous being in Moscow?"

"You're damn right he's nervous being in Moscow. And you would be, too, if you had any sense."

"How's our local station chief?"

"He looks a little better than Yaakov, but not much. Let's just say he'll be quite happy when we get on that plane tomorrow night and get out of town."

"How many cars was he able to come up with?"

"Four, just like you wanted — three old Ladas and a Volga."

"Please tell me they run, Uzi. The last thing we need is for the cars to break down tomorrow."

"Don't worry, Gabriel. They run just fine."

"Where did he get them?"

"The station picked up a small fleet of old Soviet cars and trucks for a song after the fall of communism and put them on ice. All the papers are in order."

"And the drivers?"

"Four field hands from Moscow Station. They all speak Russian."

"What time do we start leaving the hotel?"

"I go first at two-fifty. Eli goes five minutes after that. Then Yaakov five minutes later. You're the last to leave."

"It's not much time, Uzi."

"It's plenty of time. If we get here too early, we might attract unwanted attention. And that's the last thing we want."

Gabriel didn't argue. Instead, he peppered Navot with a series of questions about cell phone jammers, watch assignments, and, finally, the situation at the apartment house on the Kutuzovsky Prospekt where Elena was now staying with her mother. Navot's answer did not surprise him.

"Arkady Medvedev has placed the building under round-the-clock surveillance."

"How's he doing it?"

"Nothing too technical. Just a man in a car outside in the street."

"How often is he changing the watcher?"

"Every four hours."

"Does he change the car or just the man?"

"Just the man. The car stays in place."

Gabriel adjusted his tinted eyeglasses. His gray wig was making his scalp itch terribly.

Navot was rubbing a sore patch above his elbow. He always seemed to develop some small physical malady whenever he was anxious about an operation.

"We should assume that Arkady has instructed the watchers to follow Elena wherever she goes, including tomorrow afternoon when she leaves for the airport. If the watcher sees her making an unannounced detour to the House on the Embankment, he'll tell Arkady. And Arkady is bound to be suspicious. Do you see my point, Gabriel?"

"Yes, Uzi," Gabriel said pedantically. "I believe I do. We have to make sure the watcher doesn't follow her tomorrow or all our work could go up in flames in a Moscow minute."

"I suppose we could kill him."

"A minor traffic accident should suffice."

"Shall I tell the station chief that we need another Lada?"

"What kind of car are the watchers using?"

"An S-Class Mercedes."

"That's not really a fair fight, is it?"

"Not really."

"We'd better make it an official car, then. Something that can take a punch. Tell the station chief we want to borrow the ambassador's limo. Come to think of it, tell him we want the ambassador, too. He's really quite good, you know."

Elena Kharkov had left her mother's apartment just one time that day, a fact that Arkady Medvedev and his watchers found neither alarming nor even the slightest bit noteworthy. The outing had been brief: a quick drive to a glittering new gourmet market up the street, where, accompanied by two of her bodyguards, she had purchased the ingredients for a summer borscht. She had spent the remainder of the afternoon in the kitchen with her mother, playfully bickering over recipes, the way they always had done when Elena was young.

By evening, the soup had chilled sufficiently to eat. Mother and daughter sat together at the dining-room table, a candle and a loaf of black bread between them, images of the president's rally in Dinamo Stadium playing silently on the television in the next room. It had been nearly twenty-four hours since Elena's arrival in Moscow, yet her mother had assiduously avoided any discussion of the reason behind the unorthodox visit. She broached the topic now for the first time, not with words but by gently laying Elena's letter upon the table.

Elena looked at it a moment, then resumed eating.

"You're in trouble, my love."

"No, Mama."

"Who was the man you sent to deliver this letter?"

"He's a friend. Someone who's helping me."

"Helping you with what?"

Elena was silent.

"You're leaving your husband?"

"Yes, Mama, I'm leaving my husband."

"Has he hurt you?"

"Badly."

"Did he hit you?"

"No, never."

"Is there another woman?"

Elena nodded, eyes on her food. "She's just a child of nineteen. I'm sure Ivan will hurt her one day, too."

"You should have never married him. I begged you not to marry him, but you wouldn't listen to me."

"I know."

"He's a monster. His father was a monster and he's a monster."

"I know." Elena tried to eat some of the soup but had lost her appetite. "I'm sorry the children and I haven't been spending more time with you the last few years. Ivan wouldn't let us. It's no excuse. I should have stood up to him."

"You don't have to apologize, Elena. I know more than you think I know."

A tear spilled onto Elena's cheek. She brushed it away before her mother could see it. "I'm very sorry for the way I've behaved toward you. I hope you can forgive me."

"I forgive you, Elena. But I don't understand why you came to Moscow like this."

"I have to take care of some business before I leave Ivan. I have to protect myself and the children."

"You're not thinking about taking his money?"

"This has nothing to do with money."

Her mother didn't press the issue. She was a Party wife. She knew about secrets and walls.

"When are you planning to tell him?"

"Tomorrow night." Elena paused, then added pointedly: "When I return to France."

"Your husband isn't the sort of man who takes bad news well."

"No one knows that better than I do."

"Where are you planning to go?"

"I haven't decided yet."

"Will you stay in Europe or will you come

home to Russia?"

"It might not be safe for me in Russia anymore."

"What are you talking about?"

"I might have to take the children someplace where Ivan can't find them. Do you understand what I'm saying to you?"

The Party wife understood perfectly. "Am I ever going to see them again, Elena? Am I ever going to see my grandchildren again?"

"It might take some time. But, yes, you'll be able to see them again."

"Time? How much time? Look at me, Elena. Time is not something I have in abundance."

"I've left some money in the bottom drawer of your dresser. It's all the money I have in the world right now."

"Then I can't take it."

"Trust me, Mama. You have to take that money."

Her mother looked down and tried to eat, but now she, too, had lost her appetite. And so they sat there for a long time, clutching each other's hands across the table, faces wet with tears. Finally, her mother picked up the letter and touched it to the flame. Elena gazed at the television and saw Russia's new tsar accepting the adulation of the masses. *We cannot live as normal people,* she thought. *And we never will.*

Against all his considered judgment and in violation of all operational doctrine, written and unwritten, Gabriel did not immediately return to his room at the Ritz-Carlton Hotel. Instead, he wandered farther south, to the colony of apartment houses looming over October Square, and made his way to the building known to the locals as the House of Dogs. It had no view of the Moscow River or the Kremlin — only of its identical neighbor, and of a parking lot filled with shabby little cars, and of the Garden Ring, a euphemism if there ever was one, which thundered night and day on its northern flank. A biting wind was blowing out of the north, a reminder that the Russian "summer" had come and gone and that soon it would be winter again. The poet in him thought it appropriate. Perhaps there never had been a summer at all, he thought. Perhaps it had been an illusion, like the dream of Russian democracy.

In the small courtyard outside Entrance C, it appeared that the babushkas and the skateboard punks had declared a cessation of hostilities. Six skinny Militia boys were milling about in the doorway itself, watched over by two plainclothes FSB toughs in leather jackets. The Western reporters who had gathered at the building after the attempt on Olga Sukhova's life had given up their vigil or, more likely, had been chased away. Indeed, there was no evidence of support for Olga's cause, other than two desperate words, written in red spray paint, on the side of the building: FREE OLGA! A local wit had crossed out the word FREE and replaced it with FUCK. And who said the Russians didn't have a sense of humor?

Gabriel walked around the enormous building and, as expected, found security men standing watch at the other five entrances as well. Hiking north along the Leninsky Prospekt, he ran through the operation one final time. It was perfect, he thought. With one glaring exception. When Ivan Kharkov discovered his family and his secret papers had been stolen, he was going to take it out on someone. And that someone was likely to be Olga Sukhova.

56
SAINT-TROPEZ •
MOSCOW

The undoing of Ivan Borisovich Kharkov, real estate developer, venture capitalist, and international arms trafficker, began with a phone call. It was placed to his Saint-Tropez residence by one François Boisson, regional director of the Direction Générale de l'Aviation Civile, the French aviation authority. It appeared, said Monsieur Boisson, that there was a rather serious problem regarding recent flights by Monsieur Kharkov's airplane — problems, the director said ominously, that could not be discussed over the telephone. He then instructed Monsieur Kharkov to appear at Nice airport at one that afternoon to answer a few simple questions. If Monsieur Kharkov chose not to appear, his plane would be confiscated and held for a period of at least ninety days. After an anti-French tirade lasting precisely one minute and thirty-seven seconds, Ivan promised to come at the appointed hour.

Monsieur Boisson said he looked forward to the meeting and rang off.

Elena Kharkov learned of her husband's predicament when she telephoned Villa Soleil to wish Ivan and the children a pleasant morning. Confronted with Ivan's rage, she made a few soothing comments and assured him it had to be a misunderstanding of some sort. She then had a brief conversation with Sonia, during which she instructed the nanny to take the children to the beach. When Sonia asked whether Elena needed to speak to Ivan again, Elena hesitated, then said that, yes, she did need to speak to him. When Ivan came back on the line, she told him that she loved him very much and was looking forward to seeing him that night. But Ivan was still carrying on about his airplane and the incompetence of the French. Elena murmured, "*Dos vidanya,* Ivan," and severed the connection.

Gabriel was a man of unnatural patience, but now, during the final tedious hours before their assault on Ivan's vault of secrets, his patience abandoned him. It was fear, he thought. The kind of fear only Moscow can produce. The fear that someone was always watching. Always listening. The fear that he might find himself in Lubyanka once again and that this time he might not come out alive. The fear that others might join him there and suffer the same fate.

He attempted to suppress his fear with activity. He walked streets he loathed, ordered an elaborate lunch he barely touched, and, in the glittering GUM shopping mall near Red Square, purchased souvenirs he would leave behind. He performed these tasks alone; apparently, the FSB had no interest in Martin Stonehill, naturalized American citizen of Hamburg, Germany.

Finally, at 2:30 p.m., he returned to his room at the Ritz-Carlton and dressed for combat. His only weapons were a miniature radio and a PDA. At precisely 3:03 p.m., he boarded an elevator and rode down to the lobby. He paused briefly at the concierge's desk to collect a handful of brochures and maps, then came whirling out the revolving door into Tverskaya Street. After walking a half block, he stopped and thrust his hand toward the street, as if hailing a taxi. A silver Volga sedan immediately pulled to the curb. Gabriel climbed inside and closed the door.

"Shalom," said the man behind the wheel.

"Let's hope so."

Gabriel looked at his watch as the car shot

forward: *3:06 . . .*

Time for one last good-bye, Elena. Time to get in the car.

Elena Kharkov slipped quietly into the guest bedroom and began to pack. The mere act of folding her clothing and placing it into her bag did much to calm her raw nerves and so she performed this chore with far more care than was warranted. At 3:20, she dialed the number of Sonia's mobile phone. Receiving no answer, she was nearly overcome by a wave of panic. She dialed the number a second time — slowly, deliberately — and this time Sonia answered after three rings. In the most placid voice Elena could summon, she informed Sonia the children had had enough sun and that it was time to leave the beach. Sonia offered mild protest — the children, she said, were the happiest they had been in many days — but Elena insisted. When the call was over, she switched on the device that looked like an ordinary MP3 player and placed it in the outer compartment of her overnight bag. Then she dialed Sonia's number again. This time, the call wouldn't go through.

She finished packing and slipped into her mother's bedroom. The money was where she had left it, in the bottom of the dresser, concealed beneath a heavy woolen sweater. She closed the drawer silently and went into the sitting room. Her mother looked at Elena and attempted to smile. They had nothing more to say — they had said it all last night — and no more tears to cry.

"You'll have some tea before you leave?"

"No, Mama. There isn't time."

"Go, then," she said. "And may the angel of the Lord be looking over your shoulder."

A bodyguard, a former Alpha Group operative named Luka Osipov, was waiting for Elena outside in the corridor. He carried her suitcase downstairs and placed it in the trunk of a waiting limousine. As the car pulled away from the curb, Elena announced calmly that she needed to make a brief stop at the House on the Embankment to collect some papers from her husband's office. "I'll just be a moment or two," she said. "We'll still have plenty of time to get to Sheremetyevo in time for my flight."

As Elena Kharkov's limousine sped along the Kutuzovsky Prospekt, a second car was following carefully after it. Behind the wheel was a man named Anton Ulyanov. A former government surveillance specialist, he now worked for Arkady Medvedev, chief of Ivan Kharkov's private security service. Ulyanov had performed countless jobs for Medvedev, most of questionable ethics, but never had he been ordered to watch the wife of the man who paid his salary. He did not know why he had been given this assignment, only that it was important. *Follow her all the way to the airport,* Medvedev had told him. *And don't lose sight of her. If you do, you'll wish you'd never been born.*

Ulyanov settled fifty yards behind the limousine and switched on some music. Nothing to do now but make himself comfortable and take a nice, boring drive to Sheremetyevo. Those were the kind of jobs he liked best: the boring jobs. Leave the excitement to the heroes, he was fond of saying. One tended to live longer that way.

As it turned out, the journey would be neither long nor boring. Indeed, it would end at the Ukraina Hotel. The offending car came from Ulyanov's right, though later he would be forced to admit he never saw it. He was able to recall the moment of impact, though: a violent collision of buckling steel and shattering glass that sent his air bag exploding into his face. How long he was unconscious was never clear to him. He reckoned it was only a few seconds, because his first memory of the aftermath was the vision of a well-dressed man yelling through a blown-out window in a language he did not understand.

Anton Ulyanov did not try to communicate with the man. Instead, he began a desperate search for his mobile phone. He found it a moment later, wedged between the passenger seat and the crumpled door. The first call he made was to the Sparrow Hills apartment of Arkady Medvedev.

Upon his arrival at Côte d'Azur International Airport, Ivan Kharkov was escorted into a windowless conference room with a rectangular table and photographs of French-built aircraft on the wall. The man who had summoned him, François Boisson, was nowhere to be seen; indeed, a full thirty minutes would elapse before Boisson finally appeared. A slender man in his fifties with small eyeglasses and a bald head, he carried himself, like all French bureaucrats, with an air of condescending authority. Offering neither explanation nor apology for his tardiness, he placed a thick file at the head of the conference table and settled himself behind it. He sat there for an uncomfortably long period, fingertips pressed thoughtfully together, before finally bringing the proceedings to order.

"Two days ago, after your aircraft was refused permission to take off from this airport, we began a careful review of your flight records and passenger manifests. Unfortunately, in the process we have discovered some serious discrepancies."

"What sort of discrepancies?"

"It is our conclusion, Monsieur Kharkov, that you have been operating your aircraft as an illegal charter service. Unless you can prove to us that is not the case — and, I must stress, in France the burden of proof in such matters is entirely on *you* — then I'm afraid your aircraft will be confiscated immediately."

"Your accusation is complete nonsense," Ivan countered.

Boisson sighed and slowly lifted the cover of his impressive file. The first item he produced was a photograph of a Boeing Business Jet. "For the record, Monsieur Kharkov, is this your aircraft?" He pointed to the registration number on the aircraft's tail. "N7287IK?"

"Of course it's my plane."

Boisson touched the first character of the tail number: the *N*. "Your aircraft carries American registry," he pointed out. "When was the last time it was in the United States?"

"I couldn't say for certain. Three years at least."

"Do you not find that odd, Monsieur Kharkov?"

"No, I do not find it the least bit odd. As you well know, Monsieur Boisson, aircraft owners carry American registry because American registry ensures a high resale value."

"But according to your own records, Monsieur, you are *not* the owner of N7287IK."

"What are you talking about?"

"Your own aircraft registration lists the owner of N7287IK as a Delaware-based firm called, oddly enough, N7287 LLC. Obviously, N7287 LLC is a corporate shell maintained for no other reason than to give your plane the illusion of American ownership. Technically, you have no relationship with this company. The president of N7287 LLC is a man named Charles Hamilton. Monsieur Hamilton is an attorney in Wilmington, Delaware. He is also the owner by proxy of the aircraft you claim is yours. Monsieur Hamilton actually leases the plane to you. Isn't that correct, Monsieur Kharkov?"

"Technically," snapped Ivan, "that *is* correct, but these sorts of arrangements are

common in private aviation."

"Common, perhaps, but not entirely honest. Before we continue with this inquiry, I must insist you prove that you are the actual owner of the Boeing Business Jet with the tail number N7287IK. Perhaps the easiest way for you to do that would be to telephone your attorney and put him on the phone with me?"

"But it's Sunday morning in America."

"Then I suspect he'll be at home."

Ivan swore in Russian and picked up his mobile phone. The call failed to go through. After two more futile attempts, he looked at Boisson in frustration.

"I sometimes have trouble in this part of the building myself," the Frenchman said apologetically. He pointed toward the telephone at the opposite end of the conference table. "Feel free to use ours. I'm sure it's working just fine."

Arkady Medvedev received the call from an obviously dazed Anton Ulyanov while he was relaxing in the study of his apartment in the Sparrow Hills. After hanging up, he immediately dialed the number for Elena's driver and received no answer. After a second unsuccessful attempt, he twice tried to reach Luka Osipov, the head of Elena's small security detail, but with the same result. He slammed down the receiver in frustration and stared glumly out the window toward central Moscow. *A summons to appear at Nice airport . . . a crash on the Kutuzovsky Prospekt . . . and now Elena's bodyguards weren't answering their phones . . .* It wasn't a coincidence. Something was going on. But for the moment, there wasn't a damn thing he could do about it.

The departure of the Kharkov children from Pampelonne Beach did not go according to schedule, which surely would come as no surprise to any parent of small children. First there were the demands for a final swim. Then there was the struggle to get two sand-covered seven-year-olds into dry clothing suitable for the journey home. And finally there were the obligatory histrionics during the long walk to the cars. For Sonia Cherkasov, the Kharkov's long-suffering nanny, the task was not made any easier by the fact that she was accompanied by four armed bodyguards. Experience had taught her that, at times like these, the bodyguards were usually more trouble than the children themselves.

As a result of the delays, it was 1:45 p.m.

before the Kharkov party had boarded their cars. They followed their usual course: inland on the Route des Tamaris, then south along the D93 toward the Baie de Cavalaire. As they emerged from the traffic circle east of Ramatuelle, a gendarme stepped suddenly into the roadway ahead of them and raised a white-gloved hand. The driver of the lead car briefly considered ignoring the command, but when the gendarme gave two fierce blasts on his whistle, the driver thought better of it and pulled onto the shoulder, followed by the second car.

The gendarme, a veteran of the Saint-Tropez post, knew it was pointless to address the Russian in French. In heavily accented English, he informed the driver that he had been traveling well in excess of the posted speed limit. The driver's response — that everyone speeds in the South of France in summer — did not sit well with the gendarme, who immediately demanded to see the driver's operating permit, along with the passports of every occupant of the two vehicles.

"We didn't bring the passports."

"Why not?"

"Because we were at the beach."

"As visitors to France, you are required to carry your passports with you at all times."

"Why don't you follow us home? We can show you our passports and be done with this nonsense."

The gendarme peered into the backseat.

"Are these your children, Monsieur?"

"No, they are the children of Ivan Kharkov."

The gendarme made a face to indicate the name was not familiar to him.

"And who are you?"

"I work for Mr. Kharkov. So do my colleagues in the second car."

"In what capacity?"

"Security."

"Am I to assume that you are carrying weapons?"

The Russian driver nodded his head.

"May I see your permits, please?"

"We don't have the permits with us. They're with the passports at Mr. Kharkov's villa."

"And where is this villa?"

The gendarme, upon hearing the answer, walked back to his car and lifted his radio to his lips. A second vehicle, a Renault minivan, had already arrived on the scene and shortly thereafter was joined by what appeared to be most of the Saint-Tropez force. The Russian driver, watching this scene in his rearview mirror, sensed the situation was deteriorating rapidly. He drew a mobile phone from his pocket and tried to call the chief of Ivan's detail, but the call failed to go through. After three more attempts, he gave up in frustration and looked out the window. The gendarme was now standing there, with the flap of his holster undone and his hand wrapped around the grip of his sidearm.

"Where is your weapon, Monsieur?"

The driver reached down and silently patted his hip.

"Please remove it and place it carefully on the dash of the car." He looked at the bodyguard in the passenger seat. "You, too, Monsieur. Gun on the dash. Then I'd like you both to step out of the car very slowly and place your hands on the roof."

"What is this all about?"

"I'm afraid we have no choice but to detain you until we can sort out the matter of your passports and weapons permits. The children and their nanny can travel together in one car. You and your three colleagues will be driven separately. We can do this in a civilized manner or, if you prefer, we can do it in handcuffs. The choice is yours, Messieurs."

57
MOSCOW

On the western side of the House on the Embankment was a small park with a pretty red church in the center. It was not popular under normal circumstances, and now, with the clouds low and heavy with rain, it was largely deserted. A few yards from the church was a coppice of trees, and amid the trees was a bench with much Russian obscenity carved into its wood. Gabriel sat at one end; Shmuel Peled, embassy driver and clandestine officer of Israeli intelligence, sat at the other. Shmuel was chattering away in fluent Russian. Gabriel was not listening. He was focused instead on the voices emanating from his miniature earpiece. The voice of Yaakov Rossman, who reported that Elena Kharkov's car was now free of opposition surveillance. The voice of Eli Lavon, who reported that Elena Kharkov's car was now approaching the House on the Embankment at high speed. The voice of

Uzi Navot, who reported that Elena Kharkov was now leaving her car and proceeding into the building with Luka Osipov at her shoulder. Gabriel marked the time on his wristwatch: *3:54* . . . They were already nine minutes behind schedule.

Better hurry, Elena. We all have a plane to catch.

Word of Elena Kharkov's arrival reached London ten seconds later, not by voice but by a terse message that flashed across the billboard-sized video screen at the front of the room. Adrian Carter had been anxiously awaiting the alert and had the handset of a dedicated line to Langley pressed tightly to his ear. "She's heading into the building," he said calmly. "Take down the phones. Everything from the Moscow River south to the Garden Ring."

She crossed the lobby with Luka Osipov at her heels and entered a small foyer with a single elevator. He attempted to follow her into the waiting car but she froze him with a wave of her hand. "Wait here," she ordered, inserting a security keycard into the slot. She removed the card and pressed the button for the ninth floor. Luka Osipov stood motionless for several seconds, watching the elevator's ascent play out on the red lights of the control panel. Then he opened his mobile and tried to call the driver outside. Hearing nothing, he snapped the phone shut and swore softly. *The whole Moscow network must have crashed,* he thought. *We Russians can't do anything right.*

When the doors opened on the ninth floor, another bodyguard was waiting in the vestibule. His name was Pyotr Luzhkov and, like Luka Osipov, he was a former member of the elite Alpha Group. The expression on his pasty, dull face was one of surprise. Because of the cell phone jammer concealed in Elena's luggage, her security detail had been unable to alert him that she would be stopping by. Elena greeted him absently, then pushed past him into the entrance hall without offering any explanation for her presence. When the security man reflexively placed his hand on her arm, Elena whirled around, eyes wide with anger.

"What are you doing? How dare you touch me! Who do you think you are?"

Luzhkov removed his hand. "I'm sorry."

"You're sorry *what?*"

"I'm sorry, Mrs. Kharkov. I shouldn't have placed my hand on you."

"No, Pyotr, you should not have placed

your hand on me. Wait until Ivan finds out about this!"

She set out down the hallway toward the office. The bodyguard followed.

"I'm sorry, Mrs. Kharkov, but I'm afraid I can't allow you to enter the office unless your husband is with you."

"Except in the event of an emergency."

"That's correct."

"And I'm telling you this *is* an emergency. Go back to your post, you fool. I can't punch in the code with you looking over my shoulder."

"If there is an emergency, Mrs. Kharkov, why wasn't I notified by Arkady Medvedev?"

"You might find this difficult to believe, Pyotr, but my husband does not tell Arkady everything. He asked me to collect some important papers from his office and bring them to France. Now, ask yourself something, Pyotr: How do you think Ivan is going to react if I miss my plane because of this?"

The bodyguard held his ground. "I'm just doing my job, Mrs. Kharkov. And my instructions are very simple. No one is allowed to enter that office without clearance from Mr. Kharkov or Arkady Medvedev. And that includes you."

Elena looked toward the ceiling and sighed in exasperation. "Then I suppose you'll just have to call Arkady and tell him that I'm here." She pointed to the telephone resting on a small decorative table. "Call him, Pyotr. But do it quickly. Because if I miss my flight to France, I'm going to tell Ivan to cut out your tongue."

The guard turned his back to Elena and snatched up the receiver. A few seconds later, he reached down, brow furrowed, and rattled the switch several times.

"Something wrong, Pyotr?"

"The phone doesn't seem to be working."

"That's odd. Try my cell phone."

The guard placed the receiver back in the cradle and turned around, only to find Elena with her arm extended and a spray bottle in her hand. *The spray bottle that Gabriel had given her on the plane.* She squeezed the button once, sending a cloud of atomized liquid directly into his face. The guard struggled for several seconds to maintain his balance and for an instant Elena feared the sedative hadn't worked. Then he fell to the floor with a heavy thud, toppling the table in the process. Elena stared at him anxiously as he lay sprawled on the floor. Then she sprayed his face a second time.

That's what you get for touching me, she thought. *Swine.*

Nine floors beneath her, a fat man in a gray fedora entered the foyer for the private elevators, quietly cursing his mobile phone. He looked at Luka Osipov with an expression of mild frustration and shrugged his lumpy shoulders.

"The damn thing was working a minute ago, but when I got near the building it stopped. Perhaps it's the ghost of Stalin. My neighbor claims to have seen him wandering the halls at night. I've never had the misfortune of meeting him."

The elevator doors opened; the tubby Russian disappeared inside. Luka Osipov walked over to the lobby windows and gazed into the street. At least two other people — a woman walking along the sidewalk and a taxi driver standing next to his car — were having obvious difficulty with their cell phones. *The damn thing was working a minute ago, but when I got near the building it stopped . . .* Though Comrade Stalin was a man of great power, Luka Osipov doubted whether his ghost had anything to do with the sudden interruption in cellular communications. He suspected it was something far more tangible. Something like a signal jammer.

He tried his mobile one more time without success, then walked over to the porter's desk and asked to use his landline telephone. After ascertaining that Osipov intended to make a local call, the porter turned the instrument around and told the bodyguard to make it quick. The admonition was unnecessary. The phone wasn't working.

"It's dead," Osipov said.

"It was working a minute ago."

"Have you received any complaints from anyone in the building about trouble with their phones?"

"No, nothing."

Luka left the porter's desk and stepped outside. By the time he reached the limousine, the driver had his window down. Luka poked his head through the opening and told the man in the passenger seat to go inside and stand guard in the foyer. Then he turned toward the Kremlin and started walking. By the time he reached the middle of the Bolshoy Kamenny Bridge, his phone was working again. The first call he made was to the Sparrow Hills.

58
MOSCOW

The floor was hardwood and recently polished. Even so, it took every bit of Elena's strength to drag the two-hundred-pound unconscious body of Pyotr Luzhkov into the bathroom of the master bedroom suite. She locked the door from the inside, then made her way back to the entrance of Ivan's office. The keypad was mounted at eye level on the left side. After punching in the eight-digit access code, she placed her thumb on the scanner. An alarm chirped three times and the armored door eased slowly open. Elena stepped inside and opened her handbag.

The desk, like the man who worked there, was heavy and dark and entirely lacking in grace. It also happened to be one of Ivan's most prized possessions, for it had once belonged to Yuri Andropov, the former head of the KGB who had succeeded Leonid

Brezhnev as Soviet leader in 1982. The computer monitor and keyboard sat next to a silver-framed photograph of Ivan's father in his KGB general's uniform. The CPU was concealed beneath the desk on the floor. Elena crouched down and pressed the power button, then opened a small door on the front of the unit and plugged in the USB device that Gabriel had given her on the plane. After a few seconds, the drive engaged and the computer began to whir. Elena checked the monitor: a few characters of Hebrew, a time bar indicating that the job of copying the data files would take two minutes.

She glanced at her wristwatch, then walked over to the set of ornate bookcases on the opposite side of the room. The button was hidden behind Ivan's first edition of *Anna Karenina* — the second volume, to be precise. When pressed, the button caused the bookcases to part, revealing the door to Ivan's vault. She punched the same eight-digit code into the keypad and again placed her thumb on the scanner pad. Three chirps sounded, followed this time by the dull thud of the locks.

The interior light came on automatically as she pulled open the heavy door. Ivan's secret disks, the gray matter of his network of death, stood in a neat row on a shelf. One shelf below were some of the proceeds of that network: rubles, dollars, euros, Swiss francs. She started to reach for the money but stopped when she remembered the blood. *The blood shed by men wielding Ivan's weapons. The blood of children forced to fight in Ivan's wars.* She left the money on the shelf and took only the disks. The disks that would help Gabriel find the missiles. The disks that Gabriel would use to destroy her husband.

At the edge of Serafimovicha Street lies a broad traffic island. Like most in Moscow, it is cluttered day and night with parked cars. Some of the cars that afternoon were foreign and new; others were Russian and very old, including a battered Lada of uncertain color and registry occupied by Uzi Navot and his driver from Moscow Station. Navot did not appear happy, having witnessed several developments that had led him to conclude the operation was rapidly unraveling. He had shared that view with the rest of his teammates in the calmest voice he could manage. But now, as he watched Luka Osipov coming back over the Bolshoy Kamenny Bridge at a dead sprint, he knew that the time for composure had passed. "He's on his way back," he murmured into his wrist mike. "And it looks like we're in serious trouble."

Though Shmuel Peled had no radio, the steadily darkening expression on Gabriel's face told him everything he needed to know.

"Are we losing her, boss? Tell me we're not losing her."

"We'll know soon enough. If she comes out of that building with her handbag over her left shoulder, everything is fine. If she doesn't . . ." He left the thought unfinished.

"What do we do now?"

"We wait. And we hope to God she can talk her way back into her car."

"And if she doesn't come out?"

"Speak Russian, Shmuel. You're supposed to be speaking Russian."

The young driver resumed his ersatz Russian monologue. Gabriel stared at the western façade of the House on the Embankment and listened for the sound of Uzi Navot's voice.

Luka Osipov had gained fifteen pounds since leaving the Alpha Group and lost much of his old physical fitness. As a result, he was breathing heavily by the time he arrived back at the porter's desk in the lobby.

"I need to get into Apartment 9A immediately."

"I'm afraid that's not possible — not without a security card for the elevator and a key for the apartment itself."

"I believe a woman under my protection is in grave danger in that apartment at this very moment. And I need you to get me inside."

"I'm sorry, but it's against policy."

"Do you know who I work for, you fool?"

"You work for Mrs. Kharkov."

"No, I work for *Ivan* Kharkov. And do you know what *Ivan* Kharkov is going to do if anything happens to his wife?"

The porter swallowed hard. "I can get you up to the ninth floor but I can't get you into that apartment. Mr. Kharkov doesn't let us keep a key on file."

"Leave that part to me."

"Good luck," the porter said as he came out from behind his desk. "From what I hear, you're going to need a Red Army tank to get into that place."

Elena closed the bookcases, removed the USB device from the computer, and switched off the power. Stepping into the hallway, she glanced at her watch: *4:02 . . .* The entire thing had taken just eight minutes. She shoved the device into the bag and closed the zipper, then punched the eight-digit code into the keypad. While the heavy door swung slowly shut, she righted the fallen table and returned the telephone to its proper place. After taking one last look around to make certain everything was in order, she started for the door.

It was then she heard the pounding. A large male fist, interspersed with a large male palm. She reckoned it was the same sort of pounding the occupants of this house of horrors had heard nearly every night during the Great Terror. *How many had been dragged from this place to their deaths?* She couldn't remember the exact number now. A hundred? A thousand? What difference did it make. She only knew she might soon join them. Perhaps one day she would be the answer in a macabre Russian trivia question. *Who was the last person to be taken from the House on the Embankment and murdered? Elena Kharkov, first wife of Ivan Borisovich Kharkov . . .*

Like all those who had heard the dreaded knock, she entertained thoughts of not answering it. But she did answer. Everyone answered eventually. She did so not in fear but in a fit of feigned outrage, with her handbag over her left shoulder and her right hand wrapped around the plastic spray bottle in her coat pocket. Standing in the vestibule, his face pale with anger and damp with sweat, was Luka Osipov. A gun was in his hand and it was pointed directly at Elena's heart. She feared the gun might go off if she attempted to deploy the spray bottle, so she drew her empty hand slowly from her pocket and placed it on her hip, frowning at her bodyguard in bewilderment.

"Luka Ustinovich," she said, using his patronymic. "Whatever's gotten into you?"

"Where's Pyotr?"

"Who's Pyotr?"

"The guard who's supposed to be on duty at this flat."

"There was no one here when I arrived, you idiot. Now, let's go."

She tried to step into the vestibule. The bodyguard blocked her path.

"What game do you think you're playing, Luka? We have to get to the airport. Trust me, Luka Ustinovich, the last thing you want is for me to miss my plane."

The bodyguard said nothing. Instead, he reached into the elevator, with the gun still aimed at her abdomen, and sent the carriage back down to the lobby. Then he pushed her into the apartment and slammed the door.

59

GROSVENOR SQUARE, LONDON

Shamron's lighter flared in the gloom of the ops center, briefly illuminating his face. His eyes were focused on the large central display screen at the front of room, where Uzi Navot's last transmission from Moscow flashed with all the allure of a dead body lying in a gutter.

BG ENTERING HOTE . . . TROUBLE . . .

BG stood for bodyguard. HOTE for House on the Embankment. TROUBLE required no translation. Trouble was trouble.

The screen went black. A new message appeared.

AM ENTERING HOTE . . . ADVISE . . .

The initials AM stood for Arkady Medvedev. The word advise meant that Gabriel's meticulously planned operation was in serious danger of crashing and burning, with significant loss of life a distinct possibility.

"They're your boys," Carter said. "It's

your call."

Shamron flicked ash into his coffee cup. "We sit tight. We give her a chance."

Carter looked at the digital clock. "It is now four-fifteen, Ari. If your team is to have any chance of getting on that plane, they need to be in their cars and heading to the airport in the next ten minutes."

"Airplanes are complicated machines, Adrian. A lot of little things can go wrong with an airplane."

"It might be a good idea to get that over and done with."

Shamron picked up a secure telephone connected to the Operations Desk at King Saul Boulevard. A few terse words in Hebrew. A calm glance at Carter.

"It appears a cabin pressure warning light is now flashing in the cockpit of El Al Flight 1612. Until that problem is resolved to the satisfaction of the captain, a man who happens to be a decorated former IAF fighter pilot, that aircraft isn't going anywhere."

"Well played," said Carter.

"How long can our French friends keep Ivan tied up in Nice?"

"Monsieur Boisson is just getting started. The children, however, are another matter entirely. We have a decision to make, Ari. What do we do about the children?"

"I wouldn't want my children sitting around a gendarmerie station, would you, Adrian?"

"Can't say I would."

"Then let's take them. Who knows? Depending on what happens inside the apartment building in the next ten minutes, we may need them."

"For what?"

"I'm not going to give her up without a fight, Adrian, and you can be sure Gabriel isn't either." Shamron dropped his cigarette into his coffee cup and gave it a swirl. "Call the French. Get me Ivan's children."

Carter picked up the secure line connected to the French ops center in Paris. Shamron looked at the message screen, where Uzi Navot's last message flashed incessantly.

AM ENTERING HOTE . . . ADVISE . . .

AM ENTERING HOTE . . . ADVISE . . .

AM ENTERING HOTE . . . ADVISE . . .

They had placed Sonia and the children in a pleasant holding room and plied them with cold fruit juice and ice cream. A pretty young female gendarme remained with them at all times, more for company than for reasons of security. They watched cartoons and played a noisy game of cards that made no sense to anyone, least of all the children themselves. The chief duty officer made them honorary gendarmes for the day and even allowed Nikolai to inspect his firearm. Later, he would tell his colleagues that the boy knew rather too much about guns for a child of seven.

After receiving a telephone call from headquarters in Paris, the duty officer returned to the holding room and announced that it was time for everyone to go home. Anna and Nikolai greeted this news not with joy but tears; for them, the arrest and detention had been a great adventure and they were in no hurry to return home to their palace by the sea. They were finally coaxed into leaving with a promise they could come back to play anytime they wished. As they headed down the central corridor of the station, Anna held the hand of the female gendarme while Nikolai lectured the duty officer about the superiority of Russian-made weapons. Sonia asked after the whereabouts of the bodyguards but received no response.

They left the station not through the front entrance but through a rear door that gave onto an enclosed courtyard. Several official Renaults were parked there, along with an older-model Peugeot wagon. Seated behind the wheel, wearing a white Lacoste polo, was a man with gray hair. Seeing the children, he climbed out of the car with a tranquil smile on his face and opened the rear door. Sonia froze and turned to the duty officer in confusion.

"What's going on? Who is this man?"

"This is Monsieur Henri. He's a good man. He's going to take you and the children somewhere safe."

"I don't understand."

"I'm afraid Mr. Kharkov is in a bit of trouble at the moment. Mrs. Kharkov has made arrangements to place the children in the care of Monsieur Henri until she returns. She has asked that you remain with them. She promises you will be extremely well compensated. Do you understand what I'm saying to you, Mademoiselle?"

"I think so."

"Very good. Now, get into the car, please. And try not to look so frightened. It will only upset the children. And that is the last thing they need at a time like this."

At Moscow's Sheremetyevo 2 Airport, Chiara was standing at her post at the check-in counter when the status window on the departure board switched from ON TIME to DELAYED. Ten feet away, in the crowded passenger lounge, 187 weary voices groaned in unison. One brave soul, a bearded Orthodox Jew in a dark suit, approached the counter and demanded an explanation. "It's a minor mechanical problem," Chiara explained calmly. "The delay shouldn't be more than a few minutes." The man returned to his seat, skeptical he had been told the truth. Chiara turned and looked up at the board: *DELAYED . . .*

Walk away, Gabriel, she thought. *Turn around and walk away.*

60
MOSCOW

The clouds opened up at the same instant Gabriel's earpiece crackled with the sound of Uzi Navot's voice.

"We're history."

"What are you talking about?"

"The Old Man just issued the order to abort."

"Tell him I want ten more minutes."

"I'm not telling him anything. I'm following his order."

"You go. I'll meet you at Sheremetyevo."

"We're out of here. *Now.*"

"I'm not leaving."

"Get off the radio and into your car."

Gabriel and Peled rose in unison and walked calmly from the park in the driving rain. Peled headed to the Volga; Gabriel, to Bolotnaya Square. Navot and Lavon joined him. Navot was wearing a waxed cap but Lavon was hatless. His wispy hair was soon plastered to his scalp.

"Why are we here?" Navot demanded. "Why are we standing in the rain in this godforsaken park when we should be in our cars heading to the airport?"

"Because I'm not leaving yet, Uzi."

"Of course you are, Gabriel." Navot tapped the PDA. "It says right here you are: 'Abort at 5 p.m. Moscow time and board flight at SVO.' That's what the message says. I'm quite certain it's not a suggestion. In fact, I'm *sure* it is a direct *order* from the Memuneh himself."

Memuneh was a Hebrew word that meant "the one in charge." For as long as anyone in the Office could remember, it had been reserved for a single man: Ari Shamron.

"You can stand here in the park and shout at me until you're hoarse, Uzi, but I'm not leaving her behind."

"It's not your call, Gabriel. You made a promise to Shamron in Paris. If she doesn't come out of that building within the allotted period of time, you *leave*."

Gabriel wiped the rain from his tinted glasses. "You'd better get moving, Uzi. The traffic to Sheremetyevo can be terrible this time of night."

Navot seized Gabriel's upper arm and squeezed it hard enough for Gabriel's hand to go numb.

"What do you intend to do, Uzi? Drag me to the car?"

"If I have to."

"That might cause a bit of a spectacle, don't you think?"

"At least it will be brief. And unlike your desire to stay here in Moscow, chances are it won't be fatal."

"Let go of my arm, Uzi."

"Don't tell me what to do, Gabriel. I'm the chief of Special Ops, not you. You're nothing but an independent contractor. Therefore, you report to me. And I am telling you to get into that car and come with us to the airport."

Eli Lavon carefully removed Navot's hand from Gabriel's arm. "That's enough, Uzi. He's not getting on the plane."

Navot shot Lavon a dark look. "Thanks for the support, Eli. You Wrath of God boys always stick together, don't you?"

"I don't want him to stay behind any more than you do. I just know better than to waste my breath trying to talk him out of it. He has a hard head."

"He'll need it." The rain was now streaming off the brim of Navot's hat onto his face. "Do you know what's going to happen if I get on that plane without you? The Old Man will line me up against the wall and use me for target practice."

Gabriel held up his wristwatch so Navot could see it. "Five o'clock, Uzi. Better be running along. And take Eli with you. He's a fine watcher, but he's never been one for the rough stuff."

Navot gave Gabriel a Shamronian stare. He was done arguing.

"If I were you, I'd stay away from your hotel." He reached into his coat pocket and handed Gabriel a single key. "I've been carrying this around in case we needed a crash pad. It's an old Soviet wreck of a building near Dinamo Stadium, but it will do."

Navot recited the street address, the building number, and the number of the apartment. "Once you're inside, signal the station and bar the door. We'll put in an extraction team. With a bit of luck, you'll still be there when they arrive."

Then he turned away without another word and pounded across the rain-swept square toward his car. Lavon watched him for a moment, then looked at Gabriel.

"Sure you don't want some company?"

"Get to the airport, Eli. Get on that plane."

"What would you like me to tell your wife?"

Gabriel hesitated a moment, then said,

"Tell her I'm sorry, Eli. Tell her I'll make it up to her somehow."

"It's possible you might be making a terrible mistake."

"It won't be the first time."

"Yes, but this is Moscow. And it could be the last."

Navot's transmission appeared on the screen of the London ops center at 5:04 Moscow time: LEAVING FOR SVO . . . MINUS ONE . . . Adrian Carter swore softly and looked at Shamron, who was turning over his old Zippo lighter in his fingertips.

Two turns to the right, two turns to the left . . .

"It seems you were right," Carter said.

Shamron said nothing.

Two turns to the right, two to the left . . .

"The French say Ivan is about to blow, Ari. They say the situation at Nice is getting tenuous. They would like a resolution, one way or the other."

"Perhaps it's time to let Ivan see the scope of the dilemma he is now facing. Tell your cyberwarriors to turn the phones back on in Moscow. And tell the French to confiscate Ivan's plane. And, while they're at it, take his passport, too."

"That should get his attention."

Shamron closed his eyes.

By the time Ivan Kharkov emerged from the airport conference room at the Côte d'Azur International Airport, his anger had reached dangerous levels. It exploded into mild physical violence when he found his two bodyguards dozing on the couch. They stormed down a flight of stairs together, Ivan ranting in Russian to no one in particular, and climbed into the armored Mercedes limousine for the return trip to Saint-Tropez. When the car was two hundred feet from the building, Ivan's phone rang. It was Arkady Medvedev calling from Moscow.

"Where have you been, Ivan Borisovich?"

"Stuck at the airport, dealing with my plane."

"Do you have any idea what's been going on?"

"The French are trying to steal my plane. *And* my passport. That's what's going on, Arkady."

"They're trying to steal more than that. They've got your children, too. It's part of some elaborate operation against you. And it's not just going on there in France. Something's happening here in Moscow, too."

Ivan made no response. Arkady Medvedev

knew it was a dangerous sign. When Ivan was merely angry, he swore violently. But when he was mad enough to kill, he went dead silent. He finally instructed his chief of security to tell him everything he knew. Medvedev did so in a form of colloquial Russian that was nearly indecipherable to a Western ear.

"Where is she now, Arkady?"

"Still in the apartment."

"Who put her up to this?"

"She claims she did it on her own."

"She's lying. I need to know what I'm up against. And quickly."

"You need to get out of France."

"With no plane and no passport?"

"What do you want me to do?"

"Throw a *party*, Arkady. Somewhere outside the city. See if anyone shows up without an invitation."

"And if they do?"

"Give them a message from me. Let them know that if they fuck with Ivan Kharkov, Ivan Kharkov is going to fuck with them."

61
SHEREMETYEVO 2 AIRPORT, MOSCOW

They arrived at intervals of five minutes and made their way separately through security and passport control. Uzi Navot came last, hat pulled low over his eyes, raincoat drenched. He walked the length of the terminal twice, searching for watchers, before finally making his way to Gate A23. Lavon and Yaakov were gazing nervously out at the tarmac. Between them was an empty seat. Navot lowered himself into it and rested his attaché case on his knees. He stared hard at Chiara for a moment, like a middle-aged traveler admiring a beautiful younger woman.

"How's she doing?"

Lavon answered. "How do you *think* she's doing?"

"She has no one to blame but her husband."

"I'm sure we'll have plenty of time for recriminations later." Lavon checked the departure board. "How much longer do you think Shamron is going to hold the plane?"

"As long as he thinks he can."

"By my estimate, she's been in the hands of Arkady Medvedev for two hours now. How long do you think it took him to tear her bag apart, Uzi? How long did it take him to find Ivan's disks and Gabriel's electronic toys?"

Navot typed a brief message on his Black-Berry. Two minutes later, the status window in the departure monitor changed from DE-LAYED to NOW BOARDING. One hundred eighty-seven weary passengers began to applaud. Three anxious men stared gloomily through the window at the shimmering tarmac.

"Don't worry, Uzi. You did the right thing."

"Just don't ever tell Chiara. She'll never forgive me." Navot shook his head slowly. "It's never a good idea to bring spouses into the field. You'd think Gabriel would have learned that by now."

There was a time in Moscow, not long ago, when a man sitting alone in a parked car would have come under immediate suspicion. But that was no longer the case. These days, sitting in parked cars, or cars stuck in traffic, was what Muscovites did.

Gabriel was on the northern edge of Bolotnaya Square, next to a billboard plastered with a dour portrait of the Russian president. He did not know whether the spot was legal or illegal. He did not care. He cared only that he could see the entrance of the House on the Embankment. He left the engine running and the radio on. It sounded to Gabriel like a news analysis program of some kind: long cuts of taped remarks by the Russian president interspersed with commentary by a panel of journalists and experts. Their words were surely laudatory, for the Kremlin tolerated no other kind. *Forward as one!* as the president liked to say. And keep your criticism to yourself.

Twenty minutes into his vigil, a pair of underfed Militia officers rounded the corner, tunics glistening. Gabriel turned up the radio and nodded cordially. For a moment, he feared they might be contemplating a shakedown. Instead, they frowned at his old Volga, as if to say he wasn't worth their time on a rainy night. Next came a man with lank, dark hair, and an open bottle of Baltika beer in his hand. He shuffled over to Gabriel's window and opened his coat, revealing a veritable pharmacy underneath. Gabriel motioned for him to move on, then flicked the wipers and focused his gaze on the building. Specifically, on the lights burning in the ninth-floor apartment overlooking the Kremlin.

They went dark at 7:48 p.m. The woman who emerged from the building soon after had no handbag hanging over her left shoulder. Indeed, she had no handbag at all. She was walking more swiftly than normal; Luka Osipov, bodyguard turned captor, held one arm while a colleague held another. Arkady Medvedev walked a few steps behind, head lowered against the rain, eyes up and on the move.

A Mercedes waited at the curb. The seating arrangements had clearly been determined in advance, for the boarding process was accomplished with admirable speed and efficiency: Elena in the backseat, wedged between bodyguards; Arkady Medvedev in the front passenger seat, a mobile phone now pressed to his ear. The car crept to the end of Serafimovicha Street, then disappeared in a black blur. Gabriel counted to five and slipped the Volga into gear. Forward as one.

62
MOSCOW

They roared southward out of the city on a road that bore Lenin's name and was lined with monuments to Lenin's folly. Apartment blocks — *endless* apartments blocks. The biggest apartment blocks Gabriel had ever seen. It was as if the masters of the Communist Party, in their infinite wisdom, had decided to uproot the entire population of the world's biggest country and resettle it here, along a few wretched miles of the Leninsky Prospekt. And to think that by the end of September it would be covered beneath a blanket of snow and ice.

At that hour, the Leninsky was two different roads: inbound lanes clogged with Muscovites returning from the weekend at their dachas, outbound lanes filled with giant trucks thundering out of the capital toward the distant corners of the empire. The trucks were both his allies and enemies. One moment, they granted Gabriel a place to hide. The next, they obscured his view. Shmuel Peled had been right about the Volga — it did run decently for a twenty-year-old piece of Soviet-made junk — but it was no match for the finest automobile Bavaria had to offer. The Volga topped out at about eighty-five, and did so with much protest and pulling to the left. Its little wipers were altogether useless against the heavy rain and road spray, and the defroster fan was little more than a warm exhalation of breath against the glass. In order to see, Gabriel had to lower both front windows to create a cross draft. Each passing truck hurled water against the left side of his face.

The rain tapered, and a few rays of weak sunlight peered through a slit in the clouds near the horizon. Gabriel kept his foot pressed to the floor and his eyes fastened to the taillights of the Mercedes. His thoughts, however, were focused on the scene he had just witnessed at the House on the Embankment. *How had he managed it?* How had Arkady convinced her to walk into the car without a fight? Was it with a threat or a promise? With the truth or a lie, or some combination of both? And why were they now hurtling down the Leninsky Prospekt, into the yawning chasm of the Russian countryside?

Gabriel was pondering that final question when he felt the first impact on his rear bumper: a car, much bigger and faster than his own, headlights doused. He responded by pressing the accelerator to the floor but the Volga had nothing more to give. The car behind gave him one more tap, almost as a warning, then moved in swiftly for the kill.

What followed was the classic maneuver that every good traffic policeman knows. The aggressor initiates contact with the victim, right front bumper to left rear bumper. The aggressor then accelerates hard and the victim is sent spinning out of control. The impact of such a tactic is magnified substantially when there is a sharp imbalance in the weight and power of the two vehicles — for example, when one is an S-Class Mercedes-Benz and the other is a rattletrap old Volga already being pushed to the breaking point. How many times Gabriel's car actually rotated, he would never know. He only knew that, when it was over, the car was resting on its side in a field of mud at the edge of a pine forest and he was bleeding heavily from the nose.

Two of Arkady Medvedev's finest waded into the mud to retrieve him, though their motives were hardly altruistic. One was a skinheaded giant with a right hand like a sledgehammer. The hammer struck Gabriel only once, for once was all that was necessary. He toppled backward, into the mud, and for an instant saw upside-down pine trees. Then the trees streaked skyward toward the clouds like missiles. And Gabriel blacked out.

At that same moment, El Al Flight 1612 was rapidly gaining altitude over the suburbs of Moscow and banking hard toward the south. Uzi Navot was seated next to the window in the final row of first class, hand wrapped around a glass of whiskey, eyes scanning the vast carpet of winking yellow lights beneath him. For a few seconds, he could see it all clearly: the ring roads around the Kremlin, the snakelike course of the river, the thunderous prospekts leading like spokes into the endless expanse of the Russian interior. Then the plane knifed into the clouds and the lights of Moscow vanished. Navot pulled down his window shade and lifted the whiskey to his lips. *I should have broken his arm,* he thought. *I should have broken the little bastard's arm.*

Gabriel opened his eyes slowly. *Not eyes,* he thought. *Eye.* The left eye only. The right eye was unresponsive. The right eye was the one that had been punched by the bald giant. It was now swollen shut and crusted over with clotted blood.

Before attempting movement, he took careful stock of his situation. He was sprawled on the concrete floor of what appeared to be a warehouse, with his hands cuffed at his back and his legs in something resembling a running position, right leg lifted in front of him, left extended backward. His right shoulder was pressing painfully against the floor, as was the right side of his face. Somewhere, a light was burning, but his own corner of the building was in semidarkness. A few feet away stood a stack of large wooden crates with Cyrillic markings on the sides. Gabriel struggled to make out the words but could not. The alphabet was still like hieroglyphics to him; the crates could have been filled with tins of caviar or vials of deadly polonium and he would have never known the difference.

He rolled onto his back and lifted his knees to his chest, then levered himself into a sitting position. The exertion of the movement, combined with the fact that he was now upright, caused his right eye to begin throbbing with catastrophic pain. He reckoned the blow had fractured the orbit around the eye. For all he knew, he no longer had an eye, just an immense crater in the side of his head where once his eye had been.

He leaned against the wooden crates and looked around him. There were other stacks of crates, towering stacks of crates, receding into the distance like the apartment buildings of the Leninsky Prospekt. From his limited vantage point, Gabriel could only see two rows, but he had the impression there were many more. He doubted they were filled with caviar. Not even the gluttonous Ivan Kharkov could devour that much caviar.

He heard the sound of footsteps approaching from a distance. Two sets. Both heavy. Both male. One man significantly larger than the other. The big man was the bald giant who had hit him. The smaller man was several years older, with a fringe of iron-gray hair and a skull that looked as if it been specially designed to withstand much blunt trauma.

"Where are the children?" asked Arkady Medvedev.

"What children?" replied Gabriel.

Medvedev nodded to the giant, then stepped away as if he didn't want his clothing to be spattered with the blood. The sledgehammer crashed into Gabriel's skull a second time. Same eye, same result. Pine trees and missiles. Then nothing at all.

63
LUBYANKA SQUARE, MOSCOW

Like almost everyone else in Moscow, Colonel Grigori Bulganov of the FSB was divorced. His marriage, like Russia itself, had been characterized by wild lurches from one extreme to the other: glasnost one day, Great Terror the next. Thankfully, it had been short and had produced no offspring. Irina had won the apartment and the Volkswagen; Grigori Bulganov, his freedom. Not that he had managed to do much with it: a torrid office romance or two, the occasional afternoon in the bed of his neighbor, a mother of three who was divorced herself.

For the most part, Grigori Bulganov worked. He worked early in the morning. He worked late into the evening. He worked Saturdays. He worked Sundays. And sometimes, like now, he could even be found at his desk late on a Sunday night. His brief was counterespionage. More to the point, it was Bulganov's job to neutralize attempts by foreign intelligence services to spy on the Russian government and State-owned Russian enterprises. His assignment had been made more difficult by the activities of the FSB's sister service, the SVR. Espionage by the SVR had reached levels not seen since the height of the Cold War, which had prompted Russia's adversaries to respond in kind. Grigori Bulganov could hardly blame them. The new Russian president was fond of rattling his saber, and foreign leaders needed to know whether it had an edge to it or had turned to rust in its scabbard.

Like many FSB officers, Bulganov supplemented his government salary by selling his expertise, along with knowledge gained through his work itself, to private industry. In Bulganov's case, he served as a paid informant for a man named Arkady Medvedev, the chief of security for Russian oligarch Ivan Kharkov. Bulganov fed Medvedev a steady stream of reports dealing with potential threats to his businesses, legal and illicit. Medvedev rewarded him by keeping a secret bank account in Bulganov's name filled with cash. As a consequence of the arrangement, Grigori Bulganov had been able to penetrate Ivan Kharkov's operations in a way no other outsider ever had. In fact, Bulganov was quite confident he knew more about Ivan's arms-trafficking activities than any other intelligence officer in the world. In Russia, such knowledge could be dangerous. Sometimes, it could even be fatal, which explained why Bulganov was careful to stay on Arkady Medvedev's good side. And why, when Medvedev called his cell at 11:15 p.m. on a Sunday night, he didn't dare consider not answering it.

Grigori Bulganov did not speak for the next three minutes. Instead, he tore a sheet of notepaper into a hundred pieces while he listened to the account of what had taken place in Moscow that afternoon. He was glad Medvedev had called him. He only wished he had done it on a secure line.

"Are you sure it's him?" Bulganov asked.

"No question."

"How did he get back into the country?"

"With an American passport and a crude disguise."

"Where is he now?"

Medvedev told him the location.

"What about Ivan's wife?"

"She's here, too."

"What are your plans, Arkady?"

"I'm going to give him one more chance to answer a few questions. Then I'm going to drop him in a hole somewhere." A pause.

"Unless you'd like to do that for me, Grigori?"

"Actually, I might enjoy that. After all, he did disobey a direct order."

"How quickly can you get down here?"

"Give me an hour. I'd like to have a word with the woman, too."

"A *word,* Grigori. This matter doesn't concern you."

"I'll be brief. Just make sure she's there when I arrive."

"She'll be here."

"How many men do you have there?"

"Five."

"That's a lot of witnesses."

"Don't worry, Grigori. They're not the talkative sort."

64
KALUZHSKAYA OBLAST, RUSSIA

When Gabriel woke next, it was to the sensation of a dressing being applied to his wounded eye. He opened the one that still functioned and saw the task was being performed by none other than Arkady Medvedev. The Russian was working with a single hand. The other held a gun. A Stechkin, thought Gabriel, but he couldn't be sure. He had never cared much for Russian guns.

"Feeling sorry for me, Arkady?"

"It wouldn't stop bleeding. We were afraid you were going to die on us."

"Aren't you going to kill me anyway?"

"Of course we are, Allon. We just need a little bit of information from you first."

"And who said former KGB hoods didn't have any manners?"

Medvedev finished applying the bandage and regarded Gabriel in silence. "Aren't you going to ask me how I know your real name?" he asked finally.

"I assume you could have got it from your friends at the FSB. Or, it's possible you saved yourself a phone call by simply beating it out of Elena Kharkov. You strike me as the type who enjoys hitting women."

"Keep that up and I'll bring Dmitri back for another go at you. You're not some kid anymore, Allon. One or two blows from Dmitri and you might not come to again."

"He has a lot of wasted motion in his punch. Why don't you let me give him a couple of pointers?"

"Are you serious or is that just your Jewish sense of humor talking?"

"Our sense of humor came from living with Russians as neighbors. It helps to have a sense of humor during a pogrom. It takes the sting out of having your village burned down."

"You have a choice, Allon. You can lie there and tell jokes all night or you can start talking." The Russian removed a cigarette from a silver case and ignited it with a matching silver lighter. "You don't need this shit and neither do I. Let's just settle this like professionals."

"By professional, I suppose you mean I should tell you everything I know, so then you can kill me."

"Something like that." The Russian held the cigarette case toward Gabriel. "Would you like one?"

"They're bad for your health."

Medvedev closed the case. "Are you up for a little walk, Allon? I think you might find this place quite interesting."

"Any chance of taking off these handcuffs?"

"None whatsoever."

"I thought you would say that. Help me up, will you? Just try not to pull my shoulders out of their sockets."

Medvedev hoisted him effortlessly to his feet. Gabriel felt the room spin and for an instant thought he might topple over. Medvedev must have been thinking the same thing because he placed a steadying hand on his elbow.

"You sure you're up for this, Allon?"

"I'm sure."

"You're not going to pass out on me again, are you?"

"I'll be fine, Arkady."

Medvedev dropped his cigarette and crushed it carefully with the toe of an expensive-looking Italian loafer. Everything Medvedev was wearing looked expensive: the French suit, the English raincoat, the Swiss wristwatch. But none of it could conceal the fact that, underneath it all, he was still just a cheap KGB hood. *Just like the regime,* thought Gabriel: *KGB in nice clothing.*

They set out together between the crates. There were more than Gabriel could have imagined. They seemed to go on forever, like the warehouse itself. Hardly surprising, he thought. This was Russia, after all. World's largest country. World's largest hotel. World's largest swimming pool. World's largest warehouse.

"What's in the boxes?"

"Food."

"Really?"

"Really." Medvedev pointed toward a skyscraper of wooden crates. "That's canned tuna. Over there are canned carrots. A little farther on is the canned beef. We even have chicken soup."

"That's very impressive. Fifteen years ago, Russia was living on American handouts. Now you're feeding the world."

"We've made great strides since the fall of communism."

"What's really in the boxes, Arkady?"

Medvedev pointed toward the same skyscraper. "Those are bullets. Fifty million rounds, to be precise. Enough to kill a good portion of the Third World. There's not much chance of that, though. Your average freedom fighter isn't terribly disciplined. We don't complain. It's good for business."

Medvedev pointed to another stack. "Those are RPG-7s. Pound for pound, one of the best weapons money can buy. A great equalizer. With proper training, any twelve-year-old kid can take out a tank or an armored personnel carrier."

"And the rest?"

"Over there are mortars. Next to the mortars is our bread and butter: the AK-47. It helped us beat the Germans, then it helped us change the world. The Kalashnikov gave power to the powerless. Voice to the voiceless."

"I hear it's very popular in the rougher neighborhoods of Los Angeles, too."

Medvedev twisted his face into an expression of mock horror. "Criminals? No, Allon, we don't sell to *criminals.* Our customers are governments. Rebels. Revolutionaries."

"I never had you figured for a true believer, Arkady."

"I'm not, really. I'm just in it for the money. Just like Ivan."

They walked on in silence. Gabriel knew this wasn't a tour but a death march. Arkady Medvedev wanted something from Gabriel before they reached their destination. He wanted Ivan's children.

"You should know, Allon, that everything I am showing you is completely *legal.* We've got smaller warehouses in other parts of the country closer to the old armaments plants, but this is our central distribution facility. We've done well. We're much bigger than our competition."

"Congratulations, Arkady. Are profits still strong or did you grow too quickly?"

"Profits are fine, thank you. Despite Western claims to the contrary, arms trafficking is still a growth industry."

"How did you make out on the missile deal?"

Medvedev was silent for a moment. "What missiles are you referring to, Allon?"

"The SA-18s, Arkady. The Iglas."

"The Igla is one of the most accurate and lethal antiaircraft missiles ever produced." Medvedev's tone now had a briefing-room quality. "It is far too dangerous a system ever to be let loose into the free market. We don't deal in Iglas. Only a madman would."

"That's not what I'm told, Arkady. I hear you sold several hundred to an African country. A country that was planning to forward them at a substantial markup to some friends at al-Qaeda."

Gabriel lapsed into silence. When he spoke

again, his tone was confiding rather than confrontational.

"We know all about the Iglas, Arkady. We also know that you were against the sale from the beginning. It's not too late to help us. Tell me where those missiles are."

Medvedev made no response, other than to lead Gabriel to an empty space in the center of the warehouse floor. The area was illuminated by a light burning high in the rafters overhead. Medvedev stood there, a performer on a stage, and extended his arms.

"I'm afraid it *is* too late."

"Where are they now, Arkady?"

"In the hands of a very satisfied customer."

Medvedev stepped out of the light and gave Gabriel a firm shove in the back. Apparently, there was one more thing they had to see.

65
KALUZHSKAYA OBLAST, RUSSIA

She was secured to a straight-backed metal chair at the far end of the vast warehouse. Luka Osipov, her former bodyguard, was standing to one side, the bald giant on the other. Her blouse was torn, her cheeks aflame from repeated slaps. She stared at Gabriel's damaged eye in horror, then lowered her gaze to the floor. Medvedev took a fistful of her dark hair. It was not the sort of gesture that suggested he intended to let her live.

"Before we begin, you should know that Mrs. Kharkov has been very cooperative this evening. She has given us a full and forthright accounting of her involvement in this sorry affair, beginning with the night she eavesdropped on my telephone conversation with her husband. She has admitted to us that the operation to steal Ivan's secret papers was all *her* idea. She said you actually tried to talk her out of it."

"She's lying, Arkady. We forced her into it. We told her that her husband was going down and that if she didn't cooperate with us she was going down, too."

"That's very chivalrous of you, Allon, but it's not going to work."

Medvedev tightened his grip on Elena's hair. Elena's face remained a stoic mask.

"Unfortunately," Medvedev continued, "Mrs. Kharkov was unable to supply us with one critical piece of information: the location of her children. We were hoping you might tell us that now, so that Mrs. Kharkov might be spared additional unpleasantness. As you might expect, her husband is rather angry with her at the moment. He's ordered us to do whatever's necessary to get the answers we need."

"I told you, Arkady, I don't know where the children are. That information was kept from me."

"In case you found yourself in a situation like this?"

Medvedev tossed a mobile phone toward Gabriel. It struck him in the chest and clattered to the floor.

"Call the French. Tell them to deliver the children to Ivan's villa *tonight,* along with Ivan's passport. Then tell them to release Ivan's airplane. He'd like to return to Russia immediately."

"Let her go," Gabriel said. "Do whatever you want to me. But let Elena go."

"So she can testify against her husband in a Western courtroom? So she can publicly bemoan how Russia is becoming an authoritarian state that once again poses a grave threat to global peace? That would not only be bad for the country but bad for business. You see, Mr. Kharkov's friends in the Kremlin might find it annoying that he allowed such a situation to occur. And Mr. Kharkov tries very hard never to annoy his friends in the Kremlin."

"I promise we won't let her talk. She'll raise her children and keep her mouth shut. She's innocent."

"Ivan doesn't see it that way. Ivan sees her as a traitor. And you know what we do to traitors." Medvedev held up his Stechkin for Gabriel to see, then placed the barrel against the back of Elena's neck. "Seven grams of lead, as Stalin liked to say. That's what Elena is going to get if you don't order the French to let Ivan get on his plane tonight — *with* his children."

"I'll make that call when Elena is safely on the ground in the West."

"She isn't going anywhere."

Elena lifted her gaze from the floor and

stared directly at Gabriel.

"Don't tell him a thing, Gabriel. They're going to kill me regardless of what you do. I would rather those children be raised by anyone other than a monster like my husband." She raised her eyes toward Medvedev. "You'd better pull the trigger, Arkady, because Ivan is *never* getting those children."

Medvedev walked over to Gabriel and slammed the butt of the Stechkin into his right eye. Gabriel toppled sideways to the floor, blinded by excruciating pain. It was compounded when Medvedev buried an Italian loafer into Gabriel's solar plexus. He was lining up a second kick when a distant voice intervened in Russian. The voice was familiar to Gabriel, he was sure of it, but in his agony he could not recall where he had heard it before. It came to him a moment later, when he was finally able to breathe again. He had heard the voice two months earlier, during his first trip to Moscow. He had heard the voice in Lubyanka.

66
KALUZHSKAYA OBLAST, RUSSIA

The two men had a brief but amicable debate, as if they were quarreling over whose turn it was to pay for lunch. Because it was in Russian, Gabriel could not understand it. Nor could he see their faces. He was still lying on his side, with his abdomen exposed to Arkady Medvedev's size-eleven loafers.

When the conversation concluded, two pairs of hands lifted him to his feet. It was then he saw the face of the man he knew only as "Sergei." He looked much as he had that night in Lubyanka. The same gray suit. The same gray pallor. The same lawyerly eyes behind round spectacles. He was wearing a rather stylish raincoat. His little Lenin beard had recently been groomed.

"I thought I told you not to come back to Russia, Allon."

"If you had been doing your job, I wouldn't have had to."

"And which job is that?"

"Preventing scum like Ivan from flooding the world with weapons and missiles."

Sergei sighed heavily, as if to say this was the last way he had hoped to spend his evening. Then he took hold of Gabriel's handcuffs and gave them a sharp jerk. If Gabriel had had any feeling left in his wrists, he was certain it would have hurt like hell.

They crossed the warehouse together, Sergei trailing a step behind, and exited through a door wide enough to accommodate Ivan's freight trucks. It was raining again; three of Medvedev's security men were sheltering beneath the eaves, talking quietly in Russian. A few feet away was an official FSB sedan. Sergei inserted Gabriel into the backseat and slammed the door.

He drove with a Makarov in one hand and the radio on. Another speech by the Russian president, of course. What else? It was a small road and it ran through a thick birch forest. Tucked amid the trees were dachas — not palaces like Ivan's dacha but *real* Russian dachas. Some were the size of a quaint cottage; others were little more than toolsheds. All were surrounded by little plots of cultivated land. Gabriel thought of Olga Sukhova, tending to her radishes.

I believe in my Russia, and I want no more acts of evil committed in my name . . .

He looked into the rearview mirror and saw the eyes of Lenin.

They were searching the road behind them.

"Are we being followed, Sergei?"

"It's not Sergei. My name is Colonel Grigori Bulganov."

"How do you do, Colonel Bulganov?"

"I do just fine, Allon. Now shut your mouth."

Bulganov eased into a turnout and killed the engine. After warning Gabriel not to move, he climbed out and opened the trunk. He rummaged around the interior before coming over to Gabriel's side of the car. When he opened the door, he was holding the Makarov in one hand and a pair of rusted bolt cutters in the other.

"What are you going to do? Cut me into little pieces?"

Bulganov placed the Makarov on top of the car. "Shut up and get out."

Gabriel did as he was told. Bulganov spun him around, so that he was facing the car, and took hold of the handcuffs. Gabriel heard a single snap and his hands were free.

"Would you like to tell me what's going on, Sergei?"

"I told you, Allon — it's Grigori. Colonel Grigori Bulganov." He held out the Makarov toward Gabriel. "I assume you know how to use one of these things?"

Gabriel took hold of the gun. "Any chance of getting these cuffs off my wrists?"

"Not without the key. Besides, you'll need to be wearing them when we walk back into that warehouse. It's the only way we'll be able to get Elena out of there alive." Bulganov treated Gabriel to one of his clever smiles. "You didn't think I was actually going to let those monsters kill her, did you, Allon?"

"Of course not, *Sergei.* Why would I think a thing like that?"

"I'm sure you have a few questions."

"A couple thousand, actually."

"We'll have time for that later. Get back in the car and pretend your hands are still cuffed."

67

KALUZHSKAYA OBLAST, RUSSIA

Gabriel peered out the car window at the dachas in the trees. He did not see them. Instead, he saw a man who looked like Lenin, seated behind an interrogation table at Lubyanka. It was possible Bulganov was playing some sort of game. Possible, thought Gabriel, but not likely. The colonel had just freed his hands and given him a loaded gun — a gun he could use, if he were so inclined, to splatter the colonel's brains across the windshield.

"What were you and Arkady talking about in Russian?"

"He told me he wanted information from you."

"Did he tell you what it was?"

"No, he wanted me to take you into the woods and put a gun to your head. I was supposed to give you one more chance to talk before killing you."

"And you agreed to this?"

"It's a long story. The point is, we can use it to our advantage. We'll walk in the same door we just walked out. I'll tell Arkady you've had a change of heart. That you're willing to tell him anything he wants to know. Then, when we're close enough, I'll shoot him."

"Arkady?"

"Yes, I'll take care of Arkady. That leaves the two other gorillas. They're both ex-special forces. They know how to handle guns. I'm just an FSB counterintelligence officer. I watch spies."

Bulganov glanced into the rearview mirror.

"You can't walk into the building with the gun in your hand, Allon. You'll have to hide it somewhere you can get to it quickly. I hear you're not bad with a gun. Do you think you can get that Makarov out in time to keep those goons from killing us?"

Gabriel inserted the Makarov into the waistband of his trousers and concealed it with his coat. "Keep your gun pointed at me until you're ready. When I see it move toward Arkady, I'll take that as my cue."

"That leaves the three boys outside."

"They won't stay outside for long — not when they hear the sound of gunfire inside the warehouse. Whatever you do, don't offer them a chance to lay down their weapons and surrender. It doesn't work that way in the real world. Just turn around and start shooting. And don't miss. We won't have time to reload."

"You've only got eight rounds in that magazine."

"If I have to use more than five, we're in trouble."

"Can you see well enough?"

"I can see just fine."

"I have to admit something to you, Allon."

"What's that?"

"I've never shot anyone before."

"Just remember to pull the trigger, Grigori. The gun works much better when you pull the trigger."

The three security guards were still milling about the entrance of the warehouse when Gabriel and Bulganov returned. Someone must have found where Ivan kept the beer because all three were drinking from enormous bottles of Baltika. As Gabriel walked toward the guards, he held his right wrist in his left hand to create the illusion his hands were still cuffed. Bulganov walked a half step behind, Makarov pointed at the center of Gabriel's back. The guards seemed only moderately interested in their reappearance. Obviously, they were used to seeing condemned men being led around at the point of a gun.

It was precisely forty-two paces from the open loading door to the spot where Elena Kharkov sat chained to her metal chair. Gabriel knew this because he counted the steps in his head as he covered the distance now, with Colonel Grigori Bulganov at his side. Colonel Bulganov, who two months earlier had ordered Gabriel to be thrown down two flights of steps in Lubyanka. Colonel Bulganov, who had called himself Sergei that night and said he would kill Gabriel if he ever returned to Russia. Colonel Bulganov, who had never fired a gun in anger before and in whose hands Gabriel's life now resided.

Arkady Medvedev was standing before Elena in his shirtsleeves and screaming obscenities into her face. As Bulganov and Gabriel approached, he turned to face them, hands on his hips, Stechkin shoved down the front of his trousers. Luka Osipov and the bald giant were standing directly behind Elena, each to one side. It was hardly optimal, Gabriel thought, but because Elena was still handcuffed to the chair, there was no chance of her getting into his line of fire. Bulganov spoke in Russian to Medvedev as they moved into point-blank range. Medvedev smiled and looked at Gabriel.

"So, you've come to your senses."

"Yes, Arkady. I've come to my senses."

"Tell me then. Where are Ivan's children?"

"What children?"

Medvedev frowned and looked at Bulganov. Bulganov frowned in return and pointed his gun at Medvedev's heart. Gabriel took a step to his right while simultaneously reaching beneath his coat for the Makarov. They fired their first shots simultaneously, Bulganov into Medvedev's chest, Gabriel into the flat forehead of the bald giant. Luka Osipov responded with a futile attempt to draw his weapon. Gabriel's shot caught him just beneath the chin and exited at the base of his skull.

At that instant, Gabriel heard the sound of shattering glass: the sound of three men simultaneously dropping three bottles of Baltika beer. They came in through the doorway neatly spaced, like little floating ducklings in an arcade shooting gallery. Gabriel took them down in order: head shot, head shot, torso shot.

He spun round and looked at Elena. She was desperately trying to pull her wrists through her handcuffs, her mouth wide in a silent scream. Gabriel wanted to comfort her but could not; Arkady Medvedev was still alive and was struggling to get the Stechkin out of the front of his trousers. Gabriel kicked the gun out of Medvedev's hands and stood over him. The Russian began to pant, pink blood frothing at the side of his mouth.

"I'd like you to give Ivan a message," Gabriel said. "Will you do that for me, Arkady?"

Medvedev nodded, his breathing rapid and shallow. Gabriel raised the Makarov and fired his last three shots into the Russian's face. Message delivered.

Gabriel held Elena tightly while Bulganov searched the bodies for a key to the handcuffs. He found one, a universal, on Luka Osipov. He freed Elena's hands first, then removed the cuffs from Gabriel's hands.

"Take her out to the car," Gabriel said. "I'll be there in a minute."

"Be quick about it."

"Just go."

As Bulganov led Elena toward the door, Gabriel searched the corpse of Arkady Medvedev. He found keys, passports, and a wallet filled with cash. He ignored the money and removed a single item: a plastic card embossed with the image of a large apartment house on the banks of the Moscow River.

Bulganov had the Volga's engine running by the time Gabriel stepped outside. He climbed into the back next to Elena, whose screams were no longer silent. Gabriel held her tightly to his chest as Bulganov drove away.

Her wailing had ceased by the time they saw the sign. It stood at the intersection of two dreadful roads, rusted, crooked, and pierced by bullet holes. Two arrows pointed in opposite directions. To the left was MOCKBA, the Cyrillic spelling of Moscow. Bulganov explained what lay to the right.

"Ukraine."

"How long?"

"We can be over the border before dawn."

"We?"

"I just helped an Israeli agent kill Arkady Medvedev and five of his security men. How long do you think I'll live if I stay in Moscow? A week, if I'm lucky. I'm coming with you."

"Another defector? That's all we need."

"I suspect you'll find I'm worth my weight in gold. You see, I've been privately investigating the ties between men like Ivan Kharkov and the FSB for years. I also know a great deal about Ivan's little arms-trafficking network. Much more than you, I suspect. Are you sure you wouldn't like me to come with you, Allon?"

"We'd love the company, Colonel. Besides, it's a long drive and I don't have a clue how to get out of here."

Bulganov let his foot off the brake and started to turn to the right. Gabriel told him to stop.

"What's the problem?" Bulganov asked.

"You're going the wrong way."

"We're going to Ukraine. And Ukraine is to the right. Look at the sign."

"We have a couple of errands to run before we leave."

"Where?"

Gabriel pointed to the left.

MOCKBA . . .

68
Moscow

On the outskirts of Moscow was a super-market that never closed. If it was not the world's largest supermarket, thought Gabriel, then it was surely a close second: two acres of frozen foods, a mile of cookies and crackers, another mile of American soft drinks, one nightmarish wall hung with thousands of pork sausages. And that was just the food. At the far end of the market was a section called Home and Garden, where one could buy everything from clothing to motorcycles to lawn tractors. *Who in Moscow needed a lawn tractor?* thought Gabriel. *Who in Moscow even had a lawn?* "They're for the dachas," Elena explained. "Now that Russians have money, they don't like to dig with their hands anymore." She shrugged. "But what's the point of having a dacha if you don't get your hands dirty?"

Why the market remained open all night was a mystery because at 2 a.m. it was deserted. They walked the endless prospekts of consumer goods, quickly pulling items from the shelves: clean clothing, bandages and antiseptic, a pair of large sunglasses, enough snack food and cola to fuel an early-morning road trip. When they wheeled their cart up to the checkout stand, the drowsy female clerk looked at Gabriel's eye and winced. Elena contemptuously explained that her "husband" had crashed his car in a ditch — drunk out of his mind on vodka, of course. The checkout woman shook her head sadly as she rang up the items. "Russian men," she muttered. "They never change."

Gabriel carried the bags out to the car and climbed into the back again with Elena. Bulganov, alone in the front, told them a story as he drove toward central Moscow. It was the story of a young KGB officer who never truly believed the lies of Lenin and Stalin and who had quietly raised a glass of vodka when the empire of deception finally fell. This young officer had tried to resign after the collapse of communism but had been convinced by his mentor to stay on and help turn the KGB into a truly professional service. He had reluctantly agreed and had quickly risen through the ranks of the KGB's domestic successor, the FSB, only to see it deteriorate into something worse than the KGB had been. This young man, at great personal risk, had then joined forces with a group of officers who hoped to reform the FSB. *Quietly,* said Bulganov. *From the inside.* But they soon realized that the top brass and their masters in the Kremlin were not interested in reform. So the group went underground. And started building a dossier.

"Our dossier does not paint a pretty picture. FSB involvement in murder for hire, prostitution, and narcotics. FSB involvement in the operations of shady oligarchs. And *worse.* Who do you think planned and carried out those apartment house bombings that our president used to justify going back into Chechnya? My service is a criminal enterprise from top to bottom. And it is *running* Russia."

"How did I end up on your plate that night in Lubyanka?"

"Ironically, it was all by the book. We were watching you from the moment you hit the ground in St. Petersburg. And I must admit, you were quite good. We had no suspicions, even *after* you initiated contact with Olga Sukhova. We thought you were Natan Golani of the Israeli Ministry of Culture."

"So you didn't know Arkady and Ivan

were going to have us killed that night?"

"No, not at all. At first, I thought you were just in the wrong place at the wrong time. But when you survived the attack and saved Olga, that caused Ivan a serious problem. I almost lost you during your detention in Lubyanka. Ivan Kharkov himself was on the phone to the chief. He knew your real name and your real job. He wanted you taken out into a field and shot. The top floor ordered me to do just that. I pretended to go along and started stalling for time. Then, thankfully, your service made such a stink, you became too hot, even for the likes of Ivan Kharkov."

"How did you convince them not to kill me?"

"I told them that it would be a public-relations disaster if you died in FSB custody. I told them I didn't care what Ivan did to you once you left the country, but they couldn't lay a hand on you while you were on Russian soil. Ivan wasn't happy, but the top floor finally came around to my way of thinking. I put you in the van and got you to the border before they could change their minds. You came very close to dying that night, Allon — closer than you'll ever realize."

"Where's the dossier now?"

"Most of it's up here," he said, tapping the side of his forehead. "Whatever documentation we could copy was scanned and stored in e-mail accounts outside the country."

"How did you end up in that warehouse tonight?"

"I've been plying my trade on both sides of the street."

"You're on Ivan's payroll?"

Bulganov nodded. "It made it much easier to gather information about the FSB's shady dealings if I actually took part in some myself. It also gave me protection. The real rotten elements thought I was one of them. I know a great deal about Ivan's operation. Who knows? Maybe we know enough together to track down those missiles — *without* going back into the House on the Embankment. Even I get the creeps going into the place. It's haunted, you know. They say Stalin roams the halls at night knocking on doors."

"I'm not leaving Russia without Ivan's disks."

"You don't know if there's anything on them. You also don't know if they're even still in the apartment."

Elena intervened. "I saw Arkady put my handbag in the vault before we left."

"That was a long time ago. Ivan could have ordered someone to move them."

"He couldn't have. Only three people in the world can access that vault: Ivan, Arkady, and me. Logically, the disks have to be there."

"But getting them is going to cost valuable time. It also might mean another dead body. There's going to be a new guard in the apartment. He might even have a helper or two. In the old days, the neighbors were used to the sound of a little late-night gunfire, but not now. If we have to do any shooting, it could get ugly quickly."

"You're still a colonel in the FSB, Grigori. And FSB colonels take shit from no one."

"I don't want to be an FSB colonel anymore. I want to be one of the good guys."

"You will be," Gabriel said. "The moment you present yourself at the Ukrainian border and declare your desire to defect."

Bulganov lowered his eyes from the mirror and stared straight down the Leninsky Prospekt. "I already am a good guy," he said quietly. "I just play for a very bad team."

69
BOLOTNAYA SQUARE, MOSCOW

The Russian president frowned in disapproval as Gabriel, Elena, and Grigori Bulganov hurried across the street toward the House on the Embankment. Bulganov placed his FSB identification on the reception desk and quietly threatened to cut off the porter's hand if he touched the telephone.

"We were never here. Do you understand me?"

The terrified porter nodded. Bulganov returned his ID to his coat pocket and walked over to the private elevator, where Gabriel and Elena had already boarded a car. As the doors closed, the two men drew their Makarovs and chambered their first rounds.

The elevator was old and slow; the journey to the ninth floor seemed to last an eternity. When the doors finally opened, Elena was pressed into one corner, with Gabriel and

Bulganov, guns leveled in firing positions, shielding her body. Their precaution proved unnecessary, however, because the vestibule, like the entrance hall of the apartment, was empty. It seemed Arkady Medvedev's highly trained security guard had fallen asleep on the couch in the living room while watching a bit of pornography on Ivan's large-screen television. Gabriel woke the guard by inserting the barrel of the Makarov into his ear.

"If you are a good dog, you will live to see the sunrise. If you are a bad dog, I'm going to make a terrible mess on Ivan's couch. Which is it going to be? Good dog or bad dog?"

"Good," said the guard.

"Wise choice. Let's go."

Gabriel marched the guard into Ivan's fortified office, where Elena was already in the process of opening the interior vault. Her handbag was where Medvedev had left it. The disks were still inside. Bulganov ordered the guard into the vault and closed the steel door. Elena pressed the button behind volume 2 of *Anna Karenina* and the bookshelves slid shut. Inside, the guard began shouting in Russian, his muffled voice barely audible.

"Maybe we should give him some water," Bulganov said.

"He'll be fine for a few hours." Gabriel looked at Elena. "Is there anything else you need?"

She shook her head. Gabriel and Bulganov led the way back to the elevator, Makarovs leveled before them. The porter was still frozen in place behind the reception desk. Bulganov gave him one final reminder to keep his mouth shut, then led Gabriel and Elena out to the car.

"With a bit of luck, we can be across the border before dawn," Bulganov said as he shoved his key into the ignition. "Unless you have any more errands you'd like to run."

"I do, actually. I need you to make one final arrest while you're still an FSB officer."

"Who?"

Gabriel told him.

"It's out of the question. There's no way I can get past all that security."

"You're still a colonel in the FSB, Grigori. And FSB colonels take shit from no one."

70

MOSCOW

An Orion's Belt of lights burned on the north side of the House of Dogs; red lamps blinked in the transmission towers high atop the roof. Gabriel sat behind the wheel of Colonel Grigori Bulganov's official car. Elena sat beside him, with Colonel Grigori Bulganov's mobile phone in her hand. The colonel was not present. He was on the eleventh floor, arresting Olga Sukhova, crusading journalist from the formerly crusading *Moskovsky Gazeta.*

"Do you think she'll come?" Elena asked.

"She'll come," said Gabriel. "She has no other choice. She knows that if she ever sets foot outside that apartment, your husband will kill her."

Elena reached out and touched the bandage on Gabriel's right eye. "I did the best I could. It needs stitches. Probably more. I think that beast managed to break something."

"I'm sure he regretted his actions when he saw the gun in my hand."

"I don't think he ever saw your gun." She touched his hand. "Where did you learn to do that?"

"Unfortunately, I've had a lot of practice."

"May I make a confession?"

"Of course."

"I'm glad you killed them. I know that must sound terrible coming from the wife of a murderer, but I'm glad you killed them the way you did. Especially Arkady."

"I should have waited until you were gone. I'm sorry for that, Elena."

"Will it ever go away?"

"The memory? No, it will never go away."

She looked at the mobile phone, and checked the strength of the signal.

"So is your name really Gabriel or was that a deception, too?"

"It's my real name."

Elena smiled.

"Is there something humorous about my name?"

"No, it's a beautiful name. I was just thinking about the last words my mother said to me before I left her this afternoon: 'May the angel of the Lord be looking over your shoulder.' I suppose she was right after all."

"We can pick her up on the way out of town if you like."

"My mother? The last thing you want to do is drive to Ukraine with my mother in the backseat. Besides, there's no need to bring her out right away. Not even Ivan would harm an old woman." She scrutinized him in silence for a moment. "So are you, in fact, the angel of the Lord?"

"Do I look like the angel of the Lord?"

"I suppose not." She glanced up at the façade of the building. "Is it true you don't know where my children are?"

He shook his head. "I was lying to Arkady. I know where they are."

"Tell me."

"Not yet. I'll tell you when we're safely over the border."

"Look!" She pointed up at the building. "A light just came on. Does that mean she let him into the apartment?"

"Probably."

She looked at the mobile phone. "Ring, damn it. *Ring.*"

"Relax, Elena. It's three o'clock in the morning and an FSB colonel is telling her to pack a bag. Give her a moment to digest what's happening."

"Do you think she'll come?"

"She'll come."

Gabriel took the phone from her grasp and asked how she knew the Cassatt was a forgery.

"It was the hands."

"What about the hands?"

"The brushstrokes were too impasto."

"Sarah told me the same thing."

"You should have listened to her."

Just then the phone rang. Gabriel handed it to Elena.

"Da?" she said, then: *"Da, da."*

She looked at Gabriel.

"Flash the lights, Gabriel. She wants you to flash the headlights."

Gabriel flicked the headlamps twice. Elena spoke a few more words in Russian. The eleventh-floor window went dark.

■ ■ ■ ■

PART FOUR
THE HARVEST

■ ■ ■ ■

71
VILLA DEI FIORI, UMBRIA

The *vendemmia,* the annual harvest of the wine grapes, commenced at the Villa dei Fiori on the final Saturday in September. It coincided with the unwelcome news that the restorer was planning to return to Umbria. Count Gasparri briefly considered making the drive from Rome to inform the staff in person. In the end, he decided a quick telephone call to Margherita would suffice.

"When is he scheduled to arrive?" she asked, her voice heavy with dread.

"This is unclear."

"But of course. Will he be alone or accompanied by Francesca?"

"This is also unclear."

"Should we assume he'll be working again?"

"That is the hope," Gasparri said. "But my friends at the Vatican tell me he's been in some sort of accident. I wouldn't expect him to be in a terribly good mood."

"How will we tell the difference?"

"Be kind to him, Margherita. Apparently, the poor man's been through quite an ordeal."

And with that the line went dead. Margherita hung up the phone and headed out to the vineyards.

The poor man's been through quite an ordeal . . .

Yes, she thought. *And now he's going to take it out on us.*

The "return," as it became known to the staff, occurred late that same evening. Carlos, who lived in a stone cottage on a hill above the pasture, spotted the little Passat wagon as it turned through the gate and started down the gravel road toward the villa with its headlamps doused. He quickly telephoned Isabella, who was standing on the veranda of her residence near the stables as the blacked-out car flashed by in a cloud of dust. Her observation, though brief, yielded two critical pieces of information: the car definitely contained not one but *two* people — the restorer and the woman they knew as Francesca — and the woman was driving. Strong circumstantial evidence, she told Carlos, that the restorer had indeed suffered an accident of some sort.

The last member of the staff to see the couple that night was Margherita, who watched them cross the courtyard from her static post above the chapel. Like all house-keepers, Margherita was a natural watcher — and, like any good watcher, she took note of small details. She found it odd, to say the least, that the woman was leading the way. She also thought she could detect something different about the restorer's movements. Something vaguely hesitant in his step. She saw him once more, when he appeared in the upstairs window and gazed in her direction over the courtyard. There was no soldierly nod this time; in fact, he gave no indication that he was even aware of her presence. He just peered into the gloom, as if searching for an adversary that he knew was there but could not see.

The shutters closed with a thump and the restorer disappeared from sight. Margherita remained frozen in her window for a long time after, haunted by the image she had just seen. A man in a moonlit window with a heavy bandage over his right eye.

Unfortunately, Count Gasparri's predictions about the restorer's mood turned out to be accurate. Unlike in summer, when he had been predictably aloof, his moods now fluctuated between chilling silences and flashes of alarming temper. Francesca, while apologetic, offered few clues about how he had sustained the injury, stating only that he had suffered "a mishap" while working abroad. Naturally, the staff was left to speculate as to what had actually happened. Their theories ranged from the absurd to the mundane. They were certain of one thing: the injury had left the restorer dangerously on edge, as Anna discovered one morning when she approached him from behind while he was struggling to read the newspaper. His sudden movement gave her such a start that she vowed never to go near him again. Margherita took to singing as she went about her chores, which only seemed to annoy him more.

At first, he did not venture beyond the Etruscan walls of the garden. There, he would spend afternoons beneath the shade of the trellis, drinking his Orvieto wine and reading until his eye became too fatigued to continue. Sometimes, when it was warm, he would wander down to the pool and wade carefully into the shallow end, making certain to keep his bandaged eye above water. Other times, he would lie on his back on the chaise and toss a tennis ball into the air, for hours on end, as if testing his vision and reactions. Each time he returned to the villa, he would pause in the drawing room and stare at the empty studio. Margherita took note of the fact that he would not stand in his usual spot, directly before the easels, but several paces away. "It's as if he's trying to imagine himself working again," she told Anna. "The poor man isn't at all sure he'll ever lay his hands on another painting."

He soon felt strong enough to resume his walks. In the beginning, they were not long, nor were they conducted at a rapid pace. He wore wraparound sunglasses to cover his eyes and a cotton bucket hat pulled down to the bridge of his nose. Some days, the woman accompanied him, but usually he walked alone, with only the dogs for company. Isabella greeted him pleasantly each time he passed the stables, even though she usually received only a taciturn nod in return. His mood improved with exercise, though, and once he actually stopped for a few minutes to chat about the horses. Isabella offered to give him riding lessons when his eye had healed, but he made no response other than to turn his gaze skyward to watch a jetliner on final approach to Fiumicino Airport. "Are you afraid?" Isabella asked him. Yes, he admitted as the plane disappeared behind a khaki-colored hill. He was very afraid.

With each passing day, he walked a little farther, and by the middle of October he was able to hike to the gate and back each morning. He even began venturing into the woods again. It was during one such outing, on the first chilly day of the season, that the Villa dei Fiori echoed with a single crack of a small-caliber weapon. The restorer emerged from the trees a few moments later with a sweater knotted casually round his neck and the dogs howling with bloodlust. He informed Carlos that he had been charged by a wild boar and that the boar, unfortunately, had not survived the encounter. When Carlos looked for evidence of a gun, the restorer seemed to smile. Then he turned and set out down the gravel road toward the villa. Carlos found the animal a few minutes later. Between its eyes was a bloodless hole. Small and neat. Almost as if it had been painted with a brush.

The next morning, the Villa dei Fiori, along with the rest of Europe, awoke to the stunning news that a disaster of unimaginable proportions had been narrowly averted. The story broke first in London, where the BBC reported that Scotland Yard was conducting "major terrorism-related raids" in East London and in neighborhoods near Heathrow and Gatwick airports. Later that morning, a sober-looking British prime minister went before the cameras at Downing Street to inform the nation that the security services had disrupted a major terrorist plot aimed at simultaneously destroying several airliners in British airspace. It was not the first time a plot such as this had been uncovered in Britain. What set this one apart, though, were the weapons involved: SA-18 shoulder-launch antiaircraft missiles. British police had found twelve of the sophisticated weapons during their early-morning raids and, according to the prime minister, were frantically searching for more. He refused to say where the terrorists had obtained the missiles but pointedly reminded reporters of the name of the country where the weapons were manufactured: Russia. Finally, in a chilling endnote, the prime minister stated that the plot had been "global in scope" and warned reporters that they had a long day ahead.

Ten minutes later, in Paris, the French president strode before the cameras at the Élysée Palace and announced that a similar round of police raids had been carried out that same morning in the suburbs of Paris and in the South of France. Twenty missiles had been found thus far, ten in an apartment near Charles de Gaulle Airport and ten more on a fishing boat in Marseilles's bustling old port. Unlike the British prime minister, who had been circumspect about the origin of the missiles, the French president said it was clear to him that the weapons had been supplied to the terrorists, directly or indirectly, by a Russian source. He also suggested that the French security and intelligence services had played "a major role in foiling the plot."

Similar scenes played out in rapid succession in Madrid, Rome, Athens, Zurich, Copenhagen, and, finally, on the other side of the Atlantic, in Washington, D.C. Flanked by his senior national security staff, the president told the American people that eight SA-18 missiles had been discovered aboard a motor yacht bound for Miami from the Bahamas and six more had been found in the trunk of a car attempting to enter the United States from Canada. Four suspected terrorists had been detained and were now undergoing interrogation. Based on what had been gleaned thus far, both by American and European investigators, it appeared the plot had been timed to coincide with the Christmas holidays. American and Israeli aircraft were the primary targets of the terrorists, who were hoping to maximize casualties among "the Crusaders and the Jews." The president assured the American people that the plot had been fully disrupted and that it was safe to fly. The traveling public apparently did not agree. Within hours of the announcement, hundreds of flights were delayed or rescheduled due to an unprecedented wave of passenger cancellations. Airline analysts predicted the news would cause severe financial damage to an already-troubled industry.

By nightfall, all eyes were on Moscow, where the Kremlin had maintained a Soviet-like silence as the story unfolded. Shortly after 11 p.m., a spokesman for the Russian president finally issued a terse statement categorically denying any link between the terrorist plot and legitimate arms sales by Russia to its clients in the Middle East. If the missiles had indeed come from a Russian source, said the spokesman, then it was almost certainly a criminal act — one that would be investigated to the fullest extent possible by Russian authorities. Within a few hours, however, the veracity of the Russian statement was called into question by a dramatic newspaper report in London. It was written by someone the men of the Kremlin knew well: Olga Sukhova, the former editor in chief of *Moskovsky Gazeta.*

It was among the most intriguing aspects of the entire affair. Kept under virtual house arrest in her Moscow apartment for much of the summer, Olga Sukhova had managed to slip out of Russia undetected, purportedly with the help of an FSB colonel named Grigori Bulganov. After crossing the Ukrainian border by car, the two were spirited to a safe house in England, where they had worked closely with U.S. and British intelligence officers involved in the search for the SA-18 missiles. In exchange for her cooperation, Olga had been granted "a period of exclusivity" regarding certain details of the affair — details she published, in spectacular fashion, in London's *Telegraph* newspaper.

According to her front-page story, the missiles seized by European and American officials had originally been sold to the Democratic Republic of East Africa by Russian businessman and arms trafficker Ivan Kharkov. Kharkov had reportedly concluded the sale with the full knowledge that the weapons were to be transferred to an al-Qaeda affiliate in the Horn of Africa. The article also implicated Kharkov and his now-deceased chief of security, Arkady Medvedev, in the murders of *Gazeta* journalists Aleksandr Lubin and Boris Ostrovsky.

For the next several days, Olga Sukhova was a fixture on European and American television. So, too, was the man credited with facilitating her escape: Colonel Grigori Bulganov of the FSB. He told tales of rampant corruption inside his old service and warned that the new masters of the Kremlin were nothing but KGB thugs who planned to confront the West at every turn.

By the end of the week, he and Olga Sukhova had both signed lucrative book deals. As for the man at the center of the storm, he was nowhere to be found. Ivan Borisovich Kharkov, real estate developer, venture capitalist, and international arms trafficker, had apparently vanished into thin air.

His assets were quickly seized; his bank accounts quickly frozen. For a time, his grand palaces were surrounded day and night by reporters and cameramen. Finally, when it became clear Ivan was never coming back, the reporters moved on in search of other prey.

The list of countries where Ivan was suddenly wanted for arrest or questioning was long and somewhat ludicrous. There was irony in the situation, of course; even the most jaundiced observer had to admit it. For years, Ivan had callously fueled the deadly civil wars and conflicts of the Third World with little or no interference from the West. But only when he crossed some moral line — when he dared to sell his wares directly to the forces of global Islamic extremism — did the governments of the civilized world sit up and take notice. Even if al-Qaeda had managed to carry out its attack as planned, said one respected commentator, the death toll would have been but a tiny fraction of those killed by Ivan's guns and bullets in Africa alone.

It was assumed by all that he had taken refuge somewhere inside Russia. How he had managed to get there from France, where he was last seen, was a matter of considerable contention. French aviation officials acknowledged that Ivan's private jet had departed Côte d'Azur International Airport on the morning of August twenty-sixth, though they refused repeated requests to release a flight plan or complete manifest. The press demanded to know whether French authorities had been aware of Ivan's activities at the time of the flight. If so, they asked, why had he and his party been allowed to depart?

Confronted with a gathering media storm, French authorities were finally forced to admit that they *were* indeed aware of Ivan's involvement in the missile sale at the time of the flight in question, but "certain operational exigencies" required that Ivan be allowed to leave French soil. Those operational exigencies notwithstanding, French prosecutors now wanted Ivan back, as did their counterparts in Britain, where he faced a slew of criminal charges ranging from money laundering to involvement in a plot to commit an act of mass murder. A Kremlin spokesman dismissed the charges as "Western lies and propaganda" and pointed out that it was not possible under Russian law to extradite Mr. Kharkov to face criminal charges. The spokesman went on to say that Russian authorities were completely unaware of Mr. Kharkov's whereabouts and had no record he was even in the country.

Forty-eight hours later, when a photograph surfaced of Ivan attending a Kremlin reception for the newly reelected Russian president, the Kremlin could not be troubled for a comment. In the West, much was made of the fact that Ivan had attended the reception with a stunning young super-model named Yekatarina Mazurov rather than his elegant wife. A week later, he filed for divorce in a Russian court, accusing Elena Kharkov of sins ranging from infidelity to child abuse. Elena was not there to contest the charges. Elena, it seemed, had disappeared from the face of the earth.

None of which seemed to concern the staff of the Villa dei Fiori in Umbria, for they had more pressing matters with which to contend. There were crops to bring in and fences that needed mending. There was a horse with an injured leg and a leak in the roof that needed fixing before the heavy rains of winter. And there was a melancholy man with a patch over one eye who feared he would never be able to work again. He could do nothing now but wait. And toss his tennis ball against the Etruscan walls of the garden. And walk the dusty gravel road with the hounds at his heels.

72
VILLA DEI FIORI,
UMBRIA

Ari Shamron telephoned a week later to invite himself to lunch. He arrived in a single embassy car, with Gilah at his side. The afternoon was windy and raw, so they ate indoors in the formal dining room with an olive-wood fire blazing in the open hearth. Shamron referred to himself as Herr Heller, one of his many work names, and spoke only German in front of Anna and Margherita. When lunch was over, Chiara and Gilah helped with the dishes. Gabriel and Shamron pulled on coats and walked along the gravel road between the umbrella pines. Shamron waited until they were a hundred yards from the villa before lighting his first Turkish cigarette. "Don't tell Gilah," he said. "She's bothering me to quit again."

"She's not as naïve as you think. She knows you smoke behind her back."

"She doesn't mind as long as I make at

least *some* effort to conceal it from her."

"You should listen to her for once. Those things are going to kill you."

"I'm as old as these hills, my son. Let me enjoy myself while I'm still here."

"Why didn't you tell me Gilah was coming with you?"

"I suppose it slipped my mind. I'm not used to traveling with my wife. We're going to Vienna to listen to music next. Then we're going to London to see a play."

Shamron made it sound as if he had been sentenced to a month in solitary, with punishment rations.

"This is what people do when they retire, Ari. They travel. They relax."

"I'm not *retired.* God, I hate that word. Next, you'll accuse me of being deceased."

"Try to enjoy yourself, Ari — if not for your sake, then for Gilah's. She deserves a nice holiday in Europe. We all love you dearly, but you haven't exactly been the perfect husband and father."

"And for my sins, I am to be punished with a week of Mozart and Pinter."

They walked in silence, Gabriel with his gaze downward, Shamron trailing smoke like a steam engine.

"I hear we're sending a doctor up here tomorrow to remove your bandages."

"Is that why you came? To see the great unveiling?"

"Gilah and I thought you would like to have some family around. Were we wrong to come?"

"Of course not, Ari. I just might not be very good company. That gorilla managed to fracture my orbit and cause significant damage to my retina. Even under the best of circumstances, I'm going to have blurred vision for a while."

"And the worst?"

"Significant loss of vision in one eye. Not exactly a helpful condition for someone who makes his living restoring paintings."

"You make your *living* defending the State of Israel." Greeted by Gabriel's silence, Shamron looked up at the treetops moving in the wind. "What's wrong, Gabriel? No speech about how you're planning to leave the Office for good this time? No lecture about how you've given enough to your country and your people already?"

"I'll always be here for you, Ari — as long as I can see, of course."

"What *are* your plans?"

"I'm going to remain a guest of Count Gasparri until I wear out my welcome. And, if my vision permits, I'm going to quietly restore a few paintings for the Vatican

Museums. You may recall I was working on one when you asked me to run that little errand in Rome. Unfortunately, I had to let someone else finish it for me."

"I'm afraid I'm not terribly sympathetic. You saved thousands of lives with that little errand. That's more important than restoring a painting."

They came to the fork in the track. Shamron looked up at the large, wood-carved crucifix and shook his head slowly. "Did I mention that Gilah and I had dinner at the Vatican last night with Monsignor Donati and His Holiness?"

"No, you didn't."

"His Holiness was quite pleased that the Church was able to play a small role in Ivan's demise. He's quite anxious it remain a secret, though. He doesn't want any more dead bodies in his Basilica."

"You can see his point," said Gabriel.

"Absolutely," Shamron agreed.

It was one of the many aspects of the affair that remained secret — the fact that Ivan's children, after leaving Saint-Tropez, had been taken to an isolated priory high in the Maritime Alps. They had remained there for nearly a week — under Church protection and with the full knowledge and approval of the Supreme Pontiff — before boarding a CIA Gulfstream jet and flying clandestinely to the United States.

"Where are they?" Gabriel asked.

"Elena and the children?" Shamron dropped his cigarette and crushed it out. "I have no idea. And, quite frankly, I don't *want* to know. She's Adrian's problem now. Ivan has started more than divorce proceedings. He's created a special unit within his personal security service with one job: finding Elena and the children. He wants his children back. He wants Elena dead."

"What about Olga and Grigori?"

"Your friend Graham Seymour is hearing rumors of Russian assassins heading for British shores. Olga is locked away in a safe house outside London, surrounded by armed guards. Grigori is another story. He's told Graham he can look after himself."

"Did Graham agree to this?"

"Not entirely. He's got Grigori under full-time watch."

"*Watchers?* Watchers can't protect anyone from a Russian assassin. Grigori should be surrounded by men with guns."

"So should you." Shamron didn't bother trying to conceal his irritation. "If it were up to me, you'd be locked away someplace in Israel where Ivan would never think to look for you."

"And you wonder why I'd rather be here."

"Just don't think about setting foot outside this estate. Not until Ivan's had a chance to cool down."

"Ivan doesn't strike me as the sort to forget a grudge."

"No, he doesn't."

"Perhaps we should just kill him now and get it over with."

Shamron looked at the bandage on Gabriel's eye. "Ivan can wait, my son. You have more important things to worry about."

They had arrived at the stables. In an adjacent pen, a pair of pigs were rolling about in the mud. Shamron looked at the animals and winced in disgust.

"First a crucifix. Now pigs. What's next?"

"We have our own chapel."

Shamron ignited another cigarette. "I'm getting tired," he said. "Let's head back."

They turned around and started toward the villa. Shamron produced an envelope from the breast pocket of his leather bomber jacket and handed it to Gabriel.

"It's a letter from Elena," Shamron said. "Adrian Carter had it couriered to Tel Aviv."

"Did you read it?"

"Of course."

Gabriel removed the letter and read it for himself.

"Are you up to it?" Shamron asked.

"I'll know after the great unveiling."

"Maybe Gilah and I should stay here for a few days, just in case things don't go well."

"What about Mozart and Pinter?"

"I'd rather be here" — he looked around theatrically — "with the pigs and the crucifixes."

"Then we'd love to have you."

"Do the staff really have no idea who you are?"

"They think I'm an eccentric restorer who suffers from melancholia and mood swings."

Shamron placed his hand on Gabriel's shoulder. "It sounds to me as if they know you quite well."

73
VILLA DEI FIORI, UMBRIA

The doctor came the following morning. Israeli by way of Queens, he wore a rabbinical beard and had the small soft hands of a baby. He removed the dressing from Gabriel's eye, frowned heavily, and began snipping away the sutures.

"Let me know if anything I do hurts."

"Trust me, you'll be the first to know."

He shone a light directly into Gabriel's eye and frowned some more.

"How does it feel?"

"Like you're burning a hole in my cornea."

The doctor switched off the light.

"How does it feel now?"

"Like it's covered in cotton wool and Vaseline."

"Can you see?"

"I wouldn't go that far."

He covered Gabriel's good eye. "How many fingers am I holding up?"

"Twelve."

"Come on. How many?"

"Four, I think, but I can't be sure."

The doctor uncovered the good eye. He was holding up two fingers. He put some drops in the damaged eye that burned like battery acid and covered it with a black patch.

"I look like an idiot."

"Not for long. Your retina looks remarkably good for what you've been through. You're a very lucky man. Wear the patch on and off for a few days until your eye regains some of its strength. An hour on, an hour off. Do you understand?"

"Yes, I think I do."

"Avoid bright lights. And don't do anything that might give you unnecessary eyestrain."

"How about painting?"

"Don't even think about it. Not for at least three days."

The doctor put his light and suture cutters back in his bag and pulled the zipper closed. Gabriel thanked him for coming all the way from Tel Aviv for a five-minute job. "Just don't tell anyone you were here," he added. "If you do, that angry-looking little man over there will kill you with his bare hands."

The doctor looked at Shamron, who had managed to watch the entire proceeding without offering a single piece of advice.

"Is it true what they say about him? Was he really the one who kidnapped Eichmann?"

Gabriel nodded.

"Is it all right if I shake his hand? I want to touch the hands that grabbed hold of that monster."

"It's fine," said Gabriel. "But be careful. He bites."

He didn't want to wear the patch, but even he had to admit he looked better with it on than off. The tissue around the eye was still distorted with swelling and the new scar was raw and hideous. "You'll look like yourself eventually," Chiara assured him. "But it's going to take a while. You older men don't heal as fast."

The doctor's optimism about the pace of his recovery turned out to be accurate. By the next morning, Gabriel's vision had improved dramatically, and by the morning after it seemed almost normal. He felt ready to begin work on Elena's request but confined his efforts to only one small task: the fabrication of a stretcher, 38 3/4 inches by 29 1/4 inches. When the stretcher was finished, he pulled a linen canvas over it and covered the canvas with a layer of ground.

Then he placed the canvas on his easel and waited for it to dry.

He slept poorly that night and woke at four. He tried to fall asleep again, but it was no use, so he slipped out of bed and headed downstairs. He had always worked well in the early morning, and, despite his weakened eye, that morning was no exception. He applied the first layers of base paint, and by midday two small children were clearly visible on the canvas.

He took a break for lunch, then spent a second session before the canvas that lasted until dinner. He painted from memory, without even a photograph for reference, and with a swiftness and confidence he would not have thought possible a week earlier. Sometimes, when the house was quiet, he could almost feel her at his shoulder, whispering instructions into his ear. *Watch your brushwork on the hands,* she reminded him. *Not too impasto on the hands.* And sometimes, when his vision began to blur, he would see Elena chained to a chair in her husband's warehouse of death, a gun pressed to the side of her head. *You'd better pull the trigger, Arkady, because Ivan is never getting those children.*

Chiara and the household staff knew better than to watch him while he worked, but

Shamron and Gilah were unaware of his rules and were therefore never far from his back. Gilah's visits were brief in duration, but Shamron, with nothing else to occupy his time, became a permanent fixture in Gabriel's studio. He had always been mystified by Gabriel's ability to paint — to Shamron, it was but a parlor trick or an illusion of some sort — and he was content now to sit silently at Gabriel's side as he worked, even if it meant forgoing his cigarettes.

"I should have left you at Bezalel in 'seventy-two," he said late one night. "I should have found someone else to execute those Black September murderers. You would have been one of the greatest artists of your generation, instead of —"

"Instead of *what?*"

"Instead of an eccentric old restorer with melancholia and mood swings who lives in a villa in the middle of Umbria surrounded by pigs and crucifixes."

"I'm happy, Ari. I have Chiara."

"Keep her close, Gabriel. Remember, Ivan likes to break pretty things."

Gabriel laid down his brush, then stepped back and examined the painting for a long time, hand pressed to his chin, head tilted to one side. Chiara, who was watching from the top of the stairs, said, "Is it finished,

Signore Vianelli?"

Gabriel was silent for a moment. "Yes," he said finally. "I think it is finished."

"What are you going to do about the signature?" Shamron asked.

"I'm not sure."

"May I give you a small piece of artistic advice?"

"If you must."

"Sign it with the name your mother gave you."

He dipped the brush in black paint and signed the name *Gabriel Allon* in the bottom left corner.

"Do you think she'll like it?"

"I'm sure she will. Is it finished now?"

"Not quite," Gabriel said. "I have to bake it for thirty minutes."

"I should have left you at Bezalel," Shamron said. "You could have been great."

AUTHOR'S NOTE

Moscow Rules is a work of fiction. The names, characters, places, and incidents portrayed in this novel are the product of the author's imagination or have been used fictitiously. Any resemblance to actual persons, living or dead, businesses, companies, events, or locales is entirely coincidental.

Two Children on a Beach by Mary Cassatt does not exist and therefore could not have been forged. If it did, it would bear a striking resemblance to a picture called *Children Playing on the Beach,* which hangs in the National Gallery of Art in Washington, D.C. Visitors to the French ski resort of Courchevel will search in vain for the Hôtel Grand, for it, too, is an invention. Riviera Flight Services is fictitious, and I have tinkered with airline schedules to make them fit my story. The Novodevichy Cemetery is faithfully rendered, as is the House on the Embankment, though it is a slightly less sinister place now than I have made it out to be. The FSB is in fact the internal security service of the Russian Federation, and its multitude of sins have been widely reported. Deepest apologies to the director of the Impressionist and Modern Art department at Christie's auction house in London. I am quite certain he is nothing like Alistair Leach. To the best of my knowledge, there is no CIA safe house on N Street in Georgetown.

Moskovsky Gazeta does not exist, though, sadly, the threat to Russian journalists is all too real. According to the Committee to Protect Journalists, forty-seven reporters, editors, cameramen, and photographers have been killed in Russia since 1992, making it the third-deadliest country in the world in which to practice the craft of journalism, after Iraq and Algeria. Fourteen of those deaths occurred during the rule of Russian president Vladimir Putin, who undertook a systematic crackdown on press freedom and political dissent after coming to power in 1999. Virtually all the murders were contract killings, and few have been solved or prosecuted.

The most famous Russian reporter murdered during the rule of Vladimir Putin was

Anna Politkovskaya, who was gunned down in the elevator of her Moscow apartment house in October 2006. A vocal critic of the regime, Politkovskaya was about to publish a searing exposé detailing allegations of torture and kidnapping by the Russian military and security forces in Chechnya. Putin dismissed Anna Politkovskaya as a person of "marginal significance" and did not bother to attend her funeral. No one connected to the Kremlin did.

Six months after Politkovskaya's murder, Ivan Safronov, a highly respected military affairs writer for the *Kommersant* newspaper, was found dead in the courtyard of his Moscow apartment building. Russian police claimed he committed suicide by jumping from a fifth-floor window, even though he resided on the third floor. While conducting research in Moscow, I learned Safronov had telephoned his wife on the way home to say he was stopping to buy some oranges, hardly the act of a suicidal man. The oranges were later found scattered in the stairwell between the fourth and fifth floors, along with Safronov's cap. According to witnesses, Safronov was alive for several minutes after the fall and even attempted to stand. He would not survive the uncaring ineptitude of Moscow's ambulance service, which took thirty minutes to dispatch help. The "attendants" assumed Safronov had fallen from an open window in a drunken stupor. An autopsy found no trace of alcohol or drugs in his system.

If the brutal death of Ivan Safronov was an act of murder rather than suicide, then why was he killed and by whom? Like Anna Politkovskaya, Ivan Safronov had apparently uncovered information that Vladimir Putin's Kremlin did not want the rest of the world to know: specifically, that Russia intended to sell advanced fighter jets and missiles to its two pariah allies in the Middle East, Iran and Syria. In order to provide the Kremlin with plausible deniability it played any part in the sale, the deal was reportedly set to be conducted through an arms dealer in Belarus. Safronov is said to have confirmed details of the sale during a trip to the Middle East in the days before his death.

The promiscuity of Russian arms sales in the Middle East has been well documented. So, too, have the activities of "private" Russian arms traffickers. One such man is Viktor Bout. Often referred to as "the merchant of death" and the world's most notorious gunrunner, Bout is alleged to have sold weapons to a diverse set of clients that include the likes of Hezbollah, the Taliban, and even elements of al-Qaeda. In 2006, the U.S. Treasury Department seized some of Bout's aircraft and froze his assets. In March 2008, as I was finishing this manuscript, he was arrested in a luxury Bangkok hotel in an American-led sting operation. He is accused of offering to sell millions of dollars' worth of weaponry to the FARC rebels of Colombia, including advanced shoulder-launch antiaircraft missiles. At the time of this writing, he sits in a Thai jail cell, awaiting legal proceedings and possible extradition to the United States to face charges.

Finally, a note on the title. Many of us first became familiar with the term "Moscow Rules" when we read John le Carré's classic novel of espionage, *Smiley's People.* Though the brilliant Mr. le Carré invented much of the lexicon of his spies, the Moscow Rules were indeed a real set of Cold War operating principles and remain so today, even though the Cold War is supposedly a thing of the past. One can find written versions of the rules in various forms and in various places, though the CIA apparently has never gone to the trouble of actually placing them on paper. I am told by an officer in the Agency's national clandestine service that the rule quoted in the epigraph of this novel is accurate and is drilled into American spies throughout their training. Unfortunately, the journalists of Russia are now forced to operate by a similar set of guidelines — at least the ones who dare to question the new masters of the Kremlin.

ACKNOWLEDGMENTS

This novel, like the previous books in the Gabriel Allon series, could not have been written without the assistance of David Bull, who truly is among the finest art restorers in the world. Usually, David advises me on how to clean paintings. This time, however, he taught me how a man as gifted as Gabriel might forge one in a hurry. The technique Gabriel used for creating craquelure is a highly abbreviated version of the method developed by Han van Meegeren, a Dutchman often described as the greatest forger in history.

I am indebted to several courageous Russian journalists in Moscow who generously shared with me some of their experiences. For obvious reasons, I cannot name them here, but I stand in awe of both their courage and their dedication to freedoms we in the West take for granted. Jim Maceda of NBC News was an invaluable resource, as was Jonathan, who took me to corners of the Old Arbat I would have never found on my own. My Russian guides in St. Petersburg and Moscow gave my family the trip of a lifetime, while Tanya showed me the soul of a Leningrad girl. A very special thanks to the FSB colonel who walked me through the corridors of Lubyanka. Also, to my driver in Moscow, who poetically said of the Russians: "We cannot live as normal people." I did not realize it then but he gave me the spine of a novel.

Several Israeli and American intelligence officers spoke to me on background, and I thank them now in anonymity, which is how they would prefer it. A special thanks to J, who chose to serve his country in secret rather than use his brilliant mind to make money. We are all in his debt.

A very senior administration official generously briefed me on his own experiences dealing with the new Russia and encouraged me every step of the way. Former president George H. W. Bush, Mrs. Barbara Bush, and Jean Becker, their amazing chief of staff, offered much support and gave me an invaluable glimpse of what it is like to entertain a visiting head of state. Roger Cressey talked to me about real-life Russian arms dealers and explained how I might take down a portion of the Moscow telephone system. David Zara of Tradewind Aviation helped me steal an oligarch's airplane. Deepest gratitude to the Astoria Hotel in St. Petersburg, the Savoy Hotel in Moscow, the Métropole Hotel in Geneva, the Hôtel les Grandes Alpes in Courchevel, and the Château de la Messardière in Saint-Tropez. Please forgive any complaints by my characters; they are a surly lot who travel far too much. Also, I am forever grateful to the staff of an isolated cattle farm in the hills of Umbria. They gave my family, and my characters, a glorious summer none of us will ever forget.

I consulted hundreds of books, newspaper and magazine articles, and websites while preparing this manuscript, far too many to name here. I would be remiss, however, if I did not mention the extraordinary scholarship and reporting of Robert Service, Peter Baker, Susan Glasser, David E. Hoffman, David Remnick, Alex Goldfarb, Marina Litvinenko, Anna Politkovskaya, Hedrick Smith, Peter Landesman, Douglas Farah, Stephen Braun, and Anne Appelbaum. Anne's columns inspired me, and her Pulitzer prizewinning book, *Gulag,* is an unforgettable reminder of what lies buried in the not-so-distant Russian past.

Chris Donovan gave me a research packet from heaven. Louis Toscano made countless improvements to the manuscript, as did my copy editors, Tony Davis and Kathy Crosby. A special thanks to the remarkable team at Putnam, especially Neil Nyren, Marilyn Ducksworth, and Ivan Held, who graciously allowed me to borrow his first name for my villain. It goes without saying that none of this would have been possible without their support, but I shall say it in any case. You are all simply the best in the business.

We are blessed with many friends who fill our lives with love and laughter at critical junctures during the writing year, especially Henry and Stacey Winkler, Andrea and Tim Collins, Greg Craig and Derry Noyes, Enola Aird and Stephen L. Carter, Lisa Myers and Marcia Harrison, Mitch Glazer and Kelly Lynch, and Jane and Burt Bacharach. I listened constantly to "Painted from Memory," Burt's brilliant collaboration with Elvis Costello, while finishing the manuscript, and even managed to slip the title into the final chapter. The members of "the Peloton" were great friends and company during a long hard winter of writing. My study partners — David Gregory, Jeffrey Goldberg, Steven Weisman, Martin Indyk, Franklin Foer, Noah Oppenheim, and Erica

Brown — kept my heart focused on what is truly important, even if my thoughts were sometimes elsewhere.

I wish to extend the deepest gratitude and love to my children, Lily and Nicholas, who were at my side throughout this journey, as they have been from the beginning. Finally, my wife, Jamie Gangel, helped find the essence of the story when it eluded me and skillfully edited my early drafts. Were it not for her patience, attention to detail, and forbearance, *Moscow Rules* would not have been completed. My debt to her is immeasurable, as is my love.

ABOUT THE AUTHOR

Daniel Silva is the author of the bestselling novels *The Unlikely Spy, The Mark of the Assassin, The Marching Season, The Kill Artist, The English Assassin, The Confessor, A Death in Vienna, Prince of Fire, The Messenger,* and *The Secret Servant,* named by *Publishers Weekly* as one of the best books of 2007. He lives in Washington, D.C., with his wife, NBC News *Today* correspondent Jamie Gangel, and their two children, Lily and Nicholas.

CPSIA information can be obtained
at www.ICGtesting.com
Printed in the USA
FFHW011152240119
50292174-55330FF

9 781594 133367